The Gene Editors

The Race for Biotechnology Supremacy

The Gene Editors

The Race for Biotechnology Supremacy

Louisa Ghevaert

Troubador Publishing Ltd
Unit E2 Airfield Business Park,
Harrison Road, Market Harborough,
Leicestershire. LE16 7UL
Tel: 0116 2792299
Email: books@troubador.co.uk
Web: www.troubador.co.uk

ISBN 978 1805142 416

British Library Cataloguing in Publication Data.
A catalogue record for this book is available from the British Library.

Printed and bound by CPI Group (UK) Ltd, Croydon, CR0 4YY
Typeset in 11pt Minion Pro by Troubador Publishing Ltd, Leicester, UK

FSC www.fsc.org MIX Paper | Supporting responsible forestry FSC® C013604

Learning the lessons of life, loss and legacy

Biography

Louisa Ghevaert is a leading Fertility and Family Law expert, author and public speaker with special interests in public policy, governance, health, assisted conception and genomics.

Louisa has a BA (Hons) Degree in History from the University of Bristol, the Common Professional Entrance (CPE) and Legal Practice Course (LPC) from the College of Law, Guildford, England. She was named The Times Lawyer of the Week in October 2009 and awarded a place on The Lawyer Hot 100 List 2018 for her groundbreaking legal work on milestone cases spanning the UK and international family, fertility and medical sectors, which described her 'as an influential figure when it comes to ensuring fertility laws are fit for purpose in the 21st century'. She is a Fellow of the American Academy of Adoption and Assisted Reproduction Attorneys (AAAA) and a Fellow of the American Bar Association (ABA) Assisted Reproduction Technology Section. She lives on the World Heritage Jurassic Coast in Dorset, England and likes to travel in her spare time.

Contents

Chapter 2

Chapter 3
Summer-Autumn 2019: Strange Encounters and Military Presence

Chapter 4
Christmas 2019

Chapter 5
Winter 2019-2020

Chapter 6
Easter and Spring 2020

Chapter 7
Summer-Autumn 2020

Chapter 8

Chapter 11
Winter-Spring 2021

Chapter 12
Spring-Summer 2021

Chapter 14
Autumn 2022-Winter 2023

Prologue

Another hardback book dropped through the letterbox featuring authoritative voices and various paradigms. But was it the full story? There was so much that did not add up, resulting in incomplete and confusing mixed messages about events over the last few years. Unbeknown to Susie Miller, a seasoned forty-something UK life sciences lawyer, she was to find herself caught up and entangled in a complex and frightening web of international power and subterfuge that would dominate world events and sit at the heart of the global race for supremacy.

The real story was very different to that portrayed publicly by the authoritative voices in their hardback books and their official papers in distinguished international scientific journals. It was also very different to the official narratives produced by state governments. As Susie was to come to realise, events over the last few years and the forces behind them were more complex and deep-seated than the world at large was initially led to believe.

The origins of the Covid-19 pandemic were far more nuanced than just a zoonotic animal-to-human viral spillover event or a lab release of a new manmade virulent virus. These events and the roots of the global Covid-19 pandemic that shuttered the world economy and had officially killed nearly 7 million people by the summer of 2023 began at least in part in the early 2000s in central China. They could be traced back to a time just after the sequencing of the world's first entire human genome in 2000 and the shock of the deadly SARS virus outbreaks in China from 2002–2004 that killed 800 people and sickened 8,000 more. These events sent out seismic shockwaves and triggered an international arms race to harness and control the power, wealth and influence that rapid advances in genomics and synthetic biology promised the twenty-first-century world. This race was so important that it involved the military, Big Pharma, the Industrial Complex and information technology giants like Google. It also included government officials, private entities, the intelligence services, key scientists and international scientific collaborations, and it was a dangerous race into which Susie unwittingly stumbled and became embroiled.

A less well-understood but nonetheless significant part of the bigger picture centred round the life and scientific work of He Jiankui, an ambitious top Chinese graduate physicist. He Jiankui would eventually be jailed by the Chinese State in 2019 for illegally and recklessly creating the world's first gene-edited babies by editing their embryos in a laboratory, in an attempt to make them resistant to the HIV virus. He Jiankui's life and work represented a piece of the jigsaw puzzle that those locked fast into the twenty-first-century global race for supremacy did not wish to shine a light upon. Instead, they were keen to consign the whole shocking gene-edited baby affair in 2018 to history as the work of a rogue scientist who was subsequently condemned and imprisoned. But as Susie was to come to discover, He Jiankui's part in the bigger picture was potentially more significant, and it would begin to unlock the secrecy and obfuscation that surrounded the catastrophic world events of the last few years and start to bring meaning to the confusion and global devastation. Susie's growing understanding of the bigger picture would also result in a frightening journey of discovery that would see her sucked into a shadowy covert world for which she was not trained or ready, and the stakes for all involved could not have been higher.

Chapter 1

Winter-Spring 2019: The CFPS and Genomics

Susie Miller stretched back in her supportive black mesh office chair and ran her manicured nails through her freshly cut brown highlighted hair, a subconscious reflex when she had things on her mind. As a seasoned life sciences lawyer in her forties, she was used to being at the cutting edge of law and emerging scientific developments, as well as encountering new issues on a regular basis. However, this request was different. She paused for thought and slowly drank some milky Earl Grey tea from a favourite white Villeroy & Boch mug that was nearly always on the go on her desk. She stared out of the bay window at the cold grey mid-afternoon winter sky and wondered why Tom, from policy think tank CFPS (short for the Centre For Political Strategy), was being so persistent. Why me? she thought. And why now? Surely one of the usual suspects, a man in a stripey suit who liked the sound of his own voice and was part of the old boys' network, would have been a more obvious choice?

Why choose me to speak at this particular policy meeting at the illustrious Somerset House in London? What could she add to the debate about policy and future genomic strategy that they did not already know anyway?

Susie had worked hard to get to a point in her career, after twenty years, where she had a string of precedent-setting published legal judgements to her name and a busy specialist legal practice in life sciences. She had not come from a legal background and was the first in her family to become a lawyer. She had taken out a bank loan from NatWest to fund her law conversion course (CPE) and the legal practice course (LPC) at the College of Law following her undergraduate degree in English literature at Durham University. She had then slowly and determinedly built up her knowledge and experience over time, along with a good degree of resilience, which was needed to go the distance in law. The legal profession could be intense, brutal and bruising, and as a woman she had had to work even harder to make a name for herself. She had sacrificed a lot on the personal front to get there too, having little time for hobbies and a social life and a couple of failed relationships behind her. She was quick, with an eye for detail and the ability to drill down and get to the heart of things, which had financially and professionally served her well. Life had also taught her not to take anything for granted and that the harder you worked, the luckier you got; and there was little doubt that she had worked hard.

Even so, a request like this was unusual, as was Tom's persistence over the last three weeks. Acknowledging with some annoyance that he was unlikely to go away, she picked up the telephone handset on the corner of her desk and called him. He answered the call promptly and despite her best efforts to politely put him off, explaining that she had not attended this sort of event before and was not looking to accept a speaking engagement, he would not take no for an answer. He was clear that he and the CFPS had done their research and that they wanted her to come to the event regardless of the fact that she was not willing to speak to their heavy-hitting guest list. He added that he was going to send her a complimentary invitation straightaway, and he impressed upon her in a firm undertone the level of expectation that accompanied this. Susie was left with an undeniable understanding that she was expected to attend regardless of her own personal views on the matter.

She put the telephone handset down and sighed, before slowly taking another sip of tea from her mug. She sat back in her ergonomic chair, purchased the year before to improve her posture and ease persistent shoulder pain from too many hours spent bent over her desk. John Lewis was a lifesaver for working from home. She absentmindedly rubbed her shoulder as she digested what had just happened and looked round her office. It was a comfortable space, decorated in neutral tones, lined with hundreds of books on varied subjects and a well-used small sofa with soft pastel-coloured cushions sat in one corner. Her tidy desk was positioned next to the bay window to maximise light and give her views of the world around her. She realised that she had in effect been summoned by this political think tank to attend their event, and there was no way she was going to be able to avoid it. She felt a mixture of irritation and bemusement as to why her presence was required as she lacked the connections and personal history that usually accompanied this political world.

Faced with this realisation, Susie quickly deduced that she needed to make a plan so that she did not make a fool of herself on that day in front of a room full of important and influential people from the political class. In short, she needed to get prepared, she realised with another sigh. This required research on genomics and how scientific study of all of a person's genes and their functions was going to impact life so she could hold her own and make convincing conversation on the day. A couple of hours of internet research should do it, she thought; it was all the time she could spare anyway, given her heavy legal caseload. She could type in some key words, check out current government policy and get a sense for the future distance of travel and go from there. She was used to covering ground quickly and identifying the relevant issues, and in that moment she was grateful for her intellect. It was not something she shouted about, but she could map out issues, join up dots and construct analysis and strategies across many different subject areas with surprising ease, and people often underestimated her.

There was no time to lose, she thought to herself. She would strike whilst the iron was hot and get this research done now so that she had maximum time to mull things over in her mind and pull together her thoughts. *Thank goodness for Google,* she muttered to herself with a smile. As a junior lawyer, it had been drilled into her by those more senior that you should not rely on Google and that legal arguments and evidence needed a sound basis, underpinned by a rigorous understanding of statute, regulations and supporting case law. They were of course right to give such direction. However, over time, Susie had come to understand that Google was a very powerful tool and not something that you just used to send emails and surf in your free time for shopping or for holiday bookings. She had also read widely and voraciously every day. Her reading included numerous articles and news reports collated by her daily Google Alerts, a free content notification service by Google that matched her user's search terms on a varied range of issues about science, medicine, digital and AI technology and geopolitics, and not just law and policy. She always checked her Google Alerts first thing in the morning to ease herself into her day, and it was always a thrill to learn something new. This knowledge had been slowly and consistently filed away in her mind, and it was a useful and ever-growing resource upon which she could call. As she began this latest round of research, she realised, with some satisfaction, that she could quickly scan large amounts of data such as government tracts, extrapolate key issues and points and construct a coherent picture in her mind. As a result, the next couple of hours passed quickly and productively.

Susie stretched, got up and went to make a fresh mug of Twining's Earl Grey tea. She had tried other Earl Grey blends over the years but always returned to this, her favourite, together with her preferred Villeroy & Boch brand of mugs. It was another reflex action, something she did at regular intervals throughout the day to take a break and clear her mind. It always helped to have a short reset and come back to the desk having had a little distance and the occasional square of Lindt or Ritter Sport milk chocolate or a digestive biscuit to boost her energy levels or change up her thoughts. Yet whilst she still felt that usual buzz of a couple of hours well spent, she also felt something unfamiliar. It was a deep-seated sense of surprise and unease at just how seemingly underdeveloped and unprepared the UK was from a genomic perspective despite all of the government hype that the UK was a 'world pioneer in genomics, science and technology'. She had not gone into her research with any particular expectations, always preferring to come to a reasoned understanding, having looked at the available data. However, she had not expected to find such a large gap between what was in place from a strategic perspective and what appeared to be happening on the ground. She swallowed hard, took several sips of tea to steady herself and slow her breathing. It was not just a gap; it was a massive chasm, she thought. She felt shaken by the enormity of this realisation and its implications. Her mind then started to go into overdrive as she began to be hit by one realisation after another, each larger and more concerning than the last.

1.1 Meaning of Genomics

To begin to grasp the basics, Susie had started her internet research by looking at the science behind genomics. First, she had looked up and established a brief definition of genomics; essentially the complete set of genetic material of a human, animal, plant, or other living thing. Then she had moved on to recent developments in gene editing technology, which seemed to be where most of the current focus was. This had seemed a logical place to start to get to grips with what genomics represented. To ease herself in, she had watched a couple of carefully selected YouTube videos which had given her a visual overview and understanding of some of the basics, which she had then started to supplement with some prominent scientific articles. YouTube was great, she thought with some relief. It was a way of introducing yourself to a subject in a gentle way, allowing yourself to sit back with a mug of tea and start to let the visual learning sink in. It was also less heavy lifting than diving straight into dense text and scrabbling around trying to orientate yourself.

1.2 The Concept of Gene Editing: Computers and Humans

She quickly learnt that DNA programmes the human body and cells in the body are like computers. One of the videos she watched explained the architectural similarity between a computer and the human body, which she found fascinating. It explained that in basic terms a computer is a network of parts comprising modules (a selection of independent electronic circuits packaged onto a circuit board to provide a basic function within a computer), gates and a physical layer. It went on to explain that the human body also comprises a network of parts including cells, pathways, biochemical reactions and proteins and genes, although these are much more complex.

Next, Susie learnt that advances in genomic technology meant that it was now increasingly possible to write, code and edit DNA and change the activity of specific genes in the human body, plants, microbes and animals. The fact that you could code and edit DNA like you could computer code had come as a revelation. It had also left her feeling concerned as she realised how powerful and transformative this could be and the potential for its misuse as well. It was not much of a leap to imagine teams of technology geeks and scientists writing DNA code and making all sorts of genetic edits, and how on earth was that going to be policed, regulated and/or managed? she thought.

1.3 Personal Genomic Information: The Human Genome

She went on to read about the significance of personal genomic information. She learnt that a person's genome is a complete set of DNA and that everyone has an individual genome sequence. This is copied into our individual cells like an instruction manual. As she read on, she learnt that there are 3 billion letters in the genome and that 99.9% of the letters in the human genome are identical; so there is only 0.1% difference between people in terms of their appearance, disease risk and response to medications and environmental elements. Susie found all of this fascinating too, particularly as she read about scientific advances which meant we could sequence an entire human genome in 2019 in less than forty-eight hours for under $1,000 (and even cheaper over time). Increasingly, she learnt that this would help target diseases at source and create opportunities for genetic repairs and new curative drugs. By doing so, increasingly over time the door would open to new gene therapies to replace defective genes for a specific genetic disorder. It also offered opportunities for new cell therapies, for example, genetically engineered cells to treat cancer and target tumours in the body, promising all sorts of hope for the battle against cancer that one in two people will currently develop during their lifetime.

1.4 Genomic Technology: Research and Development

It had also been informative to watch a short YouTube video which looked at research and development using genomic technology for antibiotics, diagnostics and nanomaterials (chemical substances or materials consisting of very small particles of different shapes and sizes). She had watched in fascination as it went on to discuss the possibility of creating an inert EpiPen which could be activated using WIFI and a computer chip which could accept DNA coding. This could then in theory dispense personalised treatment anywhere in the world. If this came to pass, it would be the opposite of the Big Pharma model and it would challenge their highly powerful and successful multi-billion-dollar business model. Susie paused to reflect on the disruptive and potentially revolutionary nature of this technology and all of the vested interests, like Big Pharma and the Industrial Complex, who had so much at stake with all of this. Who would be the winners and who would be the losers? she asked herself thoughtfully.

1.5 UK Genomic Policy, 2019

Next, she worked her way through UK government policy and funding with a view to carrying out a brief comparison with the US to try and benchmark UK capabilities in genomics. This started with identifying a November 2017 UK government white paper signed by Theresa May on industrial strategy.[1] The report highlighted four grand challenges, namely (1) artificial intelligence and big data, (2) clean growth, (3) future mobility and (4) meeting the needs of an ageing population. It looked at the challenges of building better infrastructure and upskilling the workforce supported by investment from the Industrial

Strategy Challenge Fund of £725 million. However, Susie noted that it made no mention of genomics and she quickly realised that government policy had seemingly not yet fully evolved to integrate this technology across all sectors. That was a serious and fundamental problem, she thought.

It had also been illuminating to watch the UK government's Genomics Summit in Parliament on 31 October 2018, which had been jointly organised by the House of Commons Science and Technology Committee and the Department of Health and Social Care.[2] This had explained genomic infrastructure and genomic healthcare policy. It had highlighted the 100,000 Genome Project which had been launched by former Prime Minister David Cameron and how by 31 October 2018 it had succeeded in sequencing 92,000 whole human genomes. It went on to assert that this had put the UK in a brilliant position to exploit the associated learning opportunities and that they were already starting to get results of global significance, with most emphasis so far on treatment of rare diseases.

1.6 England's NHS Genomic Medicine Service (GMS)

The UK government's Genomics Summit went on to discuss the launch of the NHS Genomic Medicine Service (GMS) in England on 2 October 2018. Officials explained that this was aimed at adults with certain rare diseases or hard-to-treat cancers, who would be offered whole genome sequencing. This offer would then be extended from 2019 to all seriously ill children, including those with suspected genetic disorders and cancer. It then proceeded to explain the rollout of digital infrastructure across the NHS and how the reality of genome sequencing was a concern for some medics as a means of routinely diagnosing cancer.

The UK government's Genomics Summit also discussed

data protection issues and how data would be used for personal care and research and how it sat within the NHS charter. Then they went on to extol the promise of genomic medicine for those suffering from rare diseases and cancer and how it was right that the government seized the opportunity. As such, they discussed how they needed to garner widespread public support for genomic medicine in the UK. Susie went on to listen carefully as they explained that the 100,000 Genome Project had primarily been a science project, and the question now was how to take the genomic science and turn it into mainstream healthcare and move to preventative and personalised healthcare.

Susie was particularly struck by political commentary at the UK government's Genomics Summit that in five years 38% of UK public spending would be on NHS health spending (an eye-watering amount, she thought) and how we needed to change the model to deal with this and make the NHS financially sustainable. To achieve this, they explained that they would need to get upstream and diagnose health problems early to achieve economic and personal gains. They added that the aim was to ensure that the NHS would be the first genomic health system in the world and the question now was how to deliver it. How would they use their genomic lab and testing centres? How would they use genomics to target drug discovery? How would they make sure clinicians used the platform? How would they make it real for people? Susie was then struck by commentary that over time people would hold their genomic data and health data on their phone and other personal electronic devices and that the issue was how to make use and sense of this. This was a massive shift in policy and infrastructure, and there was a huge amount of work ahead to make it happen, she thought.

The UK government's Genomics Summit also highlighted

the revolution in genomic technology, with the reduction in price point and its ability to analyse large data sets. This represented a step change in the UK's diagnostic testing and genome sequencing capability and created what they termed the 4 P's, namely (1) prediction, (2) prevention, (3) precise diagnosis and (4) participating roles for patients. They went on to explain how the UK spent £17 billion on drugs annually on the NHS and that a large proportion of that spend was on cancer drugs, which they wanted to target. This was why the NHS had rolled out in October 2018 the Genomic Medicine Service within NHS England. Its aim was to create a standardised national approach to genomics across the NHS with equitable access to research and clinical trials, enhanced clinical interpretation and high-quality results. This would result in a change in healthcare model from lots of tests to one test (sequencing your genome), creating a platform for the future to assess individual susceptibility to toxins and drugs. Added to this, personal genomics information would be a fundamental pillar of personalised and precision medicine of the future for all consenting adults. They would have their genome sequences in their clinical records to inform diagnosis and prognosis for preventative healthcare so that we moved from crisis management to preventative medicine, emphasising that it was in the nation's interests to change the model.

All of this sounded very laudable, Susie thought. However, in reality, it led her to conclude that the deployment of genomic technology was still in its infancy in terms of UK strategy and that, at least openly, it seemed largely to be focused on personalised and precision healthcare delivery through the NHS. If her initial sense of things was right, then this was a concern.

It had also been helpful to scan news articles and commentary from around the world to sense check relevant issues, trends, points of concern and start to work out where the gaps were that would need to be addressed from a strategic perspective. In doing so, she read that BGI (formerly Beijing Genomics Institute) in China was planning to sequence 3 million human genomes over the next few years. This left Susie with the impression that China was thinking big and moving fast to scale up its genomic understanding and capability, which appeared to far outstrip what was happening in the UK.

1.7 Science Fiction to Science Fact: Discovery of CRISPR Gene Editing Technology in 2012

In carrying out this research, it became clear that rapidly evolving gene editing technology, particularly human genome-editing technology, increasingly had the capability to change not just the health of individual children, adults and families, but the future of humanity as a whole. Over time, it would have the capability to combat and prevent the onset of serious genetic diseases. It would also increasingly have the capability to overcome infertility and change our biological legacy to reduce ill health in future generations or potentially make them more resistant to diseases, environmental factors or even possess certain traits and characteristics to make them more athletic or intelligent. This technology had immense capacity for good that cut across all aspects of life when you also factored in the combined power of digital and artificial intelligence technology. However, this far exceeded the genomic narrative being put out by the UK government, Susie thought, reflecting on its Genomics Summit in Parliament on 31 October 2018 just a few months ago and its recent policy and funding strategies.

Recent advances in genomic technology now far exceeded narratives about human enhancement in films too. This included the *Terminator* franchise about human cyborgs, featuring Arnold Schwarzenegger, who had been turned into a bionic human with capabilities enhanced by electromechanical devices. They also went beyond technological ideas in Steven Spielberg's film *Minority Report* in 2002, starring Tom Cruise, in which talented mutant 'precogs', enhanced by artificial intelligence and data analytics, could predict human behaviour and prevent crimes before they were committed. They also outpaced the technological concept in *Limitless* in 2011, starring Bradley Cooper, which featured a new pharmaceutical drug which provided perfect memory recall and the ability to analyse details and information at incredible speed.

This new gene editing technology was different because it was real and not just science fiction to be immortalised in films and popular culture for our entertainment. This rapidly evolving technology was being used here and now and it was far more powerful and transformative, both an exciting and a scary prospect. What's more, this gene editing was still in its infancy as the technology to make accurate cuts in the double-helix structure of DNA to remove, add or alter sections of the DNA sequence had only been discovered seven years ago in 2012 by world-leading American and French female scientists Jennifer Doudna and Emmanuelle Charpentier. This new gene editing tool known as CRISPR-Cas9 also came with national security risks, and Susie surmised it could all too easily be used potentially to wreak devastating havoc and harm as well.

1.8 Chinese Gene-Edited Babies in 2018

Susie then read with increasing trepidation news reports of three Chinese babies whose embryos had been gene edited in a laboratory in 2018 by a young ambitious Chinese scientist called He Jiankui. Using the powerful new CRISPR-Cas9 gene editing system, discovered by Jennifer Doudna and Emmanuelle Charpentier, just six years earlier, He Jiankui reportedly tried to make the babies resistant to the AIDS HIV virus for life, by permanently editing their genomes pre-conception.[3] She had been stunned by what she read, finding it hard to digest the enormity of this scientific experiment and its implications for the babies and mankind as a whole.

Delving further into the births of Chinese gene-edited twins Lulu and Nana, Susie noted what came out in the press, just before an international genomic summit in Hong Kong in November 2018.[4] The experiment had swiftly become the subject of international scientific condemnation for irresponsibly permanently altering the human genome before the science was deemed safe and effective. He Jiankui was accused of recklessly and inaccurately permanently altering the genetic make-up of the twins and a third baby, causing unknown heritable health outcomes for them and future generations of their offspring. There was also talk that the Chinese babies might even have potentially genetically enhanced intelligence, according to some scientific reports. This was big stuff, and these scientific developments must be accompanied by power, money and influence, Susie thought to herself, and they spelled trouble. As a life sciences lawyer, the significance of this development weighed particularly heavily on her mind.

1.9 The Genomic 'Paradigm Shift'

It suddenly became important to start to capture her thoughts, and Susie quickly and deliberately began drawing on her trusty office whiteboard with a black marker pen. It was a technique she often used when she was settling her thoughts and working out litigation strategy or preparing a new paper. A series of complex spiders' webs swiftly emerged on the whiteboard. She was scared of spiders but her own spiders' webs frightened her more, and she did not like what was developing before her eyes.

As the network of webs emerged, it became clear that UK and global governance needed extensive reform to address these rapidly converging, powerful and transformative technologies. Time was of the essence and urgent action was needed now that required a paradigm shift in thinking and leadership from the top-down. This sounded crazy but it seemed clear to Susie that there was no way round this. These new technologies had crept up on us, and we had been left sleeping at the wheel and hurtling towards a cliff edge, she mused. We needed new ways of operating, and the UK needed to raise its game quickly to try and head things off at the pass.

It further became clear to Susie that to stop the UK falling off the cliff edge, an informed multi-disciplinary approach to this new challenge was essential, and it had to avoid short-term politics and current Brexit distractions. This was not going to be easy as UK politics had by 2019 descended into endless debate and increasing deadlock about how it was going to exit the European Union, and the politicians and public alike were divided, frustrated and disillusioned by it all. To achieve change and widespread reform to take account of rapid advances in genomic technology, there needed to be a high-level strategy group devising and driving a centralised approach to genomics in government politics that could co-ordinate across all sectors. This then needed to be deployed as a critical action plan. In doing so, government had to think carefully about what could be openly shared and what warranted high-level national security control. Susie deftly set this structural overhaul out in a simplistic flow chart. The simpler the better, she thought, to try and change the narrative here. Putting a slogan on the side of a bus, like they were doing as part of the UK Brexit campaigning, simply would not cut the mustard here, she thought ruefully.

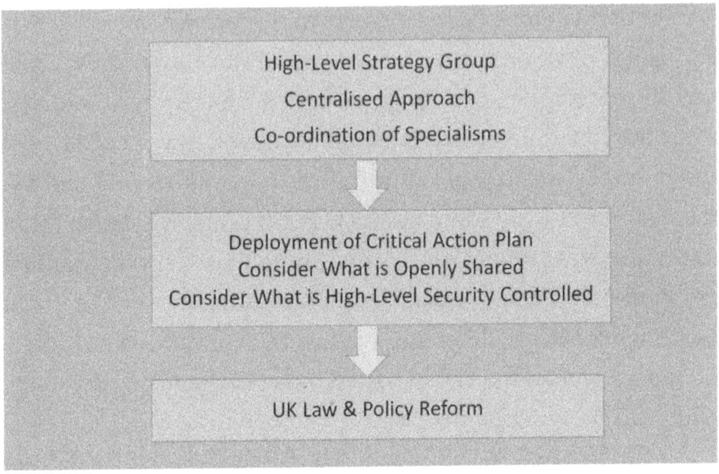

Chart 1: Overview of UK Genomic Governance Reform

Next, she visually set out what she termed the 'paradigm shift'; the change in approach required to proactively develop new law, policy and governance to address the powerful and interconnected capability and implications of genomic technology. The chart that emerged visually depicted in simplistic terms the wide-ranging extent to which genomic technology had permeated and influenced different aspects of life. Transformative and rapidly evolving genomic technology sat in the middle, driven by ongoing digital and AI capability which fed into evolving studies of epigenetics (how behaviours and environment can cause changes affecting the way genes work) and factors that switched genes on and off. Genomic technology was also driving the ongoing reproductive revolution that so many seemed blissfully unaware of, she surmised. These technologies were not very interesting or meaningful to the average person on the street, she concluded, but they impacted everything from personal genomic information, political stability and security, the economy and business and wealth, science and medicine and technology through to health, fertility and reproductive legacy. *Oh shit, this was massive and so far-reaching,* Susie muttered, as she paused and stepped back for a moment to survey her work on the whiteboard. *Shit, shit, shit,* she muttered to herself as she nervously fiddled with her black marker pen, causing black smudges to spread across her fingertips.

Next, she deftly drew a more in-depth impact assessment of genomic technological advances to illustrate the different ways they influenced life in practice. This encompassed all sorts of issues, ranging from food and water safety, genetic data attacks and big business interests to the development of the UK as a

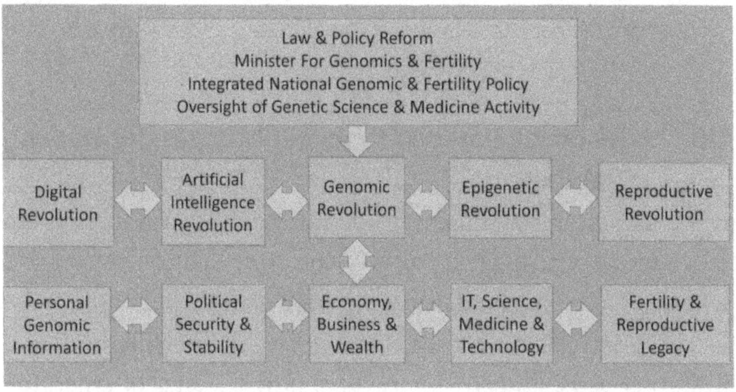

Chart 2: The 'Paradigm Shift' in Genomic UK Law, Policy & Reform

genomic capital and evolving digital and synthetic biology. Following through to its logical conclusion, it also included the UK's falling fertility levels, trends in older child-rearing, scope for genetic engineering in embryos at a preconception stage and precursor cells.

The possibilities and repercussions were literally limitless, Susie thought, and her breathing quickened, her heart pounded and she began to feel a bit lightheaded and woozy. Time for chocolate, and she reached for a half-eaten blue packet of Ritter Sport alpine milk chocolate on her desk.

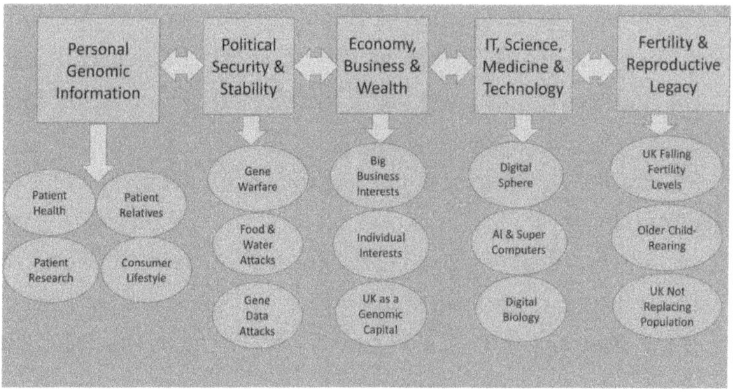

Chart 3: Impact Assessment of Genomic Technology Advances

1.10 Genomics: Personal Data and Direct-to-Consumer DNA Tests

It was also clear that there was not much public awareness about the issues around personal genomic information. How and where should personal genomic information be stored? The use of genetic data now extended far beyond personalised and preventative healthcare. There were now all sorts of emerging issues and risks with big business controlling individual data, particularly given the rapid growth in the popularity of at-home DNA testing kits by online organisations like Ancestry and 23andMe, which had amassed millions of people's genomic data.

On top of this, public behaviour had to be factored into the picture as people were merrily sharing personal information online and on social media platforms like Facebook and Instagram, which was then difficult to retract. There needed to be much greater public education and awareness of the implications and risks of disclosing not just personal information but personal genomic information as well through direct-to-consumer DNA testing to find out about personal ancestry, build family trees and trace relatives. This information could all be collected to build profiles that had the potential to be used for all sorts of purposes and all manner of surveillance and questionable purposes. This shook Susie too as it all seemed to be happening so quickly.

1.11 Cambridge Analytica Scandal

It also begged the question of what happened with the Cambridge Analytica scandal, news of which had rocked politics in the US and the UK.[5] Cambridge Analytica, a British consulting firm, had developed an app called *This Is Your Digital Life* which had been used to harvest personal data belonging to millions of Facebook users and their friends during the 2010s without their consent. This information had been deployed to build psychological profiles of US voters and then target them with political advertisements during the 2016 presidential election; an election which had ultimately resulted in Democrat candidate Hillary Clinton losing out on the US presidency to Republican Donald Trump, and it had also led to allegations that Cambridge Analytica had interfered with the Brexit campaign for Britain to leave the EU.

This alarming data breach had only come to light the year before (2018), when former employee Christopher Wylie blew the whistle on Cambridge Analytica in interviews with the *Guardian* and the *New York Times* and in three and a half hours of personal testimony before Britain's House of Commons' Select Committee on Culture. Worryingly, he had gone on to suggest that Russian intelligence agencies might have obtained this vast treasure trove of data on American voters in advance of the 2016 US presidential elections, because one of the key data scientists involved had allegedly made regular return trips to Russia. When asked why he had decided to blow the whistle, Christopher Wylie said that his views about data mining had changed when Donald Trump had been elected US President and he had realised the enormity of this technology's impact on the world. This scandal had triggered a very public apology by Facebook in 2018 for its part in data harvesting and resulted in its CEO, Mark Zuckerberg, testifying before US Congress. It had also resulted in massive fines for data breaches in the US and the UK and Cambridge Analytica filing for bankruptcy in May 2018.

Pausing for thought, Susie realised that this rapidly emerging picture of technical personal data usage, together with its rapid intersection with personalised genomic data, was getting more complex by the minute. She felt a cold shiver wash over her as she mapped out how genomics directly linked into political stability and national and international security issues, and not just health and welfare. Chocolate and tea could not possibly solve the situation here, she pondered.

1.12 Genomics and Security

The political control and exploitation of the human, animal, plant and microbial (bacteria and virus) genome in combination with rapidly evolving digital and AI technology was effectively a new central world resource. It was a succinct and simplistic assessment, but there was power and truth in simplicity. Susie also knew simplicity was an effective tool, having used it in her legal work to win arguments and cases. *Wow, this is seriously concerning*, she muttered under her breath. In simple terms, she surmised that genomics represented the fundamental building blocks and essence of life. It was like a whole new currency that promised untold wealth and influence that could potentially change the delicate balance of power around the world. This was only going to intensify in Susie's mind into a full-on territory grab in biotechnology terms and beyond. This was Davos level stuff, and yet here she was drawing it all together on a whiteboard in her office.

Then a whole new form of potential genetic terrorism began to open up in front of Susie as a next stage of terrorism, which greatly concerned her and made her hands go cold and clammy. She assessed that it was now possible to literally cut and splice together different genomic sequences to create new viruses for which there was no vaccine or cure. The potential for genomic warfare, particularly human and microbial, was arguably more difficult to control than nuclear and even cyber warfare because we lacked new forms of infrastructure to detect it and sufficient numbers of skilled people to safeguard against it. We urgently needed more national funding, genetic coders, next-generation IT security experts, biological computer-aided design software known as CAD systems, 3D chemical printers and experts in epigenetics and the human and microbial genome. We also needed more national funding for healthcare to sustain and protect the public against these new types of genomic threat. The scale of this was just massive and getting bigger by the minute.

1.13 Genomics: The Economy, Business and Wealth

Turning her attention to the impact of genomic revolution on the economy, business and wealth, on a positive note, there was the potential to ride the wave and make the UK a worldwide AI, digital and genomic capital of the world and diversify the economy for immense wealth generation. This assumed we could introduce intelligent reform. After all, London was already lauded as a financial capital of the world, and we already had some scientific and technological clusters in centres of excellence like Cambridge, Oxford and London which the UK could build upon. This was at least some good news to try and sell the situation to the 'powers that be' as the language of money mattered, she thought ruefully. In doing so, we needed to think about how our genetic data would be used and the impact of this for businesses and individuals from an employment, insurance, mortgage and even relationship perspective. Susie's breath started to quicken and she shivered again as she realised how genomics permeated and could influence so much of daily life in ways that we had yet to fully comprehend. It was like some sort of dystopian future and yet it was quickly starting to become concerningly real. What if the UK fell behind other first-world powers and did not sufficiently harness all of this technology? she asked herself. It would risk jobs and employment if it did not embrace this, reducing GDP and economic performance that it could ill afford as a nation and weakening the UK in ways it had yet to fully envisage. It was clear that the UK needed new coherent policies and the speedy deployment of national funding initiatives to start to get on top of this.

1.14 Genomics: IT, Science, Medicine and Technology

How this all fitted together from an IT, science, medicine and technology perspective also mattered. Again, Susie's mind whirred into action and she quickly drew yet another spider's web. Artificial intelligence was now a reality and she read that by 2023 a typical computer would have the same capacity as the human brain. She paused again as this sank in a bit further. Having always imagined this point would come much further into the future, it was difficult to compute the reality that it was going to happen so soon. Technological advances and change was all happening so quickly, and it was outstripping regulatory frameworks and public oversight. Super computers now connected the world by fibre optics, nation to nation and individual to individual. Computers could now quickly interpret and process genome sequences, and desktop machines could sequence a whole human genome in 2019 in just twenty-four hours for around $1,000; what's more, prices and processing times would continue to fall. Biotechnology capability was setting up in people's garages and spare rooms, and it no longer required a network of expensive centralised laboratories and armies of highly qualified scientists to staff them. Put simply, DNA was the software of life and it opened up a whole new horizon for a bright and eager generation of coders, technological geeks and scientists. Critically, she went on to surmise that DNA software makes its own hardware as it creates and replicates cells like a 3D printer. As such, it dawned on her that digital biology was a new field with a new data set that has infinite possibilities and risks. It urgently needed reform, policy and oversight before it got completely out of control, and her breathing became so rapid that she felt she might pass out if she was not careful.

1.15 Genomics: Fertility and Reproductive Legacy

Extending the continuum of her thinking to its logical conclusion also brought into focus how the field of genomics impacted fertility and reproductive legacy. Individual fertility is an increasingly precious resource and our ability to reproduce is not guaranteed. Male fertility levels in the western world had dropped by fifty percent over the last forty or fifty years, and we still did not fully understand the reasons for this.[6] The UK, like other western nations, was not sufficiently replacing its population.[7] Many individuals were leaving it longer to have children, with the average UK female age at first birth having reached thirty years and rising.[8] Demand for IVF and assisted conception had grown massively over the last fifteen years, not least because family building had become more diverse (with more same-sex couples and single people undergoing fertility treatment), reaching sixty-eight thousand annual cycles of IVF by 2019 in the UK alone.[9] On top of this, the UK, like other countries, had an ageing population that would bring with it all sorts of societal challenges and economic pressures in the years ahead. It was clear in Susie's mind that these rapidly evolving and converging revolutions would increasingly impact individual and family life. This was important too because family is a key component in the stability and future success of any society. Family is the 'squeezed middle', she thought, and this, combined with increasing fertility issues, was a ticking time bomb, and a new centralised approach was required to tackle this as well.

Over the next few days, Susie kept herself busy with her legal work and tried not to dwell too much on the enormity of her concerning findings and genomic assessments. She kept strictly to her daily *'to-do'* list, undertook her scheduled appointments and executed her legal work with her usual rigour. She also stuck to her exercise regime in the evenings, making use of her big commercial grade NordicTrack treadmill to work out some of the stresses of the day with her favourite iFIT personal trainer to maintain her petite figure. It helped to stick to a routine and commit to her usual schedule to get her work done effectively. However, she could not escape the magnitude of what she had recently discovered, and it weighed heavily on her narrow shoulders. It was like she had stepped into a different paradigm, and it was not a place that she wished to inhabit. She could not believe that she had found herself in this situation and that there seemed to be so little public or political awareness and understanding of the genomic revolution that was rapidly unfolding and the issues, challenges, vulnerabilities and risks associated with this. For the first time in her life, Susie felt overwhelmed by the sheer scale of the situation. It was very concerning to find herself so far outside of her comfort zone and in such unfamiliar territory. It occupied her subconscious, disrupted her sleep and changed her outlook on life. Suddenly life was not as safe and secure as she had thought, and her changed perspective was not widely shared, adding to a growing sense of isolation and shock that this was happening. It was like an out-of-body experience, and a very lonely one at that.

Chapter 2

2.1 CFPS: Policy and Practice

It occurred to Susie that she did not know much, if anything, about think tank CFPS and its work. Now she realised that she was committed to attending their upcoming event and that she was flying blind. She had better do some research on them and try to fix this state of affairs fast. She quickly looked them up on Google and learnt that they were a commercial think tank offering analysis and development across a range of sectors including health and social care, life sciences, economics and the environment. The CFPS was independent and cross-party, bringing together public and private sector leaders, investors, policy makers and commentators with a focus on future policy. They looked heavyweight, with strong connections across government and beyond, so at least she was not wasting her time, she thought with relief. Beyond that, Susie was unable to gauge much as this was not her world and she lacked meaningful points of reference. She figured she would just have to go with the flow for a bit and see what happened for once.

Late morning, the day before the CFPS event, Susie mustered the courage to telephone Tom to reconfirm her attendance, highlight some points and flag up some of her initial concerns. She had done her best in her limited spare time to collect her rapidly expanding thoughts about genomic strategy and put together a distilled analysis. Her key message was that the UK lacked detailed, sophisticated, joined-up centralised strategy that embedded genomics across all areas of political policy governing society and life, and it did not adequately identify the considerable vulnerabilities we faced or mitigate the risks. Despite her best efforts, the conversation did not go as well as she would have liked, and she encountered a distinct level of resistance from Tom. The conversation had been frustrating but it had not come as a complete shock. The quantum shift in thinking and level of understanding and awareness that was required to even start to get on the same page as Susie was far beyond the experience and paradigm of most people, and that was a serious problem in itself. The conversation had ended with a suggestion by Tom that she send them a short paper outlining her thoughts in more detail, although Susie had been left wondering whether this had just been a meaningless platitude. She not infrequently wished that people were better at keeping up with her train of thought, but as she had got older and following numerous professional training courses, she had come to realise that she often needed to 'dumb down' her thoughts so that other people could begin to grasp what she was saying. Despite this encounter, Susie dusted herself off. It was not the first time she had come across this. She accepted that she was not a recognised part of the political world and that, as an outsider, there was going to be a level of resistance to what she had to say. However, it did not make the situation easy, nor did she relish having to front up and attend the CFPS meeting the following day.

The next morning, Susie got up, showered and pottered round her house with breakfast TV on in the background. She fed her rescue silver tabby cat called Rina, whom she had got from the Cats Protection League a few years ago. Rina was affectionate, with a loud purr and a playful sense of humour, and she had been a good source of company over the years. Her favourite trick was to sit on Susie's chest in the evenings whilst she did some additional reading for work and purr like a lawnmower, usually ending with her paws around Susie's neck in a full-on hug. If she purred particularly loudly, her pink tongue would pop out as she only had three teeth. Apparently, her previous owners had fed her all sorts of inappropriate things and she had developed gum disease and had to have most of her teeth removed. She still liked to suck and gum to death Pringles crisps, and she literally went ballistic over fish and chips. Susie had therefore taken to buying Rina her own portion of fried fish to shut her up following an incident when she had had to banish Rina to the kitchen, where she had proceeded to hurl herself against the kitchen door in a fit of frustration with a series of yowls and thumps. Rina also loved to make it into the bedroom and curl up on the pillow next to Susie's head or sometimes in a silvery fur ball in the crook of her knee. She was a comfort and an uplifting presence in Susie's life, even when she went on protest if Susie was away from home for too long, flicking her Whiskas cat food up the walls and smearing it all over the kitchen floor.

Susie left her small characterful detached Victorian house situated on the outskirts of a smart village in Surrey in good time for the meeting. She bent down on the gravel driveway to check that Rina was not hiding under the car or blocking the driveway in another deliberate form of tabby protest to stop her leaving her all day. Having checked the coast was clear, she got into her silver Audi A3 car and drove along the narrow, windy country roads to her local train station in Godalming and caught the commuter train service to London Waterloo, which took just under fifty minutes. It was a picturesque journey and she always liked staring out across the countryside as she geared up for the day ahead in the first-class carriage to escape the noise, overcrowding and lack of seating in standard class. She had chosen her outfit with care, wearing one of her favourite black knee-length pencil skirts, with a cream silky blouse and a fitted magenta jacket and a dependable pair of well-balanced black leather high-heeled shoes by Stuart Weitzman. High heels always helped to elevate her small stature and make her feel more confident, along with a splash of purplish-red lipstick and a Mulberry handbag. The sun was out and spring was in the air and Susie wondered how things would play out, since it was unlike her typical working day. When the train pulled into Waterloo, she stepped onto the platform and sashayed her way through the crowds to the ticket barrier, across the busy concourse and joined the taxi rank for a black cab to take her the short ride over Waterloo Bridge to Somerset House, overlooking the banks of the River Thames. It was, she admitted, nice to have the opportunity to do something different and gain a small window into the world of politics. She was also glad and appreciative of the time and freedom of being out of the office and away from the demands of her legal work.

2.2 London: Somerset House

Somerset House was a stately-looking Georgian Grade I listed building, heralded as one of the great architectural treasures of the UK and Europe. It was designed to be a grand public building housing various government and public offices. It was also a popular filming location, featuring in James Bond films *Goldeneye* and *Tomorrow Never Dies* and one of Susie's particular historical favourites, *The Duchess*, starring Keira

Knightley. Susie had always wanted to pay it a visit and spend some time looking round its art galleries, having often wished she had studied history of art at university rather than English literature. Its grand stature befitted the event, she thought. She took a deep breath as she crossed the famous courtyard with all of its water fountains, up several steps and entered through a tall stone-edged door. This took her into an expansive reception area with security guards and administrative staff carefully taking down people's details and handing out plastic badges with their names and occupations. She registered her arrival with an efficient-looking woman in a Chanel-style cream jacket and fixed her name badge to her own jacket lapel, hoping that it would not leave much of a hole as it was her favourite and had cost a fortune, even in the sales.

The event started with drinks around small strategically placed tall tables in an anteroom, and Susie circulated a little and introduced herself to a few people as she slowly started to find her bearings. It was not a massive event and she got the sense that people had been carefully selected to attend, which surprised her as she had assumed it would be packed out with all sorts of political types. She was then ushered up some sweeping stairs to a table in a grand reception room with high ceilings, thick patterned carpet and a selection of old-fashioned oil paintings of fierce and important-looking men on the walls; no women yet, she noted. A meal followed, with a small salmon terrine for the starter, followed by beef Wellington and greens and a lemon cheesecake for dessert. Susie's appetite was failing due to nerves, and the waitress took away her half-eaten plates one after the other.

Then came an introduction by the CFPS' CEO followed by a keynote speech from a scientific expert in genomics and then a selection of short speeches by prominent thought leaders, investors and policymakers. The event perpetuated the idea that it was part of the Establishment. It followed Chatham House Rules, to foster free discussion and debate, and delegates in smart suits and business attire were busy mingling and discussing ideas and networking amongst themselves. She had been placed prominently next to the top table, where all the guest speakers and organisers were sat. She also discovered that she was sat next to a delegate from the CFPS, whom it seemed was intent upon making her feel welcome and part of the action. He was in his early forties, charming and very attentive, and he spent time asking her about herself, her work and her interests and she made polite conversation. She explained a little about her personal background and that she had practised life sciences law for twenty years.

After some short speeches and a lively question-and-answer session in which she managed to ask one question to be seen to be contributing to the debate and somewhat justifying her presence, she circulated more freely. The delegates were mainly middle-aged or older men, she noticed, although there were some women too. Growing in confidence, she shared a few thoughts and concerns with the keynote speaker about rapidly developing digital and AI technology and its convergence with genomics, national security, business and economics, health and reproduction. She quickly sketched out a flowchart on a napkin to illustrate her point, although she got the distinct impression that she was not really being listened to, and this just fuelled her growing sense of imposter syndrome. Despite this, she did speak with two other delegates, a man and a woman whom she had not met before, who quietly agreed with her and expressed their concerns too. The man volunteered that it was now relatively easy for rogue actors to capture someone's personal genetic information from, say, a used cup or glass, or even a toilet seat, and use this to potentially embark upon new forms of terrorism as a next step on from cyber warfare. Susie took some comfort from this conversation that she was not the only person who was concerned about all of this. However, there was little opportunity to have any in-depth discussions before the meeting came to a close and everybody departed to go about the rest of their day.

Over the next couple of days, Susie was left with a consistent nagging feeling that she needed to try and do more to raise the alert and share her concerns with the CFPS more fully in the hope that the penny would drop and they would start to take action. As a key political think tank, they were well placed to do something and she did not know what else to do as this was outside her usual realms of experience. It was not as if her network of contacts was bursting at the seams with people from the political world.

Over Easter, Susie had long-standing friends to stay from London for a relaxed and boozy weekend. Rory and his partner were full of life and loved good food, travel and the arts. They lived busy lives in London and they loved to come and stay in the country for some rest and recuperation from time to time. Rory should have been an actor but had taken the decision to become a university lecturer for more stability and to provide for his family. He had married young and quickly had two children in his twenties. Later in life, he had come out as gay and was now happily settled with Steve, and they liked nothing better than to party, drink and have fun when the opportunity presented itself. They were good for Susie and they livened up her world with intelligent conversation, wit and a great sense of humour, and she felt able to let her hair down with them in a way she rarely did with others. They were always interested to hear what was going on with her and, over a choice bottle of red wine from The Sunday Times Wine Club and dinner, she told them about her recent invitation from the CFPS and briefly outlined some of her concerns. They listened and she could see that they found the whole thing unsettling, but despite this they asked a few questions and talked through their thoughts out loud, aided by a few large glasses of Californian white label Zinfandel followed by some expensive-looking brandy she had been given by a grateful client last Christmas. They concluded, somewhat inebriated, that she should write up a briefing note and send it to the CFPS. After all, what did she have to lose? They added that it might help ease her mind and then at least she would have done everything that she could in practical terms. They went on to say that she should try to lighten up a bit and start to live a little as she had worked too hard for too long, which she could not disagree with. The topic of conversation then moved on to more light-hearted topics involving holiday plans, upcoming birthday celebrations and bookings at swanky restaurants in town with lustworthy menus and wine lists.

After Rory and Steve had left on Sunday afternoon, she stripped the spare bed, put on a load of washing and flicked the kettle on for a much-needed mug of tea. The house seemed much quieter and bigger now they had left and it was just her and Rina again. Whilst she adored them both and always looked forward to their visits, she recognised that she liked her own company and needed space to think. The weekend break had done her some good and she felt more energised and positive than she had of late. Encouraged by their visit, Susie decided to spend the rest of the Easter bank holiday weekend doing some more research. This, she told herself, would help her decide one way or another what to do and whether or not to follow things up with the CFPS with a briefing note. Picking up her freshly made mug of Earl Grey tea, she padded down the hall and into her office, accompanied by Rina who, after some initial fidgeting, curled up on the sofa for a snooze.

Susie decided to try and get a better sense of what was happening on the technology and genomic front in the US, to start to build a fuller understanding of the international picture and double-check her earlier assessment. Diving back into Google, she learnt that the US had a far bigger budget and a more sophisticated and joined-up infrastructure, having come across an official 2011 US White House paper on genomics. It had a picture of the White House on the front with different logos around it, featuring amongst others the FBI, Google and the US Department of Defense. This discovery surprised Susie and she paused, sat back in her chair and wondered why these different agencies were all in the picture together, stretching as far back as eight years ago (and she suspected well before that as well). This level of interconnection and convergence of power and wealth was significant, she told herself, and she made a mental note.

After a while, Susie carefully drafted an email to the CFPS, thanking them for inviting her and articulating in more detail her concerns that the UK lacked a sufficiently detailed, sophisticated, joined-up centralised strategy that embedded genomics across all areas of political policy in a short PowerPoint presentation attachment. She let out a slow sigh of relief as she finally pressed send on her computer laptop and the email disappeared from view. She had managed to knock up the presentation in just a couple of hours, setting out her thoughts in a series of colourful flowcharts and bullet points. It was easier and quicker than working up a written briefing note, and it was easier to navigate as you could switch back and forth through the different slides and get a visual sense for things, which was simply not possible with dense written text. There, she had done it. She had sent her assessment to the CFPS and the ball was now firmly in their court. It felt good to have acted on her thoughts, although she was nervous as she had not done anything like this before. It felt out of character and yet also necessary.

She felt Rina brush against the side of her leg and looked at her Omega constellation wristwatch to check the time. It was five o'clock and Rina wanted feeding and some attention. Susie got up from her chair and padded across her home office, down the parquet-floored hall and into the kitchen with its big glass bi-fold doors overlooking a small patio and the immaculate garden onto fields at the bottom. It was the quintessential English country garden and the expansive views that had sold the house to Susie, and she employed a trusty old local gardener to do the gardening as she did not have the time to do it herself. She realised that she was an absolute sucker for a beautiful garden and a restful setting because it helped to calm the fast-paced energy of her mind and shape her thoughts. She loved to hear the wind rustle in the trees and hear birdsong at all hours of the day, catch glimpses of squirrels scuttling across the lawn and up into the trees and hear owls screeching in the evenings. It came from having grown up in a pretty village in the country close to the North Yorkshire Moors national park. She had spent many hours as a child on walks and bike rides round the local country paths and trips to the North Yorkshire Moors with her mum and another family from the village with girls her own age. A favourite haunt had been a beauty spot called Sheepwash, located on Cod Beck which flows into the Cod Beck Reservoir near Osmotherley, where they would park the car and pass the day with a picnic beside a little stream. The water was crystal clear and cold yet shallow enough to make it accessible for paddling, and many happy times were spent there playing and hunting for big fat yellow and green native caterpillars amid the purple heather flowers and gorse. Life had been a lot simpler back then, she thought.

Susie was surprised and thankful that her email garnered some interest from one of the senior executives at the CFPS, a man called Matt, who having reviewed the email replied a few days later. He invited her to participate in a scheduled telephone call with him and a selection of his colleagues to discuss the issues raised about a week later. On the one hand, she was surprised that they had taken the time to consider her thinking and analysis and set time aside in their diaries. On the other hand, she supposed that they were perhaps just curious enough to want to know more so they could pump her for information. Their world was all a bit of a closed shop and mystery to Susie. It was full of people connected through background, school and Oxbridge, and it was difficult to break through their barriers and inhabit their world. This was a weakness in Susie's eyes as she felt the relatively closed nature of the political world limited their knowledge and understanding, particularly in scientific and technological developments at the heart of government and that this was not good from a policymaking and strategic perspective. The 'old school tie' had a lot to answer for.

A week later, the meeting started with the usual introductions, and her key point of contact, Tom, invited Susie to take them all through her short PowerPoint presentation in more detail. It was a strange and at times uncomfortable experience and at the end of the meeting she was left with mixed feelings. They had asked a lot of questions, made notes and at times interrupted her train of speech, which had made it difficult for her to get her points across in the way that she had wanted. They had also been rather taken aback when they had learnt how it had only taken a few hours of her time to do the research and knock up the PowerPoint presentation. Susie sensed that they felt rather unsettled by what she was telling them and that it was all a bit much to deal with. Their main comments were that she had turned traditional policymaking on its head for the next twenty-five years and that it generated a huge amount of work in terms of seeking to embed genomics into all areas of strategy and government. Matt told her that her multidisciplinary recommendations and plans for policy and governance far exceeded what they could achieve on the ground, particularly the national security aspects. He then proceeded to tell her that they needed to go away and make funding pitches in order to take matters forward, adding that if they were able to make progress, they would return to her to look at potential for a work collaboration. Susie let it be known that she was interested in doing some policy work and that she would like to try her hand at this. Matt retorted that she should stick with her legal work, although he talked about welcoming her more closely into their ranks and giving her access to their reading materials and library. In the weeks that followed, Susie was left to focus on her legal practice and it all went quiet. There was no further follow-up from the CFPS, other than to make arrangements for her to speak and horizon scan on developments in life sciences at a policy forum later in the autumn. Susie politely accepted their invitation, feeling a bit more confident about speaking on the back of attending their last event.

Chapter 3

Summer-Autumn 2019: Strange Encounters and Military Presence

Following the call with the CFPS, Susie had not been able to shake off her ongoing unease, concerns and thoughts on the genomic front. She could not just shut it all off and carry on with her legal work as if nothing had happened, try as she might. It still weighed heavily on her mind when she was not completely absorbed with her day job. It particularly came to mind in the evenings as she tried to make better sense of it all and she realised she still had so much to learn. She just could not get the births of the Chinese gene-edited babies out of her thoughts either; the significance of what had happened there blew her mind. Their genomes, along with an unknown third baby known as Amy, had been permanently altered, which was absolutely massive not just for them but for future generations and mankind as a whole. A red line had been crossed and from her perspective as a life sciences lawyer, it was huge. Yet it had all seemed to have gone quiet after the Chinese scientist had been arrested and was now in the process of being prosecuted by the Chinese authorities. She wondered what else the Chinese were doing on the genomic front, and she made a mental note to take a look at some point. Was the editing of the three Chinese babies' genomes an isolated incident or was there more to this than first met the eye? she wondered. The whole affair seemed incongruous and a bit odd.

3.1 Global Genomic Regulations

When she next found some spare time, Susie learnt about the Nuremberg Code, which was a set of ethical research principles for human experimentation first created by the war crimes court held in Nuremberg after the Second World War.[10] These arose from the case of *United States of America v. Karl Brandt, et al.*, which tried German physicians responsible for conducting unethical and inhumane medical procedures during the war on people in concentration camps and the forced sterilisation of over 3.5 million Germans. It was hailed as a landmark document in medical and research ethics, but she noted it had not been officially accepted as law by any nation, or as official ethics guidelines by any association.

The Declaration of Helsinki was also an important part of the historical record.[11] This was published in 1964 by the World Medical Association (the WMA), seventeen years after the shocking news broke of the eugenic experiments carried out by the Nazis during the Second World War. Like the Nuremberg Code, its aim was to prevent human subjects from being mistreated. It codified various ethical standards in respect of clinical research on human individuals. But it was not a legally binding document as the WMA did not have any legal authority, and it only carried weight when cited in national regulations. Susie went on to learn that the US subsequently announced in 2006 that it was going to remove all reference to the Helsinki Declaration in its national regulations.

The Universal Declaration on the Human Genome and Human Rights, which was adopted unanimously at the United Nations Educational, Scientific and Cultural Organization's (UNESCO's) 29th General Conference on 11 November 1997, was also an important part of the timeline.[12] Susie was particularly struck by several articles, including:

Article 1

The human genome underlies the fundamental unity of all members of the human family, as well as the recognition of their inherent dignity and diversity. In a symbolic sense it is the heritage of humanity.

Article 2

(a) Everyone has a right to respect for their dignity and for their rights regardless of their genetic characteristics.

(b) That dignity makes it imperative not to reduce individuals to their genetic characteristics and to respect their uniqueness and diversity...

Article 5

(a) Research, treatment or diagnosis affecting an individual's genome shall be undertaken only after the rigorous and prior assessment of the potential risks and benefits pertaining thereto and in accordance with any other requirement of national law.

(b) In all cases, the prior, free and informed consent of the person concerned shall be obtained. If the latter is not in a position to consent, consent or authorization shall be obtained in the manner prescribed by the law, guided by the person's best interest.

Reading that the human genome was said, in a symbolic sense, to be the 'heritage of humanity' was real food for thought. However, despite all of her reading, she still had questions about the current state of play of genomic regulation and governance, since these Declarations were just that and they had been published years ago.

3.2 US Genomics Policy & Appropriations Bill, 2019

In an attempt to try and make better sense of matters, Susie vowed to undertake some further research on genomics in the US. The US were world leaders in life sciences, and as a first-world power, it was always helpful to get to grips with where they sat in the overall scheme of things. The next free weekend she had, she decided to focus her energies on genomic funding, telling herself that if she followed the money this would give her a better picture of what was happening on the ground. After all, you could not accomplish much without money these days. It was an effective way in as her Google searches had produced few other meaningful leads. She wished she had more in-depth scientific expertise and a degree in something like natural sciences to help her better understand the scientific world. Nevertheless, she was not going to let this put her off, and she clicked on a few more links that took her to the latest draft US appropriations bill.

The US appropriations bill made fascinating reading because it laid out what the US was spending its money on, and the amounts at stake were massive, particularly in areas like defence. She trawled through this looking for headings and words that related to technology and genomics. It was not long before she realised that the US was at a pivotal point in its political approach to funding and regulation of human genome modification. Reading round the appropriations bill, she learnt that the draft federal spending bill had in the last few days been subject to an amendment to drop the ban on federal funding for human genome modifications in embryos. If this passed into law, it would enable the US Food and Drugs Administration (FDA) to approve human clinical trials and mark the start of a more liberal approach to human genomic science and practice in the US. This coincided with recent rapid innovation in science and technology in the genomic sector, not least the news that broke in November 2018 of the world's first gene-edited Chinese twin babies, Lulu and Nana. This was surely not a coincidence.

In further research, Susie discovered that in 2015, a provision had been inserted into the US federal spending bill for the US government in 2016 banning the FDA from funding clinical trials that created or modified the human genome in embryos.[13] This brought US policy in line with conservative thinking across the world which viewed human genome modification as a slippery slope towards eugenics and human genetic engineering. In effect, regulation of this important area sat within the US' wide-ranging federal spending bill. If US restrictions on funding of human genome modification in embryos were removed, it would represent a significant policy U-turn in just four years, and this would be significant in more ways than one. Given rapidly evolving genomic technology, there needed to be careful and in-depth consideration of the issues and debate to develop regulatory frameworks and policy that kept pace with developments. Susie could not help but think that it was just not enough for regulation to come down to this one provision buried in the US federal spending bill. She kept a close eye on US political developments in this regard over the next few weeks. It transpired that the proposed lifting of the federal funding ban on human genome modification of embryos was not lifted in the end.[14] Susie was relieved when this happened, thinking that at least there would now be more time and an opportunity for the US to consider and debate genomic policy in more detail before making any significant changes.

Another article looked at US regulations on genomics.[15] It reiterated that there was no federal legislation governing human genetic engineering. That said, there was US federal control on (1) the allocation of federal funding for research projects, (2) running gene therapy clinical trials and (3) FDA approval in terms of marketing a product. As such, access to federal funding or permission to run clinical trials or commercially marketed gene therapies required FDA approval. The article went on to make clear that as of 2019 the official stance of the US FDA was that federal money could be used to research somatic cell gene therapy (cells in the body which will not confer heritable changes in DNA to subsequent generations). However, federal money could not be used to research germline (cells including eggs, sperm and embryos which could be carried on to subsequent generations) cell gene therapy. However, Susie's attention was also drawn to comments in the article which went on to say that in theory it was possible to operate a privately funded laboratory to conduct non-clinical, human gene therapy research in the US. That was an interesting loophole, she thought, and she wondered if that was something that could be potentially exploited in some way, and she also wondered somewhat vaguely about the potential for dangerous gene-therapy research activity happening under the radar away from public scrutiny and regulation.

Summer marched on and Susie's legal work intensified over the next couple of months ahead of the High Court summer recess in August. Her time was taken up with a few big cases and some court hearings which kept her busy, and there was little time to do or think about much else. She was glad that her days were so full, and the routine of her work schedule came as a comfort. After a long day in her office, there was usually just enough time to sit out on her patio in the evening in the company of Earl Grey tea or occasionally a glass of wine and enjoy the last of the summer sun whilst Rina pottered round the garden chasing bugs and butterflies. Friends and family were also more sociable at this time of year and she was kept busy with the local village fete, visits to see her aged parents and summer drinks and events for work at which she was expected to make an appearance. There also seemed to be a never-ending stream of text messages and WhatsApp calls to negotiate with friends.

3.3 London: Royal Courts of Justice

Towards the end of summer, as Susie was coming to the end of her inevitable summer litigation push, she prepped for a particularly difficult court hearing at the High Court in London. She always enjoyed her trips to the Royal Courts of Justice, a large and imposing Victorian gothic building that stood proudly on the Strand. Its entrance hall never failed to impress, with its stunning vaulted ceiling, its elaborate tiled floor and beautiful stained-glass windows. It always felt cool and calm as you stepped inside, just like a cathedral, despite the challenging nature of the legal work undertaken there every day in its numerous court rooms. It always gave a sense of occasion to proceedings. There was always lots to look at too, whether it was people watching, looking out for someone in the public eye or an ancient legal and judicial costume in a large glass display case tucked away in the narrow hallways. It was often in the news too when big cases came to trial, and it had been forever memorialised in the first *Bridget Jones* film, starring Renée Zellweger, when she was sent to court to interview a famous human rights barrister played by Colin Firth. That said, it was not the most practical of buildings, with lots of stone steps to negotiate and too few lifts and toilets from Susie's perspective. It could also be freezing sat outside court in the large waiting areas in the depths of winter.

As Susie sat at a large wooden table in one of the cavernous stone-floored waiting areas, talking through case strategy and developments with a leading QC barrister, she began to notice a woman behaving oddly in close vicinity to her. The woman was propped up against a stone pillar and was staring at her keenly and then looking at her mobile phone intently. Susie looked at the woman, who was small, with piercing blue eyes, dark shoulder-length curly hair and a Middle Eastern look about her. Susie did not recognise her and was sure she had not seen her before. All of a sudden, the woman walked rapidly past her and started to take a call in one of the small meeting rooms behind her, occasionally sticking her head out of the doorway to look at Susie again whilst still talking in an urgent fashion to someone. It was like she wanted Susie to notice her, she thought to herself. The woman did not look as if she was involved in one of the listed cases that day either, which was a bit strange. It was almost as if she was reporting back to someone. However, there was little time to dwell on this as Susie's case was called into court for hearing and the demands of litigation took over.

Susie did not give the strange encounter much further thought, putting it down to a one-off thing that was probably nothing to do with her. As the weeks passed, she decided that it would be a good idea to start to prepare her presentation for the CFPS forum well in advance of the event itself in October. It was not going to be a legal audience and the delegates would be investors, policymakers, scientists and the like, so she realised that she would have to take a different approach, with less emphasis on the law itself and more focus on trends and horizon scanning. She decided to do something different with her presentation and put some of her recent research and analysis into practice to start to develop new genomic strategy for the fertility sector. Having worked out the distance of travel in her mind, it was then relatively easy to translate this into a PowerPoint presentation. First, she set out a new UK governance structure with a series of flowcharts, and then she set out a new model for fertility treatment delivery which embedded genomics into its work flow. This should give them something new and interesting to focus on, she thought, and it might appeal to all the private equity delegates who were in the business of buying up hospitals, clinics and pharmaceutical and genomic start-ups. She was glad she had decided not to leave it to the last minute because the CFPS contacted her a few weeks beforehand asking to see her presentation in advance, which had surprised her. Normally, she turned in her presentation at the last minute, squeezed in amid her busy court work. However, she went along with their request nonetheless, not wanting to seem uncooperative.

3.4 Twitter US Military Presence

Whilst she was in the kitchen waiting for her M&S lasagne for one to cook the night before the forum, Susie suddenly noticed some unusual activity on her Twitter account. She spotted several important-looking men from the US army in amongst her usual sector followers. As she scrolled back through her followers, she noticed a few more, along with some other tough, scary-looking foreign men not in military uniform, who did not look like her usual type of follower either. One of them looked Russian and another looked as if they could be Eastern European, but it was hard to be sure, and she definitely would not want to come across them in a dark alley late at night, she thought. She looked at the military accounts more carefully and then instinctively turned to Google to do some searches to try and find out a bit more information and satisfy her curiosity. She discovered that they were mainly high-ranking US army officers and this took her aback, all highly qualified with specialist experience. One was in cyber, whilst another seemed to run one of the US army's main scientific research laboratories, and the most recent one had a wide range of experience in training, logistics and policy.

Susie wondered what they were doing on her Twitter account, and she suddenly felt anxious and more than a little worried. She racked her brains and wondered about the timing of this and if it had anything to do with her dealings with the CFPS and her research, given the national security aspects she had identified. She could not think of anything else it could be, although she was struggling to see what had triggered this state of affairs. Admittedly, her research over the last few months had been more wide-ranging than usual, encompassing genomics as well as human rights law and international funding and governance. She supposed it could be linked to the briefing note she had sent the CFPS earlier in the year, although that had just given a short overview. Even so, it was quite something for them to appear like this, she thought. She was just a lawyer after all. Maybe they were just 'bots', she thought. However, as she could not shake her feeling of unease, she telephoned a friend, Tony, from the village, who was retired ex-armed services, and he called round later that evening for a chat and a drink. He was good like that and always happy to lend a hand when she needed to move something heavy or put the garden furniture away for the winter. He was excellent company, sociable and could make conversation easily, which she figured came in part from all of his military training and time served as an officer. He was also a perfect choice in this instance. She would pick his brains and see what he thought about it all as he had decades of experience and knowledge under his belt. She also trusted and valued his opinion.

After a quick catch-up about news in the village, Susie, slightly hesitantly, showed Tony her Twitter feed on her mobile phone and her Google search results on her iPad over a glass of red wine from an open bottle in the kitchen. She felt self-conscious and a bit silly, as if she was making a mountain out of a molehill as they stood chatting in the kitchen. *It was bound to be nothing, just some 'bots' or spoof accounts*, a voice in her head told her. She was not much of a drama queen and she did not discuss her work much since most of it was highly confidential anyway. It was also well known that no one really liked lawyers and on top of that, life sciences stuff was far removed from most people's lives. In fact, Susie tended to keep to herself these days, preferring her own company much of the time. Dealing with other lawyers all day was hard work and as she got older, she had become increasingly disillusioned with all the politics, egos and aggressive competitive behaviour that she witnessed.

3.5 C4I Military Communications Systems

However, Tony seemed surprised and he quickly put down his glass of wine and started to look at her screens carefully. Then he looked up at her. She could see from his face and body language that he was taking it seriously, which instantly sent her stress levels right up. Tony suddenly seemed on alert and to shift into an altogether different gear, and he slowly and carefully pointed out to her that one of the military accounts was marked C4I, which he said was heavyweight stuff. Susie asked him what he meant by that and what it stood for, feeling a bit self-conscious and embarrassed in the process. Tony briskly explained that it was an acronym for 'command, control, communications, computers, and intelligence' in the defence industry. C4I military communications systems operated in the US Air Force, Army and Navy and the Australian Navy and Air Force, and there was a system running at RAF Mildenhall in the UK. *That might explain why I had seen another account on my Twitter feed of a US army man staring back at me in headphones with computer kit in the background*, she said almost under her breath but just loud enough for Tony to hear.

Tony looked at her quizzically and began to gently ask her about her work and what on earth had been happening. Susie was taken aback by this news and what Tony was saying and she began to wish that she did not have to go to London and give her presentation the following day. She recounted that she had previously been invited by the CFPS to attend a policy event at Somerset House in London and thereafter she had sent them a briefing note and was due to speak at one of their policy forums the next day. She added that she had joined up a few dots as a result of her research and this had sparked an interest in genomics. However, she felt that this level of military presence should not be felt by someone like her, and she admitted that she was starting to feel increasingly stressed out by it. Seeing this, Tony spent a bit of time doing his best to calm her down and telling her not to worry and instead focus on the job in hand and delivering a successful presentation at the forum. He added that he was around if she wanted to chat again later and with that he left, saying that he was expected home for dinner. After he had left, the rest of the evening passed in a bit of a blur as she packed her overnight bag, got her outfit ready for the following day and checked her work emails.

The next day, Susie took her usual route in the car to Godalming train station, with Eurythmics blasting from her top-of-the-range Bang & Olufsen speakers to cheer herself up and lighten her mood. She travelled into London Waterloo and then on to the venue for the forum, which was in a hotel across town, involving a long taxi ride in a black cab. When she got there, she signed into reception and then made her way up to her room for the night, since she was the first speaker of the day and she wanted to arrive in good time and make the best of the networking opportunity. She passed a quiet and uneventful night, with an early meal in the hotel restaurant, a long bath and a good book. She slept reasonably well considering the pillows were a bit hard and she was away from home.

Susie got up early the next morning, put on her best black suit and after a light breakfast made her way to the conference hall. There was already a buzz when she got there, and she mingled with all sorts of different people including management consultants, scientists and thought leaders. The event was attended by around one hundred delegates from all over Europe and it had a distinctly international feel. She got the impression there were business people with deep pockets looking to pick up market intelligence which they could exploit for maximum gain. They were certainly not her usual crowd. Her presentation lasted around fifteen minutes and she delivered it smoothly and efficiently, hoping it was all worth it. The audience seemed engaged, which was a relief, and afterwards a couple of people came up to her to say how interesting it had been. However, she noticed that the rest of the speaker sessions were more based in the present than her own forward-looking presentation and they were arguably more conservative, which was unsettling, and she was relieved when the day came to an end and she could make her way home.

3.6 Senior US Military Officer on Twitter

The weekend following the forum gave Susie time to review her Twitter account in more detail and reflect on events over the last few days. One recent follower stood out to her: a good-looking senior US military officer. She wondered what this was all about and whether or not to follow him back and see if anything happened. She was not sure what to do and she hesitated, rechecking her account numerous times that Saturday. Eventually, she decided to follow the account back, which was completely out of character and rather daring compared with her usually cautious approach to life. She was not a massive social media user, seeing it much more as a work tool, and she had never done anything like this before. Probably nothing would happen, she told herself. She then sat down on the sofa with an M&S pizza and Rina next to her to take her mind off things with a film. She scanned Netflix and decided on a political thriller, telling herself that there was nothing like a good film to occupy her thoughts and help her switch off. Rina loved Saturday night sofa time and as soon as Susie had finished eating she jumped onto her chest, where she proceeded to get closer and closer to Susie's face with ever-louder purrs of delight before settling down with her paws round her neck.

The next morning, Susie got up around 8.30am and pottered into the kitchen to feed Rina and make her first mug of Earl Grey tea of the day. She could not function before this and Rina was unbearable if she was not fed before 9am. Then, with a mug in one hand and a slice of granary toast and marmalade in the other, she wandered into her office and sat down on her sofa. Rina materialised a few minutes later, looking pleased with herself, and proceeded to curl up next to her and start to wash herself loudly. Susie stroked her with one hand to settle her down whilst she switched her mobile on to check her emails and Google alerts. When she had checked through these and made sure there was nothing urgent that needed to be dealt with, she moved on to her Twitter account. As she was scrolling through this, a direct message appeared from the senior US military officer's account. This stopped Susie in her tracks and she tentatively checked it, feeling both intrigued and nervous at the same time. He introduced himself and asked her how her day was going. She paused for a minute before replying, saying that she was well. He replied again, this time saying that he was posted overseas, where he was in charge of troops and on peacekeeping duty in the area, and asking what she did. She replied, not wanting to seem rude, explaining that she was a UK life sciences lawyer. All the time, she had in the back of her mind that this could be a spoof account and she did not want to do or say anything compromising as she had her safety and reputation to consider. He sent another friendly message, and not wanting to get drawn into things further she politely made her excuses and signed out, feeling a bit flustered and bewildered.

Over the course of the next few days, the senior US military officer proceeded to send her messages, wanting to get to know her. He told her that he was divorced, with children at a military school in the US, and asked her whether she was single or married with kids. Susie was a bit surprised by this and retorted that she liked to keep her account professional and she did not give away personal information like that. There, she hoped that was enough to nip that in the bud. She did not know for sure who he was or what his motives were, and she did not want to get herself into any danger here. She was clear that she did not want to seem too rude and she hoped he understood. It all went quiet for a few days and Susie was left feeling a bit in two minds about the situation. He had been very charming and, if he was who he said he was, he was clearly doing a difficult job with great responsibility, miles from home, trying to make the world a safer place. That could not be easy and the long postings abroad must seem arduous at times. On the spur of the moment, the following week, she sent him a message sending her best wishes and thanking him for his peacekeeping work, as much as anything to make herself feel better as she was not sure she had handled their last exchange particularly well. He replied a couple of days later saying he had been away on a mission and that he was glad to hear from her. He then messaged her again over the next few days. Late one evening, she got a longer message from him expressing feelings for her and saying that he wanted to spend quality time with her after his mission had ended and really get to know her. Susie panicked, as this was not what she wanted to happen at all. She did not know the man and she realised she has been rather naïve. She took a deep breath and sent him back a final message thanking him for his interest but making it clear that she did not want to meet him or take things further. It all seemed a bit surreal and very unusual, and she was left wondering what was really happening. She could not decide whether it was just one of those things in life that happened or whether there had been a different agenda at work. She did not want to be used and she did not want to put herself in harm's way or be made a fool of by an opportunistic social media scammer.

Fortunately, it all then went quiet and she was relieved. A week or so later, following some late-night internet surfing, she noticed that President Trump had made a last-minute trip to visit the US military troops stationed overseas under the command of the senior US military officer. She watched some footage of President Trump standing in a huge hanger addressing hundreds of service personnel. With such an important visit from the US President, there would have been a lot of security and checks, and she thought to herself that this would have increased focus on his day job. The timing of this was fortuitous as it had probably helped divert his attention away from her and kept him really busy, she thought (if it had been a genuine account), and she breathed a sigh of relief. However, it had been a strange encounter and she was left feeling rather bemused by it all, recognising it was unusual for someone purporting to be a high-ranking US military officer and other military people to take an interest in a civilian, and a foreign civilian at that. It was definitely odd and it did not add up, and she could not decide whether there was a more serious agenda behind it all. Perhaps she would never know, she told herself; after all, she was fairly inconsequential in the grand scheme of things. She was not in the defence world and she did not mix regularly in the international circles of the elite. All she could do was chalk it up to experience, she thought, and get on with life.

3.7 BGI

The following weekend, Susie came across an illuminating article about Chinese genetics company BGI (formerly known as Beijing Genomics Institute).[16] On the front was a photo of BGI's co-founder chairman Wang Jian. The article reported that at BGI there was a big emphasis on health. Employees were expected to undertake regular high-intensity exercise using the company's exercise equipment in its open-plan offices and breakout areas. The company discouraged its employees from using elevators and, if people did, there were signs instructing them to do squats. The article went on to report that there was an in-house café which served low-calorie healthy meals and that out-of-hours employees undertook hikes up and down mountains since physical fitness was a component of the annual review process and influenced bonus awards. The article stated that employees (the majority of whom were just over age thirty) and their families were also encouraged to undertake regular tests, including genetic tests, for a range of illnesses including cancer, heart disease and dementia. Additional steps, including monitoring and prevention plans, were implemented for those with concerning test results in the hope that everyone at BGI could live to age ninety-nine or older. Susie also noted with interest how the article went on to report Jian as saying that genomic sequencing costs were becoming cheaper and more reliable and research was getting to the point where genetic findings could underpin treatments. As a result, China's government was encouraging large-scale deployment of genome sequencing and she wondered what this meant in practice.

The article also summarised BGI's history. BGI originally started as a state-backed laboratory in 1999 to assist the Human Genome Project and sequence the first-ever human genome. In 2007, the report said that Jian and his co-founders split from the Chinese Academy of Sciences, a state-controlled organisation for high-level scientific research, to create a private company focused on genome sequencing in Shenzhen. They went on to publish the first genome sequence of an Asian person in 2008 in scientific journal *Nature*. In 2011, they created the Cognitive Genomics Laboratory, gathering a multi-national group of scientists to investigate the genetic basis for intelligence. In doing so, they studied people with high IQs and compared them with a group of people of average intellect, although the article reported the work was never finished, which left Susie wondering why.[17]

The article went on to explain that in 2012, BGI offered $118 million to acquire Complete Genomics, a sequencing-machine manufacturer in Silicon Valley that was not making a profit; with the aim to acquire its technology so that it could build and sell its own sequencers reportedly to undercut competitors' costs. The article further reported that this garnered lots of attention in the US at the time and that US genomics company Illumina mounted an unsuccessful counterbid along with a Washington DC lobbying campaign before the US authorities approved the deal despite concerns that it could give China a strategic advantage on the genomics front.[18]

As Susie read on, she was also interested to read that the article described BGI's structures as 'opaque', which made it difficult for others to understand the full extent of its operation, finances and ownership. She noted the article asserted that it was said that BGI was privately owned and that Jian, who was reported to have a net worth estimated by Forbes at $1.2 billion, was the largest shareholder and that BGI had no special relationship with Beijing. However, the article went on to report that BGI received substantial loans from the government's China Development Bank and operated a 'biorepository' of frozen tissue samples as well as the China National GeneBank (CNGB) on behalf of the Chinese State. She further noted that the article reported that the genomic revolution would continue to advance, raising as yet unresolved issues about its future deployment.[19]

3.8 Chinese Genetic Testing Activity

In a *New York Times* article about the Chinese State's mass collection of genomic information from Uighur minorities, Susie noted that it reported that Uighurs and others were being caught up in a vast Chinese campaign of surveillance and oppression, allegedly to track down those who did not conform and reduce crime and terrorism across China.[20] The article reported that from 2016–2017 nearly 36 million people took part in Xinhua, where officials took DNA samples, images of irises and other personal data, and Susie was astounded by the sheer scale of this activity. The article also reported that Chinese officials were building a broad nationwide database of DNA samples from other ethnic groups, including from the US, and samples from a global database called the 1000 Genomes Project, and she wondered what would come of that and where it would lead. The *New York Times* article went on to report that the Chinese campaign was using US technology and that this had given rise to at least one US company announcing it would no longer sell its equipment in Xinjiang, where most of the reported campaign against the Uighurs was taking place. The article also raised concerns about genetic samples being uploaded to global genomic databases in the absence of obtaining valid informed consent from the individuals involved, asserting that this challenged scientific norms.

All of this reading about developments in China left Susie pondering as she realised there was much she did not know. But from her initial limited reading, she could see that things were developing quickly in China and that was an issue for the western world. She was left with lingering concerns about the issues ahead if the West did not keep abreast of what the Chinese were doing.

Chapter 4

Christmas 2019

Life seemed rather mundane in the run-up to Christmas after all the intrigue on Twitter, and things felt a bit flat. Gathering her spirits together as best she could, Susie carried on with her legal work and tried to put events over the last few months behind her. It had been a rollercoaster of a journey and it would feel good to catch her breath and steady the ship, she told herself firmly. There was the usual village carol service by candlelight followed by mulled wine and mince pies to attend in the old Norman church. She always did her best to attend this as it showed willing with the rest of the villagers and helped kick-start the festive season. It also delivered a special and calming atmosphere, with the soft candlelight dancing round the church and the joyful familiarity of the Christmas carols bringing back happy childhood memories.

Then there were all the Christmas presents to organise for family and friends, which was a time-consuming and frankly stressful exercise. There was never enough time to spend a day shopping in London, or even Guildford, hanging out with a friend and buying gifts. Instead, Susie had to squeeze in online shopping late at night, which was neither enjoyable nor one of her strengths. She was always amazed when she managed to order anything halfway decent and usually resorted to presents consisting of food and drink, perfume, slippers, cookbooks and gadgets, thankful for the John Lewis website. She usually went away over Christmas too, and this year was no different. It alleviated all of the family politics and meant she did not have to play host and spend days cooking and catering. It was also a good time to go away as the courts shut down over Christmas and New Year, save for emergency work. It provided an opportunity to go somewhere hot and recharge her batteries away from the cold, dark and wet weather in the UK and meant she started the year on a positive note. She liked to go to the Caribbean and this year she was going to Barbados with her on-off boyfriend, Michael, whom she had known since her university days.

4.1 CRISPR-Cas9 and a Genetic Arms Race

The weekend before she flew out to Barbados, Susie came across an article in the *Telegraph* over breakfast about the female scientist Jennifer Doudna, who it reported had 'unleashed the gene genie'.[21] The article immediately caught her attention, not least because it also contained a photograph of the Chinese scientist He Jiankui, who had created the world's first gene-edited babies in 2018. The article started by explaining that Jennifer Doudna had discovered a gene-editing technique called CRISPR-Cas9 which was producing new experimental therapies to correct genetic conditions like sickle cell anaemia and beta thalassaemia, which stop red blood cells carrying the right amount of oxygen for the human body's needs. It went on to report how in theory this new technology had almost limitless potential as it could precisely cut out parts of DNA and insert customised replacements. It likened DNA to the book of life written into human cells in the body with CRISPR-Cas9 acting as a word processor. Susie noted the article went on to report that CRISPR-Cas9 technology was easy to use, so easy that scientists could order CRISPR molecules on their phone designed to target any part of DNA in the human body as easily as ordering a takeaway meal. *Wow,* Susie muttered to herself as she paused to reflect on the seeming ease with which this new powerful and transformative technology could be used.

The *Telegraph* article reported that Jennifer Doudna was worried about the power that this technology had unleashed. It went on to refer to a new film about CRISPR-Cas9 technology in which Jennifer spoke of her panic and nightmares about eugenics. The article also referred to the Chinese gene-edited babies and how the Chinese scientist He Jiankui had crossed not just a line but a 'chasm'. It reported that the implications of the gene edits were not fully known, given the complex interactions with other genes and the environment, and that they would be passed on to future generations with the risk that this could cause problems in the second, third or fourth generations of offspring. The article went on to report Jennifer's horror at this incident and concerns that it could lead to the technology attracting a 'Dr Frankenstein stigma'.

Then, Susie's heart started to beat faster as she spotted some further comments in the article by Jennifer Doudna, who referred to the risk of a genetic arms race to perfect the human species. She quickly read on that because of these implications, the Pentagon had added gene-editing technology to its list of 'weapons of mass destruction' and was now investigating 'antidotes' to counter genetic arms developed by enemy players. The article went on to report that Jennifer was now in receipt of funding by the US government to find ways to reverse her own technology, before ending by reporting that human gene editing was coming and it was 'just a question of how and when'.

There it was in black and white in the mainstream press, the link between CRISPR-Cas9 gene-editing technology and a genetic arms race, Susie thought. It also spelled out how the US military categorised this technology as a weapon of mass destruction and US state funding was now being thrown at this to develop countermeasures.

Bingo, Susie thought as she sat back on the sofa with a bump to catch her breath. She now had a user-friendly reputable article in the *Telegraph* depicting a clear link between this genomic technology, human gene editing and the US military. It paralleled her own set of connections and assessment mapped out in a series of spiders' webs on her office whiteboard. It also gave a potential explanation for her own encounters with seemingly heavyweight military personnel. On the one hand, it was a relief to have the article as it helped to dispel worries that her concerns had all been in her head and she was just paranoid. On the other hand, it also lent additional weight to her assessment and her growing concerns about genomics. It seemed that her instincts were right and in that moment it felt as if she had been hit by a tidal wave. It felt as if her world had shifted further on its axis and that there was no going back from this.

4.2 Barbados, December 2019

It therefore came as a big relief when she was able to pack up her suitcase and head for the airport with Michael for her annual Christmas holiday. She had never been more glad to get away from everything and take a break. She was also glad to have Michael's company, time and attention. She recognised that she had been working too hard and was subject to far too much stress for her own good. She felt exhausted and she recognised that if she did not get some rest and relaxation it would catch up with her in the new year and she would probably end up with a bad bout of flu or something equally nasty for being too run-down.

Happily, Barbados was wonderful and she loved her holiday after all the hard work she had put in during the year. As a true patriot, she always travelled by British Airways and she liked the familiarity of having British food, newspapers and staff on board; it made her feel safer somehow during the flight. It was a real luxury not to have to worry about legal casework or have to check her emails every hour too. It was an opportunity to mentally unwind and reflect on her goals and wishes for the year ahead, something she liked to do every Christmas, and she realised she was incredibly lucky to be in a position to do so. The weather in Barbados was great, with lots of sun and beautiful golden sunsets over the Caribbean Sea every evening. The locals were friendly and this engendered a laid-back vibe amongst the guests too. She indulged in fresh fish and seafood most nights, washed down with the odd glass of chilled white wine and sparkling water, and she really allowed herself to relax with Michael on the open-air restaurant terrace. One of her favourite meals was the seafood *cioppino* which comprised spiced tomato, grilled garlic bread and lava sauce. Another favourite was the restaurant's seafood broil with prawns, clams, mussels, wine, parsley, butter and fries, although she would have to watch her cholesterol levels when she got home, she thought ruefully.

Together with Michael, she spent time lounging on the beach in the mornings and in a shady corner by the large and elegant hotel pool in the afternoons with a selection of holiday reading. Her favourite was the recently released autobiography *Becoming Michelle Obama*, which gave a fascinating insight into politics in America and life in the White House, and the latest Margaret Atwood novel *The Testaments*; both written by strong, successful and independently minded women, she thought with satisfaction. The hotel they had chosen was small and boutique on the platinum west coast of the island in St James near the iconic Sandy Lane Hotel, where the likes of Simon Cowell and

Rihanna stayed and where Simon Cowell organised an annual New Year's party. The other guests were smart, successful types who were looking to take a break from their busy lives too. It was, she thought, looking round her with a smile, her happy place, as she adjusted her wide-brimmed sun hat and lay back on her sun lounger with a cool sparkling water with ice and lemon.

On Christmas morning, Susie took a leisurely breakfast with Michael on the hotel terrace, which had been bedecked with local handmade decorations, and enjoyed the festive carols playing softly in the background. She wore a new pink pastel caftan over her bikini and a fresh pair of open-toed Sketchers sandals. She indulged in a fresh fruit cocktail packed with mango and pineapple followed by a basket of Caribbean-style pastries, whilst Michael tucked into a spicy-looking breakfast concoction of some sort with gusto. It was bliss to kick back on the deck overlooking the gentle laps of the Caribbean Sea over a second pot of Earl Grey tea whilst Michael enjoyed another coffee, she thought. The staff were in a good mood too and she and Michael signed up for a special Christmas banquet that evening, pre-ordering their mains and booking their favourite table overlooking the beach. Later in the day, as she and Michael relaxed in their room to avoid the heat of the afternoon sun, they opened a couple of presents that they had brought with them. Susie was thrilled when Michael presented her with a lovely pair of white gold earrings, and he was equally pleased with the Cartier keyring she had bought him.

To mix things up after Christmas Day and Boxing Day spent at the hotel, Susie hired a bright red compact automatic car with air conditioning for a couple of days. She and Michael drove round the island via the capital Bridgetown to take in the rugged scenery and Atlantic coast on the east side. The coastline was much more dramatic and much less populated, which surprised her after all the hustle and bustle of the west coast. It had a completely different feel altogether and it felt rather wild and untamed in comparison. They stopped off for a long lazy lunch at a rum distillery, enjoying a short tour and sampling the different rums on offer as well as picking up a couple of bottles to take back home to the UK; friends and family always appreciated some rum, she thought with a smile. She and Michael also called into the famous Lime Grove lifestyle centre in Holetown on the way back to wander round the luxury boutiques, check out the designer jewellery and watches and enjoy a cool drink in the main square. It was a completely different world and she looked and felt better for the time away. Michael was good company too and he knew how to give her some space and make a great travel companion. He was well dressed, made lively conversation in the evenings and he adored her; he always had. She was glad that he was there with her and she told herself she would worry about how to handle Michael when she got back home. The reality was that she liked her life as it was in many respects. She liked her freedom and she was now rather settled in her ways and daily routine. She did not really want to have to compromise, and she certainly did not want Michael to move in. She shuddered at the thought of having to deal with someone else in her personal space every day; that was just not for her. She sensed that Michael knew deep down how she felt about him, but even so, she did not relish having to have a conversation about it and see the look of disappointment in his eyes.

Another day, Susie booked them both onto a luxury catamaran trip round the island with lunch. It was one of the highlights of the holiday and something she liked to do every time she visited the Caribbean. Last time, she had gone for a sunset cruise and so this time she picked a day cruise instead. There were a handful of other well-heeled guests and the staff on board gave exceptional service, plying everyone with drinks and providing entertaining conversation. There was chilled music playing in the background and a relaxed party atmosphere developed on board, especially after a couple of potent alcoholic rum mixers along with shrieks of laughter from the crew every time they poured saying, 'One, two, three, floor.' They met some interesting people, including an itinerant bohemian family of three from the USA and an extended family from the UK, who had visited the island every year for the last fifteen years. The trip started with an opportunity to snorkel and feed the friendly turtles, who came right up to the side of the boat. The Caribbean Sea water was warm and crystal clear and she felt invigorated after twenty minutes in the water. Later that morning, they stopped off at a deserted beach where they were able to wade through the shallow water and explore the untouched white sandy coastline for half an hour whilst the staff served up a delicious buffet of freshly cooked fish and local food at lunchtime. It also gave her a fresh perspective on things, with the gentle sea breeze washing over her face, and she vowed that she would make more time to enjoy herself and live a little when she got back home. Life was short and after twenty years in law, she found herself wanting to do more and widen her horizons. Yes, she told herself, that was her goal and she would do her best to stick to it.

4.3 Man on the Beach

During the mornings, Michael would take some time to go swimming in the Caribbean Sea whilst Susie settled into her reading on the beautiful private white sandy beach by their hotel. The hotel produced an informative news bulletin which she liked to scan every day as they did not stock newspapers and there were no televisions showing the news in the public areas of the hotel either. She suspected this was a deliberate decision by the hotel team to provide a relaxing environment for their guests away from the strains of world affairs, whilst still providing a small stream of news for those that wanted to keep up to speed.

As she wandered back to her sun lounger with the latest edition one morning, she noticed one of the local beach sellers heading purposely towards her. There was nothing she could do but wait to be accosted by the man with his big bag of handmade bracelets and other bits and bobs. It was an uncomfortable experience for her, as she was not confident at handling herself with a seasoned local in this way and he made her feel guilty when she did not want to buy anything, despite the fact she did not have any cash on her. In the end, she agreed to purchase an overpriced bracelet which Michael would pay for after his swim, to keep the local beach seller happy and show willing.

As she sat back on her sun lounger in relief, she looked around and caught the eye of a man standing up next to his lounger in front of her. His female companion was talking happily with the vendor and he was tall looking, fit and maybe in his late forties or possibly early fifties, she thought, although it was hard to tell in the heat. All of a sudden, she stiffened as she heard the beach seller ask the man what he did for a living and he replied that he was in the armed services. The man then looked over at her again with a studied air and took in what she was reading and the news bulletin on the table next to her drink and she hurriedly looked down at her book. She felt an all-too-familiar cold shiver come over her again like the previous times and she did not like it. *Stop it*, she muttered to herself firmly, sensing she was starting to get paranoid and imagine things. Just because the man was in the armed services it did not mean it had anything to do with her. He was just enjoying a well-earned break with his lover. However, it gave her an unpleasant jolt and reminded her of all her research findings and the previous strange encounters with the military she had had in recent months. She tried not to dwell on this for the rest of the day, although it shook her up and it took until dinner that evening to relax in Michael's company and get over it.

4.4 Man at Barbados International Airport

Having returned to Sir Grantley Adams International Airport in Barbados on New Year's Eve for their flight home feeling refreshed, Susie looked round the waiting area to see lots of happy and relaxed-looking people and families. Many sported a golden tan and it was a good-natured crowd of families and couples, she thought to herself with a smile. Returning with one last decent cup of Earl Grey tea before they boarded their premium economy flight home, she rummaged through her bag to find their passports and boarding passes as she was the unofficial keeper of the paperwork. As she brought them out of her bag and looked up, she saw a man sitting close by on her left-hand side. He had a buzz cut, massive shoulders and a powerful-looking physique, and he could definitely take someone out with ease if he wanted to, she thought. He looked as if he should be some sort of commando and with that her back stiffened, her senses became heightened and she quickly started to pay more attention. He was Caucasian and blond from what she could see, with sharp bright blue eyes, and he was travelling on his own, unlike everyone else around her waiting for their British Airways flight to the UK. He had a battered black rucksack to the side of him with an old well-used neck rest hanging off one corner, and she noticed that he had been watching her intently as she got their passports out, which made her shiver and she felt her stress levels begin to rise.

She tried not to stare and instead made light conversation with Michael for a few minutes whilst the passengers in business class and the rows in front of her were called to board the flight. She was sure that the man was listening to everything that she was saying by the way he was leaning towards her and it all felt a bit menacing. Finally, as their rows were called, she gathered her belongings together and dropped her used cup of tea into the bin. He then suddenly jumped up, pushed through the snaking queue of passengers waiting to get their boarding passes checked and headed for the bin, with his rucksack swinging over his shoulder. She had an uneasy feeling that he was going straight for her cup, before she checked herself. That was just more paranoia about things and she had to stop thinking like that, she thought to herself. Nonetheless, she turned to Michael and pointed the man out as they joined the back of the queue. Michael looked round and as they got on the plane and took their seats, they both kept an eye on the door. The man did not appear to have got on the flight and the last she had seen of him was his back heading down the waiting area towards the exit at speed. Susie wondered for a moment whether she was being watched, and if so by whom and for what reason, and her stomach churned as she snapped her seat belt shut and waited for the flight to take off. Even Michael, who was so laid-back in life, had to confess there had been something odd about the incident, and he agreed with her that the man had not got on the plane.

Chapter 5

Winter 2019-2020

Feeling rejuvenated after her holiday, Susie felt sufficiently refreshed to carry on with her reading and research about genomics in her free time. There was still so much to learn and make sense of, and she was like a dog with a bone about it all. She came across an interesting article about lethal flu strains and dirty radiation bombs and the extent to which the human race could survive these.[22] At first glance, it all sounded a bit extreme, but she nonetheless persevered with the article to see what else it had to say. Then it began to discuss bioterrorism and a biological arms race, which piqued her interest and built on the *Telegraph* article she had read the previous month. The article proceeded to report how CRISPR-Cas9 technology could be used as a counter-terrorism measure and a defence program and had peacetime applications against flu, high-dose radiation and cancer treatment. The article went on to report that we needed additional better biodefence measures too, including better protective masks, clothing, air and water filtration systems, detection and identification devices and decontamination systems. These were needed, the article reported, because the human body's immune defence system could quickly become overcome by weaponised pathogens.

Reflecting on the significance of this, it was clear that the article was essentially warning about the risk of a manmade virus that could be used as a biological weapon. This was a really concerning prospect, she thought, because we would all be like sitting ducks, and nobody wanted to be in that position. It also fed into Susie's growing concerns about the risks of genomic technology and the creation of manmade cut and spliced viruses in laboratories around the world. She had been really unnerved by the whole thing since she had started her research last year, and she was not someone who was easily swayed. Then there was the decision by the US Pentagon to add CRISPR-Cas9 genomic technology to its list of 'weapons of mass destruction'. On top of this, there was a fundamental lack of effective global regulation of this rapidly evolving and incredibly powerful and transformative technology. It did not bode well, she thought gloomily, and in that moment she felt more helpless and alone in her thoughts than ever.

5.1 Chinese Genomic Policy and BGI

Continuing with her research, she started to gain a better sense of the sheer scale of the Chinese focus on and fascination with genetics and genetic testing for babies and newborns. This was seemingly far more extensive than that which was happening in the UK and across many parts of the western world. She read that making China one of the world's most scientifically advanced nations was key to Chinese President Xi Jinping's ambitions for the Chinese State to become an indisputable world power; with genomic technology sitting at the heart of its strategy.[23]

Susie read that Chinese genetics company the BGI group was one of the world's largest producers of genetic research and that it believed that genomics was about to become central to modern medicine.[24] Here was another reference to BGI, she thought, as she recollected her previous reading about this large, complex and reportedly opaque organisation. BGI manufactured genomic sequencing equipment, sold diagnostic tests and performed research for drug companies, and its co-founder and chairman, Wang Jian, allegedly had a massive $1.2 billion shareholding in the company.[25] She also read reports that Wang Jian predicted entire human genome sequencing would be repeated throughout a person's lifetime to inform health decisions, eating habits, guide medical treatments and even choice of partner.[26] These assertions resonated with the UK's genomic healthcare initiatives, but she was concerned that the Chinese approach would far exceed these, particularly if it started crossing into people's dating choices and decisions about a life partner.

BGI also operated a biorepository of frozen tissue samples and it operated the China National GeneBank, a digitised genetic databank on behalf of the Chinese State.[27] She also read reports that China had systematically collected genetic information about members of the Uighur minority community, allegedly without proper consent, from as far back as 2016; being a key part of the Chinese State's campaign to make the community more subservient to the Chinese Communist Party. She read reports that the Chinese State had detained a million Uighurs in 're-education camps', having blamed them for a series of terrorist attacks across the country.[28] She then read with a shudder that China was reportedly using genomic technology to map the genes of its people and identify different ethnic groups, for example, Han, Uighur and Tibetan, and that there were concerns that this technology was also being used for the purposes of surveillance and tracking individuals to tighten its authoritarian rule.[29]

This research made Susie realise just how different the Chinese approach to genomic technology and policy was in practice compared with the western world. The ideology was different in that the Chinese were using genomic technology according to news reports to suppress and control its people, not just focus on healthcare improvements. The Chinese had also made genomics a central part of its strategy to assert itself as an indisputable world power and she wondered what precisely this meant for the rest of the world. If the Chinese State was reportedly prepared to suppress, track and control its own people by means of genomic technology, how could it be harnessed globally to maximum advantage? Given the delicate international balance of power and finite level of global resources, what changes could this bring, and what did the rest of the world potentially have to lose? These were big and important questions, and she wondered what was being done to address them.

5.2 International Genomic Policy and Governance

To further develop her understanding of recent genomic international regulation initiatives, Susie also took some time to read about the World Health Organization (WHO), which included the Chinese. Then there was also a separate international commission set up by the UK Royal Society, the US National Academy of Sciences and the US National Academy of Medicine. The Commissions' aim was to develop principles, criteria and standards for the clinical use of genome editing of the human germline, should it be considered acceptable by the public. She learnt that it had convened its second commission meeting from 14–15 November 2019 in London, with the first commission meeting having taken place from 1-3 December 2015 in Washington DC.[30]

From the WHO's perspective, it had on 29 August 2019 made a start at greater regulation by launching via the WHO Expert Advisory Committee a global registry on human genome editing.[31] This used an existing International Clinical

Trials Register Platform (ICTRP) to include both somatic (affecting cells in the body) and germline (cells in eggs and sperm containing the genetic information that is passed down from one generation to the next) genome-editing clinical trials. In doing so, the committee called on all relevant research and development initiatives to register their trials. This followed on from an announcement on 14 December 2018 by a WHO advisory committee that it would develop standards for governance and oversight of human genome editing. It produced its first report of its advisory committee's work on 18–19 March 2019, comprising a global multidisciplinary expert panel which was tasked with looking at the scientific, ethical, social and legal challenges associated with human genome editing.[32] In doing so, the committee agreed that it was irresponsible at this time for anyone to proceed with clinical applications of human genome editing. This was rather late in the day, given the Chinese gene-edited baby affair, she thought dryly. It went on to report that over the following two years it would consult with a wide range of stakeholders and provide recommendations for a comprehensive governance framework for its use at an international, regional, national and local level.

5.3 UK Genomic Policy, 2020

Another article mid-January 2020 reported the UK government's publication in December 2019 entitled *Growing the Bioeconomy: A national bioeconomy strategy to 2030.*[33] It defined the bioeconomy as 'the economic potential of harnessing the power of bioscience and biotechnology'. The UK bioeconomy encompassed up to 5 million jobs in the UK, with an estimated worth of £220 billion. She noted that the government had ambitions to make the UK a global leader in bio-based solutions, predicting that the UK bioeconomy would double in size in the next 10–15 years and with the global market for biorefineries alone set to soar to £550 billion by 2021. In doing so, this would create a strong bioeconomy to harness the power of bioscience and biotechnology and transform approaches to food, chemicals, materials, energy and fuel production, health and the environment. Susie noted with interest that to be successful in this regard there needed to be continued collaboration between government, industry and research organisations. She sat back and reflected on the synergy and close collaboration between these entities. She was also struck by comments that although the technology and ideas existed, there was still a need for better high-level investment and better collaboration and knowledge exchange between the various different parties. She read it was also no secret that there was a nationwide STEM shortage and that we needed to ensure that we had a workforce equipped with the skills that the bioeconomy demanded right now. Too true, she thought, it was one thing to talk the talk but quite another to walk the walk. This policy also aligned with her policy and governance discussions with the CFPS think tank last year, and she was relieved to see there had been some further strategic movement in this regard, albeit there was still a long way to go.

5.4 Coronavirus Outbreak, 2020

Mid to late January 2020 came round quickly, despite the cold, wet English winter weather, and holiday time in Barbados seemed like a lifetime ago. Susie liked to keep a close eye on the news, not least because it could impact her specialist legal practice in life sciences. New technological advances in genomics and pharmaceuticals were happening all the time, and it paid dividends to be well informed and stay one step ahead. As a result of her voracious reading habit and news addiction, she soon became aware of increasing numbers of reports of a strange and deadly SARS-like virus in Wuhan in China.

5.5 2003 SARS Outbreak

She instantly picked up on this strange new pneumonia-like virus outbreak in Wuhan with a strong sense of foreboding. As a non-scientist, she was more aware than most of the risks of a virus outbreak because she had spent three weeks in China, including a visit to Wuhan, as a tourist back in 2003, just as the SARS epidemic had emerged.[34] The SARS virus outbreak had badly disrupted her trip and left her marooned in southern China in a quarantine hotel whilst the holiday operator frantically worked out a way to get her and the rest of her stranded tour group home. The Chinese authorities had closed down the famous Terracotta Warriors Museum near the city of Xi'an in China's landlocked Shaanxi Province which bordered Hubai Province and stopped her visit to Hong Kong, which had been very disappointing; she had always wanted to see the Terracotta Warriors in person and it had been a long-held goal of hers to visit Hong Kong. She and the rest of the tour group had only learnt of this as they came to the end of an epic cruise down the Yangtze River Gorges, which she had wanted to experience before the stunning landscape was forever flooded with the world's largest dam, the Three Gorges Dam, coming into operation to produce hydroelectric power. Costing upwards of $40 billion, the dam was heralded at the time as a major source of renewable energy for a power-hungry nation and a means to prevent floods downstream. However, it came at massive ecological cost in China, reportedly submerging more than 1,500 cities, towns and villages, and more than 1.3 million local people were forced to relocate along with massive loss of animal and plant habitats.[35] It had also been an impressive reminder of the power of the Chinese State, who were able to accomplish this immense feat in a manner that simply would not have been possible in the UK or most other countries around the world.

As a result of the 2003 SARS outbreak, the Chinese authorities had cancelled flights from Beijing and Hong Kong back to the UK, and Susie and the rest of her tour group had eventually got home via a flight out of Shanghai. At one point, they had been left sitting on a plane following an internal flight for over two hours, and then they had all been temperature checked before they were let off and allowed to travel on to their quarantine hotel. It had been a stressful experience and she had seen first-hand the panic SARS caused, with all the Chinese people they came into contact with masked up and genuinely scared to come near their tourist party in case they caught the virus, got sick and died. It had all felt a bit surreal as she and the rest of her tour group had had no experience of dealing with deadly virus outbreaks back then and some of the party had taken it badly, accusing the Chinese staff of overreacting. The quarantine hotel had been opened up at short notice to accommodate just them and it had been ropey in places compared with the previous hotels they had stayed in, and the food had been fairly grim; so much so that one couple amongst them had in protest checked themselves into the far more luxurious five-star Grand Hyatt Hotel down the road at their own expense.

5.6 The City of Wuhan: Virus Epicentre, 2020

Susie therefore felt an eerie and chilling sense of foreboding about this new unknown SARS-like virus outbreak, given the scale of the death and misery it seemed to be causing in Wuhan. China had first alerted the World Health Organization (WHO) to about twenty-seven cases of 'viral pneumonia' in Wuhan on 31 December 2019. The draft genome sequence for the virus was first published on Saturday, 11 January 2020 on virological.org, with China officially making the sequence public the following day.[36] Scientists from all over the world then started to download the genome sequence in a frantic flurry of activity as the scramble began to learn more about the virus, create diagnostic tools and work towards a vaccine. There were reports that the hospitals in Wuhan were full and overflowing, that people lay collapsed in the streets and bodies were laid outside apartment buildings. News reports said that 11 million people in Wuhan, plus other cities in Hubai Province, had been placed into forced quarantine by the Chinese authorities on 23 January 2020.[37] Wuhan was the largest and most densely populated city in central China and the seventh-most populous Chinese city, and so a virus outbreak of this magnitude was really bad news, she thought. Within hours of the Wuhan lockdown, travel restrictions were also imposed on the nearby cities of Huanggang and Ezhou, and then imposed on all fifteen other cities in Hubei, affecting a total of about 57 million people. She had not witnessed anything like it, and the WHO called the Wuhan lockdown 'unprecedented' and said it showed 'how committed the authorities were to containing a viral breakout'.

There were early reports that the true scale of the deaths was much higher than the Chinese authorities were admitting. With growing concern, Susie suspected that the real death toll was potentially much higher, based on her own knowledge and experience of how things happened in China. By 21 January 2020, she had read a report that the virus had spread to countries outside of China, but there had only been 314 confirmed cases globally and six deaths reported in Wuhan.[38] Based on satellite imagery of crematoriums with furnaces belching out smoke round the clock seven days a week, she noted that it was reported in some quarters that the true number of Chinese deaths was much worse. Then there was worrying footage on the news of new Chinese emergency field hospitals being built in just ten days to treat the sick. This in itself was evidence that the Chinese State recognised the deadly nature of this new unknown virus and that it was racing to deal with a tsunami of deaths, despite what it was saying publicly.

This outbreak could not have come at a worse time, Susie thought, as it coincided with the Chinese New Year public holiday celebrations on 25 January 2020 and the massive movement of people across China to visit family and friends. She knew from her own travels that Wuhan was a large transport hub in Hubai Province in central China and that this killer virus, for which there was no cure, could quickly and easily spread all around China and worldwide via internal and international flights and train links. It was like watching a train crash in slow motion, she thought, with rapidly growing concern. She found herself bouncing up and down on the sofa in frustration shouting at the television, much to Rina's surprise, to immediately shut down flights from Wuhan and China to the UK. No one was going to listen to her but she knew it made sense, despite the fact that there was little prospect of the UK authorities taking such drastic action.

5.7 The WHO Declares Human-to-Human Virus Transmission and A PHEIC, January 2020

On 22 January 2020, the WHO issued a statement on Twitter saying that there was evidence of human-to-human transmission of the virus in Wuhan, but more investigation was needed to understand the full extent of this.[39] This did not sit comfortably with Susie, and she worried that the international community was not reacting nearly quickly enough to this serious and rapidly evolving situation.

Then on 22–23 January 2020, the WHO Director-General convened an Emergency Committee (EC) under the International Health Regulations (IHR 2005).[40] Its purpose was to assess whether the virus outbreak constituted a Public Health Emergency of International Concern (PHEIC). A PHEIC is defined by the IHR 2005 as an extraordinary event that may constitute a public health risk to other countries through international spread of disease and which may require an international coordinated response. In other words, an emerging viral outbreak of concern that needed to be taken seriously by the international community. Unfortunately, the independent committee members from around the world could not reach a consensus based on the available evidence and so it was agreed that they would reconvene within a further ten days after receiving more information. Susie clenched her teeth in frustration when she heard this on the news.

Eventually, on 30 January 2020, the WHO issued a PHEIC.[41] The WHO also issued a situation report stating that there were more than 7,700 total confirmed cases of the new SARS-like virus worldwide, with the majority of these in China, and eighty-two cases reported in eighteen countries outside China.[42] Susie realised with increasing dread that this dangerous virus outbreak was far more worrying than the SARS outbreak had been in 2002–2004, which had infected approximately 8,000 people in total with just under 800 fatalities. In contrast, this new SARS-like virus had seemingly infected the same number or more in just the last four weeks, and the mortality rate had yet to be fully understood. In reality, the number of infections and deaths was likely to be far larger than the official numbers reported so far, she thought grimly. It had also spread like wildfire to eighteen different countries, and that trajectory would likely continue as it was not contained nor under control. Logic also dictated that the greater the number of people that got sick, the greater the number of fatalities we were likely to see, given the lack of diagnostics and vaccine capability. This was getting more concerning by the minute, and it seemed like her worst fears were coming true.

5.8 Major-General Chen Wei of the People's Liberation Army

Given her heightened sense of alert and her first-hand experience of the SARS virus outbreak in 2003, Susie started to home in even closer on the developing situation in China. She read that on 1 February 2020, the People's Liberation Army Daily, the official online media arm of the Chinese Army, reported that Major-General Chen Wei of the Chinese People's Liberation Army (PLA) and the virologist who led the Institute of Bioengineering at the Chinese Academy of Military Medical Sciences had been called in to oversee operations at the Wuhan Institute of Virology (WIV) in Wuhan, which was at the epicentre of the viral outbreak.[43 44]

The WIV was China's only mainland BS Level 4 laboratory, where the world's most deadly viruses and pathogens were worked on and where a leading Chinese scientist called Shi Zhengli undertook dangerous gain-of-function experiments on coronaviruses found in bats. The *People's Liberation Army Daily* reported that Major-General Chen Wei's role was to develop a vaccine and lead the response to this deadly new virus.

Susie also read reports that Major-General Chen Wei was China's premier expert in biological and chemical warfare, and that realisation hit her hard. Major-General Chen Wei's experience with coronaviruses dated back to the 2003 SARS outbreak, and her scientific work had been personally recognised in 2015 when she had been awarded the title Major-General by Chinese President Xi Jinping.[45] Susie sat back and reflected on the fact that the PLA's top military biological and chemicals expert was now running China's only mainland Biosecurity (BS) Level 4 virology lab, which also housed an important virus database containing genome sequences of thousands of viruses. She realised that the swift arrival of the PLA in Wuhan represented a military presence right at the epicentre of this new, unknown and deadly virus. The location of the WIV laboratory and its work on novel coronaviruses in Wuhan was either a mighty big coincidence or it was somehow connected to this deadly virus outbreak, she thought. This was despite Shi Zhengli's loud protestations that the virus had not leaked out under her watch as director at the WIV laboratory.

5.9 Is the Virus Manmade?

This line of thinking triggered all sorts of thoughts in Susie's mind. She had, since last summer, been aware of unusual things happening around her, and then there had been all those military accounts on her Twitter feed and that encounter with the senior US military officer. On top of that, there had been the incident at Barbados Airport with the unknown man who had looked like he was some sort of military commando. Now, the PLA were all over Wuhan, having dispatched hundreds of military medics to the Wuhan coronavirus frontline and placed their top expert in biological and chemical warfare in charge of the WIV laboratory. This got her thinking about the origins of the virus and she suddenly suspected that it might potentially be manmade, possibly with some sort of military association. All of her instincts, based on all of her reading to date and the impact of this novel virus, suggested that this might potentially be the case. Susie had learnt to trust her instincts over the years as they were often right, based on her wide-ranging accumulated knowledge over the last twenty years and her ability to join up the dots. It was like having a personal computer in her head, which could be both really helpful and also really annoying. *Whoa*, she thought, and she rubbed a painful knot that had sprung up in her shoulder as this sunk in. The more she thought about it, the more it potentially made sense and the less likely it seemed to her that this was some form of natural zoonotic viral spillover event from an animal host. After all, there had been little convincing evidence about the source of the virus to her mind, despite China's explanation that it had crossed from animal to human (zoonotic spread) in a wet market, the Huanan Seafood Wholesale Market in Wuhan, which they had hastily closed down and disinfected on 1 January. What if she was right? This would potentially have massive implications for the whole world as this deadly virus, for which there was currently no vaccine, threatened to wreak mass disruption and devastation and upset the delicate world order.

It followed that if this deadly virus was heading towards the UK and was about to do here what it was doing in Wuhan, that was quite frankly terrifying, and her own health and life could be in jeopardy along with that of her family and friends. There was so much to learn, and it was like a whole new world had opened up as national security, biosecurity and defence was not something she knew a great deal about. She urgently needed to do some more research to inform her thinking one way or another. More and more, she was coming across the military and they seemed to be an ever-increasing presence, and she felt more concerned and chilled to the bone than ever.

5.10 The Wuhan Institute of Virology and EcoHealth Alliance

The next weekend, Susie set time aside to research this new SARS-like virus and the Wuhan Institute of Virology (WIV) in more detail. Working from her study with a steady stream of Earl Grey tea, she learnt that it was China's first mainland Biosafety (BS) Level 4 laboratory. This was the highest level of biosecurity containment classification where the world's most deadly pathogens were worked on. Notably, the WIV had only recently opened in January 2018, and there had reportedly been worries about training and safety standards from the start. It had been built in collaboration with the French as part of an international agreement on the prevention and control of emerging infectious diseases at a reported cost of 300 million yuan (US$44 million).[46] However, the French had subsequently been eased out of the picture and the Chinese authorities had taken over by the time the facility opened.

The WIV was also where Shi Zhengli, known as 'Bat Woman', conducted world-leading coronavirus research collected from bats in southern China and other places. Susie read that Bat Woman had been working in partnership with a British zoologist called Dr Peter Daszak, who was the president of a US non-profit agency called EcoHealth Alliance. This came as a big surprise and she wondered how a British scientist came to find himself in this position of influence, running a US-based organisation conducting research and outreach programs on global health, conservation and international development in more than thirty countries around the world. She went on to learn that Dr Daszak's research had been instrumental in identifying and predicting the origins and impact of emerging diseases across the globe and identifying the bat origin of SARS. It also got her wondering why this US non-profit agency was funding Chinese research on bats in China and whether this had any correlation to the recent virus outbreak in Wuhan. This all seemed odd to her, and it did not make sense, given the state of US-Chinese politics and the increasingly complex anti-China stance, coupled with trade disputes, adopted by President Trump who was all about 'putting America First' and growing US businesses and jobs. She filed this information away and made a mental note to look further into this when she had more time.

5.11 UK COBR Meetings

Political developments and responses to the virus outbreak in the UK and in the US unfolded at a rapid pace. Susie learnt about the role played by SAGE, a subcommittee of COBR (Civil Contingencies Committee), otherwise known as COBRA, which is brought together to deal with large-scale emergencies like natural disasters, a terrorist attack or a disease outbreak. COBR is the acronym for Cabinet Office Briefing Rooms, a series of rooms located in the Cabinet Office at 70 Whitehall in London. The first COBR meeting took place in the 1970s to oversee the UK government's response to the 1972 miners' strike. Further COBR events were triggered by the 1980 Iranian Embassy siege, the 2001 foot and mouth outbreak, the 11 September 2001 attacks (commonly known as 9/11), the 7 July 2005 London bombings, the refugee crisis in Calais, the Paris attacks in 2015 and the Manchester Arena bombing at an Ariana Grande music concert in 2017.

A first precautionary UK SAGE meeting was convened on 22 January 2020, which coincided with the WHO statement saying that there was evidence of human-to-human transmission of the virus in Wuhan.[47] More meetings then followed in quick succession as a result of developing concerns about this deadly new virus outbreak and what this meant for the UK. Susie further noted grimly in the weeks that followed the excoriating media coverage that Prime Minister Boris Johnson had missed the first five COBR meetings, which reportedly only served to put the UK government's response to the rapidly emerging global coronavirus pandemic further on the back foot.

5.12 The Diamond Princess Cruise Liner, February 2020

On 5 February 2020, Susie watched the news in shock as a large tourist cruise ship called the *Diamond Princess* quarantined 3,700 passengers and staff in Tokyo Bay after a two-week trip to China, Vietnam and Taiwan.[48] News had reached the cruise liner on 2 February 2020 that an elderly passenger in his eighties had disembarked the ship in Hong Kong eight days earlier and then tested positive for the new SARS-like virus. The captain had then been instructed to sail the cruise liner to Tokyo Bay, so that passengers and crew could be screened. On 3 February 2020, a team of health workers had sailed out to the *Diamond Princess* and spent that night and the next day visiting each cabin and asking if people were feverish or coughing, taking temperatures and swabbing throats. The first set of test results came back with ten reportedly positive for the new SARS-like virus to which no one had immunity. The boat was then placed in quarantine for fourteen days off Japan when Japanese authorities prevented the passengers and crew from disembarking at the port of Yokohama for fear of spreading the virus. At that point, Japan had only identified twenty cases of the virus and it was due to host the Summer Olympics a few months later and so it was intent on eliminating this disease risk as far as possible.

The plight of the *Diamond Princess* cruise liner had effectively become an international incident and a serious quarantine nightmare. There was frequent coverage about this developing situation, and Susie watched in horror from the comfort of her sofa as news reports came in that 218 people on board the ship had gone on to test positive for the virus. The thought of being trapped on a cruise ship in close proximity to other guests and staff who had already contracted the virus, knowing that you might get it and fall seriously ill too, or worse still die, was a terrifying prospect and enough to put you off holidaying on a cruise ship anytime soon, she thought. There were heart-wrenching TV interviews with frightened-looking passengers in their cabins on the cruise liner pleading with authorities to evacuate them and it was awful to watch. Lots of the passengers were over sixty too, which made the situation worse as they were more vulnerable to the deadly virus, she thought. Eventually, over time, passengers and crew were evacuated and either sent to hospital facilities for medical treatment or flown home to yet more quarantine. The whole incident left her wondering if this was a sign of much worse things to come as the virus continued to spread around the world. Deep down, her gut instinct told her this was just the start.

5.13 Death of Chinese Doctor Dr Li Wenliang, 7 February 2020

News reports came in on 7 February 2020 that the brave Chinese doctor, Dr Li Wenliang, had died.[49] He had reportedly first raised the alarm to fellow Chinese doctors on a chat group on 30 December 2019 about a cluster of a new SARS-like virus at Wuhan Central Hospital in Wuhan before contracting the virus himself. He had then reportedly been reprimanded by the Chinese authorities in early January 2020 for his actions and he had been required to sign a statement denouncing his warning as an unfounded rumour of what had then turned out to be true. Susie noted sadly that there were belated outpourings of public support around the world marking Li Wenliang's bravery.

This sad news was a poignant reminder of just how deadly the virus could be and that no one was immune. If medics could get sick and die too, this was really bad news, and she wondered how the UK and the National Health Service would cope if the virus took hold here. Would we have enough personal protective equipment (PPE) to keep staff safe? Would we have enough oxygen and ventilators to support those suffering with the virus? Would we need to build new field hospitals too, like the Chinese, to accommodate an avalanche of sick patients? These thoughts and concerns kept Susie awake at night and left her feeling exhausted and sluggish when she woke up in the morning, despite copious amounts of Earl Grey tea.

5.14 The Virus is Named Covid-19

On 11 February 2020, the new SARS-like virus was officially named 'Covid-19', an acronym that stood for coronavirus disease 2019.[50] It was, Susie thought, a more user-friendly name, and it was quickly adopted and helped to de-politicise references to the pandemic. Throughout February, there were ongoing discussions about what caused the virus, and she did her best to keep her eyes and ears open about this in amongst her busy legal workload. The question as to whether it was zoonotic spread or potentially a lab release of a virulent manmade virus kept going round and round her head, and it occupied her thoughts at all hours of the day and night. There were also ongoing fears that the number of people infected and dying with the virus in China was being seriously under-reported, which really concerned her and played on her mind. If this virus was potentially manmade and the result of a lab release, this could just be the start of a global pandemic of unprecedented proportions, she thought in trepidation.

5.15 The WHO Declares a Global Pandemic on 11 March 2020

On 11 March 2020, the coronavirus outbreak was labelled a global pandemic by the WHO and Susie's worst fears started to become even more real. 'This is not just a public health crisis, it is a crisis that will touch every sector – so every sector and every individual must be involved in the fight,' said Dr Tedros Adhanom Ghebreyesus, WHO Director-General, at a media briefing.[51] Dr Tedros called on governments to change the course of the outbreak by taking 'urgent and aggressive action'. He went on to say, 'Pandemic is not a word to use lightly or carelessly. It is a word that, if misused, can cause unreasonable fear, or unjustified acceptance that the fight is over, leading to unnecessary suffering and death.'[52] It was chilling to hear this and it stoked Susie's fears to an altogether new level of concern.

5.16 The US Declares a National Emergency and Travel Restrictions on 13 March 2020

Susie did her best to keep an eye on the US response to the Covid-19 pandemic as well, given their size, wealth and political status as one of the key leaders of the democratic free world. To begin with, Republican President Donald Trump was seen playing down the coronavirus outbreak and making public addresses that it was 'all going to be just fine' and it was 'a problem that's going to go away'. Over time, President Trump was increasingly flanked by Dr Tony Fauci, the director of the National Institute of Allergy and Infectious Diseases (NIAID). He served under President Trump as one of the lead members of the White House Coronavirus Task Force and she noticed he was steadily becoming more visible and a public health spokesperson for the Office of the President during the pandemic. This was paralleled by the likes of Professor Chris Whitty, Chief Medical Officer for England and the UK government's Chief Medical Adviser, and Professor Jonathan Van-Tam, Deputy Chief Medical Officer, who were doing their best to support the UK government pandemic response and provide scientific guidance.

On 17 January 2020, the US Center for Disease Control and Prevention (CDC) announced that it would begin screening passengers at three US airports, namely JFK International, San Francisco International and Los Angeles International airports.[53] These airports were selected because they had the most flights between the US and Wuhan in China. Then on 21 January 2020, the CDC confirmed the US' first coronavirus case involving a Washington State resident who had returned from Wuhan in China on 15 January.[54] On 2 February 2020, global air travel started to be restricted and those travelling to the US from Hubei Province faced a two-week home-based quarantine. This was followed by an announcement by President Trump on 13 March 2020 of a US national emergency due to the coronavirus outbreak.[55] The same day, the US banned non-American citizens who had visited twenty-six European countries within fourteen days of coming to the United States, although Susie noted that people travelling from the UK and the Republic of Ireland were for the time being exempt. However, it was only a question of time, she thought, before UK and Irish citizens were banned from entry to the US too.

5.17 UK Travel Restrictions Announced on 17 March 2020

It frustrated Susie even more to see that the US were busy shutting down international travel whilst the best the UK could do was get the Foreign Secretary, Dominic Raab, to issue travel advice on 17 March 2020 against all but non-essential travel, initially for a period of thirty days, saying:[56]

> *UK travellers abroad now face widespread international border restrictions and lockdowns in various countries. The speed and range of those measures across other countries is unprecedented. So I have taken the decision to advise British nationals against all non-essential international travel...*
>
> *UK inward and outward travel has already fallen by a significant amount since the outbreak of coronavirus. Ryanair, Virgin and EasyJet have cut flights by 80% this month and IAG has decreased capacity by 75%.*

It seemed crazy to Susie that the UK's borders were being left open. As an island nation, the UK had the advantage of being able to seal off its borders far more effectively than other landlocked countries across Europe, and that advantage was being squandered, she thought crossly. The UK government had missed a small window of opportunity that had been available back in early January 2020 to really jump on this virus, aggressively contact trace anyone that had come into contact with it and drive down numbers to eliminate the disease risk amongst the general public pending the development of a vaccine. She could not help but wonder whether the UK response would have been different if a woman prime minister had been in charge, noting the way in which New Zealand's female prime minister, Jacinda Ardern, went in hard and fast, closing its borders and effectively shielding its population from the spread of the virus. Time would tell, but she was not optimistic for the UK's chances faced with the virulence and speed with which this deadly virus was spreading.

5.18 Publication of 'The Proximal Origin of SARS COV-2' on 17 March 2020

This coincided on 17 March 2020 with the publication of a significant new scientific paper in *Nature Medicine* entitled *The Proximal Origin of SARS COV-2.*[57] The paper was co-authored by five heavyweight scientists from the USA, UK and Australia, and it was an important early read on what was thought to be the cause of this new deadly virus. In the paper, the scientists asserted that it was improbable that SARS-CoV-2 had emerged through laboratory manipulation of a related SARS-CoV-like coronavirus. Instead, the scientists set out two scenarios that could plausibly explain the origin of SARS-CoV-2: (i) natural selection in an animal host before zoonotic transfer; and (ii) natural selection in humans following zoonotic transfer. Susie sat back and digested this, acutely aware that she did not have a formal scientific background and that these scientists were seemingly far better placed to assess the origins of Covid-19 than she was. However, their scientific assessment sat at odds with her own views and suspicions. It left her feeling uneasy and frustrated because it quickly set the tone and framed the mainstream narrative about the Covid-19 outbreak and stifled open debate about the possibility of a manmade virus lab release. She noted with annoyance that anyone who tried to discuss a potential lab release was labelled a conspiracy theorist, and that could spell professional death for people's careers, she thought. Whilst she appreciated the world was at a pivotal point in the absence of effective medications and a vaccine to combat the virus, she still worried that this narrative might not be an accurate picture of what was really going on. This troubled her and left many unanswered questions to her way of thinking.

5.19 Italy is Overrun by Covid-19, 2020

Susie also watched with growing concern as Covid-19 hit Italy as this was a northern European country, much closer to home in the UK. On 30 January 2020, the first two cases of Covid-19 were confirmed in Rome.[58] A Chinese couple from Wuhan had reportedly arrived in Italy on 23 January via Milan Malpensa Airport, travelled from the airport to Verona, then to Parma, arriving in Rome on 28 January 2020. The following day, the couple had developed a cough and a fever and were hospitalised, having tested positive for SARS-CoV-2. On 30 January 2020, the Italian government suspended all flights to and from China and declared a state of emergency for the next six months.[59] During February and March 2020, clusters of Covid-19 developed in northern Italy. Starting on 8 March, the region of Lombardy, together with fourteen additional northern and central provinces in Piedmont, Emilia-Romagna, Veneto and Marche, was put under lockdown. Two days later, the Italian government extended the lockdown to the whole country.[60] However, the news coverage got worse and worse and Susie watched one report after another showing the Italian health service being overrun, with Covid-19 intensive care wards full of the sick and the dying. There were also reports that Italy was struggling to keep pace with the numbers of people needing to be buried. This was truly awful, she thought, and her heart went out to the Italian people.

5.20 The Term 'Proning'

It was from the Italian news reports that the general public first learnt about the term 'proning'. This was a manual procedure which placed patients in respiratory distress on their stomachs in intensive care to take pressure off their lungs and help them breathe. Graphic images of unconscious patients in hospital gowns and bare feet being turned over into a prone position on hospital beds by teams of Italian medical staff in full PPE were truly distressing to watch on TV. These patients were fathers, mothers, brothers and sisters of normal people, and they were now left fighting for their lives, with their futures hanging in the balance. Susie could not get these harrowing images out of her mind, nor the distinctive bleeps and noise of the intensive care units. It was also very upsetting to see reports of distressed families in Italy waiting for ambulance crew to take away their sick or deceased loved ones. It was like something out of a science fiction film, except it was real and it was now science fact. News reports also came in regularly saying that the virus would take off in the UK in just a matter of weeks. No amount of Earl Grey tea or chocolate was going to stop that from happening, she thought, as she reached for yet another bar of Ritter Sport alpine milk chocolate to try and steady her nerves.

5.21 The UK Goes into Nationwide Lockdown on 23 March 2020

On 10 March 2020 came news reports that Nadine Dorries, a UK junior health minister, had become the first MP to test positive for Covid-19.[61] This really brought it home to know that it was spreading in London and through the corridors of political power at Westminster. Here we go, thought Susie through gritted teeth, as it now seemed inevitable that the UK was next to be hit by this viral tsunami. She wondered how long it would be before other members of the UK government were struck down by the virus and got sick too.

On 16 March 2020, UK Prime Minister Boris Johnson started daily press briefings, urging everybody in the UK to work from home and avoid pubs and restaurants to give the National Health Service (the NHS) time to cope with the pandemic. It was strange to watch the news briefings and it all felt very alarming. On 23 March 2020, Boris Johnson gave a televised address in which he instructed Britons to stay at home and only leave to buy food, to exercise once a day, or to go to work if they absolutely could not work from home.[62] He went on to make clear that people would face police fines if they failed to comply with these new measures. Covid-19 had effectively locked down the UK, and Susie watched on grimly as non-essential shops and services closed their doors to the public and she started her own period of lockdown and working from home in the company of just Rina. It was a surreal and scary moment, accompanied by uncertainty on a scale Susie had not known before.

5.22 Britain's Prime Minister Boris Johnson Contracts Covid-19 on 27 March 2020

On 27 March 2020, a news announcement came that both the UK Prime Minister Boris Johnson and Health Secretary Matt Hancock had tested positive for Covid-19.[63] Susie was not surprised to hear this, given the virulence of the virus and the fact that Boris Johnson in particular had been reportedly rather cavalier about infection control, insisting that he was not going to stop shaking hands with people as he went about his official political duties. Both men had frequently been in the news together and they would have been working in close proximity in Westminster over the last few weeks, she thought.

Susie had also at first been bemused by Prime Minister Boris Johnson's 'don't worry about shaking hands' line until it had dawned on her that this suggested a genuine lack of experience and understanding about virology and pandemic control amongst UK government politicians. This had potentially been made worse by the fact that Boris Johnson had missed the first five COBR meetings convened to deal with the virus, she thought dryly. Unlike Asian countries who had previous experience with SARS and MERS, the UK had not really seen anything like this before and there had been no past experience to fall back on beyond contingency planning for an influenza pandemic back in 2016.

Over the days that followed, Boris Johnson gave short social media updates on Twitter from his upstairs flat at Number 10 Downing Street in London where he was self-isolating, looking poorly, away from his heavily pregnant fiancée Carrie Symonds. Eventually, on Sunday, 5 April 2020, he was admitted to St Thomas' Hospital in London after suffering ten days of symptoms, including a high fever.[64] On 7 April, news broke from grave-looking media reporters that Boris Johnson's condition had worsened, and he had been moved into intensive care and that Foreign Secretary Dominic Raab was going to deputise for him.[65] News reports said Boris Johnson had been given oxygen late on Monday afternoon, before being taken to intensive care. However, they stressed that importantly he had not been sedated or put on a ventilator. This put the country into an even more sombre mood as people watched events unfold from their televisions at home as the nationwide lockdown continued. Susie heaved a sigh of relief along with the rest of the UK when Boris Johnson pulled through and was eventually discharged from hospital on 14 April 2020 and sent to his government country retreat, Chequers, to continue his recovery.[66] It sent an important message that the virus was survivable and that despite the deaths being reported, there was hope if you succumbed and fell sick. It was a small ray of hope in an otherwise dark moment in time.

5.23 Britain During its First Lockdown In 2020

Susie was immensely grateful for the comfort and outside space her house offered her in the Surrey countryside. Unusually, the UK experienced a blisteringly hot heatwave at the beginning of April 2020, which helped take the edge off the shock and worry of being in lockdown. It almost felt like a mini holiday until the reality of the situation kicked back in with worrying news reports about growing numbers of people that were getting sick and being hospitalised across the UK. She could at least potter out into the garden with Rina and take in the sun and listen to the birds and wildlife. She could stretch her legs round her garden and enjoy the hot weather in peace from a comfortable garden chair with lots of cushions. She felt guilty and terribly sorry for all those people in overcrowded housing, particularly those with young families stuck in flats or homes without gardens, and those in densely packed housing in towns and cities who were only able to leave their homes once a day for an hour of exercise. She could not imagine what that must be like, and she shuddered, although the media did their best to cover the trials and tribulations of single parents with young children in high-rise flats. How you kept young children entertained day after day in those cramped conditions alluded her. She also felt concerned for those that were not able to work from home and particularly key workers like ambulance crew, nurses and doctors, who had to face this deadly virus on the Covid-19 frontline every day without respite.

Chapter 6

Easter and Spring 2020

In the run-up to the nationwide lockdown declared in the UK, Susie managed to deal with a complex court case in person in London. The mood at court was sombre and there was a palpable sense of doom and gloom. Lawyers and clients alike were jittery and anxious about the horrific level of sickness and deaths in Italy caused by the Covid-19 pandemic. Everyone was worried about whether, or when, it would spread to the UK following incessant news coverage that the pandemic would hit in just a few weeks' time like an avalanche. Conversations in the corridors and waiting areas outside court talked about using hand sanitiser, whether to shake hands, ability to work from home and social distancing, which all seemed strange and surreal. The normal energy at court was subdued, and people looked dazed and out of sorts, in themselves and with the world around them.

6.1 Strange Men at a London Restaurant

Following a demanding High Court hearing, Susie and her QC barrister made their way to a nearby restaurant for a well-earned late lunch. They crossed the zebra crossing on the Strand outside the main entrance to the Royal Courts of Justice and briskly cut through the lunchtime crowds to a restaurant on the corner. Inside, they were ushered through the bar to a spacious seating area at the back, where they gratefully sat down at a table in the corner and looked at the menu. The waitress was attentive and rattled off the mainly fish specials for the day. Susie chose a fish finger sandwich, preferring something light at lunchtime as a large, heavy meal tended to slow her down and make her sleepy. Conversation flowed easily after the demands of court.

After a time, Susie looked up and noticed two men sat at a table across from them by the window. A little while later, she noticed that they were leaning in and talking to each other intently and then glancing over in her direction. She could not put her finger on it precisely, but she just had a sixth sense that there was something a bit off about them, and their expressions did not seem very pleasant. The men wore camel-coloured raincoats and she had an odd feeling about them. There was just something in the way they were behaving, their body language and their glances her way. It did not look as if they were enjoying a casual lunch, and the fact that they were still wearing their coats was unsettling. The feeling did not last long, though, as conversation with the QC took over and when she looked up again the two men had gone. It did not look as if they had eaten anything either, which was strange too, she thought, as she left the restaurant and headed to Waterloo train station to go home. The journey back home was stressful and uncomfortable. A man started to cough profusely in a seat near her on the opposite side of the carriage and she worried whether he had Covid-19 and whether he was exposing her to the virus as well. She had not known what to do and had felt very unprotected sat there in the carriage. It had started to rain too, which served to dampen her mood still further.

Susie was therefore relieved when she finally reached her

front door later that evening, only to find that Rina had been busy smearing her Whiskas cat food all over the kitchen floor again. Rina had mastered the art of pushing her bowl across the floor and scooping out the wet food with her paw and rubbing it in. Susie knew it was another tabby protest for having been left all day after some long hours at work that week. That cat had some serious separation anxiety issues, she thought, as she surveyed the mess in dismay. There was little she could do to stop it from happening as Rina only had three teeth left and could only eat soft food. Susie had already tried upgrading her plastic bowls to heavier ones made of pottery to make it more difficult for Rina to move them across the floor, but this had not really made much difference. This was all she needed, and she sighed as she calculated it would take her a good twenty minutes to clear it all up and calm Rina down before she could get on with her own dinner. At least Rina had not managed to flick it up the walls too, which had necessitated her repainting the kitchen with washable paint last year. It was at times like this she wondered why she kept a pet, she thought wearily, and it definitely called for an early night.

6.2 Britain Stockpiles Food

Over the next few days, Susie decided to stock up on food in case of shortages and restrictions in the UK. She was now convinced that the UK would have to face the tidal wave of the virus that was about to hit them. She took a trip in her silver Audi to Sainsbury's in Godalming and loaded up her trolley with Earl Grey tea bags, chocolate, toilet roll, baked beans, pasta, tinned goods and lots of frozen food. Looking round the aisles, other people seemed to be stocking up too, with trollies piled high and similar looks of intent on their faces. She noticed that some items were already starting to run out quickly, like paracetamol and handwash. Other people were doing the same as her, she thought grimly. This fuelled her fears and instinctively she added in a few extra bottles of fruit juice, some liquid soap and her favourite San Pellegrino sparkling water for good measure. She knew it would not be enough if the worst happened, but it made her feel better to be doing something rather than nothing. She also bought lots more cat food for Rina just in case. Later that day on the news, she saw news reports of nationwide food shortages and shots of empty supermarket shelves. News reporters explained that rationing of certain items was now being introduced in stores, although there were no shortages per se, and the situation would settle once people stopped panic buying. Susie also noted that online supermarket delivery slots were booked out too, and she wondered how the old, frail and disabled would cope as a result. It was no time to be anything other than fit and healthy, she thought, given what lay ahead.

6.3 Covid-19 Symptoms

It was just as well that Susie had done a big shop and stocked up because a few days later she started to feel unwell and took to her bed at the beginning of April 2020. It did not come as a massive shock after all of the news coverage and the incident with the man who had coughed all the way home on the train from London following her last court hearing. She developed an irritating dry cough, headache, sore throat, temperature and had the most debilitating diarrhoea. She ached all over too and suffered with really bad brain fog. These symptoms went on for days and she got weaker and weaker, unable to eat properly or concentrate on anything much and she sank into a weird state of lethargy. In desperation, she took out her iPad and slowly did some Google searches about Covid-19 symptoms, reading some early scientific papers before concluding that she had caught the virus. There was no community testing and so she could not be sure, since formal testing was only taking place in hospital. However, she was as sure as she could be that the virus had got her. Whilst she felt terrible, she was fortunate that her oxygen levels were good, and she was not left gasping for breath. The GP had called round to see her and checked her vital signs and prescribed some antibiotics to stop the diarrhoea following a stool test. It was just a question of riding it out and keeping hydrated with some blackcurrant rehydration sachets from the bathroom cupboard.

Susie put her ability to maintain her oxygen levels and avoid hospital admission down to her mother's insistence that she learn a wind instrument as a child. This had done wonders stopping her childhood asthma. After about ten days, and once the antibiotics kicked in, she turned a corner and slowly started to feel better. She was able to get out of bed and make her way down to the sofa and watch some television with Rina for company. However, she was really shocked and surprised by just how much the virus had taken out of her. It left her with a lasting sense that it had penetrated deep into all sorts of different cells in her body, and it felt unlike anything else she had encountered. She was left feeling exhausted and it was such an effort to get up and down the stairs, leaving her breathless after only a few steps. It was going to take a while to get over this, she thought, as she looked at herself in the bathroom mirror. She was white and gaunt-looking and she had lost a noticeable amount of weight, which had temporarily aged her. Her hair was dull and brittle-looking too, and annoyingly she could not go to the hairdressers as they had all been shuttered by the government along with all non-essential shops and services. At least she was not going out anytime soon, so that saved her from public embarrassment, she told herself with a half-hearted smile.

6.4 US Diplomatic Visits to the WIV in 2018

As Susie started to get back on her feet later in April 2020, she could not stop herself from doing further research. Her recent illness had made her even more determined to try to get to the bottom of the Covid-19 pandemic. It now felt really personal, having experienced first-hand just how sick and wretched it could make you feel even if you recovered. She was now even more convinced that it might potentially be a virulent manmade virus that had leaked from a laboratory, given the way it had seeped deep into the cells in her body and sickened her in a manner she had never previously experienced.

In the course of her research, Susie learnt that the US Embassy in Beijing had sent US science diplomats to visit the Wuhan Institute of Virology (the WIV) BS Level 4 laboratory several times between January and March 2018.[67] She read that the US officials had reportedly been so concerned by what they found that they had sent two diplomatic cables categorised as sensitive but unclassified back to Washington DC warning about inadequate safety at the newly opened WIV lab, which was conducting risky studies on coronaviruses from bats.[68] One of the cables reportedly warned that the WIV's work on bat coronaviruses and their potential human transmission represented a risk of a new SARS-like pandemic.[69] Furthermore, they had reportedly raised concerns that the WIV had a serious shortage of appropriately trained technicians and investigators needed to safely operate a BS Level 4 laboratory. Moreover, the cables also reportedly warned that the Chinese researchers had found that various SARS-like coronaviruses could interact with the human receptor ACE2 and that the research strongly suggested that SARS-like coronaviruses from bats could be transmitted to humans to cause SARS-like diseases.[70] She was surprised that US Embassy officials had been let into China's only BS Level 4 laboratory, and she wondered how that had come about.

The same news report also stated that the Chinese researchers at the WIV had been receiving assistance from the Galveston National Laboratory at the University of Texas Medical Branch and other US organisations.[71] Here was even more evidence of US-Chinese scientific collaboration around genomics and viruses, she thought, again wondering how this had come about, given the increasingly strained US-China political situation. It felt odd to Susie, but she could not quite put her finger on why she felt that way.

6.5 Working From Home

As her strength slowly returned, Susie spent her time working from home and switching to digital working and remote court hearings as part of the ongoing nationwide lockdown. She had to learn to generate digital court bundles at speed and operate new IT platforms to video conference with clients, the court and colleagues. She also had to prepare and film a life sciences legal lecture from home on her mobile phone as the annual sector conference had switched to an online event when lockdown shuttered the UK. It was much harder work filming a lecture than giving it live, Susie thought, and she disliked the way she looked when she played the clips back. She still looked pale and drawn and the brain fog had not fully gone, which meant the whole exercise had taken three times as long as it should have done. When she spoke with the conference organiser, Laura, she had been surprised that Laura had suffered with the virus so badly too. Apparently, it had left Laura in need of hospital care.

In fact, working from home took all of Susie's focus and energy and there was little opportunity to do much else and even less reason to venture outside. Michael had been good at delivering food parcels to her door and she had managed to order a few online supermarket shops by staying up really late to book slots despite the massive competition for these. With a weary sigh as another day unfolded with increasing monotony, she realised that she had not left home for several weeks. Whilst this was uncharacteristic, these were unprecedented times, and life had changed beyond all measure and come to a standstill in many respects. She wondered if life would ever be the same again as she watched the daily news and the rising statistics of those that were sick, in hospital or who had died. The UK government mandate to stay at home and protect the NHS was tedious but necessary, she told herself, fearing the alternative if such measures were not strictly observed by the public.

6.6 Man at the Backdoor

As she pottered into the kitchen one lunchtime in May 2020 around 1pm, Susie noticed with a sudden jolt a strange man standing in her back porch. He stared at her and smiled through the backdoor window as she stopped in surprise and put her mug down on the granite kitchen worktop. Caught off guard and without thinking things through fully, she slowly went over to the backdoor and unlocked it to see what the man wanted. What was he doing in her porch in the middle of the national lockdown she asked herself. Her house was well set back from the road up a long gravel driveway in the village, and so he could hardly claim he was just passing by. She looked at him more closely and noted that he was tall, around 5 foot 11 or 6 foot, lean and fit-looking with dark hair and blue eyes. She reckoned he was in his forties, maybe mid to late forties at a push. He was very charming and well spoken, and he started to ask whether her house was number three as he had some masks to deliver, pointing to a couple in his right hand. Susie took a deep breath and explained that she was not house number three, that her house was Brook House and that she could not help him with directions.

Susie started to feel anxious and realised that she had never seen the man before and he did not seem local. She became acutely aware that she was all alone in her house with an unfamiliar man in front of her and she suddenly felt very small and vulnerable. Her heart began to pound, and the strain made her feel a bit wobbly as she gripped the backdoor handle a bit tighter. It all felt strange and unfamiliar as few people turned up unannounced at her home even without a national lockdown. Starting to think more quickly, she decided the best course of action was to appear as friendly as possible and hope that he would just leave. He was looking at her as if appraising her appearance, and she felt self-conscious as she was dressed in an old skirt and baggy top and still looked haggard after her recent bout of Covid-19. After what felt like a long few minutes, he took his leave and slowly ambled off down her driveway back onto the road. Susie closed the door quickly, locked it firmly and heaved a huge sigh of relief. Her heart was still pounding, and she somehow felt as if she had had a lucky escape, although she was not sure why.

She flicked the kettle on for a much-needed mug of Earl Grey tea to calm her nerves and she forced herself to make a light sandwich of smoked salmon and cucumber from the fridge on granary bread. She liked to eat her main meal in the evening, usually around 7.30pm, as her workdays were long and intense. As she flopped onto the duck-egg blue velvet sofa in the sitting room for lunch, she saw her iPad on the coffee table. Having picked at her sandwich, she could not help but run through in her mind the conversation she had just had with the unknown man in the porch. After the isolation of the last few weeks, it had been strange in itself to find someone at the door and engage in conversation. Intuitively, she sensed that this had been another in a series of unusual encounters and she had a growing feeling that she was being watched. She realised that she had not set foot out of her house for several weeks and she wondered whether the man had been sent around to check on her whereabouts. Maybe they knew she had been ill and wanted to check if she was still alive and kicking, because her mobile phone signal had been static and home based. That sounded crazy, though, she thought crossly. Nonetheless, she picked up her iPad and decided to double-check whether her house had a number.

Assuming her house was not number three, it was just a random thing and nothing to be concerned about, she told herself firmly. That would put the whole incident to rest.

Susie sat back on the sofa and did a Google search of her house details and took in a sharp intake of breath when the results confirmed that her house was indeed number three. She paused for a moment as the significance of this slowly sank in. She had only known her home as Brook House and rightly or wrongly she had not been aware of its number before. If her house was number three, then the man's story did not add up as she was definitely not expecting any visitors or masks. It dawned on her that it might just have been an excuse, and she wondered how long he had been in her porch before she had entered the kitchen and what he was doing visiting her home. All sorts of thoughts suddenly rushed through her mind, and it occurred to her that he might have been an intelligence officer or some sort of plainclothes official and she shuddered at the thought. She felt shaken to the core by what had just happened on her own doorstep and her mind began to whirr into overdrive. She felt more concerned and anxious than ever despite being in the comfort of her own home, and yet another strange encounter with an unknown man. This was getting serious, and she swallowed hard, not knowing what to do for the best.

6.7 US President Donald Trump Claims Evidence that Covid-19 Originated in a Chinese Lab

On 30 April 2020, Susie noted that US President Donald Trump claimed there was evidence that Covid-19 had originated in a Chinese lab.[72] *Wow, that was a serious development*, she muttered under her breath. This followed persistent references by him from March onwards that Covid-19 was a 'Chinese virus' despite the best efforts of other US politicos and Dr Anthony Fauci to counter this. It was all getting contentious despite the

WHO advising against using terms that linked the virus to China or the city of Wuhan, where it was first detected, to avoid discrimination and politicisation of the situation. Susie took this all in, as here was the President of the US announcing that there was evidence that Covid-19 might be the result of a manmade lab leak in China. Susie wondered what evidence President Trump had seen and she wondered what the US authorities knew that she did not, given that important scientific paper in *Nature Medicine* entitled *The Proximal Origin of SARS COV-2* the previous month. She also wondered whether this had something to do with the strange encounters she had been having, and the nagging feeling that she was being watched grew stronger. If the Covid-19 pandemic was potentially the result of a lab release of a manmade virus, as she suspected might be the case, this was really serious and it did not bode well. If this was widely found to be true, it could cause havoc politically at a time when the world lacked a functional vaccine and it could ignite World War Three. That was a truly terrifying thought, and it might explain the encounters she had been having, she surmised.

On 4 May 2020, Susie noted that the official global Covid-19 death toll had passed 250,000, although in reality she reckoned it was far worse than that. On 7 May 2020, the Bank of England reported that the UK economy was set to shrink by 14% in 2020, which was depressing and worrying.[73] The same day, the United Nations (UN) warned that the Covid-19 pandemic could potentially cause multiple famines around the world, which only added to Susie's concerns about the future.[74] The following day, 8 May 2020, the UN Secretary-General António Guterres announced that Covid-19 had released a 'tsunami of hate' across the world, with increased xenophobia and scapegoating, which all played into Susie's growing fears about the state of international geopolitics.[75] The world was slowly beginning to splinter apart.

It therefore came as a bit of a relief to Susie the following day, 10 May 2020, when Prime Minister Boris Johnson announced plans for the easing of lockdown, which included allowing unlimited exercise and going back to work if you couldn't work from home.[76] She had no intentions of returning to London or mixing with lots of people again anytime soon, although she would make an exception for Michael, she thought with a smile. She had missed not being able to see him in person and that had caught her off guard, since she prided herself on being independent and self-reliant. Michael had been a familiar figure in her life and at a time like this, there was lots to appreciate in Michael, she realised.

Chapter 7

Summer-Autumn 2020

After the UK-wide lockdown restrictions began to ease in late spring 2020, Susie heaved a sigh of relief along with the rest of England, Wales, Scotland and Northern Ireland. It had been a long hard slog and a real shock to the system to be locked down at home for so long. From 13 May 2020, the Covid-19 restrictions were slowly relaxed, and people were allowed to leave home for outdoor recreation. Then on 1 June 2020, restrictions were further eased with a less onerous requirement to be at home overnight and to enable groups of up to six people to meet outside. The official government thinking was that the virus was much less likely to spread outside in the open air, compared with cramped and often poorly ventilated indoor spaces. After weeks on end at home alone and the nasty and debilitating bout of Covid-19 that she had endured, Susie was ready to socialise a bit, and she decided to invite her neighbour Tony and his wife, Emilia, round for drinks in the garden. They were always good company and there was the added advantage that she could pick up where she had left off with Tony before Christmas and pick his brains about her growing concerns. It would be good to have Tony as a sounding board, she thought.

7.1 Drinks in the Garden with Tony and Emilia

The following Saturday, Susie arranged her garden table and chairs in a sunny spot and got out a selection of drinks and snacks whilst Rina prowled anxiously round her ankles. Tony and Emilia were right on time, she thought with a smile, as Tony marched straight-backed up the garden brandishing a bottle of red wine in his right hand with Emilia in tow in a relaxed-looking yellow sundress. They quickly settled round the table and Susie enjoyed their chatty, light-hearted conversation and was glad for the opportunity to reconnect with them face to face. It was so much nicer than discussions over Zoom, she thought, and it felt much more like life had been before the pandemic had wreaked havoc like a category five hurricane. The sun was shining, and a soft breeze rustled in the trees and for a short while it felt as if life was slowly getting back to normal after all the horrors the world had witnessed over recent months.

After an hour or so, Susie turned to Tony and plucked up the courage to say that she had been doing some more research about genomics and she had further clarified her thoughts since their last conversation before Christmas. She was keen not to squander the opportunity to catch Tony face to face and air her thoughts after all that had been running through her mind and the unusual encounters she had been having. The visit by the strange man at her backdoor a few weeks ago had only served to stiffen her resolve to try to make sense of things. Him turning up unannounced at her home like that had definitely raised more questions in her mind, and made matters feel more real and personal. It had been a shock and it had unnerved her to encounter a visit like that in her own home during a national state-mandated lockdown, although the man had been very charming. Susie wondered where to begin, since there was so much that could be said, given the turbulence of recent months. Somewhat hesitantly, she went on to explain that despite the official narrative, she was increasingly concerned that the Covid-19 pandemic might potentially be the result of a lab release of a manmade virulent gain-of-function virus in Wuhan in China. Saying this out loud made Susie feel vulnerable and anxious. She also felt uncomfortable articulating her concerns because they went against the international scientific community's established view. Yet somehow, despite this, she felt spurred on because she trusted her gut instincts, which had so far rarely let her down in life.

On hearing what Susie had to say, Tony slowly sat back in his chair and looked her steadily in the eyes before carefully asking her why she had come to this conclusion. Sensing the serious note in Tony's voice and the noticeable change in his body language, she swallowed hard before proceeding. She began to summarise her collective thinking based on her personal experience of the 2003 SARS outbreak in China, her research findings and the fact that Major-General Chen Wei of the Chinese People's Liberation Army (PLA) and the virologist who led the Institute of Bioengineering at the Chinese Academy of Military Medical Sciences had been called in to oversee operations at the Wuhan Institute of Virology (WIV) in Wuhan since early January 2020. She added that the Chinese military presence and control of what had previously ostensibly appeared to be a civilian institution was troubling to her mind, as was all the secrecy surrounding the WIV and its scientific research. Added to this, there had so far been no convincing evidence that the Covid-19 pandemic was the result of a zoonotic viral spillover event, and all the searches of the Chinese wet market in Wuhan and other animals had drawn a blank. It all led her to conclude that there might potentially have been a lab release of an unknown manmade virus.

Susie went on to share her concerns that the Chinese military might also potentially have been conducting secret 'dual-use technology' research involving risky laboratory animal experiments to develop virulent gain-of-function viruses and corresponding vaccines over a period of years. On top of that, she recounted that there had been reports of serious safety concerns raised by US officials about work practices and research conducted at the WIV dating back as far as the beginning of 2018 when it first opened. Moreover, the WIV had reportedly and mysteriously closed its viral genetic database to the outside world on 12 September 2019, which was an unusual move in her mind and potentially an attempt by the Chinese State to cover its tracks and protect its viral research and development work. Then there was the fact that the original Covid-19 genomic sequence was 96.2% the same as a SAR-CoV-like virus found in bats in a mine in southern China in 2013 and shipped back to the WIV laboratory run by Shi Zenghli in Wuhan. She ended by saying it simply did not pass the smell test as far as she was concerned, regardless of what the world's leading scientists and politicians were saying about the origins of the pandemic.

Tony reflected thoughtfully on what Susie said before slowly and calmly responding that she might be on to something with this. He had known her for a number of years and he instinctively knew that she was not one to make mountains out of molehills. He asked her if she had any evidence to support what she was saying, and Susie explained that she had a growing pile of news reports, articles and scientific papers which gave weight to her thinking. Susie was taken aback by Tony's calm and measured response. She had not been expecting a reaction like that from him and she was surprised that he had not instantly dismissed her thoughts and concerns out of hand. In some ways, it made her feel even more unsettled and worried about everything and in that moment, she felt more out of her depth than ever. It was concerning to think that the pandemic might potentially be a lab release of an engineered virus that might also have been designed to cause mass disruption and destruction. Tony asked for copies of a few articles, saying that he would make some gentle enquiries with some of his old contacts. This took Susie further aback, since naively she had not been aware that Tony still had some skin in the game after his retirement from the armed forces. She silently scolded herself over this, realising that armed forces servicemen like him were highly trained for all eventualities and that they never truly went off grid, even after retirement.

Sensing that the conversation had come to a natural pause and not wanting to bore Emilia, Susie then steered the conversation on to some more banal topics for the next hour or so. After a while, Rina appeared out of the flowerbeds and went straight for Tony for some attention, like the true tabby diva that she was. Tony and Emilia had fed Rina a few times whilst Susie had been away on work trips or to stay over at Michael's house and so Rina considered them to be friends. She jumped confidently up onto Tony's lap and proceeded to cuddle him and purr. The more Tony petted and stroked her, the louder her purr became until she looked and sounded quite ridiculous, Susie thought with a smile. Tony did not seem to mind and Emilia giggled at the spectacle Rina was making of herself, remarking that they missed having a pet cat of their own after their last one had been run over outside their home last year. All in all, their friendly conversation was a good way to finish off their get-together and, having finished the last of the red wine, Tony and Emilia were happy to take their leave and wind their way home for the evening.

7.2 Event 201: Pandemic Preparedness Exercise, October 2019

In the course of her further research one weekend, Susie came across reports of Event 201.[77] Event 201 was a high-level tabletop simulation of a global pandemic caused by a new coronavirus that took place on 18 October 2019, just a few weeks before news emerged of the SARS-CoV-2 outbreak in Wuhan, China in December 2019. It was hosted by the John Hopkins Center for Health Security in partnership with the Bill & Melinda Gates Foundation and World Economic Forum. It was reported as an invitation-only event attended by medical professionals, policy experts and business analysts who were tasked with considering how different organisations would respond to a deadly new virus pandemic modelled on the SARS virus, which in the scenario killed 65 million people over eighteen months. The scenario simulated a novel virus outbreak transmitted from bats to pigs to people, originating in Brazil and then quickly spread around the world by air travel. Notably, it stated that there was no possibility of a vaccine being available in the first year, although there was a fictional antiviral drug that could help the sick, but it would not stop disease transmission.[78] The timing of Event 201 was either coincidental, just before news of the Covid-19 outbreak emerged, or it might potentially have foreseen the emergence of the pandemic (although there was no evidence of this), she thought.

Looking more closely at the attendees, they were reported to be 'prominent individuals from global business, government, and public health'. It made interesting reading when she considered each attendee's profile and their role in the wider complex inter-dependent international landscape. The first listed attendee was Latoya D Abbott, the Senior Director of Global Occupational Health Services for Marriott International who 'advises hotel properties on the handling of infectious disease outbreaks' and who 'serves as the occupational health representative on the crisis team, advising on crises including natural disasters, infectious disease outbreaks and violence or terrorist activity'.[79] It was thought-provoking when she listened to Ms Abbott in video recordings of Event 201 report that travel and trade restrictions implemented as a result of a global pandemic would result in 'crippling losses' for the hotel industry 'which in itself make up 5 percent of GDP';[80] as well as reinforcing the economic fallout and global financial crisis that would be caused by a pandemic.

The next listed attendee at Event 201 was Sofia Borges, the UN Foundation's Senior Vice President and Head of the New York Office where 'she serves as chief liaison with United Nations leadership and the diplomatic community, working to identify new opportunities for building and deepening partnerships with a range of stakeholders'.[81] The reference to the diplomatic community stood out, not just because of the need to manage pandemic politics but also because of the importance of building strategic partnerships to deal with the multifaceted needs and issues caused by a pandemic behind the scenes, Susie thought.

Then came Brad Connett, President of the Henry Schein's US Medical Group, a leading provider of products and services to support the medical community.[82] This would include things like personal protective equipment (PPE), ventilators and medical supplies needed to combat a viral outbreak, all critical to providing population healthcare, she thought. Next on the list was Dr Chris Elias, President of the Global Development Program at the Bill & Melinda Gates Foundation, whose role was to 'accelerate the delivery of proven healthcare products and solutions to those who need them'.[83] It was sobering to hear him report in video recordings of the event the reality that there wasn't the logistics capability in the US or through the UN to set up a global stockpile and strategic allocation of medical supplies and pandemic antivirals. As such, there needed to be international collaboration between the World Health Organization and the private sector, which runs the supply chains.[84] This in turn made Susie ponder who in the private sector would be the winners and losers in terms of power, wealth and influence in this regard and the extent to which events like this would help forge that landscape.

Timothy Grant Evans was listed next, having joined McGill University the month before (September 2019) as the Director and Associate Dean of the School of Population and Global Health (SPGH) in the Faculty of Medicine and Associate Vice Principal (Global Policy and Innovation). This followed a six-year tenure as the Senior Director of the Health Nutrition Global Practice at the World Bank Group. Notably, Susie thought, he was listed as having been co-founder of the Global Alliance on Vaccines and Immunization (GAVI) 'as well as efforts to increase access to HIV treatment'.[85] So, even prior to the Covid-19 outbreak, there had been a focus on vaccine development and delivery as a means of combatting novel viral disease, she thought, and she wondered what initiatives had been happening in the background around this (openly or otherwise).

She was also very interested to see that Professor George Fu Gao, a Chinese scientist, was an attendee. Professor Gao was the Director-General at the Chinese Center for Disease Control and Prevention; a professor in the Institute of Microbiology, Chinese Academy of Sciences; President of the Chinese Society of Biotechnology and President of the Asian Federation of Biotechnology. His expertise was listed as '...focused on the enveloped virus entry and release, especially influenza virus interspecies transmission (host jump), structure-based drug-design, and structural immunology. He is also interested in virus ecology, especially the relationship between influenza virus and migratory birds or live poultry markets and the bat-derived virus ecology and molecular biology.'[86] This high-level involvement by Professor Gao had parallels with the US-China scientific collaboration at the WIV, she thought, and indicated another link between the Chinese scientific community and the West. She also wondered, with the benefit of hindsight, whether Professor Gao had any understanding at the time of Event 201 about matters which might have contributed to the emergence of the SARS-CoV-2 virus outbreak in Wuhan, China in the weeks that followed.

Next on the list was Dr Avril Haines. Susie's attention was immediately drawn to the fact that she was listed during the last US administration as '...Assistant to the President and Principal Deputy National Security Advisor. She also served as the Deputy Director of the Central Intelligence Agency and Legal Advisor to the National Security Council'.[87] As such, Dr Haines had high-level connections within the US intelligence community, providing another link between scientific work on pathogens and viruses, viral outbreaks and national and international security considerations, she thought. There was that dual-use concept again, providing further insight into a complex landscape and set of relationships between the intelligence, political and scientific communities.

The inclusion of Jane Halton as a listed attendee at Event 201 was also interesting. Amongst a variety of high-level positions, she was a member of the Australian Strategic Policy Institute (ASPI), which had just published an in-depth report on Chinese Genomic Surveillance in June 2020, Susie thought. It also listed her as '...Chairman of the Coalition for Epidemic Preparedness Innovations' and having 'nearly 15 years as Secretary of the Department of Finance and Secretary of the Department of Health and Ageing' and '...previously she was Executive Co-ordinator (Deputy Secretary) of the Department of the Prime Minister and Cabinet. She has extensive experience in public health and delivery, the delivery of the Australian government budget, and the management and performance of Australian government agencies'. It went on to state that she '...has held a number of significant roles in global health governance, including as chair of the board of the World Health Organization (WHO), president of the World Health Assembly, and chair of the Organisation for Economic Co-operation and Development (OECD) health committee'.[88] Ms Halton therefore had a great deal of experience and links within the higher echelons of Australian politics and governance as well as internationally through the WHO, the World Health Assembly and the OECD, she thought. Susie was also mindful that Australia was a strategic ally of the US and the UK, providing another example of the complex international political and public health landscape.

It surprised Susie at first when she noted that Matthew J Harrington was also included as an attendee at Event 201. He was listed as '...the global chief operating officer at Edelman, an industry-leading communications firm that partners with businesses and organizations to evolve, promote, and protect their brands and reputations. In concert with his overseeing global operations, Mr Harrington advises leaders of some of the world's largest and most complex companies on corporate positioning, reputation management, crises communications, merger and acquisition and IPOs'.[89] This left her wondering whose 'brands and reputations' would be the focus of promotion and protection during a global pandemic and the reasons behind this; presumably partly motivated by power, wealth and influence, she thought soberly.

Martin Knuchel was listed next as Senior Director and Head of Crisis, Emergency & Business Continuity Management for Lufthansa Group Airlines. He was further listed as '...responsible for emergency operations with partner airlines and is the leader of the Swiss International Air Lines crisis team. He directs emergency training for staff worldwide, and he is responsible for interfacing with national and international organizations, including the Swiss foreign ministry, the Swiss health ministry, and embassies and authorities in various countries'.[90] As such, he seemed again very well connected from an international perspective, as well as having links with the Swiss foreign and health ministries and various embassies; all important when dealing with the logistical, political and health impacts caused by an international pandemic, she thought.

The involvement of Eduardo Martinez as an attendee at Event 201 was also noteworthy. He was the President of the UPS Foundation and UPS Chief Diversity & Inclusion Officer and was listed as '...responsible for the operations and management of its global philanthropic, employee engagement, and corporate relations programs, which invests in more than 4,300 organizations and communities across 170 countries'. His profile went on to state that '...Currently he serves on the WEF's managing the Risk and Impact of Future Epidemics Steering Committee... and on the UN Global Logistics Cluster's Logistics Emergency Team Steering Council and on the executive committees of the United Nations Office for Coordination Humanitarian Affairs (UNOCHA) Connecting Business Initiative and the Global Health Security Agenda's Private Sector Round Table' amongst other organisations.[91] This gave further insight into the scale and reach of those in positions of power and tasked with dealing with the international fallout of a global pandemic, she thought.

Stephen C Redd was the next attendee listed at Event 201. He was a rear admiral and the Deputy Director for Public Health Service and Implementation Science at the Centers for Disease Control and Prevention (CDC) and listed as someone who '...currently oversees the Center for Preparedness and Response; the Center for Global Health; the Center for State, Tribal, Local and Territorial Support; and the Office of Minority

Health and Health Equity'. Susie was interested to note that he had previously '...served as incident commander for the 2009 H1N1 [novel influenza virus] pandemic response, which was the longest activation of CDC's Emergency Operations Center at the time. As the leader of the response, involving more than 3,000 CDC staff, he aided in the effort to vaccinate 81 million people against H1N1 in the United States'.[92] He therefore had in-depth experience of mounting a mass response to a viral pandemic across the US. She noted that he had a military background, reinforced by his attendance at Event 201 in his rear admiral military uniform as seen in video recordings of the discussions. Once again, here was a military presence, she thought, and another link between viruses, viral outbreaks and the military sphere. It also made her ponder when he participated in the debate about the risks of a pandemic causing a global financial crisis by saying, 'Governments need to be willing to do things that are outside of their historical perspective and it's really a war footing we need to be on.'[93]

The final three attendees listed at Event 201 were also interesting. Hasti Taghi served in a chief of staff capacity at a major media company and had led strategic initiatives in partnership with the World Economic Forum. Adrian Thomas served as Vice President Global Public Health at Johnson & Johnson. In this role, he was described as '...responsible for global health programs and strategy addressing Global Health Security threats and pandemic preparedness including antimicrobial resistance (AMR), Multi Drug Resistant Tuberculosis (MDRTB), Ebola, Denghe Fever, HIV vaccines amongst others' and having '...a special interest in the fields of disease area strategy, public health, market access and pharmaceutical policy'. The final attendee, Lavan Thiru, was part of the Monetary Authority of Singapore.[94]

Overall, Event 201 was divided into four different segments dealing with medical countermeasures, trade and travel and the economic and financial impact of the crisis and communications. It was the fourth segment on dealing with misinformation and disinformation which gave Susie most food for thought. This session focused on controlling information and the narrative around the pandemic and she noted Stephen Redd's comments about collecting and analysing social media data and wondered what the implications of this might be:[95]

> *We are all susceptible to misinformation based on our own beliefs and experience. With social media platforms there's an opportunity to understand who it is that is susceptible and in what form to this misinformation. So, there's an opportunity to collect data from that communication mechanism.*

She also noted what Dr Avril Haines had to say about tackling misinformation and disinformation, noting that she was vocal on these issues:[96]

> *One of the things we want to do is work with telecommunication companies to actually ensure everyone has access to the kind of communications that we are interested in providing. That is going to be critical in dealing with the explosion of the disease.*
>
> *If you have a trusted source I believe in the idea that we shouldn't be trying to control communication but rather flood the zone with a trusted source which is then influential with community leaders as well as health workers on these issues in order to amplify the message that is coming through. I certainly see the value of communicating constantly on these issues so as to continue to deal with the vacuum that can be created in this circumstance.*

For all of the dis-information that will be out it is going to be important to have a response to those questions and concerns. I understand from staff that there are also intelligence sources identifying multiple foreign mis-information campaigns and so on but it's all part of a larger piece which is to say everywhere there is something which comes out that is in fact false information and is starting to hamper our ability to address the pandemic then we need to be able to respond quickly to that.

If you have a state sponsored dis-information campaign there are obviously additional tools which you can bring to bear to try to address that situation. Not the least bringing together other countries to effectively take action against them for the kind of campaigns that they are propagating. But generally, I would say that the line between dis-information and misinformation is not always an easy one to find and the reality is the greatest way to impact this in my experience is not to let it sit. In other words, find your trusted interlocutors that are capable of saying this is not acceptable and this is in fact the truth and here is information and the community of survivors is one example, employers, trusted faith leaders, health workers and so on can be part of that. In addition, obviously you want to work with the private sector and those who are spreading information generally to see that they can either bring things down that are in fact lies or false information that is being put forward as a way of minimising it. Having a national source and an international source of trusted sources in really guiding everyone to that information is one of the most effective ways to deal with the situation.

With the benefit of hindsight, these strategies resonated with Susie as they had clearly gone on to be applied by governments when the SARS-CoV-2 pandemic hit. Key spokespeople had been appointed to disseminate public health information and the 'flood strategy' had been applied in the daily public health updates governments delivered. In addition, steps had been taken to check and manage the accuracy of information posted online and through social media platforms to counter misinformation and disinformation and deliver the messages that governments wanted to disseminate.

The expertise and connections of the attendees at Event 201 was seriously high-level stuff and it must have taken some time to arrange, Susie pondered. She wondered what had triggered its organisation and motivated this elite group of influential people to carry out this exercise in October 2019, just a few weeks before the SARS CoV-2 outbreak in China. It also depicted a complex picture where public and global health merged with political, intelligence, scientific, economic, logistical and media sectors. Furthermore, Event 201 went on to publish a call to action and a list of recommended actions for a scenario which subsequently came to pass just a few weeks later when Covid-19 struck:[97]

> *The next severe pandemic will not only cause great illness and loss of life but could also trigger major cascading economic and societal consequences that could contribute greatly to global impact and suffering. Efforts to prevent such consequences or respond to them as they unfold will require unprecedented levels of collaboration between governments, international organizations and the private sector. However, there are major unmet global vulnerabilities and international system challenges posed by pandemics that will require new robust forms of public-private cooperation to address.*
>
> *The Event 201 pandemic exercise, conducted on October 18, 2019, vividly demonstrated a number of these*

important gaps in pandemic preparedness as well as some of the elements of the solutions between public and private sectors that will be needed to fill them. The John Hopkins Center for Health Security, World Economic Forum and Bill & Melinda Gates Foundation jointly propose the following:

1. *Governments, international organizations, and businesses should plan now for how essential corporate capabilities will be utilized during a large-scale pandemic…*
2. *Industry, national governments, and international organizations should work together to enhance internationally held stockpiles of medical countermeasures (MCMs) to enable rapid and equitable distribution during a severe pandemic…*
3. *Countries, international organizations, and global transportation companies should work together to maintain travel and trade during severe pandemics. Travel and trade are essential to the global economy as well as to national and even local economies, and they should be maintained even in the face of a pandemic…*
4. *Governments should provide more resources and support for the development and surge manufacturing of vaccines, therapeutics, and diagnostics that will be needed during a severe pandemic…*
5. *Global business should recognise the economic burden of pandemics and fight for stronger preparedness…*
6. *International organizations should prioritize reducing economic impacts of epidemics and pandemics…*
7. *Governments and the private sector should assign a greater priority to developing methods to combat mis-and disinformation prior to the next pandemic response.*

7.3 Social Media

It was around this time that Susie decided to raise her game for work purposes on the social media front. Since the UK-wide Covid-19 lockdown, everything had quickly gone digital and it made sense to look to increase her professional profile online. She therefore decided to take the plunge and launch an Instagram account to promote her work, something she had previously not had the time or opportunity to consider. After all, she was a lawyer and not a marketing expert. It was a whole new world, she thought, as she scanned various accounts to get a better feel for how things worked on the platform. There was quite a lot to it, with posts, reels and Insta Lives, and clearly some people were using it very successfully for maximum impact. The hardest thing, she realised, would be to come up with suitable imagery to use, since she was not in a position from a professional perspective to post endless bikini shots or pictures of herself living the high life at a steady stream of trendy parties. All she could do was set up an account and see how things went. She already had various other online platforms and so she could take it slowly.

However, almost immediately, Susie realised with mounting concern that a US military account had followed her Instagram profile. The man was dressed in US army uniform and, following a quick Google search and a brief look at some YouTube footage of the man, the account holder purported to be from the US Army National Guard. Susie's heart sank and she felt an all-too-familiar feeling of dread mounting inside her. What was the US National Guard doing sniffing round her account and what was its role? She did some more research and learnt that the US National Guard had a unique role amongst the US armed forces in that it could perform state as well as federal functions. She learnt that it is a state-based military force that becomes part of the reserve components of the United States Army and the United States Air Force when activated for federal missions. The man was a long-serving sergeant in the US National Guard, who had previously completed a tour in Iraq and, according to the video clip Susie watched, was also helping to recruit civilians into the National Guard. He had a bachelor's degree in psychology, had studied for a qualification in Spanish at the Defense Language Institute Foreign Language Center and was currently studying for a master's degree in psychology. He was highly trained and experienced, she thought, and she wondered what he was doing lurking on her Instagram account. She had hoped that the military presence had died off and that they had lost interest in her and moved on to other things. Clearly, this was not the case, and they were now actively appearing on her new Instagram account as well, which felt deliberate and persistent. Susie wondered if there was some sort of message in all of this. It was hard to think that this account was just a 'bot', given the man's profile and track record. It left Susie feeling even more convinced that she was under surveillance by the US military.

Over the next few days and weeks, other accounts started to follow Susie on Instagram, which unsettled her further. One account purported to be that of a high-ranking member of an important and powerful Arab family, with various video clips of the man carrying out official duties and participating in various sports matches on horseback. Susie did not know what to make of this and was left bemused as it was so far outside her comfort zone. She did not know what to do for the best, not knowing whether to ignore the account or follow back. She certainly did not want to come across as rude, but equally she did not want to do anything which could compromise herself and her reputation. Eventually, she tentatively followed back and the account holder immediately responded. After a short exchange, Susie asked him why he was messaging her. He replied saying that he wanted to get to know her and exchange ideas. Susie politely refused and explained it was a work account, at which point the man became more persistent and asked her for an email account. Susie knew better than to provide an email address in case he sent some sort of compromising material that could cause trouble for her and, feeling increasingly uncomfortable about the situation, she blocked the account. She sat back with a sigh and hoped that there would be no ramifications. She definitely did not want to create any enemies and end up with a stalker on her hands. However, a few days later, a second account was set up with a picture saying in large words, 'I haven't forgotten you'. This menacing message shook her and made her worry even more about a stalker and for her safety. This was getting really unpleasant, she thought, and she felt powerless in the face of it all, although she hastily blocked the account.

Unfortunately, the strange activity on her Instagram account did not stop there. In the weeks that followed, Susie noticed a man whom she had previously seen on her Twitter feed set up two Instagram accounts to follow her. They both had different photos, but they were definitely the same man, she thought. Susie did not like this development and she acted quickly to block both accounts. After that, she spotted two more US military accounts following her, one of which sent her another message saying he wanted to get to know her. She did not respond, but it was stressful and uncomfortable and it was all starting to get to her and affect her sleep patterns again. It left her wondering what was at the root of this and why they were being so persistent with her. In some ways, the Covid-19 pandemic had acted as a bit of a buffer since she had not been able to travel for work and so there had been little opportunity for real-life encounters, although there had still been the strange visit by that man at her backdoor in May 2020, she thought with a shudder.

Given all of this activity and since the incident with the

senior US military officer on Twitter, Susie found that she was devoting more time than she had envisaged to social media. In addition to checking her Google alerts each morning, she also surfed her social media accounts every night in bed before she went to sleep. This was partly to double-check for unusual activity and partly because for the last year or so she had found it increasingly difficult to wind down in the evenings and fall asleep. During her late-night surfing sessions, she followed scientific debate and politics about the Covid-19 pandemic, and this had expanded her understanding and widened her horizons in lots of different ways. It had been a fascinating journey in the evenings and she had soaked up information and scientific analysis like a sponge, notwithstanding the regular late hours she was keeping. Over a period of months, it provided another way to further shape her evolving thoughts and sense-check her general understanding of what was happening. It was during one of these surfing sessions that she came across a small series of posts claiming that Covid-19 was a manmade virus that combined elements of HIV virus with a SARS-CoV-like virus, which allegedly made it more virulent and helped to explain why it kept mutating and spreading. The posts were not widely taken up and it was difficult to know if they were just a random theory or whether there was more to them. Nonetheless, Susie made a mental note, thinking it was an interesting angle even if it was one she was not yet able to assess for accuracy. Then she sighed again in frustration, wishing that she was scientifically trained before her head hit the pillow for the night.

Chapter 8

8.1 CCR5

Susie went on to experience a sudden peak in the demands of her legal work over the summer of 2020. People were slowly coming out of hibernation after the shock of the first Covid-19 lockdown and one of her cases had been listed for an online court hearing. This was going to be interesting, she thought, and sure enough there were all sorts of hoops to jump through to get the technology to work and ensure that all the various parties were present and ready to go for a video hearing before the presiding high court judge. She kept her head down and put in the hours to get through the workload, finding that most things were taking much longer to achieve in this new pandemic reality. It was exhausting working on the legal frontline, she thought, having been classified as a key worker along with others across the legal profession. That said, it was still far better than being a doctor or nurse and having to work twelve-hour shifts in restrictive PPE on the Covid-19 frontline in hospital, literally risking your life to save the lives of others every day, she thought.

The summer passed quickly from a work perspective, although there was a bit of respite when the court system had its summer recess in August. As part of her daily work routine, Susie always scanned her Google alerts for new developments across science, medicine, politics, law and policy as well as a range of other issues. It was her favourite way to wake up with her first mug of Earl Grey tea of the day, and she loved the buzz of discovering something new and honing her thoughts on a particular issue that could help her legal practice or understanding of the world. One morning, mid-July 2020, she sat down at her desk with her usual mug of tea and came across a Google alert with a link to a new science paper by a group of Indian scientists.[98] The paper looked at whether the genetic makeup of people might be playing a role in susceptibility to Covid-19 disease or poor prognosis. It reported that the role of biochemical receptors in cells in the body in inducing susceptibility to Covid-19 infection and death could not be ruled out. She went on to read in the paper that C-C Chemokine Receptor 5 (CCR5) was known to be responsible for the induction of inflammation in a wide range of infectious diseases, including: Human Immunodeficiency Virus (HIV), Hepatitis C Virus (HCV) and Hepatitis B Virus (HBV), West Nile Virus (WNV) and Tick-Borne Encephalitis Virus (TBEV). This was interesting stuff, she thought, and clearly CCR5 was noteworthy. The Indian paper went on to highlight a significant association of the CCR5 Δ32 genetic variant with susceptibility and death from Covid-19 infection.

Reflecting on this, it made sense that some people were genetically more susceptible to viruses than others, including viruses like Covid-19. We were certainly seeing this in the way Covid-19 was playing out in different population cohorts, with some people getting severe disease progressing to death, whilst others only experienced mild disease or were asymptomatic.

Susie filed this information away and made a mental note to keep an eye out for more information along these lines. Whilst she was not a virologist or a specialist in immunology, this seemed like a logical train of thought and something to bear in mind. It resonated with her and she had learnt through all her reading and work over the years to take note when this happened.

Then, at the end of August 2020, another Google alert highlighted a further scientific paper which built on her understanding about genetic variants and susceptibility to disease. This paper reported emerging results that an uncontrolled immune response leading to a life-threatening condition called a 'cytokine storm' was a major driver of severe disease caused by Covid-19. It went on to report that the role of different variations in DNA sequences within, as well as outside, CCR5 in HIV/AIDS may be worth considering. The paper further reported that the CCR5 receptor, and a nearby gene cluster where many other chemokine receptors were located, may contribute to susceptibility to Covid-19 and its treatment.[99] From this, Susie extrapolated that CCR5 gene functionality codes for a protein C-C chemokine receptor type 5 (CCR5), which is essential for HIV infection of the white blood cells and acts as a co-receptor to HIV.

She also noted reports in the same paper that mutation in the gene CCR5 (called CCR5 Δ32) confers resistance to HIV; resistance being higher when mutations are in two genetic copies and weaker in only one genetic copy. The CCR5 Δ32 allele was found predominantly in European populations, with rare occurrences in other populations. This could be significant, she thought, if ethnicity and predisposition to disease were also relevant in terms of what was playing out in terms of the Covid-19 pandemic. It also raised questions about the potential risk of viruses being developed to target specific ethnic groups and cohorts of people, she thought soberly.

This collective reading suddenly triggered all sorts of thoughts and alarm bells in the back of her mind. Could this potentially have more deep-seated implications, she tentatively asked herself, and her mind started to whirr into overdrive like a powerful race car on the open road. Quickly, she remembered that the Chinese gene-edited babies in 2018 had reportedly had their genomes edited to make them immune to HIV/AIDS virus. Then she remembered from her scientific reading that the HIV/AIDS virus used the CCR5 receptor to enter cells in the body and that, significantly, those people (around 10% of those of northern European descent) who possessed the CCR5 Δ32 allele mutation were reportedly immune to HIV/AIDS infection. She then recalled from her late-night social media surfing a few posts claiming that Covid-19 was a manmade virus which mixed elements of the HIV virus with a SARS-CoV-like virus. Suddenly it was like a bomb had gone off inside Susie's head. She was hit by an almost overwhelming sense that there might potentially be a link between genetic susceptibility to severe Covid-19 disease and death and the Chinese scientific research undertaken by biophysicist He Jiankui in gene editing the three Chinese babies in 2018 to try to make them immune to HIV/AIDS and related Chinese scientific research.

If she was right, then the Chinese gene-edited baby affair in 2018 was potentially no random or rogue clinical experiment, she thought; it might then fit into a much bigger picture, and she swallowed hard. If you could potentially gene edit humans to make them immune to HIV and more or less immune to other viruses, this was important from a public health and national security perspective as well. Here was that 'dual-use' technology concept again. *Shit, shit, shit*, she muttered and her hand shook as she reached for her mug of Earl Grey tea. The magnitude of her growing sense that the Covid-19 pandemic, the epicentre of which had started in Wuhan in China, and Chinese scientific research and the Chinese gene-edited babies might potentially be linked threw her completely off guard. In fact, it took her breath away and completely stopped her in her tracks for the next hour or so as she tried to unjumble her thoughts. Her gut was telling her that there might potentially be a connection when you stripped everything bare, removed the confusion and joined up the dots. Her heart was pounding so hard that it was difficult to breathe and her chest felt painful and tight.

Susie got up from her desk to stretch her legs and try and clear the overwhelming enormity of her thoughts. She stopped for a moment or two to look out of the window and gaze at the view. It helped to steady her breathing, slow her heartbeat and short-circuit the mounting panic inside her. She watched a beautiful group of birds as they swooped and swirled across the sky in graceful waves until her breathing slowed and her brain felt more ordered again. Then, with as much determination as she could muster, she slowly walked over to her whiteboard and frantically began to draw a series of further spiders' webs, building in CCR5 gene functionality that codes for a protein that HIV uses to enter cells, HIV virus research and Covid-19 with her black marker pen. These translated her rapidly evolving thoughts and concepts into a visual network of interconnected points. It was a relief to capture, order and download these from her mind. It would provide a useful reference to help organise and shape her analysis moving forward, she thought, recognising the still overwhelming need to make sense of recent world events and the chaos, loss and disruption that was continuing to unfold.

With that, Susie wandered down her hallway to the kitchen to flick on the kettle and dig out some chocolate. It might still be early, but it was definitely one of those moments that required chocolate, she told herself. Chocolate always helped to calm her nerves and cheer her up, and it was why she always tried to keep a supply in the house, just in case. As the kettle boiled and she opened yet another packet of Earl Grey teabags, Rina came shooting through the cat flap with a thud and a loud meow; she certainly knew how to make an entrance and get attention, thought Susie, with a wry smile. Rina seemed to instinctively sense the heightened stress and anxiety that Susie was feeling and she instantly fussed around Susie's ankles, purring. Susie bent down to stroke her and then picked her up for a much-needed cuddle as she waited for her mug of tea to brew. She must put Rina on a bit of a diet, she thought, somewhat absentmindedly, as she removed her teabag. Her furry tabby friend was getting too heavy and she did not want to get into trouble with the vet on their next visit or create unnecessary health problems for Rina. However, the thought of putting Rina on a diet and restricting favourite treats filled her with dread.

Returning to her thoughts with a heavy jolt, Susie quickly realised that she needed to do more in-depth research to check and inform her latest thinking and analysis. This included more research into (1) the Chinese gene-edited baby affair and the life and work of the Chinese scientist He Jiankui and (2) CCR5 and the science around the HIV/AIDS virus and (3) scientific research at the Wuhan Institute of Virology (WIV). Her legal training over many years had taught her to do her homework and not to assume anything. If she was potentially right, then there might be a much bigger picture surrounding the Covid-19 pandemic and some serious forces behind events in recent years, and that was a frankly terrifying prospect, she thought. It might also explain why there had been such an unusual and persistent military presence around her over the last year or so. Her preoccupation with the Chinese gene-edited babies had resonated with her from the outset, given her legal practice in life sciences. The whole affair had seemed strange to her and that sense that something was 'off' had stayed with her. She reasoned that it was possible that this might potentially have hit a nerve with the US military and others along with her growing interest in genomics and its governance. She shivered violently as she mulled this all over in her mind, feeling very small and alone.

It had always struck her as odd that of all the genes to look to edit on a permanent basis, the Chinese scientist He Jiankui had chosen to edit the CCR5 gene to try to make the babies immune to HIV. He had sought to justify his work on the basis that the babies' fathers were HIV positive and so by gene editing the embryos in the laboratory before implantation, he was trying to ensure the babies would be born free of the disease, avoid discrimination and be resistant to HIV throughout their lives. He had even prepared some video clips explaining this ahead of the Second International Human Genome Editing Conference in Hong Kong in November 2018, emphasising the social justice dimension to his work in striving to help those marginalised elements of society at risk or suffering from HIV.[100] However, Susie had been acutely aware that it was already possible to prevent the transmission of HIV by way of sperm-washing procedures during fertility treatment, and there were also powerful antiretroviral medicines which stopped the HIV virus replicating in the body and being transmitted to others even though they could not eliminate it completely. To Susie's way of thinking, it would therefore have made more sense to choose a different gene to edit in the genome of the world's first permanently gene-edited babies to prevent them developing some serious condition for which there was no cure, or even common potentially fatal conditions like cancer or heart disease. The whole incident involving the gene editing of the CCR5 gene in the Chinese babies' embryos in 2018 had just not sat comfortably with her at all and she had not been entirely sure why at first. Putting it bluntly, it had not passed the smell test, and a lingering whiff had hung over the incident. Now, however, it might potentially be starting to make more sense, she thought, and that was both exhilarating and incredibly unnerving.

Following some further internet research, Susie learnt that in early June 2019, before the Covid-19 outbreak, a well-known scientific journal had published an article using the genotyping and death register information of approximately 410,000 individuals of British ancestry to investigate the effects of the CCR5 Δ32 mutation. It estimated a 21% increase in all-cause mortality rate in individuals who were homozygous (having two identical copies of a gene) for the CCR5 Δ32 allele, being a significant finding, she thought.[101] She read on in associated commentary that having two copies of the Δ32 allele mutation of the CCR5 gene on the one hand seemed to protect against HIV, but on the other hand reportedly gave them a 21% increase in their overall mortality rate. British commentary went on to say that these results highlighted the need to better understand the impact of introducing genetic mutations upon human health. The commentary also referenced the work of the Chinese scientist He Jiankui in gene editing the world's first gene-edited babies in 2018 by editing the CCR5 gene in their embryos. It reported that in doing so he had aimed to mimic the effect of the naturally occurring CCR5 Δ32 mutation. The commentator added that previous studies suggested that people with this genetic mutation may be more at risk of contracting certain infectious diseases, such as influenza.[102] Susie then discovered that the accuracy of this scientific research had subsequently been called into question, having overlooked sampling bias in UK Biobank's data. This resulted in the research being retracted four months later.

Following further research, she discovered additional scientific commentary in early June 2019 about the significance of possessing the CCR5 Δ32 genetic mutation. An eminent British professor of genetics reported in a Science Media Centre press release that having mutations in both copies of the CCR5 Δ32 may result in a shorter lifespan than on average, although conferring resistance to HIV infection. He calculated that their chances of dying before they were aged seventy-six were increased by over 20%.[103] Another professor went on to say that not having a full working copy of the gene could cause problems in other ways too, and it had been suggested that it could result in an increased susceptibility to influenza. Here was another reference to infectious disease resistance and virus susceptibility, thought Susie. She surmised that on the one hand editing the CCR5 gene might confer immunity to the HIV virus, but on the other hand might create increased risk of contracting influenza; the significance of which was not lost on her since she knew that influenza killed hundreds of thousands of people each year globally. The professor added that humans have two copies of genes for a reason and that there was still a lot they did not know and understand about the functionality of the CCR5 gene.

Susie carefully mulled over in her mind what this all meant. It seemed apparent in basic terms that there were two sides of the coin involving the scientific study of human genetics and viruses, namely (1) infectious disease susceptibility and (2) resistance/functional treatments. This in turn ran parallel with emerging dual-use biotechnology. On the one hand, you could use rapidly evolving gene-editing technology to make viruses more virulent using a variety of gain-of-function techniques and even potentially as biological weapons. Then, on the other hand, you could look to develop vaccines and other functional treatments to counter these virulent new viruses. As such, Susie began to gain a sense that this duality might be playing out somehow in the scientific research surrounding CCR5, and her gut instinct told her that this might be significant to the bigger picture. She sensed that she might be 'in the zone', so to speak, although she had yet to fully settle and clarify her thoughts.

Western scientists were saying that there was still much that was not known about the CCR5 gene and its functionality. But what if the Chinese State and its scientists knew more than they were letting on about this? That was serious food for thought, she thought, and her levels of stress and anxiety started to shoot up even further as she stared intently at her latest spider's web-like drawings on her whiteboard and she shuddered hard yet again.

The next opportunity she had, Susie set some time aside to learn more about the life and work of Chinese scientist He Jiankui. She figured that if she had a better knowledge of the man, she could gain a better sense of his work. She could also maybe glean more understanding about the confusing and opaque bigger picture. Once again, she recognised with some frustration that she remained at a disadvantage as she was not scientifically trained. Nonetheless, she told herself stubbornly, reading up on the life and work of scientist He Jiankui might give her an 'in', so to speak, and a point of reference from which she could build out. The more she read and delved into matters, the more there appeared to be obfuscation, confusion and denials about the origins of the Covid-19 pandemic and events over the last few years, a pattern that repeated itself throughout history in different guises. *Shit, shit, shit*, she muttered to herself. This was getting really serious, and she wondered where it would all lead.

In 2006, for example, He Jiankui earned his undergraduate physics degree from the University of Science and Technology of China in Hefi. His undergraduate studies had been made possible with the benefit of scholarship funding as he reportedly came from a modest family background in a small Chinese farming community in Hunan Province. She discovered that He Jiankui was reportedly hardworking and talented, possessing an ability to learn quickly and a photographic memory; attributes that could serve him and the Chinese State well, she thought dryly. Like other top scholars at the time, he was then sent by the Chinese authorities to the US to expand his education and scientific expertise in one of the leading US scientific institutions.[104] She sat back and reflected on the strategy behind this. For the Chinese, it provided an effective way to send out talented Chinese nationals so that they could learn new scientific techniques which could then be funnelled back to China for future use by the Chinese State. She supposed that from the US' perspective, it was an opportunity to forge links with Chinese scientists and try and gain some further insight into Chinese affairs and penetrate the authoritarian rule of the Chinese State; a symbiotic relationship of sorts.

8.2 He Jiankui 2007-2010: Rice University in Houston, Texas

Susie found out that He Jiankui moved to the US to increase his knowledge and study for a PhD in biophysics. He was placed under the supervision of Professor Michael Deem, then the John W. Cox Professor of Biochemical and Genetic Engineering and Professor of Physics and Astronomy, at Rice University in Houston, Texas.[105] The decision to place He Jiankui under the tutelage of Professor Michael Deem at Rice University in the US had been a strategic move by the Chinese State, she reasoned as she dived deeper into her research. She concluded that it was astute and carefully executed for two reasons.

Firstly, the study of biophysics offered greater scientific opportunities, in Susie's mind, given the sequencing of the entire human genome just a few years earlier in 2000 and the race to develop effective gene editing technologies. This tied in with central Chinese genomic policy to harness genomics to make the Chinese State an indisputable world power. As such, it was a smart move on He Jiankui's part and one that would offer future opportunities to advance his scientific career, she thought.

Secondly, Susie discovered after considerable internet and YouTube research an interview of Professor Michael Deem on YouTube delivering the Professional Progress Award lecture at the American Institute of Chemical Engineers' (AIChE) annual meeting in Minneapolis in October 2011. On watching this, she saw Professor Deem explain that he was in receipt of key military funding. He explained that the funding was provided by the US Defense Advanced Research Projects Agency (DARPA), a research and development agency of the US Department of Defense responsible for the development of emerging technologies for use by the US military. She further learnt that Professor Deem's groundbreaking work, along with that of other mathematicians and biologists over six years or so, used maths and biology to assess the landscape of viruses, their evolution and ability to mutate to improve their fitness to survive. It encompassed physical theories of pathogen evolution and vaccine design.[106] Susie noted from her previous reading that these were important components in the international race to manage public health and develop 'dual-use technology', including for national security purposes. Ah, here was that double-sided coin again, noting the inter-relationship between virus mutation and infectious disease transmission on the one hand and vaccines and treatment functionality on the other hand to counter these.

Susie surmised that He Jiankui's reported strong work ethic and photographic memory enabled him to hoover up all that his hard-won scientific placement had to offer at Rice University in Houston, Texas. She then deduced that the legacy of his time spent in the US had likely helped to shape his work and might have set in motion the events that played a part in the international biotechnology race to manipulate and control the human, animal, plant and microbial genome. In doing so, she began to break down events to make them more manageable to explain in bite-sized chunks. She found that it always helped to distil things down to clarify complex situations and thinking and make it more accessible for herself and others.

To start with, Susie learnt that He Jiankui worked closely with Professor Michael Deem and in 2010 they published a scientific paper together identifying a cluster of DNA sequences in bacteria that acted as a sort of immune system to repel infections and silence genes.[107] They also researched and published a scientific paper together that analysed the evolution of influenza genetic sequences in September 2010, which Susie noted was funded by DARPA.[108] This paper acknowledged that 'influenza viruses are hyper-mutating' and that 'influenza has a high evolution rate, which makes vaccine design challenging'. As such, the paper considered 'an approach for early detection of new dominant strains, which would appear to be useful for annual influenza vaccine selection' and looked at flu seasons and vaccine strains in certain places around the world, including specifically Wuhan in China. Furthermore, she noted that He Jiankui and Michael Deem produced a scientific paper comparing the factors impacting recessions and the world trade network and the correlation with the spread of viral diseases, stating in a scientific paper in *Physical Review Letters* entitled *Structure and Response in the World Trade Network*, published 5 November 2010:[109]

> *...the modular structure that exists at multiple scales affects how recessions propagate in the trade network, just as modular structure of person-to-person contacts affects how diseases spread in a population. We examine how the network structure affects the propagation of a recession throughout the world.*

This was important work, she thought. As she paused to reflect on this, it resonated with what was currently happening as a result of the Covid-19 pandemic and the immense global economic disruption being caused to 'just-in-time' supply chains, the shuttering of businesses and people's livelihoods and the strain placed on state finances and global economic markets. She was also interested to note that He Jiankui had been conducting work looking at viral transmission, including hyper-mutating viruses like influenza, vaccine design and the impact and correlation of a virus outbreak on the world trade network, some of which appeared to have been funded by DARPA, a scheme responsible for the development of emerging technologies for use by the US military.

Susie was further interested to come across a scientific paper co-authored by Michael Deem in 2010 entitled *Theoretical Aspects of Immunity*. The paper's Abstract explained in more detail the work undertaken to develop theories that 'quantify the immune system dynamics'. The paper went on to look at the role played by two major components of the immune system, namely T cells and B cells, as well as the immune system's structural design. It went on to state:[110]

> *The Deem group has developed a random energy theory that describes the dynamics of the immune system and the interaction between influenza antigens and antibodies... The model is population based, considering a population of B cells in one person, a population of viruses, and a population of individual people. The random energy model permits study of the immune response at the level of individual antibodies and antigens.*

This was complex and high-level research, thought Susie. It looked at the structural components and workings of the human immune system and its responses to viruses like influenza, which reportedly causes a worldwide annual mortality rate of

250,000–500,000, as well as dengue fever which was said to cause approximately 50 to 100 million cases annually with a conservative estimate of 25,000 mortalities annually.[111]

8.3 He Jiankui, 2011: Stanford University, California

Having earned his PhD in 2010, He Jiankui had then reportedly started to hone his interest in genetics, particularly gene-editing technologies. Susie figured that he had likely realised the great promise that this technology held, which was smart and forward thinking. The following year, 2011, she discovered that the young and ambitious He Jiankui went on to become a post-doctorate scholar in the laboratory of Professor Steven Quake at Stanford University.[112] There, he further expanded his knowledge and network of scientific contacts in the US and fostered that oddly symbiotic relationship amongst the international scientific community; a sort of soft power that elicited all sorts of scientific opportunities, tensions and conflicts for those in the know.

8.4 He Jiankui's Return to China, 2012: Chinese State Funding Under the Peacock Plan

Susie went on read that the collaborative work of He Jiankui and Professor Michael Deem preceded the transformative scientific 2012 discovery of CRISPR Cas-9 gene-editing technology by Jennifer Doudna and Emmanuelle Charpentier; for which they became the first women in history to be awarded the Nobel Prize for Chemistry in 2020. He Jiankui was therefore well placed, arguably even at the forefront of the race, to use and apply these and related techniques in his own subsequent cutting-edge scientific work. Then, in line with Chinese State policy, having acquired new overseas scientific knowledge and skills, he was reportedly lured back to China in 2012 by Chinese State funding under the Peacock Plan. He was appointed to the faculty of the Southern University of Science and Technology (SUSTech) in

Shenzhen in Guangdong, a coastal province in southern China. There, reportedly armed with $6 million of Chinese State start-up funding, He Jiankui launched Direct Genomics, a company which licensed a technology he had reportedly acquired from a defunct US enterprise to sequence single molecules of DNA as a diagnostic tool for cancer or genetic abnormalities in embryos.[113]

So, Susie thought, there were indications and evidence as early as 2012 that He Jiankui had developed an interest in the science and genetics around embryos; some six years before he went on to infamously gene edit the embryos of the three Chinese babies. This followed his previous research into virus transmission, human immunity and vaccine design in collaboration with Professor Michael Deem. This did not necessarily feel entirely coincidental in Susie's mind against the backdrop of all her reading and her growing understanding of genomics and international events. Others might disagree, she thought, but there were potential patterns and connections in her mind, and it was enough to spur her on to test her instincts and build further analysis to help elucidate matters further.

8.5 Chinese CRISPR Gene-Editing Technology Research in Monkeys, 2014

By 2014, Susie learnt that Chinese scientists were the first in the world to harness the power of CRISPR Cas-9 gene-editing technology in research in monkeys. This, to Susie's mind, illustrated the speed, determination and scale with which the Chinese deployed this new powerful and transformative biotechnology. Susie read that He Jiankui collaborated with a team of Chinese scientists to enhance understanding of immune system complexity and immune-related diseases in humans. In that study, they reportedly found that the immune repertoire of the rhesus monkey is highly diversified, close to that found in humans, and this could be applied in investigating T cell responses (part of the immune system) during virulent influenza virus infection.[114] There was yet another reference to influenza, viruses and immunity, and she made a mental note.

As such, Susie surmised that this groundbreaking research, which no doubt increased the Chinese's understanding of the human body's immune system, might have been used for both public health purposes and potentially for 'dual-use' technological development by the Chinese State and military. This might not have been something the Chinese scientists, including He Jiankui, were aware of in conducting their experiments, but it did not mean that their work was not potentially being deployed for other purposes too. Scientists were often deeply invested in the minutiae of their work, effectively siloed in their endeavours, leaving scope for other actors to manipulate the bigger picture and wield the associated power, wealth and influence in the upper echelons of the global elite.

8.6 He Jiankui 2016–2017: Gene-editing Research in Embryos of Rodents, Monkeys and Humans

During 2016–17, Susie learnt that He Jiankui's scientific research progressed at pace to gene edit the embryos of rodents, monkeys and humans in Chinese proof-of-concept experiments. She read that some gene-edited rodent and monkey embryos actually resulted in live births, reflecting that this was achieved only four to five years after CRISPR Cas-9 gene-editing technology was first discovered. *Wow, that was fast*, she muttered. She also learnt that He Jiankui went on to report his unpublished research findings at an international scientific Cold Spring Harbour Laboratory meeting in the US in 2017. Other eminent scientists at this meeting included the likes of Jennifer Doudna. In giving a presentation, He Jiankui reportedly discussed his CCR5 gene-editing work in mice, monkeys and over 300 non-viable human embryos discarded from IVF.[115] That guy meant business, Susie thought, in reportedly gene-editing 300 human embryos; that was not just a handful of embryos he was concerned with.

It was later reported that the rest of the scientists present at the Cold Spring Harbour Laboratory meeting had no idea that He Jiankui would move on to actual clinical trials in humans using gene-edited embryos. She wondered how or why they had missed the signs. The articles that she read reported that the scientists had downplayed his research because he was reportedly young and because he did not have a prolific list of published articles behind him in prominent scientific journals.[116] That seemed a bit narrow-minded, she thought. However, by the same token, she knew that scientific careers were built and sustained through article publication and funding, and scientists often sat in their own individual spheres or operated in small collaborative groups to undertake their complex and highly competitive work. As such, she could see how they might well have failed to appreciate the very different centralised scientific strategy being increasingly and rapidly deployed by the Chinese State. It was not necessarily obvious, but it was there if you could join up the dots, she thought. Added to which, she had the benefit of hindsight, which the other scientists did not have at the time.

8.7 He Jiankui, 2017: Chinese Thousand Talents Program

By 2017, He Jiankui's scientific work and expertise in gene editing had reportedly led to him being included in the Chinese State's prestigious Thousand Talents Program.[117] This was the central Chinese government's top science program, which it claimed was the 'world's most prestigious and influential state science program'. Its aim was to advance specific scientific areas, like gene editing and the genetic industry, which the Chinese State considered to be of primary importance in the global race to lead the scientific and genomic revolution. As such, this likely put He Jiankui in a position of some significance from a scientific perspective in China, despite what was later said and done about him. Susie wondered whether this had given He Jiankui more or less freedom to pursue his scientific work. It also raised questions about the extent to which his work was kept under review and sanctioned by the Chinese authorities. It was not the case that he was simply an unknown scientist who somehow slipped through the net in China, she thought.

8.8 He Jiankui 2017-2018: Conception and Birth of the Three Chinese Gene-Edited Babies

Over 2017 and 2018, He Jiankui reportedly rushed ahead full throttle with translating his scientific work gene editing embryos in the lab and in animals into humans as another groundbreaking proof-of-concept experiment. He Jiankui reportedly submitted a medical ethics approval to the Shenzhen Harmonicare Women and Children's Hospital outlining the proposed CCR5 genome edit of human embryos.[118] He then reportedly proceeded to work with a Beijing AIDS advocacy group to recruit married couples where the husband tested positive for HIV and where the family had encountered HIV-related stigma and discrimination for his research trial.[119] [120] The couples reportedly agreed to the experiment because in China HIV positive fathers were not usually allowed to have children using IVF. Thereafter, she read that a total of five married women reportedly had between eleven and thirteen gene-edited embryos transferred.[121] In doing so, He Jiankui became the first scientist in the world to gene edit human embryos and cross a red line by successfully impregnating three Chinese women with these. Two of the women subsequently became pregnant and gave birth to twins Lulu and Nana in November 2018 and a third subsequent baby called Amy; to which news the international community reacted in horror and condemnation when it broke at the Second International Summit on Human Genome Editing in Hong Kong, deeming it a reckless, unnecessary and inaccurate scientific experiment that subjected the gene-edited babies to unknown health risks and a dangerous permanent alteration of the human genome.[122]

Susie went on to read that Lulu and Nana reportedly carried both functional and mutant copies of the CCR5 gene, meaning He Jiankui's gene-editing experiment had not been complete. In addition, she learnt that there are various forms of HIV that use a different receptor instead of CCR5. As a result, his clinical experiment did not necessarily protect Lulu and Nana from all forms of HIV.[123]

The controversy around the alleged role of two figures who some sources claimed were present around the time consent was obtained from the participants for He Jiankui's groundbreaking human genome editing trial also made for interesting reading. Reports alleged that these two men were US Professor Michael Deem at Rice University in Houston, Texas along with a Chinese individual called Yu Jun, who was a member of the Chinese Academy of Sciences (CAS) and co-founder of the Beijing Genomics Institute.[124] She read disputed accounts about their alleged presence, role and understanding of what happened at the time, and she noted that Professor Michael Deem was subsequently put under investigation by Rice University for his part in the affair. The alleged presence of these two important men, one a US citizen and the other reportedly working at Chinese genomics company Beijing Institute of Genomics and a member of CAS, struck a chord with Susie and she wondered about their alleged presence and potential involvement.[125] Professor Michael Deem was He Jiankui's former work mentor and colleague, but the connection was more opaque where Yu Jun was concerned. She further noted that the Chinese authorities later condemned He Jiankui's experiment to create the world's first gene-edited humans and claimed it had been done without their knowledge or approval 'in the pursuit of personal fame and gain'.[126] There were conflicting narratives here, obfuscation and denials at play once again, she thought.

8.9 He Jiankui, 2019: Conviction, Assisted Reproductive Technology Ban and Imprisonment

From further research into the fate of the Chinese scientists involved, Susie learnt that He Jiankui was sentenced in late December 2019 to three years in jail and a 3 million-*yuan* fine (US$425,000) for the illegal creation of the three gene-edited babies Lulu, Nana and Amy. The other two scientists received an eighteen-month prison sentence, a 500,000-*yuan* fine and were banned from working in assisted reproductive technology for life.[127] [128] However, there was a lack of transparency around the whole affair, with little Chinese press coverage. The court hearing was held in private, the ruling of which had been published just ahead of New Year in 2019. This was potentially a time that had been picked when most people were away from work and spending time with family, Susie thought wryly, to minimise impact when the news broke. Another tactic? she wondered. She also noted that the Chinese scientists had been banned from engaging in assisted reproductive technology and prohibited from applying for public research funds by the Ministry of Science and Technology and banned for life from using human genetic resources.

These sentences sent a clear message of disapproval by the Chinese State in response to the Chinese gene-edited baby affair. However, Susie was still left wondering if this might potentially be a bit of a smokescreen, suspecting that in practice it might be difficult to do anything undetected and unsanctioned in China. Furthermore, it left her wondering why He Jiankui chose to announce his work at an international genomic conference and expose himself to prosecution in the face of a Chinese 2003 assisted reproductive technology regulation that banned the use of genetically manipulated human gametes, zygotes and embryos for the purpose of reproduction, unless he believed his work had been officially sanctioned in China. He was either incredibly naïve, which some accounts said was the case, or he had perhaps been led to believe that what he was doing was acceptable or at least tolerated. She went on to read some further reports which said that *MIT Technology Review* broke the story of the gene-edited babies based on information from the Chinese clinical trials registry just before the conference, effectively forcing He Jiankui's hand to disclose his work and the birth of Lulu, Nana and Amy. Susie was further interested to note that the three Chinese scientists were in the end not found criminally liable for the implantation of the genetically edited embryos per se but were instead convicted of undertaking a medical activity without the appropriate licence.[129] It all sounded a bit contrived, she thought, and cobbled together after the event to save face when an international storm blew up and the world reacted with abject horror and condemnation to the news of the birth of the gene-edited Chinese babies.

Once again, Susie was left feeling that the Chinese gene-edited baby incident did not pass the smell test and that there might potentially be more to it than first met the eye. Susie knew from her previous reading and her own visit that life, work and society were heavily controlled and scrutinised in China. On top of this, He Jiankui had been in receipt of Chinese State funding for some aspects of his scientific work, although she noted from her research that there were reports that he had allegedly used his own funds and obscured funding for his clinical genome-editing trial in humans. Then there was the alleged presence of US citizen Professor Michael Deem, He Jiankui's former academic supervisor and mentor, and she wondered what (if anything) lay behind this; here was another example of seemingly ongoing scientific US-Chinese scientific links which puzzled Susie, given the growing competition and political tensions between the two nations. Moreover, Yu Jun was allegedly there too and she wondered if this had anything to do with his membership and role within CAS, the national academy of the People's Republic of China for natural sciences. The role of CAS was to act as the national scientific think tank and academic governing body, providing an advisory and appraisal role for science and technology progress. If Susie's line of reasoning was potentially on to something, this might be indicative of links between He Jiankui's clinical human genome-editing trial and the Chinese State, which the Chinese State had been keen to dispel after the event. All of this left Susie feeling uneasy and her stress levels began to rise.

Chapter 9

September 2020

By August and September 2020, Susie had noticed that the US military presence was getting even more intense on her social media. She felt increasingly bombarded by military and other accounts, and she felt more and more worried about the situation and her own safety. It was getting really stressful and overwhelming, and it was making it difficult to sleep at night. It was also inhibiting her ability to promote her profile on social media for fear of stirring up even more unusual activity. She wondered whether the US military and others had realised that she had joined up some dots and was potentially beginning to make more sense of the bigger picture. If they had been monitoring her activity online, then it was not much of a leap to get to that conclusion, she thought soberly.

After a particularly miserable weekend with it all towards the end of September of 2020, Susie started Monday morning with the mindset that something had to give. It was just not sustainable to keep going like this and to have to carry so much pressure and anxiety about the situation. Her instincts told her that she needed to try and get the situation on a firmer footing. People were getting more and more persistent in their attempts to reach her and find out what she knew, and she did not want the situation to escalate any further; after all, she suspected she had already been followed at court and someone had turned up at her home. If her assessment was right, then there was good reason to be concerned. The question was, how could she start to address this?

9.1 Social Media Activity

Susie sat back in her office chair and racked her brains. The first thing she thought was to try and check whether the online cat and mouse game involving military accounts on social media was just automated 'bots' or whether there was more to it than that. Susie therefore decided to search for an official and authenticated senior US military account. She then selected an account for a high-ranking US army officer and followed it. If that account followed her back and started to try and make contact, it would be from a verified source and this would help rule out concerns about 'bots', fake accounts and scammers, she thought. It was at least something, and that was better than doing nothing at this stage, although she had to admit it was a fairly unsophisticated step. She was fed up with all the ongoing activity in the fringes and she wondered why whoever was behind all of this strange activity was not reaching out to her in a more conventional manner. Instead, this ongoing shadowy presence just lurked like a bad cloud overhead and she felt as if she was going round and round in circles. It was exhausting and it needed to stop, she thought. She had run out of patience, energy and time to keep putting up with it all.

After following the verified high-ranking US army account, Susie did her best to put matters to one side and focus on getting on with her day job. Fortunately, the complexity of her legal caseload required her full attention, and this gave some relief from the enormity of the situation, which weighed her down when her mind was not fully occupied with work. The next day, she nervously checked her social media account and her heart started to pound as she discovered a new military account had appeared. She stared closely at the screen and saw that it was a private account for the high-ranking verified US military general she had followed yesterday. As such, it was not an official account and Susie was unable to verify its authenticity. *Damn*, she muttered, *I am back to square one again,* and she reached out for a sip of Earl Grey tea to steady her nerves, realising that her simplistic test had just failed.

Susie then sat back on her office chair and wondered what her next move should be. Was this just an automated 'bot' that had been triggered when she had followed the official military account the day before? Was it just a random coincidence or scammer or was someone testing the water and trying to make contact? It was difficult to know and maybe this was intentional, she reasoned. She did not want to be caught out and compromised, nor make herself feel more vulnerable than she already did. She also did not want to encourage trouble if she could help it. After considerable soul-searching and with mounting frustration and disappointment, she decided to just ignore the account and see what happened, although she had to admit that it did look out of place following her account. The next day, she noticed with surprise that a whole bunch of other military accounts that had been following her had suddenly disappeared. That was really odd, Susie thought, and she wondered what it meant, wishing yet again that she could make more sense of the situation. Had they been warned off by the presence of this new private account for the high-ranking US military officer? If so, did this tell her anything about the authenticity of the account? Was someone wanting to try and open dialogue with her and if so who? Susie was left feeling in a quandary and did not know what to do for the best, although she sensed that the new military account would not stick around for long as it was looking increasingly out of place. Sure enough, after a couple of days, the account disappeared and she thought with a sigh that that was that.

Then to Susie's considerable surprise, a week later, the same private account for the high-ranking US military officer reappeared and started to follow her again. This was getting beyond a joke, she thought, rather helplessly. It felt like a deliberate move and she felt anxious in case there was something more behind it, and she did not want to cause offence or miss something. After taking a deep breath, she took the plunge and followed the account back, not knowing whether this was for the best or not. Shortly afterwards, she received a direct message from someone purporting to be the high-ranking US military officer. It was a friendly message and Susie replied carefully, not wanting to appear rude but at the same time on high alert, given the situation as a whole. Fairly quickly, she received further messages wanting to get to know her and asking if she was single. *Oh, here we go again,* Susie muttered crossly. This was adopting a similar pattern to situations she had encountered previously, all of which involved someone wanting to get to know her on a private basis. It all felt rather patronising to say the least. As before, she did not entertain matters any further. She quickly closed the situation down by politely explaining that it was a work account and that she did not share her private information. However, the incident left her feeling confused and wondering if it was just a game for whoever was behind this or whether there was some ulterior motive.

Not to be easily defeated, Susie decided to try to test the waters again a few days later. She decided to take a slightly different approach and followed a high-ranking UK British military verified account. Once again, a private account for the military officer appeared and, upon following it back, the individual sought to befriend her on a personal level. Yet again, she closed the situation down as politely as she could. It was so frustrating and she wondered if this was merely an attempt to distract and wear her down or see if she would drop her guard so they could somehow exploit the situation. Alternatively, was this someone's way of trying to reach out since she was still not mixing much or travelling and was largely working from home? It was difficult to know, but she was left feeling more wary than ever, having established the same pattern of activity with both the US military account and the separate UK military account.

9.2 RAF Wyton

Sitting back in her office chair, Susie wondered what her next move should be. She thought hard and concluded that the best thing she could do to protect herself was to get 'on the grid'. If the UK military authorities were made aware of the situation and she shared her analysis with them then it could help alleviate matters. It was a bold move, she thought, and not something she had ever needed to contemplate before despite her twenty-year legal career. It would require some bravery and she would need to stick her head above the parapet, but it had to be better than leaving things as they were, given how intense the situation had become. The next question was, how was she going to achieve this and who would she approach? It was not like she could easily reach out to someone. After a while, and thanks to her voracious reading habit, she recalled a small but illuminating article in *The Sunday Times* a week or so before about a military cyber intelligence unit run by a lieutenant general at Defence Intelligence RAF Wyton in Cambridgeshire.[130] Given the military presence on her social media, it seemed logical in Susie's mind to try and make enquiries with UK military intelligence. According to the article, the unit at RAF Wyton comprised 650 intelligence experts and it had been expanded around March or April 2020 as the Covid-19 pandemic had started to escalate to recruit an additional seventeen military reservists who worked in the medical, biotech and pharmaceutical industries. The article had gone on to report that the team were tasked with monitoring Covid-19 infections in foreign countries, especially those where governments were trying to hide what was happening and track criminal gangs trying to sell fake PPE, medical supplies and drugs to the NHS. It had also reported that several analysts who usually monitored rocket technology were also being drafted in because of their expertise in maths and modelling. She recalled that the article went on to report that not even the Americans had anything equivalent which comprised every military service, secret agency and representatives of all of the 'Five Eyes' allies, namely the US, Canada, Australia, New Zealand and the UK.

It had been very interesting to read in the article the lieutenant general's assessment that the future of intelligence work was to analyse publicly available or so-called 'open source' information. He had explained that this was increasingly providing the basis of their understanding to which they added classified intelligence. He went on to estimate that 80% of their understanding would be generated in this way, with secret intelligence adding further detail, depth and insight. Susie had found this fascinating and she had quickly drawn parallels with her own research and analysis, given all that she was learning through open source internet research. This had shed some fresh light and given new perspective on her own research and view of world affairs. If the military were adopting a similar approach, she realised that she was in good company. Clearly, there was still the matter of accuracy in terms of the research and analysis itself. However, over recent months, Susie had been able to analyse vast amounts of information and identify themes, patterns and distance of travel by means of multiple checks and verification based on her growing understanding and points of reference. If she was on the right track, then there was a possibility that she could make increasingly accurate assessments thanks to the power of the internet, she thought. It had been eerie to realise this capability within herself, the extent of which she was still discovering as she went along. Every so often, she would read something or join up the dots and that would then set off a train of new thoughts and connections that expanded her growing insight and understanding of the bigger interconnected picture. It was as annoying as it was fruitful, and she was not yet entirely comfortable with this capability, which seemed to be unleashing itself at pace and taking on a power all of its own. It was difficult to switch off or even dial it down, and it was taking more and more effort to try and distract herself and rest. It was only when her mind was fully occupied with complex legal work or an interesting film or programme on Netflix that she was able to achieve some respite.

Given the unexplained ongoing military presence on her social media, particularly her Instagram account of late, Susie decided that she would try and contact the lieutenant general's military unit at RAF Wyton. It was a bold move and entirely out of character, but it made sense in her mind and she needed to do something. They might be able to assess what was going on and it would send a clear message that she was intent upon addressing the situation. It might also shed some further light on the situation and provide a pathway forward. It was time to call in the big guns, she thought. She therefore turned to the internet and did a Google search for RAF Wyton. On locating their telephone number, she picked up the telephone and dialled the number, willing herself to keep calm. A man answered the telephone and she explained who she was and that she wished to speak to the lieutenant general in charge of the unit or a member of his team about some unusual military activity she was experiencing and her concerns that she was under surveillance. The man explained that he would need to pass this on. He took down Susie's contact details and the call ended. All Susie could do was wait and see whether anything came of this. At least she had made the call and raised a flag. The ball was now in their court, she thought grimly.

An hour or so later, Susie's telephone rang, and she heard a well-spoken educated male voice introduce himself as the legal advisor to the lieutenant general in charge at RAF Wyton. Susie was surprised to hear from him and relieved at the same time. Part of her had prepared for no response at all, and so to receive a call like this was at least something, she told herself. He asked her to explain what had been happening and what had prompted her to call. Susie took a deep breath and proceeded to summarise in chronological terms the history of strange encounters that led her to believe that she was under surveillance, the ongoing persistent military presence on her social media and her fears for her safety. She also briefly explained her concerns about genomic technology and the need for law reform. The military officer listened carefully and then he told her that it was perfectly possibly that she was under surveillance by foreign entities but stressed it was not the UK. He went on to explain that as Susie had a public profile and she was a civilian, they were unable to assist any further, but he suggested Susie contact her local MP for help, recognising the issues she had raised. Susie thanked the military officer for his time, help and guidance and said that she would follow up with her MP as a next step.

9.3 Discussions with MP

Susie sat back after the call and reflected thoughtfully on what had just happened. Her call for help had been received and it had registered, she thought. The officer she had just spoken to had been friendly and done his best to reassure her about the

US military presence and suggested she contact her local MP to make further enquiries on her behalf. In doing so, her call and concerns had not been ignored or dismissed out of hand. The UK military officer had not denied or sidestepped the issues she had raised either. So, to some extent, her objectives had been met in that she had raised a red flag and got herself 'on the grid'. She sighed in relief at this point, telling herself things could have been worse and that she had made a not insignificant step forward. The next step was to try and reach out to her local MP and see what, if anything, could be achieved with their help.

After a quick sandwich and yet another mug of Earl Grey tea, Susie fired up Google to track down the best way to contact her local Conservative MP. She called up her local constituency details and discovered that she needed to write in by email with her name, address, contact details and a short summary of the issue she wished to raise. Due to the Covid-19 pandemic, her MP was not offering in-person meetings and in some cases a telephone call would be arranged instead. This then left the no small matter of how best to explain the situation effectively in an email. This would take a bit of time, she thought with a sigh. Nothing about the situation she found herself in was easy and she was weary, feeling up against it all the time and forever swimming against the tide. She felt a wave of sadness sweep over her that took her breath away for a moment. She had not ever expected to find herself in this situation. She was just a lawyer who had worked hard and she was not someone who had consciously signed up for a life like this, like those in the military or intelligence world. At least they had a community of colleagues, infrastructure, training and support around them, she thought wistfully. She, on the other hand, had no such support day after day, which was exhausting. It did not seem fair, but then life wasn't fair, she told herself firmly. She was incredibly lucky to have received the education that she did and to have been able to practise law for over twenty years, and it was important to recognise that and remain grateful, she told herself sternly. There was no space in life to feel sorry for yourself when you had received so much and enjoyed so much that so many others could only dream about.

After a much-needed pep talk, Susie called up a blank Word document on her laptop and began to draft a letter to her MP. It was a strange experience to find herself doing this, but she nonetheless gritted her teeth and pushed on with the task, telling herself it was important to keep going. She had over the years coined a phrase which had served her well when times were tough, 'never give up and never give in', and it helped to repeat this under her breath from time to time. Today was one of those days, she thought grimly. She then gathered herself together and dug deep as she constructed her letter. Firstly, she introduced herself and explained that it followed a telephone call that afternoon with the lawyer to the UK military general at RAF Wyton. Susie then explained that in the course of her work about fertility and genomics, considerable unwelcome attention, surveillance and approaches by a range of individuals and military personnel had been generated. She explained that this had included activity across her digital platforms and unexplained and concerning 'real-life' situations. Susie went on to explain that this was adversely affecting her online profile, her sense of security and her private and family life. She then highlighted a critical absence of integrated, multidisciplinary and forward-looking law, policy and practice in the UK with which to address the rapidly evolving digital, artificial intelligence, genomic, epigenetic and reproductive revolutions.

Susie sat back in her office chair to survey the progress that she had made with her letter to her local MP. She stared out of her office window for a few moments as she reflected on the next points and the assistance that she was going to ask for. The sun was low, even though it was only mid-afternoon, and the birds were noisily circling overhead as the remaining daylight faded into a beautiful pink and purple early evening dusk. This sight never failed to impress Susie and she loved the countryside views that she was so fortunate to enjoy from her home at Brook House. It had been the country setting and the views that had sold the house to her in the first place. Then after a few minutes, she refocused and distilled her call for assistance into a request for understanding as to whether she was classified as a 'Person of Interest' and if so by whom, on what basis and what further steps should be taken. Then she highlighted the critical law and policy matters not currently answered by the state and put forward some proposals to respond to the rapidly evolving digital, artificial, genomic, epigenetic and reproductive revolutions. Firstly, it should create a top-level multidisciplinary strategy group that operated on a continuous basis in the UK with an extended remit beyond that of the government's Scientific Advisory Group for Emergencies (Sage) to help bring about paradigm shifts in thinking, leadership and governance from the top down. Secondly, it should create a new Ministry for Genomics and Fertility, providing integrated national genomic and fertility policy and political strategy and unified future direction for the fertility sector. Thirdly, it should bring about root and branch law reform in the UK. She concluded the letter with a short further reading list of links to various articles she had written for good measure. After carefully proof reading the letter and a further short break to clear her head, she pressed send and the email disappeared from her screen.

She did not know whether or not she felt relief or just more stress about the situation. A rush of adrenalin was pumping through her body and her hands felt clammy to the touch. On the one hand, she had taken another step forward to raise a red flag about her situation and take action. On the other hand, she had now upped the stakes and she was not sure what would happen from here. It was unchartered territory and it was not a path to adopt lightly. In this moment, Susie felt really small and alone and she felt another wave of sadness flood over her. Trying to do the right thing was never easy and in difficult times like these, it came at very considerable cost. Life would be much easier if she were to take a far more cavalier attitude to things, but that was not the sort of life she led.

After sending off the email to her local MP, Susie did her best to clear her head and focus on other things. She buried herself in her legal work and kept busy, sticking to her exercise schedule on her treadmill in the evenings and trying to limit her late-night internet surfing habit. She also spent some time in the kitchen, preparing fresh and healthy meals as she realised she should be doing more to take care of herself. She noticed that her hair was looking dull and rather brittle again and her nails were fragile and snapping, sure signs of stress and being a bit run-down. She made the effort to change her bed more frequently too so that she could sink into fresh-smelling sheets at night in the hope of achieving a better night's sleep. Following her exercise routine and a good meal, she also tried to hunker down on the sofa a bit with Rina to watch some lightweight television and improve her popular culture. She was not a big fan of, nor did she have the time to follow, the ins and outs of regular weekly soap operas beloved by millions across the country, but she did like programmes such as *The Great British Bake Off*, *MasterChef* and the odd drama series.

A few days later, Susie received an email reply from her local MP's assistant advising that her MP would forward her email to the Home Secretary to try and establish whether she was classified as a 'Person of Interest' and for any other helpful advice that could be offered. The email said that if she had not already contacted the local police regarding her concerns about her personal safety, then this was something to consider. The email went on to explain that her MP would also contact the Secretary of State for Health for his response to her suggestion for a new Ministry for Genomics and Fertility and that if the Secretary of State expressed an interest, they would try and get contact details of individual(s) for her to approach to take matters forward. She was pleased to have received a response from her MP, given their busy workload, but at the same time it did not provide an opportunity for a discussion, which is what she had been hoping for. After a few minutes' thought, she therefore picked up the telephone and called her MP's office to see whether or not there was any scope for a telephone meeting with her MP, reminding herself of the phrase, 'if you do not ask, you did not get in life'. After a short but productive conversation with her MP's assistant, it was left that the assistant would speak to her MP to see if they were willing to offer Susie a telephone appointment. Susie hung up after the call, feeling she had done all that she could in seeking to progress matters through her MP. She felt relieved that she had persevered with this, although it did not drastically alleviate her ongoing stress levels to any great extent.

About a week later, Susie received a short follow-up email from her local MP's assistant explaining that her MP was willing to offer her a twenty-minute telephone appointment later that week. Susie responded quickly by accepting this and then adding the appointment to her Outlook calendar on her laptop. The telephone appointment passed quickly in that there was only limited time to explain the background to what had been happening and explore the way forward. It took a bit of time too for her MP to rest into the discussion and at first Susie was concerned that she would simply run out of time if her MP strictly adhered to the twenty-minute appointment time. The tone of the call was very formal and this made it difficult to gauge how things were going, particularly as Susie could not assess her MP's body language or facial expressions. Luckily, the call was extended a bit and after a while her MP began to engage a little more and propose some further steps. It was agreed that Susie would put together a written timeline of events and email this over, together with a selection of screenshots of military and other unexplained followers on her social media accounts.

Following the call, Susie rested back in her chair to reflect on the conversation and gather her thoughts more fully. She had not had any preconceptions about the call, having never done this sort of thing before. As such, she did not have a mental checklist to which to refer beyond the letter she had sent her MP. Then as she made herself another mug of Earl Grey tea in the kitchen and cracked open a fresh packet of chocolate digestives, she went back over the conversation in her mind. Her MP had been businesslike. Susie had got the distinct impression that her MP did not have an in-depth knowledge or understanding of the issues she was trying to raise, which was perhaps not surprising. She had also noted a few comments from her MP towards the end of the call about it all being rather complex. Nonetheless, her MP's suggestion to prepare a written timeline and put together screenshots of some of the strange people she had encountered on her digital platforms were constructive and she therefore set about doing just that.

The preparation of the written timeline was relatively straightforward in that she could piece together the timeline fairly quickly by looking back through her diary and then providing accompanying information. Preparing the screenshots of some of the strange people on her digital platforms took longer. She found it a sobering exercise as she scrolled back through her accounts and revisited the sorts of people who were there, and it made the hairs on the back of her neck stand up as they were just so far removed from the world which she inhabited. They were not the sort of people you would meet at the village fete or in your local Sainsbury's supermarket, she thought grimly. The first account she screenshotted was for a retired executive officer to a former chief of staff of the United States Army who now delivered strategic direction on C4I technology solutions to the defence industry. The second one related to another high-ranking US military account for US Cybercom, which made her swallow hard. The third was another US military account, which appeared to be the head of one of the US Army's research laboratories. Then she screenshotted another account for yet another retired high-ranking US military officer who seemed rather strangely to have been chief of the US Army Dental Corps. Then she came across another high-ranking military account, this time from Norway, with a photo of a man in uniform with stars all up his shoulder lapels, suggesting he was a military general. As Susie scrolled on through her accounts, she found further accounts for US servicemen in army combat uniform, one of whom she noticed had popped up on more than one of her social media platforms, which unnerved her all over again. Then, as Susie scrolled on, she started to come across account after account of unidentified, strong, fit-looking men who looked as if they could have connections to military or intelligence services.

After that, Susie came across more accounts of foreign men from all over the place, including what looked like Eastern Europe, South Africa, Western Europe and Asia. She realised that these accounts reflected a global presence and it was hard in the face of all these accounts to attribute this to coincidence. Instead, it appeared to indicate that she was right to feel under surveillance, something the lawyer to the general at the military unit at RAF Wyton had said was possible. This got Susie wondering whether they were all just 'bot' accounts or whether they were actual accounts for some of these individuals. She had no way of knowing and it was frustrating and concerning, she thought, although her gut instinct was telling her that some of them at least looked real. After a few hours' work, she was relieved to finally send everything off by email to her MP. She then raided the fridge for a light supper, which was all she could stomach after the stress of the day.

The following Friday, Susie wandered into her office and sat down with her morning mug of Earl Grey tea as she scrolled through her daily Google alerts. It was how she liked to start her day and that morning was no exception. She liked Friday mornings as the prospect of the weekend ahead offered some respite after what was always a busy working week. However, she stopped in her tracks as a Google alert caught her attention. She suddenly went cold as her eyes scanned the link to a recently published scientific paper and it was like a light bulb went on inside her head. The scientific article was titled *CCR5 Δ32 minorallele is associated with susceptibility to SARS-CoV-2 infection and death: An epidemiological investigation.*[131] It reported that the role of the immune system and the CCR5 receptor in producing an uncontrolled inflammatory response (a 'cytokine storm') to Covid-19 was becoming clearer. Susie's eye had then been caught by sections in the article that looked at the role of CCR5 in HIV/AIDS and other diseases. This suddenly triggered a potential link in Susie's mind between the Chinese gene-edited baby affair, whose embryos had been genetically edited to try to make them resistant to HIV/AIDS, and the Covid-19 pandemic. Susie then began to work through in her mind a 'dual-use' line of thinking that the SARS-CoV-2 virus might potentially be a manmade Chinese gain-of-function virus that leaked from a laboratory in Wuhan and that the Chinese scientist He Jiankui had (potentially unknowingly) been working on a way to edit embryos to prevent people from contracting the disease; a sort of proof-of-concept experiment as a disease resistance countermeasure (not just to prevent the transmission of HIV). Susie sat back in her chair as this line of thinking sank in a bit. She felt utterly shell-shocked by the enormity of it and she had a growing sense that she might potentially be on to something with this. It would potentially give wider significance to the CCR5 gene edit in the Chinese babies. It might also potentially explain why there had been such a high level of military presence on her digital platforms, which coincided with when she started to read up on the Chinese gene-edited babies. If she was right in her thinking, then the presentation that he was looking to find a cure for HIV might potentially have been a smokescreen designed to detract from a far more significant and serious picture.

Susie felt her worst fears might potentially be coming true. Her line of thinking quite literally flattened her for the best part of an hour. She felt positively bludgeoned by it all. In fact, she felt shaken to her core by what she had just thought through. She was also concerned that she was now sitting on sensitive knowledge that was not widely known. In that moment, she felt utterly alone. The question now was what to do about it all. She did not want to be left holding this information on her own; it made her feel too vulnerable and downright unsafe. Her attempts to 'get on grid' had only been partially successful, and her immediate thoughts were to ratchet things up and try and get hold of the security services as she had got as far as she could with the help of her MP.

9.4 MI5

Where to start? Susie thought. It was not an everyday occurrence to try and contact the security services. It felt strangely surreal to even be thinking along these lines and she questioned how on earth things had got to this point. It was another step into the unknown and it was uncomfortable to say the least. She had to trust that it was the right thing to do and have faith that it would be all right, she told herself firmly. With that, she swallowed hard and googled the security services and, sure enough, a webpage popped up with a contact telephone number. *Well, that was not so hard*, she muttered under her breath.

There was no time to procrastinate, Susie thought. She had to strike whilst the iron was hot and follow through before she lost her nerve. With that, she took another big breath and picked up the telephone handset on her desk and punched in the security services' telephone number. A moment later, she heard the line ring and then a youngish-sounding male voice answered. It worked, Susie thought somewhat incredulously; she had got through to someone. She quickly took the plunge and began to outline her concerns that she was somehow under surveillance, her discussions with the military intelligence unit at RAF Wyton, her MP and her growing concerns about genomic technology and events surrounding the Covid-19 pandemic. Every so often, the male voice interjected and asked some questions as he tried to follow the conversation. Susie was not sure to what extent what she was saying was registering. After what seemed like a long explanation, but which in reality took only a few minutes, the male voice said that the information would be passed on for consideration and someone would be in touch. With that, the call abruptly ended.

Susie sat back in her chair with a sigh. Well, that was a first, she thought. She had officially stuck her head above the parapet with the security services and she did not know whether to laugh or cry in that moment. Presumably now they would run some checks and decide what to do next. Would they be in touch? she wondered. On balance, Susie was far from convinced that they would follow up with her and then what? She was not a big scientific fish, nor was she an obvious source of information or so-called 'intelligence'. If they ignored her request, it was going to get harder to know what to do, she realised soberly.

The next few days were fairly torturous for Susie. She was like a cat on hot bricks and the weekend seemed to pass so slowly. When Monday came and went, her heart sank and she felt dejected by the lack of progress or news. However, she was not ready to be defeated or give in just yet, she decided through gritted teeth. She had been through too much already and lost too much sleep over it all to just let things slide now. Spurring herself on, she picked up the telephone handset and dialled the security services once more. A woman answered her call this time in an efficient way and asked about the nature of her call. She explained briefly that she was following up her last call as she hadn't heard anything further. Then, somewhat more boldly, she went on to ask why she had not been contacted, given the serious nature of her approach. The woman paused and then said that Susie's file was currently with a colleague and that she would follow up with them after the call. Well, that was something, Susie thought. There was now a file and it was sitting on someone's desk for consideration. With that, the woman brought the call to a close and the call ended abruptly once again.

Susie got up from her desk chair and stretched slowly. She paused to stare out of her study window at the afternoon sky. Autumn was here and the leaves on the trees were changing colour, whilst the days were drawing in fast, she thought. With that, she wandered down the hallway to make a much-needed mug of Earl Grey tea and dig out a fresh stash of chocolate. Rina sat up in delight from her bed across the kitchen and slowly wandered over to say hello, rubbing herself around Susie's ankles in the hope she would get some food. *'It's too early for dinner,'* Susie told Rina firmly, feeling a little bit mean and guilty as she stretched out to reach the chocolate for herself. She could swear the irony of the situation was not lost on Rina either as she poured the boiling water into her mug and squeezed the teabag briefly, munching on a square of chocolate as she did so.

Chapter 10

Another evening passed slowly in the company of Rina. Susie struggled to keep her thoughts in check and so she decided the best thing to do was to bury herself in a film, even though it was a weekday evening. It helped to pass the time and at bedtime, she managed to resist the urge for once to do some late-night internet surfing. She was tired emotionally as well as physically and what she needed was a good night's sleep. Whether she would achieve this was another matter, but it was worth a go, she thought, as Rina curled up on the other side of the bed.

The next morning, she followed her usual morning routine. She made breakfast, fed Rina and sat down at her desk first thing with a fresh mug of Earl Grey tea. She fired up her laptop and scanned the day's Google alerts. Then she started to prepare for a 10am video meeting. It was going to be a busy morning and for that she was grateful. Just before 9.30am, her telephone rang and she answered it in a rather preoccupied manner. A mature male voice introduced himself in a businesslike fashion as being from the local counter-terrorism police unit and said he had been asked by the security services to make contact. He went on to ask calmly if they could visit her that morning. She sat up straight with a start, feeling rather stunned. She found herself explaining that she had a scheduled meeting just about to start at 10am and so she was not actually available that morning, but that she would be free after 12 noon. The man paused and said he was not sure that was convenient and then proceeded to ask her if she was available the following morning. Susie gulped and apologised, saying she had another meeting the following morning too. After another pause, the man then replied that they would attend her house at 12.15pm that day. She thanked him very much and went on to ask if he would like some directions as her house was quite hard to find. She could hear him smiling down the telephone at that point and he went on to say that they knew where she was and that they would be with her at 12.15 pm. The call ended and she ran through the conversation in her mind. They were coming to see her at home in a couple of hours' time; not much notice, she thought, to get herself together and prepared, particularly as she had a video meeting to get through first. She also kicked herself a bit for checking whether they needed directions; of course they didn't need them – they were the security services, and finding people was all in a day's work for them.

Following the call, she had to work really hard to stay focused and get through her morning meeting effectively. It had taken additional effort to hold the line and she found herself looking at her watch at regular intervals. She did, however, manage to conclude her meeting at 12 noon sharp, which was a relief as this was not the day for a meeting to overrun. This gave her a few minutes to gather up her laptop and get to the kitchen and put the kettle on before they arrived. There was more room at the kitchen table and it felt a little more neutral than her home office. The kettle had just boiled when she heard the doorbell go. As she opened her front door, she was met by two men. One was slim, in his forties, dressed in a dark well-fitting suit. The other was much taller and well built, in his fifties, and looked like he could handle himself, she thought. They did not shake hands although they smiled politely at her. She welcomed them in and quickly discussed social distancing arrangements in the kitchen and whether they would like the backdoor kept open to improve air ventilation. Once they were settled, she proceeded to make them each a hot drink. The younger man did not have any official ID on him and she was pretty sure his name, Charles, was a pseudonym. The other man produced his police ID and introduced himself to her more formerly and gave his name as Andrew.

As they all gathered around the large kitchen table, she wondered how things would play out. The two men started by asking her to tell them about herself. It was an open question and she was not really sure where to start, nor was she accustomed to talking about herself like this. She was far more comfortable and used to discussing legal work and case strategy. However, she realised this was different and that she would have to open up about herself if this was going to go anywhere. They were looking to get a better feel for her, much as she liked to do with clients, before getting down to the specifics. She figured that the best thing to do was to provide a brief personal history. She proceeded to summarise her background, career, personal situation and skillset. The men listened carefully and made notes in their black books as she went along.

Then, the younger of the two men, Charles, broached her calls to the security services and calmly explained that they had spoken with her MP before their visit to see her today. He went on to say that he gathered that she had put together a PowerPoint presentation of her findings, which they were here to see. Susie was somewhat taken aback by the direct nature of his comments, but she was also not surprised that they had done their homework too. After all, here they were sat in her kitchen and she was sure they did not do this every time they received a call from a member of the public.

With that, she explained to Charles that she was mindful of the complex dynamics and the need to navigate matters carefully. They nodded in response and relaxed a little, which Susie took as a good sign. She opened up her laptop and called up her PowerPoint presentation. As she did so, Charles commented that Susie would need to bear in mind that they were not scientists nor were they technical experts in genomics. She nodded, commenting that they should be fine to follow her presentation and that she would be happy to answer any questions they might have. The older man, Andrew, then pointedly asked her where she had got her information from. She looked at him steadily, explaining that it was all open source material, which he duly noted and made a note of in his little black book. He then asked if she evidenced this in her presentation and she nodded with an encouraging smile, explaining that there were electronic references and links at the back of the PowerPoint presentation to which they could refer. With that, Andrew seemed satisfied with her answers and he sat back in his chair and made a few further written notes. After a few minutes nervously fiddling with the mouse, which did not immediately work, she was ready and she started to run through her findings slide by slide.

10.1 First PowerPoint Presentation

Susie started with a brief introduction to set the scene. She explained that CRISPR Cas-9 gene-editing technology had only been invented in 2012, just eight years ago, and so it was new in technological terms.[132] [133] By 2014, just two years later, the Chinese had started to harness CRISPR technology in monkeys. The following year, 2015, a Chinese team of scientists collaborated with the subsequently discredited scientist He Jiankui in a study of monkeys to enhance understanding of immune system complexity and immune-related diseases in humans. She went on to explain that between 2016 and 2017, He Jiankui carried out CRISPR Cas-9 experiments to edit the embryos of rodents, monkeys and humans, being a so-called 'proof-of-concept'.

Susie explained that in 2018 He Jiankui proceeded to announce the birth of the world's first gene-edited twin babies (Lulu and Nana) at the Second International Summit on Human Genome Editing in Hong Kong, who were said to be resistant to HIV with an altered CCR5 gene (another proof-of-concept).[134] [135] [136] She explained that this might have been a smokescreen and that the clinical experiment might potentially have had wider significance beyond gene edits to try to make the Chinese babies resistant to HIV/AIDS. She added that the Chinese scientist He Jiankui might (potentially unknowingly) have been working on a way to gene edit embryos to prevent people from contracting viral diseases more widely (or the converse); a sort of proof-of-concept experiment relevant to potential virulent gain-of-function viruses (not just to prevent the transmission of HIV).

The news of the gene-edited babies had been met by international condemnation that He Jiankui was a rogue scientist, and this resulted in his prosecution by the Chinese authorities and imprisonment for three years in December 2019.[137] [138] She added that in December 2019, the Covid-19 virus outbreak came to light in Wuhan. This coincided with reports of alleged gain-of-function virus experiments being undertaken at the Wuhan Institute of Virology. There followed a global pandemic which up to now had resulted in the loss of life of upwards of 1 million people and global economic and wider disruption.[139]

10.2 Correlation Between Chinese Gene-Edited Babies and Covid-19 Virus

Susie then highlighted a potential correlation between the Chinese gene-edited babies and the Covid-19 virus, stressing the word virus. She explained that in 2015 He Jiankui had collaborated with Chinese scientists in a study that found that the immune repertoire of the rhesus monkey is highly diversified, close to that in humans and could be applied in investigating T-Cell responses during virulent influenza virus infection.[140] [141]

Next, Susie explained that between 2016 and 2017, He Jiankui began CRISPR Cas-9 gene-editing experiments in the embryos of rodents, monkeys and humans. She explained that some gene-edited rodent and monkey embryos even resulted in live births. This work was said to have been reported orally by He Jiankui at a Cold Spring Harbour Laboratory meeting in July 2017 but was not scientifically published.[142] [143] Then, in 2018, He Jiankui created the world's first gene-edited babies as proof of principle. The headline was that they were said to be resistant to HIV, but she explained there were reports that they might also be more susceptible to influenza-type viral infection as a result of their altered CCR5 gene.[144] [145] She added that the 2019–20 global Covid-19 virus outbreak caused severe infection, which was understood to have genetic links, including the role of the CCR5 gene, in contributing to inflammatory 'cytokine storms' in the human body.[146] [147] [148]

10.3 Implications of CCR5 Gene Editing

She then proceeded to explore some of the potential implications of CCR5 gene-editing experiments. She explained that He Jiankui had presented the CCR5 gene edit as a treatment to prevent HIV. Could this potentially over time develop a commercial value and global sales? If so, there could be benefit and gain in areas like

Africa to obtain world resources and geopolitical expansion. She went on to say that there might also be potential 'backdoor susceptibility' to Covid-19-type infections, which would then require Covid-19-type treatments and vaccines, driving further commercial global sales. She added that the Covid-19 pandemic had already caused a massive uptake in demand for genomic testing. She explained that the Chinese had developed a Fire Eye genomic laboratory and associated technology capability which could be rolled out internationally for commercial gain. As a result, the Chinese now had a biopolitical influence in more than eighty countries.[149] With this, China had increased access to global genomic data. She went on to say that the Covid-19 pandemic had also caused global disruption and economic loss, which could also potentially fuel Chinese geopolitical ambitions in the South China Sea, Taiwan and Hong Kong. She thought that the younger of the two security officers, Charles, looked thoughtful at this point, although Andrew still remained fairly impassive and harder to read.

10.4 Covid-19 Origins

Susie moved on, noting that both officers were listening carefully and continuing to make notes. She explained that there was an ongoing question about whether Covid-19 was a natural occurrence. She pointed out that in 2018, China had opened its first mainland biosecurity level 4 (BSL-4) laboratory.[150] This is the highest containment level laboratory cleared to work on dangerous airborne pathogens that have no known cures or vaccines. This had given rise to a further ongoing question about whether the Wuhan Institute of Virology (the WIV) had played a role in the Covid-19 viral outbreak in Wuhan, China. Genomic gain-of-function experiments on coronaviruses had seemingly been undertaken at the WIV by lead Chinese scientist Shi Zhengli (Bat Woman) working on bats. The WIV had published the closest known relative to SARS CoV-2 in the form of virus RaTG13 with a 96.2% similarity identified in a scientific study between 2011 and 2012.[151] This type of gain-of-function research was undertaken to understand how bat coronaviruses could mutate to attack humans and with a view to then designing vaccines to counter this.

Another hypothesis that required interrogation was whether there might have been an accidental release of the Covid-19 virus at the WIV earlier than first thought in, say, October 2019. If so, this was earlier than the current public narrative that the virus had emerged in December 2019, but it potentially made sense that the virus had been circulating for a while before it exploded into a full outbreak. Charles became more interested at this point and made eye contact with Susie. She explained that she had come across reports from telephone and aerial records that indicated that there might have been some sort of incident at the WIV in October 2019, resulting in the closure of operations there for a few days. Charles nodded thoughtfully and Susie noted that this seemed to resonate with him as he made some further notes in his little black book.

Susie added that there was also a further potential hypothesis that there might have been a deliberate release of the Covid-19 virus (however unlikely that might seem), adding that this would be a different matter altogether.

10.5 Chinese Biophysicist He Jiankui

Susie then explained that she then wanted to take them through the life of Chinese biophysicist He Jiankui, the architect of the three Chinese gene-edited babies, reminding them of her initial comments that there might potentially be a correlation between the CCR5 gene edit and the Covid-19 virus pandemic.

He Jiankui had studied for an undergraduate physics degree at the University of Science and Technology of China in Hefi, reportedly with the benefit of scholarship funding. He received his undergraduate degree in 2006. Then in 2007, as a top Chinese graduate, he had been sent to the US to study for a PhD in biophysics under the tutelage of Professor Michael Deem at Rice University in Texas. He received his PhD in 2010 and shifted his focus to genetics, particularly gene-editing technologies, most likely due to their greater future potential. She added that in 2011, he then became a post-doctoral scholar in the laboratory of Professor Steven Quake at Stanford University in California.[152] [153]

What was interesting was that in 2010, Professor Michael Deem and He Jiankui published a paper in a scientific publication that explored the evolutionary properties of the CRISPR bacterial immune system. Susie added that other papers from He Jiankui analysed the evolution of animal body plans and the correlation between a viral pandemic and economic recession in terms of the World Trade Network. Hearing this, Charles scribbled further notes in his black book and shot a glance at his colleague across the table. With that, Susie began to think that what she had to say was being taken seriously and appeared to be of some interest. She then explained that He Jiankui had gone on to study influenza genetic sequences within the Department of Bioengineering at Stanford University School of Medicine, resulting in the publication of a further scientific paper in 2013.[154]

Susie quickly went on to explain that in 2011, He Jiankui reportedly announced on a blog that he and the Southern University of Science and Technology (SUSTECH) University in Shenzhen, China would start a joint laboratory to find disease-specific genes that control immune responses. The following year, 2012, He Jiankui returned to China and was appointed to the faculty of SUSTECH in Shenzhen in Guangdong Province.[155] [156] She explained that in the same year, He Jiankui reportedly launched a company called Direct Genomics in Shenzen, China, with $6 million start-up funding from the Peacock Plan; one of several programs to lure scientific researchers back to China. In doing so, Direct Genomics licensed a technology to sequence single molecules of DNA as a diagnostic tool for cancer or genetic abnormalities in embryos.[157] [158]

Having paused for a moment to check that both men were following and keeping up, Susie explained that in 2017, He Jiankui reportedly became part of the Chinese government's prestigious Thousand Talents program.[159] [160] This is China's central government's top science program, which claims to be the 'world's most prestigious and influential state science program', involving almost every department of government. Its aim is to advance specific scientific and financial areas, such as gene technologies and the genetic industry, which the Chinese State considers to be of primary strategic importance. In other words, Susie suggested it was a big deal when He Jiankui hit the Thousand Talents program in China. Charles looked at Susie again rather thoughtfully at this point.

Moving on, she explained that in July 2017, He Jiankui attended a scientific meeting in the US at Cold Harbour Laboratory with leading US scientist Jennifer Doudna and others. Charles nodded at this point, clearly familiar with the Cold Harbour Scientific Laboratory meetings, she thought. She smiled to herself, appreciating that he obviously knew far more than he was letting on to her, which was not overly surprising. She went on to explain that He Jiankui delivered a talk on 'Evaluating the safety of germline genome editing in human, monkey and mouse embryos'. He discussed his CCR5 gene-editing work in mice, rodents, monkeys and over 300 non-viable human embryos discarded from IVF.[161] [162] The reports of this meeting indicated that leading attending scientists like Jennifer Doudna and others had no idea that he would move on to clinical trials since he had not published much in peer-related journals.

These high-level discussions required focus and Susie took a moment to stare briefly out of the window and sip her mug of tea to catch her breath. She was intent on remaining focused as she delivered her presentation, recognising that it was an important exercise in more ways than one. She then explained that between 2017 and 2018, He Jiankui reportedly submitted a medical ethics approval application to the Shenzhen Harmonicare Women and Children's Hospital outlining the planned CCR5 genetic edits of human embryos. He Jiankui then reportedly worked with a Beijing Aids advocacy group to recruit participants. He reportedly subsequently transferred to five women a total of eleven to thirteen embryos for implantation, two of whom became pregnant and subsequently gave birth.[163 164]

Looking in more detail at the events surrounding his actions, there were some reported indications of what was to come. In April 2018, He Jiankui allegedly told contacts linked to the company Direct Genomics that a woman was pregnant with CRISPR gene-edited embryos. In October 2018, the Chinese gene-edited twins Lulu and Nana were believed to have been born in the north of China, and a third pregnancy was confirmed in November 2018. On 22 November 2018, He Jiankui reportedly sent an email to scientist Jennifer Doudna to announce the birth of gene-edited twins, just three days before the Second International Summit on Human Genome Editing in Hong Kong was due to happen. He subsequently went on to present his work and clinical results at the summit.[165 166]

10.6 Global Response to News of Gene-Edited Babies, 2018

Susie moved to a further slide addressing the global reaction to news of the Chinese gene-edited babies and the response of leading scientists. She noted that this made the two officers sit up a little straighter as they began to realise that she had drilled down into the specifics of this as well. They seemed somewhat reassured by this, she thought to herself. She explained that Professor David Baltimore, chair of the Second International Summit on the genome editing organising committee reportedly asserted that the research was a 'failure of self-regulation by the scientific community, because of a lack of transparency'.[167] [168]

Professor Robin Lovell-Badge, a leading British scientist who had moderated He Jiankui's panel session at the summit, reportedly questioned the selection of editing the CCR5 gene, commenting on how little was known about it and, given some research, suggesting that it could have made the babies more susceptible to influenza and enhanced cognitive capabilities. Susie then paused, looked directly at the officers and explained that He Jiankui had reportedly responded by saying that CCR5 genes had been 'studied for decades'. Charles shifted in his seat on hearing this, shot another quick look at his colleague and made some further notes in his black book. That had resonated with them, Susie thought to herself.

Professor David Lui from the US Broad Institute had reportedly questioned whether the research satisfied an 'unmet need' which warranted such a serious clinical experiment. He pointed out that sperm-washing technology could prevent prenatal paternal transmission of HIV. Susie added that Jennifer Doudna was reportedly 'horrified' when she learnt the news too.[169] [170]

Susie moved on, wanting to keep up momentum at this stage. The two officers were engaging well, she thought, and were seemingly interested in the analysis of the scientists' responses to the whole affair. Susie explained that the summit's organising committee issued a statement saying:[171] [172]

The organizing committee concludes that the scientific understanding and technical requirements for clinical practice remain too uncertain and the risks too great to permit clinical trials of germline editing at this time.

The only scientist who reportedly appeared to lend any support to He Jiankui's work was Professor George Church at Harvard Medical School in the US, who reportedly said:[173] [174]

I'd just as well not hang myself out to dry with someone I barely know, but I feel an obligation to be balanced about it. I'm sitting in the middle and everyone else is so extreme that it makes me look like his buddy. He's just an acquaintance. But it seems like a bullying situation to me. The most serious thing I've heard is that he didn't do the paperwork right. He wouldn't be the first person who got the paperwork wrong. It's just that the stakes are higher. If it had gone south and someone had been damaged, maybe these would be some point. Like what happened with Jesse Gelsinger [who died in a 1999 gene therapy experiment gone wrong]. But is this a Jesse Gelsinger or a Louise Brown 'the first baby born through in vitro fertilization' event? That's probably what it boils down to.

Susie pushed on, explaining that the Chinese response had immediately condemned He Jiankui's research. On 26 November 2018, the Chinese government announced that there would be an investigation and suggested that there were several fairly vague regulations that He Jiankui's work may have violated.[175] [176] On 21 January 2019, the official Chinese news agency published a short statement saying:[177] [178]

A preliminary investigation into the claimed 'genetically edited babies' shows that Chinese researcher He Jiankui

> *had defied government bans and conducted the research in the pursuit of personal fame and gain.*

Susie added that SUSTECH University had then seemingly fired He Jiankui the same day from his university post.

10.7 Implications of CCR5 Gene Mutation

Moving on, she explained that on 3 June 2019, *Nature Medicine* published a study using the genotyping and death register information of 409,693 individuals of British ancestry to investigate fitness effects of the CCR5-Δ32 mutation. It estimated a 21% increase in all-cause mortality rates in individuals who are homozygous (possessing two identical alleles of a particular gene) for the CCR5-Δ32 mutation.[179]

She paused for a moment whilst she let the security officers soak everything in. She was conscious that she was moving through her presentation at pace and there was a lot for them to absorb and consider. They were continuing to follow, she thought, which was something. They were good listeners and they were clearly highly trained in their own areas, whatever that be in. They had not given much away about themselves or their overall work, and she supposed that was standard operational procedure. Their job was to gather information and assess risks and not divulge too much. Instead, it was a question of communicating the information she had put together and not expect much in return. The main thing was to share the load, she told herself, and impart her concerns in the hope that all the shadowy activity in the fringes would start to lessen. She hoped that was not too much to ask as a small quid pro quo at this juncture. She was showing willing and trying to do the right thing, which she hoped would not go unrecognised.

Adding to the picture, she explained that the UK Science Media Centre had issued a press release on 3 June 2019 on expert reaction on mutations to the CCR5 gene and mortality. In the publication *Nature Medicine*, Professor David Curtis, Honorary Professor at University City London (UCL) genetic Institute, said:[180]

> *This study suggests that people who have damaging mutations in both copies of their CCR5 gene may tend to have slightly shorter life spans on average. Such people are highly resistant to HIV infection and even those who only have a mutation in one copy of the gene are partially protected against HIV. However, it seems that not having a working copy of the gene may cause problems in other ways, for example it has been suggested that this might result in increased susceptibility to influenza. Overall, this makes sense. Human beings have CCR5 genes for a reason, even if we do not yet know the fully details about its functionality. Human beings have evolved to possess a CCR5 gene and this means that it must be providing us with some benefit.*

Professor Jonathan Ball, Professor of Molecular Virology at the University of Nottingham, said at the time:[181]

> *To infect a cell, most circulating strains of HIV hijack a protein, found on the surface of white blood cells, called CCR5. Our genomes contain two copies of the CCR5 gene, and it is well established that those people where both copies of CCR5 are defective are highly resistant to HIV, raising the possibility that it might even be possible to prevent or cure HIV infection by genetically engineering a person's CCR5 gene. Indeed, this was the stated reasoning behind the recent announcement of the gene-edited babies born in China: a proclamation that caused an almost*

universal uproar – not least because the full impacts of carrying defective CCR5 genes are not fully understood.

What this study shows is that when both copies of the gene are defective, your chances of dying before the age of 76 are increased by over 20%. In other words, these data suggest that any intervention designed to knock out your CCR5 gene, as in the case of the Chinese gene-edited babies, is not without measurable risk of premature death. However, the current study stops short of telling us why this genetic defect is associated with early demise.

Professor Robin Lovell-Badge, group leader at the Francis Crick Institute, added:[182]

This is a well worked study, indicating that participants in the UK Biobank project have on average a reduced lifespan if they carry two copies of (are homozygous for) the delta-32 variant of the CCR5 gene. This is a mutation that truncates the protein it encodes, and it has been known for a while that this confers resistance to the HIV virus and AIDS. The virus uses the normal CCR5 protein as a receptor to gain entry into cells of the immune system, but if this was all it did, one might have suspected that the delta-32 mutation might on average increase average lifespan. But clearly CCR5 likely has many other roles, and these are still being discovered. It has roles in the immune system and individuals homozygous for the delta-32 variant are known to be more susceptible to some other viruses, such as West Nile Virus and there is some suggestion that they are also more susceptible to the bad effects of influenza, although this is challenged in other studies. There is also evidence from studies in mice and humans that being homozygous for the delta-32 variant may have a positive effect on some cognitive abilities and to make the brain more robust to the effects of stroke. The CCR5 gene is expressed within the brain, but it is really not clear what its normal function is here, and it is likely that mutations in the gene also have bad effects.

10.8 China's Genomics Strategy: To Be the Global Leader

Changing direction, Susie then outlined China's genomic strategy in crops and plants. She showed a timeline illustrating the scale of China's recent plant and crop genomic activity. She explained that in August 2013, China's leading plant scientist, Gao Caixia, was the first to modify plant DNA with CRISPR technology following its landmark scientific discovery by Jennifer Doudna and others in 2012.[183]

Adding to the picture, in July 2014, the Chinese did early genetic editing of plant DNA to establish proof of principle in rice. Then they moved on to gene edits in wheat and corn as reported in the scientific publication *Nature Biotechnology*.[184]

10.9 Chinese Acquisition of Syngenta

In 2016, the Chinese government announced its five-year plan to back genome editing in plants. This plan was then cemented by its purchase of Syngenta in 2016, taking advantage of its industry-leading R&D and manufacturing capability and leading status in the global agricultural technology field.[185] Susie explained that China's expansion overseas and Chinese state-owned company ChemChina's purchase of Switzerland-based Syngenta, one of the world's four largest agribusinesses for $43 billion, was a significant move and was reportedly the most that China had spent acquiring a foreign company. Having reached this point in time in 2020, the Chinese State reportedly had more than twenty scientific teams using

CRISPR technology to modify crops at scale.[186] Syngenta was now reportedly amongst the most active corporate acquirers in agrifoodtech. For example, in 2019, it reportedly acquired Ukrainian digital crop monitoring start-up Cropio for an undisclosed amount. Prior to this, it reportedly acquired farm management software providers including Strider in Brazil and Farmshots and AgConnections in the US. It had also reportedly invested in Indian farmer-to-business platform Farmlink, whilst its venture capital arm Syngenta ventures had reportedly backed dozens of start-ups including, most recently, Israeli precision weed sprayer Greeneye.[187]

Charles looked at Susie and commented that this was not new. He was clearly less interested in this aspect of China's genomic policy. She acknowledged his comments, adding that what it did show was the sheer speed, scale and sophisticated breadth of their genomic policy across multiple sectors. She then quickly explained that China's acquisition of Syngenta reportedly created a close relationship between government, industry and academia, emphasising that this pattern is replicated in other strategic sectors identified by the Chinese State. In doing so, the Chinese State is enabled to direct intellectual property from university laboratories and companies it has acquired to help support its 1.4 billion population. Was this with the aim of becoming food self-reliant? It also provided commercial value on crops on the world market. It further potentially provided the capability to undermine or restrict overseas crop supply. In doing so, she went on to say that there was a recent news report that China was engaged in becoming the world's only superpower by any means necessary and using a multi-pronged disruption campaign; according to the Director of the FBI, Christopher Wray, when speaking to the Hudson Institute in Washington DC just a few months ago on 7 July 2020.[188]

10.10 Beijing Genomics Institute (BGI)

Susie pushed on, explaining that Beijing Genomics Institute (BGI), a Chinese gene-sequencing and biomedical firm, had reportedly developed close links with the European scientific community since it was founded in 1999 to participate in the Human Genome Project; an international project to determine the DNA sequence of the entire human genome. She explained that BGI reportedly received a $1.5 billion line of credit from the state-run China Development Bank in 2009 to purchase 128 DNA sequencers from California-based genomics company to build its business.[189] [190] [191] In 2012, BGI reportedly opened its first European Genome Research Centre in Copenhagen, in Denmark. Susie added that BGI was reportedly a complex company that had a large and expanding global reach, noting that Charles looked thoughtful again at this point.

Building on this, Susie began to explain that BGI was reportedly using the Covid-19 pandemic to further expand its footprint. BGI led the genetic testing effort in China following its Covid-19 outbreak, including the deployment of its 'Fire Eye' laboratories in Shenzhen, Beijing and other cities by offering 2,000-square metre automated biosecurity level-2 PCR testing laboratories.[192] [193] [194] In the last six months of 2020, BGI had reportedly sold 35 million rapid Covid-19 kits to 180 countries and built fifty-eight laboratories in eighteen countries including Sweden, Serbia, Saudi Arabia and the UAE.[195] [196] [197] In doing so, BGI was reportedly distributing gene-sequencing technology that US security officials say could threaten national security. Its sequencers are used to analyse genetic material which in turn can unlock powerful personal information.[198] [199] [200] This was reportedly leading to increasing concerns about genetic and medical data privacy and worldwide genetic data at China's fingertips.[201] [202] [203]

BGI, a Shenzhen-based company, was also reportedly linked to the Chinese State. Susie explained that it operates China's national genetic database and research in government-affiliated key laboratories.[204] [205] [206] A co-founder of Beijing Genomics Institute, Yu Jun PhD, was reportedly part of He Jiankui's alleged 'circle of trust' and was allegedly an observer during at least one of the informed consent sessions held by He Jiankui leading to the implantation of human genome-edited embryos and subsequent birth of the Chinese gene-edited babies. She added that Yu Jun was also reported to be a member of the Chinese Academy of Sciences.[207] [208] [209] Charles looked up at Susie and took this in. Seeing this, Susie explained that this indicated that there might potentially have been awareness of what He Jiankui was doing at a senior level of the Chinese scientific community and state.

BGI also reportedly stated in stock market filings that it aims to help the Chinese Communist Party achieve its goal *to* 'seize the commanding heights of international biotechnology competition' and that this was coming under increasing scrutiny.[210] [211] [212] This was not least because BGI had reportedly sold the Chinese State supplies to collect and analyse DNA from millions of men and boys with no serious criminal history.[213] [214] [215] Susie explained that this raised questions about population surveillance, health and global ambition. She went on to say that according to an article in *BioNews* on 22 June 2020, just a few months ago, Chinese authorities were reportedly collecting blood samples from across the country to build a genetic map of its 700 million males.[216] [217] A recent Australian Strategic Policy Institute (ASPI) report described how Chinese law enforcement had been collecting samples to build a DNA database to trace a man's male relatives using blood, saliva or other genetic material. This ASPI report also stated that the Chinese database contained biometric samples and detailed multi-generational genealogies from 5–10% of the country's male population from which they could build family trees for all Chinese patrilineal families.[218] [219] It was also being reported that there was a continuation of

Chinese efforts to use genetics to control its people, causing concerns about repression of civil and human rights.[220 221]

Susie then sat back for a moment and looked Charles in the eye, saying slowly that having genetically mapped their own population, the Chinese State was building an understanding of its people's genetic predisposition to viruses and diseases. This might present potential concerns that the Chinese State might now turn its attention to genetically mapping the populations of other countries for its own ends; which, if so, would be a significant development that should not be underestimated.

10.11 CCR5 Gene Associated with Susceptibility to Covid-19 and Death

As time was ticking by and the two men could only keep listening for so long, Susie explained that a very recent scientific study on 10 July 2020 sought to address an important issue: *CCR5 Δ32 mutation is associated with susceptibility to SARS-CoV-2 infection and death: an epidemiological investigation.*[222] She explained that she had been very interested to read that the scientific paper highlighted a significant association of CCR5 Δ32 variant with susceptibility and mortality from SARS CoV-2 infection. It also reported that inclusion of the presence of two or more variant forms of a specific DNA sequence for the CCR5 gene could further highlight the role of CCR5 in Covid-19 pathogenesis (the process by which an infection leads to disease). It went on to report that the mechanism of CCR5 allele offering predisposition to SARS CoV-2 infection susceptibility and death of patients was not known.

A scientific study published on 26 August 2020 had also made an interesting read in that it stated that emerging results indicated that an uncontrolled immune response, leading to a life-threatening condition called a 'cytokine storm,' is the major pathology in severe Covid-19.[223] It reported that the role of certain genetic variants within as well as outside CCR5 in HIV/AIDS may also be worth considering. It stated that the CCR5 receptor and a nearby cluster where many other chemokine receptors are located may be potentially involved in Covid-19 treatment and may contribute to susceptibility to the complications of the disease. It went on to report that the CCR5 Δ32 allele is found predominantly in European populations (which Susie emphasised) with rare occurrences in Asians and native populations from Africa, the Americas and Oceania.[224]

Susie summed up to the two official men saying that this gave weight to an emerging picture that there might potentially be a connection between the CCR5 gene and Covid-19 and the Chinese gene-edited babies. If so, this would then raise all sorts of questions and issues about genomic technology and research and development.

10.12 US-China Genomic Activity

Pressing on at pace, she highlighted a *Newsweek* article on 28 April 2020 earlier that year. It reported that the National Institute for Allergy and Infectious Diseases (NIAD), the organisation led by Dr Anthony Fauci, funded scientists at the Wuhan Institute of Virology and other institutions for work on gain-of-function research on bat coronaviruses. It reported that in 2019, with the backing of NIAD, the National Institutes of Health reportedly committed to $3.7 million over six years for research that included some gain-of-function work. The program reportedly followed another $3.7 million five-year project for collecting and studying bat coronaviruses, which ended in 2019, bringing the reported total to $7.4 million. Susie added that Dr Fauci had also been a prominent top advisor to US President Trump during the Covid-19 pandemic.[225]

A CNBC news article dated 16 October 2020 also reported that the United States government, using a confidential process, had blocked a Chinese entity from purchasing a fertility clinic in San Diego. This action to protect a US fertility clinic reportedly revealed concerns about Chinese access to Americans' medical data stored in fertility clinics, which can include families' intimate biological and personal information. The action was reportedly taken by the secretive Committee on Foreign Investment in the United States (CFIUS). The article went on to report that John Demers, Head of the Department of Justice's National Security Division and one of the nation's top spy hunters, said, 'Your genetic material, your biological material, is among the most intimate information about you, who you are, what your vulnerabilities may be, what your illnesses have been in the past, what your family medical history is.'[226]

The CNBC article also made significant reading because it reported that the United States had two concerns when it came to Chinese ownership of US fertility clinics. Firstly, it reported that US officials believe that the Chinese might use the data from fertility clinics to amass a large database of biological information that could be used against Americans, with John Demers reported to have stated:[227]

> *That can be used from a counterintelligence perspective to either coerce you or convince you to help the Chinese... I'd be worried that the Chinese were going to get sensitive personal information about individual Americans, whether it's their financial information, their healthcare information, their genetic information, all of which they could use from an intelligence perspective, to target that person.*

That same CNBC article reported John Demers' concerns that the Chinese military might use data from fertility clinics to create a military threat, saying:[228]

> *I'm not saying that we've seen this, but the worst case would be the development of some kind of biological weapon… If you had all of the data of a population, you might be able to see what the population is most vulnerable to and then develop something that's taking advantage of that vulnerability.*

The article went on to report a CNBC investigation which found that four of the roughly dozen clinics in the San Diego area already had investors with links to China. The San Diego region was replete with some of the nation's most sensitive military facilities, such as Marine Corps Air Station Mirama, known as 'Fighter Town USA', made famous in the movie *Top Gun,* and Naval Base San Diego, home port of the US Pacific Fleet.[229]

10.13 New Genomics Governance Proposal

As she started to reach the end of her presentation, she explained that given this rapidly evolving genomic landscape, the adoption of new paradigms was required to bring about new effective genomic governance in the UK. There was a critical need for a top-level multidisciplinary group of experts that operate on a continuous basis (unlike SAGE) and not just during emergencies. This should comprise critical thinkers who sit outside the elected political elite to inform law and policymakers and shape the future more quickly and effectively. It should be tasked with driving innovation and identifying and mitigating risk with joined-up thinking between the genomic, technology, science, healthcare, fertility, education, economic and other sectors in the UK. It would help respond effectively to the rapidly evolving interconnected digital, artificial, genomic, epigenetic and reproductive technological advances. Susie explained that the UK would also benefit from a Ministry for

Genomics and Fertility to create and drive forward strategic change leading to root and branch reform in the UK.

There was also a critical need for continued close collaboration internationally. Susie went on to say that we also needed effective genomic infrastructure, technology and genetic surveillance mechanisms to track genetic changes and the spread of new viruses and diseases in the UK and internationally. The UK could also look at effective genomic security at its borders, which would capitalise on our geographical advantage as island nations. Furthermore, consideration could be given to tighter control over UK genomic data and scientific research and publications to prevent sensitive genomic information falling into the wrong hands for use for nefarious purposes.

10.14 UK Genomic Outlook, 2020

Susie then moved on to address current genomic considerations. She explained that Mr McCallum, the director-general of MI5, was on record in the press on 14 October 2020 discussing China. He reportedly stated that they had tried to steal UK intellectual property and target technology and infrastructure and they represented the greatest long-term threat saying:[230]

> *If the question is which countries' intelligence services cause the most aggravation to the UK in October 2020, the answer is Russia.*
>
> *If the question is which state will be shaping our world across the next decade, presenting big opportunities and big challenges, the answer is China.*
>
> *You might think in terms of the Russian intelligence services providing bursts of bad weather, while China is changing the climate.*

10.15 First PowerPoint Conclusions

Susie summed up by saying that China reportedly had a concerted plan to become the global leader in genomics. She then summarised various key points to round things off.

The edits to the CCR5 gene of twins Lulu and Nana, born in November 2018, were carried out with the aim of making them resistant to HIV, but might also reportedly have made them more susceptible to coronaviruses and influenza.

Mutations in the CCR5 gene are also reportedly emerging as a 'major driver of pathology in severe Covid-19'. This CCR5 gene activity in populations around the world is triggered by viral attack and raises potential questions about gain-of-function viral research on coronaviruses and their capacity to impact global health and security now and in the future.

Susie then looked up at both of the two security officers in turn to gauge their final response. They looked weary and sombre, and the younger of the two, Charles, commented that they had a lot of work to do. *Wow*, thought Susie; that was telling. They had clearly listened hard and it seemed that what she had to say had hit home. Then Andrew leant forward and calmly asked Susie if she had a copy of the presentation on a memory stick which they could take away. She was taken aback by that request and her instinctive reaction was to shake her head and say she did not. She had not been prepared for that request and the thought of handing over her presentation to them at such short notice was daunting. Andrew looked at her more kindly in an attempt to offer some reassurance, and Charles said that their intention was to send the presentation up the chain of command to the head of the security services. In that moment, Susie gulped and swallowed hard as she realised that they meant business.

She stared out of the window in an attempt to settle her thoughts and think through what to do next. She had been concerned about raising her head above the parapet and this request raised the stakes. In sharing her presentation face to face today, she still had some control over who saw it. If she gave it to these officers, it could be seen by all sorts of people, and that thought left her feeling vulnerable, exposed and anxious. She looked back at the men and said that she would give some thought to sending them a copy of her presentation. She added that she also wanted to update it a bit further. She then proceeded to explain that if she sent it to them, it would be on the understanding that it was being shared on a 'need-to-know' basis. The older officer acknowledged Susie's sentiments in this regard.

As the meeting drew to a close, the two officers relaxed a little more in Susie's company. She sensed that they had come away with a meaningful understanding of her research and concerns and that they were going to take action. In short, it had not been a wasted journey for them. The older officer, Andrew, turned to her and said that as a matter of courtesy she should contact her local MP and let them know about today's meeting. She nodded and said that she would do so. The older man took note and reiterated that they would wait to hear from her with a copy of her presentation. She thanked them for their time, adding that there had just been something about the whole Chinese gene-edited baby affair that had made her look more closely. Its justification as an AIDS prevention measure had seemed incongruous, knowing as she did through her work that HIV transmission could be stopped by sperm washing before undergoing fertility treatment and through use of antiretrovirals. Andrew shot a look at Charles and his expression briefly changed to one of concern. So, thought Susie, she was not the only one concerned by this. She then thanked the officers again for their time and with that they were gone. She watched them walk down her driveway at pace, out through her gates, and disappear across the village.

Chapter 11

Winter-Spring 2021

The days and weeks that followed Susie's meeting with the two security officers passed in a bit of a haze. She had asked them if they could do something about the strange activity on her social media accounts and she began to notice a definite reduction, which came as a bit of a relief. Having sent off a copy of her presentation a day or so after their visit, she did not hear further from them other than a short acknowledgment from Andrew. Well, that was to be expected, she told herself. It was not a two-way street; that was not how they operated. The main thing was that she had shared her analysis and put herself firmly on the grid.

The problem was, however, that Susie could not stop herself from revisiting her analysis. It was like her thoughts had a mind of their own. Every time she read something, or she reviewed her Google alerts for work, she seemed to see new things and more dots started to join up. Pictures just started to form in her head and the whole picture continued to grow and become more nuanced by the day; so much so that she ended up drawing more complex spiders' webs on her whiteboard to relieve the pressure and free up headspace.

As her understanding grew over time, she began to get a clearer sense of a sophisticated civil-military fusion of genomic strategy and activity in the US and China, with their associated worldwide health and national security implications. She also worked out that this strategic picture was underpinned by complex and interlinked national and international genomic networks and key figures. This was driving a rapidly developing narrative around infectious disease, associated risks and countermeasures.

As she mulled everything over in her mind, her research seemed to suggest that the Covid-19 outbreak in Wuhan in China between October and December 2019 might potentially have been a laboratory release of a gain-of-function and/or recombinant virus programme. There was a lack of convincing zoonotic disease-spread evidence with which to come to any other reasoned conclusion at present, she thought. She also wondered whether Chinese activity might have been a factor in its emergence in Wuhan. Why did the Wuhan Institute of Virology (the WIV) close its viral database on 12 September 2019? To her way of thinking, it demonstrated a lack of transparency about its virus programmes. Susie surmised that this might have been for national security reasons to protect other unknown virus and R&D capability. She also kept having a nagging concern about the timing of the virus database shutdown just before the Covid-19 breakdown; might it be indicative of an even earlier potential laboratory release of a gain-of-function and/or recombinant virus programme or perhaps a series of incidents?

She also had concerns about the escalating genomic situation in China. She thought about China's recent inauguration of a new biosecurity law on 15 April 2021, concluding that in part it was to support the announcement by their Deputy Minister of Science and Technology of the construction of three more BSL-4 and thirty-three more BSL-3 laboratories across China. It suggested a ramping-up of Chinese genomic technology, research and development, with the associated risk of viral lab leaks in future, she thought. She was also painfully aware that existing global regulation was insufficient from a genomic perspective.[231]

From a UK perspective, Susie concluded that we needed sophisticated genomic infrastructure both within the UK and internationally. This would help provide greater oversight of scientific activity and key players. There also needed to be a firm grip of the rapidly evolving genomic and fertility sector landscape. Additionally, closer oversight was required around the security of genomic information at UK fertility clinics, national hospitals and with direct-to-consumer DNA tests.

She also concluded that there needed to be improved national genomic defence capability and policy. To achieve this, there needed to be priority genomic funding for the security services and military, tighter UK border controls and self-sufficiency in genomic testing, vaccines, equipment, manpower, skills and enforceable sophisticated community management.

Added to this, there was an ongoing significant risk of further pandemic disruption and loss of life with virulent new viruses that evade current vaccines and treatments. In the cold light of day, that was a depressing and concerning thought, given all the chaos, disruption, loss and change over recent months. It created ongoing uncertainty and risk, which was difficult to adjust to and live with, she thought sadly. It was a heavy load to carry and it continued to change her outlook on life in ways that caught her by surprise and created fresh worry and stress on a daily basis.

11.1 US: Genomic Infrastructure and Governance

Without even really trying, Susie found herself creating another chart on her office whiteboard that simplistically mapped out US genomic infrastructure and governance. Stepping back to survey her work, she began to see a complex interconnected picture emerge. It sent a chill down her spine and she clenched her fists to steady her breathing. Making sense of this when so much of what was said was confusing and contradictory made her really uneasy.

The chart simplistically demonstrated the flow of money and control exercised by the military and other key people in positions of authority in terms of infectious diseases and virus research and development. It also potentially helped explain why Susie had been experiencing so much military activity on her social media and potentially the real-life encounters she had experienced as well.

The chart also highlighted the role played by scientist Peter Daszak, a British citizen and president of US agency EcoHealth Alliance. Susie reasoned that this brought with it its own complex and internationally nuanced factors and relationships. It was all so murky, she thought, before reminding herself that that was probably the whole point. There was definitely a lot more to this than first met the eye.

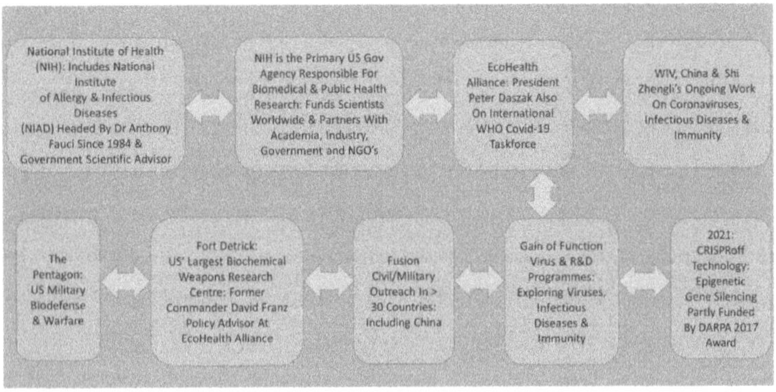

Chart 4: US Genomic Infrastructure & Governance (Simplified)

11.2 China: Genomics and Governance

Susie then found herself constructing a simplified chart of Chinese genomics and governance by way of a comparison.

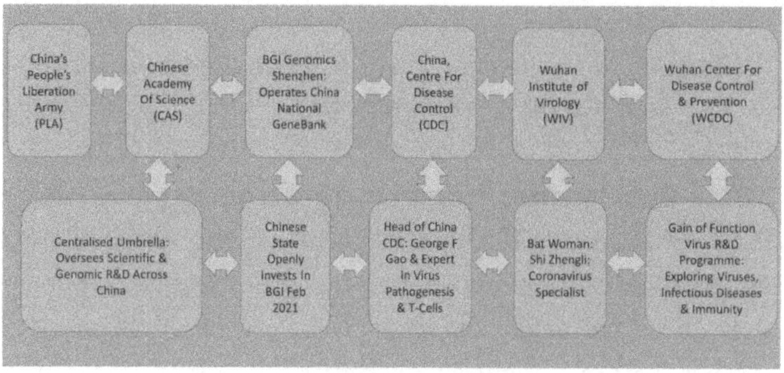

Chart 5: China Genomics & Governance (Simplified)

In doing so, she was struck by the part played by Chinese scientist George F Gao. She was surprised to learn from her reading about the extent of his links with the UK. He had reportedly studied at Oxford University from 1991 to 1994 and earned a PhD. Then from 1994 to 1999 he had reportedly undertaken postdoctoral research at Oxford University. Thereafter, he had reportedly taught at Oxford University from 2001 to 2004 as a lecturer, doctoral and group leader. Then from 2010, he had reportedly been an adjunct professor at Oxford University.[232] Here was that Chinese strategy at play again, she thought, sending top Chinese scientists overseas to take up prominent research and university postings and build understanding, networks and skills which could all be channelled back to the Chinese State. She figured that the British had to have some skin in the game with all of this too, hence why this was allowed to happen on British soil.

She was further interested to read that George F Gao had expertise in immunity and viruses like influenza:[233]

He is well known for his scientific contributions to the understanding of the molecular recognition of immune receptors to their ligands and molecular basis of the pathogenicity of pathogens, in particular, influenza viruses and other enveloped viruses, which provide insight into drug and antibody development and the prevention and control of infections worldwide.

11.3 BGI: Genomic Infrastructure and Activity

Susie was also mindful that she kept coming across reports about Chinese genomics company BGI. They seemed to pop up all the time and before she knew it, she was busy mapping out another chart on her office whiteboard.

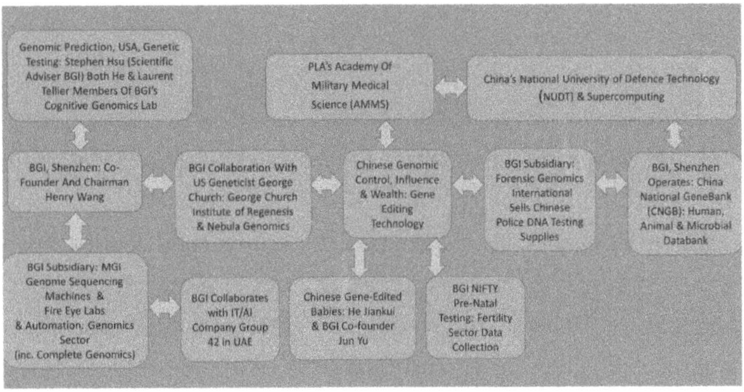

Chart 6: BGI Genomic Infrastructure & Activity

It was a complex landscape, even in simplistic terms. It also started to indicate to Susie the scale and breadth of BGI's activities and influence. She swallowed hard as she looked at the level of sophistication this seemingly showed. She also found herself wondering to what extent the rest of the western world was on top of this and developing its own infrastructure to counterbalance it all.

11.4 Coronavirus, HIV, CCR5 and CRISPR Cas-9

Susie then started to map out scientific research on coronaviruses, HIV, CCR5 and CRISPR Cas-9 technology. She found visual representations helpful in bringing matters to life and this was no different.

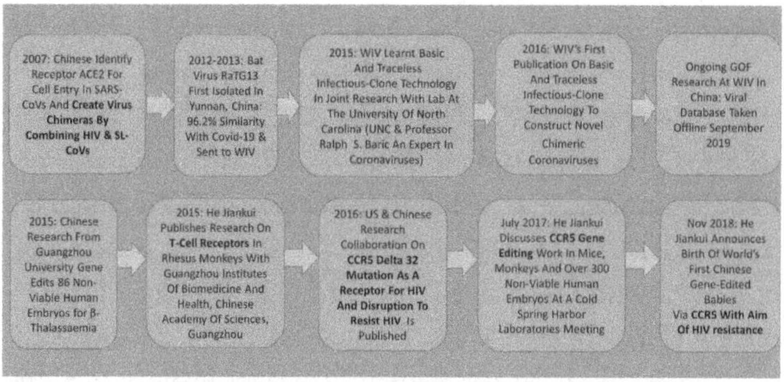

Chart 7: Coronavirus, HIV, CCR5 & CRISPR CAS-9

She worked out from her reading that in November 2007, the Chinese had published a scientific paper led by the State Key Laboratory of Virology, the Wuhan Institute of Virology and the Chinese Academy of Sciences. This work had been funded by a State Key Program for Basic Research Grants through the Chinese Ministry of Science and Technology. This was in effect a special fund from the President of the Chinese Academy of Sciences and the Knowledge Innovation Program Key Project of the Chinese Academy of Sciences to Shi Zhengli (Bat Woman). It was therefore considered important work by the Chinese State, she concluded.[234]

She also learnt that this scientific work had identified that SARS-CoV viruses use the ACE2 receptor for cell entry. This research had identified a group of SARS-like CoVs (SL-CoVs) in horseshoe bats known to be responsible for their receptor binding properties. Then she had learnt that they had investigated the receptor usage of SL-CoVs by combining a human immunodeficiency virus (HIV) with cell lines expressing the AC2 molecules of human, civet and horseshoe bats. In other words, they had created a series of chimera viruses (viruses that contain genetic material from two or more distinct viruses). These 'cut and spliced' chimeric viruses had inserted different sequences of SARS-CoVs into a SL-CoV backbone to enhance their ability to infect humans. These viruses then gained the ability to enter cells via the human ACE2 receptor. They also reported that minimal inserts were sufficient to convert SL-CoVs from non-ACE2 binding to human ACE2 binding. So, from as far back as 2007, there was evidence of the creation of virulent viruses capable of penetrating the human body by mixing HIV with SL-CoVs by Chinese scientists, she thought.

A scientific paper in March 2016 also made interesting reading in that it was a Chinese/US collaboration with George F Gao as a co-author. It had looked at the epidemiology and manner of development of human coronaviruses and genetic recombination. It reported that CoV infections primarily involve the upper respiratory tract and the gastrointestinal tract. It identified that CoV infections could vary from mild to severe, including bronchitis and pneumonia with renal failure, infection of the liver and brain. It reported that diarrhoea was observed in approximately 30–40% of SARS infections. As such, Susie deduced that key symptoms of CoV infections were clearly set out in this paper in 2016 and arguably should have been more widely understood when the global Covid-19 pandemic hit.[235]

A Chinese scientific paper made further interesting reading from September 2016 in *PLOS Pathogens*, featuring amongst others: George F Gao, China National GeneBank-Shenzhen, BGI-Shenzhen and the Chinese Academy of Sciences. Here were key Chinese scientists and institutions all working together in an organised manner, she thought soberly. Dr Zhengli Shi (Bat

Woman) at the Wuhan Institute of Virology, Chinese Academy of Sciences had provided kidney cell lines. Beijing Genomics Institute (BGI-Shenzhen) had provided assistance with genomic sequencing and data analysis. The work had identified a novel coronavirus called Ro-BatCoV GCCDC1, representing a virus that evolved through recombination of two separate viruses. The paper reported that this shed new light on mechanisms of viral evolution.[236]

Another scientific study in December 2017 was a follow-up Chinese paper on the dynamic evolution of virus Ro-BatCoV GCCDC1 which was reportedly in persistent circulation in bats in a specific cave of South China (Yunnan Province). What had struck Susie was that it appeared to demonstrate long-term Chinese work collaborations, suggesting (to her way of thinking) centralised and sophisticated genomic and scientific management. George F Gao was a co-author of this follow-up paper and he had by then become head of the China Center for Disease Control and Prevention (CDC). He had also been elected to the Chinese Academy of Sciences.[237]

11.5 T-Cell Functionality and Viruses

Spurred on by this, Susie had drilled down to learn more about the work of Chinese scientist George F Gao. It soon became clear that he was an expert in T-cell immunity and viruses. Interesting stuff, she told herself, in the grand scheme of things. She read that in November 2017, a Chinese paper was published with George F Gao as a co-author and featuring the Chinese Academy of Sciences (CAS) entitled *Human T-cell immunity against emerging and re-emerging viruses.* It tracked the history and knowledge of T-cell immunity.[238] It also identified the pivotal role of an individual's T-cell immunity in the alleviation of symptoms and the clearance of new viruses. It observed similar immune features that correlate with disease severity in patients with infectious diseases; essentially high levels of inflammatory reaction termed ‘pro-inflammatory cytokines and chemokines’ and extensive tissue infiltration of immune cells. It went on to report that after contracting H7N9 influenza virus, patients developed severe respiratory illness including acute respiratory syndrome and pneumonia and showed high T-cell responses and inflammatory cytokines in lungs and in the blood. It also reported that in H7N9 hospitalised patients, it was observed that early robust CD8+ T-cell responses correlated with rapid recovery from severe H7N9 influenza disease.

The same scientific paper went on to report that genetic immunity variations were modulated (affected by) receptor binding and recognition. It stated that CD8+ T-cells played a protective part in flavivirus infection (a family of viruses including Dengue, Yellow Fever, Japanese Encephalitis, West Nile Encephalitis, Tick-Borne Encephalitis and Zika). It reported that animals lacking CD8+ T-cells showed reduced viral clearance capacity. It went on to report robust T-cell responses might play a pivotal role in virus clearance, having observed a strong T-cell response against the MERS-CoV S protein. The paper also stated, worryingly from Susie’s perspective, the continued general lack of understanding about immunity:

> *Although the timely characterization of the T-cell immunity of the emerging or re-emerging viruses provides beneficial references for clinical intervention or vaccine development, many aspects of the general mechanism of cell-mediated immunity in these viral diseases remains poorly understood.*

She then came across another scientific article published in December 2018 and co-written by the Wuhan Institute of Virology (the WIV) and the Chinese Academy of Sciences (CAS) called *On the Centenary of the Spanish Flu: being Prepared for the next Pandemic,* which had also been co-authored by George F Gao.[239] It stated that CAS had been a backbone force in the fight against influenza since 2005. Susie was also struck by the warnings about the risk of an unpredictable pandemic and the lead time required to develop vaccines:

> *Given the substantial lead time and the lack of available vaccines ahead of any unpredictable pandemic, major efforts are needed to develop new universal vaccines that stimulate broadly reactive antibodies or T-cells against conserved epitopes to confer heterotypic protection against different subtypes of influenza viruses.*

11.6 The Wuhan Institute of Virology (The WIV)

As her limited spare time allowed, Susie also turned her attention in more detail to what had reportedly been happening at the Wuhan Institute of Virology (the WIV). She learnt that the WIV possessed the bat virus RaTG13, the most closely reported virus to Covid-19 with a 96.2% similarity.[240] She read that RaTG13 virus was first isolated in 2013 in Yunnan Province in China.[241] She also read accounts that the WIV had reportedly begun its gain-of-function research programme in bat viruses (to study them and make them more virulent using a variety of genomic technology techniques) in 2015. She then paused for thought when she went on to learn that the scientists at the WIV learnt basic and traceless infections-clone technology from a joint research programme with a laboratory at the University of North Carolina (UNC) led by Dr Ralph S Baric in the United States in 2015.[242] This technology enabled scientists to manipulate and clone viruses without leaving any obvious clues that this had been done. That had concerned her, realising that this was one way to create a nasty virulent virus that presumably could not be readily traced back in origins should it be deployed; a useful tool for any potential biowarfare manufacturer too, she thought tersely. This then rapidly led to the WIV's first publication on basic and traceless infectious-clone technology to construct novel chimeric coronaviruses which appeared in 2016.[243]

She then focused on the WIV's decision to shut down its virus database in September 2019, resulting in a lack of transparency about its work. She still could not shake a nagging feeling that this might be significant. To her way of thinking, it was a potential way to protect research and development programmes and prevent these from being accessible to others. It also raised questions about the timing of this decision and whether it was potentially trying to hide something in particular. There could be multiple reasons for this, including potentially: sensitive Chinese State biotechnology programmes, a lucrative commercial cache of scientific R&D, a laboratory incident and a way to try to obscure the origins of the Covid-19 pandemic. All food for thought, she told herself.

11.7 CCR5 Functionality

Susie also started to look more closely at CCR5, learning that in humans the CCR5 gene encoded the CCR5 protein. C-C chemokine receptor 5 (CCR5) is a protein on the surface of white blood cells that is involved in the immune system as it acts as a receptor for chemokines (signalling proteins to activate cells to fight infection). She learnt that C-C chemokine receptor type 5 (CCR5) is a key player in HIV infection as the virus binds to it and spreads from cell to cell. Susie found that a 2010 Italian scientific paper was published representing a large study involving over 2,000 HIV-positive and healthy people.[244] It identified that CCR5 is a key target in the prevention of HIV and other immune-based diseases. That paper stated that CCR5 was shown to play an important role in the priming of T-cell immune responses. The paper also stated that natural autoimmunity to the CCR5 co-receptor exists. Reduced or abolished expression of the CCR5 receptor had been found in Caucasians and other ethnic groups; being groups of people who were homozygous delta-32 individuals and substantially resistant to HIV infection. It also went on to say that some hypotheses suggested they could also have increased resistance to plague or smallpox.

That same 2010 scientific paper also reported that the scientists had knocked out CCR5 in mice and then infected them with West Nile Virus. All of the mice succumbed to the infection, with the majority of the non-genetically altered mice recovering. In contrast, the CCR5 deficient mice failed to control virus replication due to reduced immune response. It also mentioned that CCR5 deficiency was shown to play a protective role in rheumatoid arthritis, supporting the use of agents to prevent the effect of CCR5 in clinical treatment of autoimmune, inflammatory-based disorders. It went on to say that CCR5 blockage may prevent T-cell migration, a key pathway in the inflammatory process causing pain, tissue damage and disability.

Working through that 2010 paper, she also read that HIV entry was complex but that it often involved chemokine receptor CCR5. It stated that intestinal tissues are populated dendritic cells and T-cells, which play a role in immune surveillance. The majority of these types of cells express CD4 and CCR5 molecules and therefore offer a large and convenient population of target cells for HIV. It went on to report that these layers offer poor resistance to virus penetration. It proceeded to explain how the gut surface is considerably larger (up to 400 square metres, i.e. the surface of a tennis court) and composed of a single layer of cells and is therefore less resistant. It also reported that GALT (gut-associated lymphoid tissues) host up to 90% of CD4+ and CD8 lymphocytes (white blood cells), making it a more important immune organ than even blood. That certainly put a different perspective on gut and intestinal function, Susie thought.

However, what really stood out for Susie was a statement in the 2010 paper which indicated that HIV was notorious for its ability to overcome immune defences and antiretroviral therapy by random gene mutation and selection of drug-resistant viral strains. In other words, HIV kept mutating as a means of evading immunity and replicating.

Building on this, Susie came across a scientific paper in 2016, being a US and Chinese collaboration on CCR5 delta 32 mutation.[245] Its stated aim was to understand more about the CCR5 gene as a receptor for HIV and as a means of disrupting and resisting HIV. She read about a German patient known as the 'Berlin patient' who was HIV-positive and who had undergone a stem cell transplant in 2009 to cure leukaemia. The treatment had used stem cells from a donor with the CCR5 genetic deletion, which blocks the most common form of HIV from establishing infection. It sent the patient's leukaemia into remission and reduced his HIV viral load, essentially curing him of HIV. The article went on to report that 'The success of Berlin patient stimulates the scientists' interest to disrupt CCR5 gene and even integrated HIV genome by up-to-date genome editing techniques'. It also reiterated that the average frequency of the CCR5 delta 32 mutation is around 10% in European populations but is virtually absent in African, American Indian and Asian populations.

Susie was then fascinated to read an extract describing the work of US scientist Carl June who used modified HIV virus as a genetic engineering tool in his cancer research, which read.[246]

Carl June explained how this viral delivery system works in an episode of a podcast called CureTalks: "In the cancer field the problem was how to make T-cells attack your own cancer, but not attack your body. And we didn't have an efficient way to genetically alter those T-cells. And it turns out that HIV is evolved to do exactly that. I mean, it infects people, it goes into their immune system, into T-cells. But the natural HIV virus, as people know, destroys T-cells eventually. So a number of investigators over the years developed HIV and modified it so that it would be a tool to insert genes into T-cells rather than kill them."

In the 1990s, when June stated working with HIV, he had to seek approval from the RAC committee in Washington to use the virus as a genetic engineering tool. The committee flagged 'all kinds of issues' according to June. They were worried that HIV 'might recombine and could make some sort of an Armageddon-like virus...'

Now gene therapy experiments with a modified version of HIV, called lentivirus, have become routine.

She read on and learnt that:[247]

Carl June's team hoped to synthetically replicate the Berlin patient effect: they wanted to produce targeted damage to the CCR5 gene. The June laboratory already knew how to manufacture T-cells, and they just needed a good tool for the job. They began collaborating with Sangamo Therapeutics, a company in California, that had been promoting zinc fingers [a gene-editing technique] to edit the human genome. Together this interdisciplinary team started engineering resistance to HIV into living blood cells in the hopes of producing a cure.

Building on this, Susie gained what she considered to be

meaningful clarity when she read a further report on HIV. Specifically, it reported that HIV evolves extremely rapidly, exhibiting the highest recorded biological mutation rate currently known to science. It went on to say that this essentially renders HIV a 'moving target', which also contributes to the inability of the host to control and clear the virus in natural infection.[248] *Bingo*, she muttered. It was like another light bulb had gone on inside her mind. This was another connection that potentially linked the whole Chinese gene-edited baby affair, the Covid-19 pandemic and gain-of-function virus research. It was becoming clearer in her mind and seemed to indicate that her initial analysis and concerns had potentially been right. If so, it started to make sense of a far bigger picture and a concerning world she had not wanted to inhabit. It also upped the stakes massively and she realised with mounting dread that it made her potentially more, rather than less, vulnerable to others in the know.

11.8 He Jiankui's Scientific Research

Delving deeper into the life and work of Chinese scientist He Jiankui, another account reported that he possessed a photographic memory.[249] She read further accounts that his PhD was diverse and interdisciplinary, encompassing what was termed the 'modularity, diversity and stochasticity of evolutionary processes over the last 4 billion years'.[250] Susie went on to work out that he had used statistical models and differential equations to study seemingly unrelated systems including the: structure of animal bodies, dynamics of global financial markets, emergent strains of influenza virus and adaptive immune systems in bacteria. This left her under no illusion that he was one bright guy.

It was also illuminating to look in more detail at a scientific paper He Jiankui published in May 2015 on T-cell receptor chains in rhesus monkeys with South University of Science and Technology, Shenzhen and China State Key Laboratory of Respiratory Disease, Center for Infection and Immunity, Guangzhou Institutes of Biomedicine and Health, Chinese Academy of Sciences, Guangzhou.[251] The stated aim of the scientific work was to enhance understanding of immune system complexity and immune-related diseases in humans. Susie learnt that He Jiankui's research was funded by the Knowledge Innovation Program of the Chinese Academy of Sciences and the Science Technology Planning Projects of Guangzhou[252]. Having dug deeper, Susie had then worked out that the Wuhan Institute of Virology (the WIV), Guangzhou Institutes of Biomedicine and Health and the Chinese Academy of Sciences all had a long interlinked history, having come across the following report:[253]

> *The predecessor of Wuhan Institute of Virology, Chinese Academy of Sciences was the Wuhan Institute of Microbiology... At the beginning of 1961, Wuhan branch institute and the Guangzhou branch institute merged to set up the Zhongnan Branch of Chinese Academy of Sciences, Wuhan Microbiology Research Laboratory was hence renamed as Wuhan Institute of Microbiology, Chinese Academy of Sciences. In October 1962, it was again renamed to Wuhan Institute of Microbiology, Chinese Academy of Sciences. In 1966, the local branch institute of Chinese Academy of Sciences was cancelled. In 1970, Wuhan Institute of Microbiology, Chinese Academy of Sciences was placed under the leadership of Hubei Province, changed its name to Hubei Provincial Institute of Microbiology. In 1978 on the eve of holding the National Science and Technology Conference, it returned to the Chinese Academy of Sciences, known as Wuhan Institute of Virology, Chinese Academy of Sciences.*

Sitting back from this, Susie deduced that He Jiankui had therefore likely been operating under the umbrella of CAS and had Chinese State funding for some of his scientific work. This put him much closer to the central scientific heart of things in China and seemed to contradict subsequent official reports following news breaking of the birth of the Chinese gene-edited babies to international condemnation.

11.9 Fort Detrick

Squeezing in further research in her limited spare time, Susie had learnt over many years that it was often worth looking at the wider picture. As such, she cast her mind in a different direction and decided to look a little deeper into US genomic activity. She sensed that if the Chinese were running biological research and development programmes then the US would likely be doing so too. That stood to reason, she thought.

With this in mind, she started to look at Fort Detrick in the US. This was the US Army's Medical Research Institute of Infectious Diseases (USARID) based at Fort Detrick, Maryland. It housed the US' largest research centre for biochemical weapons. She read that it had the ability to bypass the Biological Weapons Convention (BWC) restrictions and public scrutiny. It then surprised her to read that the US Center for Disease Control (CDC) had sent USARID at Fort Detrick a desist letter in July 2019.[254] That had made her pause for a minute and question what had happened to warrant that.

Reading on, Susie read that an incident reportedly occurred in July 2019. The scientific work in question was reported to have involved dangerous microbes which were stopped due to a series of safety violations found by the CDC. In a statement, CDC officials refused to release further information citing 'national security reasons'.[255] That was interesting, Susie thought, biosafety incidents could happen anywhere at any time. Following further reading, she found that the CDC had reportedly found several problems with new procedures used to decontaminate waste water. Reportedly, Fort Detrick had used a steam sterilisation system to treat waste, but this had been damaged following storm flooding the previous year, so the facility changed to a new chemical-based decontamination system. However, the CDC inspectors reportedly found the new procedures were insufficient, with mechanical failures causing leaks and failures amongst staff to follow the rules.[256]

Susie was interested in further reading to learn that the Laboratory Response Network at Fort Detrick was responsible for determining unknown material and was essentially equivalent to the UK's scientific research facility at Porton Down in Wiltshire. She read on and learnt that the US Army's Medical Research Institute of Infectious Diseases, based at Fort Detrick, said that its primary mission was 'to protect the warfighter from biological threats', although its scientists also investigated outbreaks of diseases amongst civilians and other threats to public health.[257]

In the course of this reading, Susie came across some further snippets of information which made her pause. She read an account that there were US military links with EcoHealth Alliance and that these were not just reportedly limited to money and mindset. It went on to report that one noteworthy policy advisor to EcoHealth Alliance was David Franz. It added that David Franz was former commander of Fort Detrick, the principal US government biowarfare/biodefense facility.[258] *Wow,* thought Susie, here was a further report of what appeared to be complex interrelated forces below the surface. It shook her as she let this sink in and slowly added to the picture she was slowly building.

11.10 EcoHealth Alliance, Dr Peter Daszak and Funding

A letter in science publication *Nature* on 28 November 2013 entitled *Isolation and characterization of a bat SARS-like coronavirus that uses the ACE2 receptor* also stood out.[259] This study was a collaboration amongst others by Dr Peter Daszak and Zheng-Li Shi. They reported whole-genome sequences of two novel bat coronaviruses from Chinese horseshoe bats in Yunnan, China, called RsSHC014 and Rs3367. These were far more closely related to SARS-CoV viruses than any previously identified, it reported, particularly in the receptor binding domain of the spike protein which enabled viruses to penetrate its host. It went on to report that it was the first recorded isolation of a live SL-CoV virus from bat faecal samples which uses ACE2 receptors from humans, civets and Chinese horseshoe bats for cell entry. They went on to state that this was the first identification of an SL-CoV capable of expressing ACE2 as an entry receptor into cells.

The letter also reported that the results provided the strongest evidence to date that Chinese horseshoe bats are natural reservoirs of SARS-CoV and that intermediary hosts may not be required for direct human infection. It went on to state that to understand the evolutionary origin of these two novel SL-CoV strains, they conducted recombination analysis, effectively mixing genome sequences of bat SL-CoV strains and human and civet SARS-CoV strains. Critically, Susie noted that they replaced the receptor binding domain of one of the SL-CoV's protein with SARS-CoVs which conferred the ability to use human ACE2 and replicate efficiently in mice. In other words, they made the virus more virulent and transmissible to humans.

What also interested Susie about the letter was the research funding arrangements. She noticed that this work had been funded by State Key Program for Basic Research, National Natural Science Foundation of China, NIH/National Science Foundation (NSF) 'Ecology and Evolution of Infectious Diseases' award from the NIH Fogarty International Center supported by International Influenza Funds from the Office of the Secretary of the

Department of Health and Human Services (USAID) and United States Agency for International Development (USAID) Emerging Pandemic Threats PREDICT.[260] Here was further evidence of scientific collaboration between the US and the Chinese and complex high-level intertwined financial arrangements.

This got Susie thinking and she dug deeper into the financial funding arrangements at EcoHealth Alliance. She discovered an NIH funding award to EcoHealth Alliance operated by project leader Dr Peter Daszak from June 2014 to May 2019 totalling $666,442.[261] This was for 'Understanding the risk of bat coronavirus emergence' as a significant threat to global health. The aims of this stated research were also interesting, Susie thought:[262]

> *Aim 1: Assess CoV spillover potential at high risk human-wildlife interfaces in China. This will include quantifying the nature and frequency of contact people have with bats and other wildlife; serological and molecular screening of people working in wet markets and highly exposed to wildlife; screening wild-caught and market-sampled bats from 30+ species for CoVs using molecular assays; and genomic characterization and isolation of novel CoVs.*
>
> *Aim2: Develop predictive models of bat CoV emergence risk and host range. A combined modeling approach will include phylogenetic analyses of host receptors and novel CoV genes (including functional receptor binding domains); a fused ecological and evolutionary model to predict host-range and viral sharing; and mathematical matrix models to examine evolutionary and transmission dynamics.*
>
> *Aim 3: Test predictions of CoV inter-species transmission. Predictive models of host range (i.e. emergence potential)*

> *will be tested experimentally using reverse genetics, pseudovirus and receptor binding assays, and virus infection experiments across a range of cell cultures from different species and humanized mice.*

What Susie went on to notice keenly were the NIH spending categories: biotechnology, emerging infectious diseases, genetics and infectious diseases. Its project terms also included: chimeric proteins, genetic recombination, virus diseases, biosecurity, coronavirus receptor, pandemic disease, public health relevance and receptor binding.[263]

Then she came across a report which allegedly found buried under 'Privacy Policy' under a section titled *EcoHealth Alliance Policy Regarding Conflict of Interest Research* that it was the 'recipient of various grant awards from federal agencies including the National Institute of Health, the National Science Foundation, US Fish and Wildlife Service, and the US Agency for International Development and the Department of Defense'. There it was, she thought, further alleged evidence of the complex civil US military and NIH funding arrangements to EcoHealth Alliance to undertake dangerous and risky gain-of-function scientific work on SL-CoVs on bat viruses in China.[264]

It reported that a meticulous investigation of US government databases had allegedly revealed that Pentagon funding for EcoHealth Alliance from 2013 to 2020, including contracts, grants and subcontracts, was just under $39 million. Of this, it alleged that $34.6 million was from the Defense Threat Reduction Agency (DTRA), which is a branch of the Department of Defense which states it is tasked to 'counter and deter weapons of mass destruction and improvised threat networks'. It went on to allege that most of the remaining money to EcoHealth Alliance was from USAID (State Department), comprising at least $64,700.00. It added that these two sources totalled over $103 million in funding to EcoHealth Alliance.[265]

This same report went on to allege that another $20 million came from Health and Human Services ($13 million, which includes National Institutes of Health and Centers for Disease Control), National Science Foundation ($2.6. million), Department of Homeland Security ($2.3 million), Department of Commerce ($1.2 million), Department of Agriculture ($0.6 million) and Department of Interior ($0.3 million). It went on to allege that the total US government funding for EcoHealth Alliance stood at $123 million, approximately one third of which came from the Pentagon directly.[266] *Wow*, muttered Susie. If this was accurate in its analysis, it might also potentially explain the high-level military activity she had been experiencing over recent months. It might all potentially be connected.

Susie could not quite believe what she was seeing as she read on. The report proceeded to highlight four significant points. Firstly, it alleged that EcoHealth and Dr Peter Daszak's non-profit work was closely affiliated with the military. Secondly, it alleged that EcoHealth attempted to conceal these military connections. Thirdly, it alleged that through militaristic language and analogies, Dr Daszak and his colleagues promoted what was often referred to as 'securitization'. In this case, securitisation of infectious diseases and of global public health. It went on to allege that they argued that pandemics constitute a 'vast and existential threat' as a way to justify their scientific research. Susie then paused for thought when it went on to allege that David Franz was part of UNSCOM, which inspected Iraq for alleged bioweapons.[267]

11.11 The Rise of BGI

As time allowed, Susie also dug deeper into her understanding of Beijing Genomics Institute (BGI).[268] She read that BGI's co-founder and chairman, Henry Wang/Wang Jian, was a prominent geneticist. She noted that he had reportedly spent six years as a research fellow in the US during the 1980s and '90s – a familiar pattern, she told herself, one that had subsequently been replicated by He Jiankui.

In 2009, BGI had reportedly received a $1.5 billion line of credit from the state-run China Development Bank, after which it purchased 128 DNA sequencers from a California genomics company.[269] She read on and came across a statement reportedly from BGI Chairman Henry Yang at an international conference at the China National GeneBank in 2018: 'Within ten years we aim to sequence the DNA of every important plant species, within twenty years we want to sequence every human on the planet, within thirty years we aim to sequence every form of life.'[270] The magnitude of this being possible and being discussed like this was scary, thought Susie.

She went on to read more about the international conference at the China National GeneBank in 2018. She read an account that alleged 'Henry Yang was flush with cash. He was chairman of a gene sequencing company that had just generated $14.5 billion in market capital after going public on the Shenzhen Stock Exchange'.[271] She read in the same account that BGI '...was already operating facilities to process samples in Europe, the US, Africa and Asia'.[272] She read on that 'Yang's headline surprise for the opening ceremony was the George Church Institute for Regenesis: a bold project to reanimate extinct species'.[273] She read on that '...other startling projects were already in motion. For example, BGI... were starting to target genes for athletic performance and high-altitude that could be optimized in humans'.[274] She carried on and noted it alleged that 'Privately, one of BGI's founders, Jun Yu, was offering advice to Dr He as he embarked on his controversial project. In public, Yang signalled the company's intention to reengineer the human species'.[275] She also read that BGI reportedly had multiple connections to the Chinese State government, including the Chinese Academy of Sciences and the Ministry of Science and Technology.[276] She also read an account which alleged that 'Hundreds of people were in the audience… –talented scientists from Europe, Australia, the United States, Asia and all parts of China. BGI was actively recruiting the best and the brightest into new collaboration projects'.[277] The account also alleged that 'Yang's vision of collecting the DNA of every human on earth was not simply pie in the sky. BGI was already 70% of the way toward its goal of sequencing all important agricultural plants. The facility already had over 3 million complete human genomes stored inside, more than any other facility on the planet. The China National GeneBank was steadily expanding its DNA archive'.[278]

Susie then put together a timeline concerning BGI, which charted its swift rise to power and prominence:

1999 BGI, a state-backed laboratory, is created to participate in the international Human Genome Project.

2003 The finished version of the first human genome sequence is completed.

2003 BGI first established a formal relationship with James Watson (who discovered the DNA double helix) and created the James D. Watson Institute of Genome Sciences in collaboration with Zhejiang University.[279]

2007 BGI splits from the Chinese Academy of Sciences, the state-controlled umbrella for high-level research to create a private company focusing on sequencing and moves to Shenzhen, China's entrepreneurial hothouse.[280]

2009 BGI receives $1.5 billion line of credit from state-run China Development Bank.

2012 BGI purchases Complete Genomics for $118 million, a sequencing machine manufacturer in Silicon Valley. This gave China the ability to build its own sequencers and sell them (having previously bought them from a US sequencing company).[281]

2013 The launch of BGI's Cognitive Genomics Laboratory – to study the DNA of highly intelligent people, collecting samples from 2,200 individuals (now believed to be defunct).[282]

2014 BGI's first gene-sequencing machine is given clearance by China's FDA.[283]

2016 The Chinese government launches the National GeneBank administered by BGI.[284]

2017 BGI is listed on the Shenzhen stock exchange.[285]

She did not stop there. She started to delve even deeper into BGI's activities. She read that the BGI Group, reportedly the world's largest genomics company, had allegedly worked with China's military on research that ranged from mass testing for respiratory pathogens to brain science.[286] She also found a report of a review of more than forty publicly available documents and research papers in Chinese and English allegedly showing BGI's links to the People's Liberation Army (PLA), including research with China's top military supercomputing experts.[287] It went on to report that material allegedly showed that the links between the Chinese military and BGI ran deep, illustrating how China had moved to integrate private technology companies into military-related research under President Xi Jinping.[288]

A report also came to light that the US government had recently been warned by an expert panel that adversary companies and non-state actors might fund and target genetic weaknesses in the US population and that a competitor such as China could use genetics to augment the strength of its own military personnel.[289] The report went on to say that a senior fellow at a US think tank, who had provided testimony to US congressional committees, had told Reuters that China's military had pushed research on brain science, gene editing and the creation of artificial genomes that could have a future application in future bioweapons.[290]

She then came across a report about a technology industry panel on artificial intelligence, appointed by the US government and chaired by former Google Chief Executive Eric Schmidt, which raised the alarm in October 2020 about China's financial support for its biotechnology sector, its advantages in collecting biological data and the PLA's interest in potential military applications. She read that the panel, which was due to deliver its final report in March 2021, warned about adversaries using artificial intelligence to identify genetic weaknesses in a population and engineering pathogens to exploit them, as well as genetic research designed to enhance soldiers' mental or physical strength. She read on that the panel allegedly recommended that the US government 'take more aggressive public posture regarding BGI', citing national security risks posed by the company's links to the Chinese government and its trove of genomic data.[291]

Susie also read a report that IT cloud computing company G42 (Group 42 Emirati Company), founded in 2018, was allegedly working with BGI on a project for collecting genetic data of the UAE citizens to 'generate the highest quality, most comprehensive genome data'. She read on that G42 Emirati comprises a multidisciplinary and diverse team of data scientists and engineers. The company was reported to perform fundamental AI research and development process on big data, AI and machine learning, via its subsidiary the Inception Institute of Artificial Intelligence.[292]

It was also reported that BGI jointly allegedly held a dozen patents for tests that screen for genomes linked to disease with the military university, the PLA's Academy of Military Medical Science; being the top medical research institute of the PLA and PLA Hospitals.[293] One patent was allegedly granted in 2015 to BGI and the Academy of Military Science for a low-cost test kit to detect respiratory pathogens, including SARS (Severe Acute Respiratory Syndrome) and coronaviruses.[294] BGI's chief infectious disease scientist, Chen Weijun, was allegedly listed as an inventor on the patent documents. Chen was also amongst the first scientists to sequence Covid-19, taking samples from a military hospital in Wuhan, according to sequence data later shared internationally.[295]

Diving deeper into BGI's activities, the complex interrelated picture expanded even further. She read on in the same account which alleged that four BGI researchers had also been jointly affiliated with another military institution, the National University of Defence Technology (NUDT).[296] It reported that Hunan-based NUDT was allegedly under the direct leadership of China's Central Military Commission, the top-level body that steers the Chinese military and headed by President Xi Jinping.[297] NUDT was reportedly on a US blacklist as a threat to national security because its Tianhe-2 supercomputer, one of the world's most powerful, was used to simulate nuclear explosions according to a Department of Commerce Listing. As such, that listing reportedly restricted US companies from supplying NUDT with technology.[298] She read on that one researcher was allegedly instrumental in developing software to speed up BGI's sequencing of human genomes using supercomputing developed by NUDT. That researcher had reportedly won military awards for his work. He was also allegedly a member of an expert group advising the Central Military Commission's Science and Technology Commission, set up in 2016 when President Xi Jinping began promoting a strategy to integrate China's civilian and military research.[299] Susie read on that the same Chinese researcher was reportedly also shown in patent applications in 2020 to be a member of the PLA's Institute of Military Medicine.[300] She also read that the head of the NUDT's supercomputer programme and a major general in the PLA had also reportedly published seven scientific papers either co-authored with BGI or crediting them for providing data and source code.[301]

There were also reports that BGI had sold Chinese police DNA testing supplies through its subsidiary Forensic Genomics International to collect and analyse DNA from millions of Chinese men and boys (Australian Strategic Policy Institute (ASPI) Report). This allegedly violated human rights.[302] She read a further report that:[303]

> *BGI has actively used gene-sequencing technologies to help the Chinese police with crime scene investigations. Their spin-off company Forensic Genomics International (FGI), operates with oversight from China's Ministry of Justice domestically and in multiple countries around the world... to sequence the DNA of Chinese political activists, migrants and Muslim Uyghurs.*

Further reports stated that *'At other BGI facilities – dotted throughout Shenzhen, Hong Kong, other parts of Asia, Europe and the United States – there were scores of other freezers, gene sequencers and severs for data storage. Underground caves were being excavated to expand safe cold-storage capacity for the future'*.[304] She read on that in 2017, BGI reportedly generated $332 million from sales of sequencing machines, laboratory accessories and sample processing… just behind the $418 million of Thermo Fisher.[305]

Then Susie stopped short in her tracks as she came across a report about 'One of BGI's most successful commercial products: a genetic test for pregnant mothers called NIFTY (which stands for Non-Invasive Fetal TrisomeY test), which offers the opportunity to sequence the DNA of a baby even before it is born'.[306] She read that NIFTY had apparently been used in more than sixty-two countries in Asia, the Americas and the Middle East. She learnt that NIFTY is a blood test that can pick up Down's syndrome and other genetic conditions. It is not as risky as amniocentesis since it uses fragments of fetal DNA in the mother's bloodstream, so avoiding risk of miscarriage. She read on that NIFTY can also screen for some types of body diversity, for example, when boys have an extra X chromosome, known as Klinefelter syndrome, found in one in every 500 newborn babies, most of whom are infertile.[307]

Following further research, Susie read that BGI had reportedly received substantial government loans from the China Development Bank.[308] She read that by April 2020, it was reported that BGI had stored 5 million whole human genomes in the China National GeneBank.[309] She also came across a further account which stated:[310]

> *Dr. Xin Liu, the associate director of BGI, told me that the NIFTY test is playing an important role in helping the company assemble the enormous collection of human DNA. But the way that they collected these gene sequences was not transparent. The whole genome of each mother who took the NIFTY test was collected, along with the genes of each woman's unborn children. I reviewed*

the legalese on the standard 'NIFTY test Request and Consent Form' and found it difficult to understand. Most patients and even health care practitioners probably do not understand that they are giving a sample to the China National GeneBank.

She was fascinated and stunned to read a further account of BGI which stated:[311]

As we continued on the tour, our guide made another big claim: BGI has assembled 'the world's largest DNA 'writing' platform'. They planned to transition from reading gene sequences to rewriting genomes, to move "from design to synthesis". The goal was large-scale genetic engineering.

She read on from the same account:[312]

A multimedia display illustrated the workflow for producing a genetically modified baby. Simply inject CRISPR into a freshly fertilized egg and then let the cells divide into a later-stage embryo. After sequencing the DNA of the newly synthetic embryo, checking to make sure that the cells have the desired changes, it can be implanted in the mother or a human surrogate who can carry the baby to term. The display summarized BGI's aspirations: 'Safe, efficient, high-speed, and targeted editing pipeline with scaled-up industrial capacity.

Well before Dr. Jiankui He suddenly grabbed international headlines, it was clear to anyone who was paying attention that Chinese scientists were taking the lead in the race to genetically engineer humans. Broad shifts in global economic, political, and cultural influence were clearly afoot. Chinese entrepreneurs and scientists were busy upsetting the status quo of science, technology, and society.'

This research concerned Susie and she paused for reflection about this reported activity in the fertility sector; her sector of work and one for which she felt responsibility. Susie then read on from the same account:[313]

Doctors and scientists from all over the world are already relying on BGI to sequence their DNA samples. In Copenhagen I visited the local BGI laboratory, where technicians told me about their workflow for processing genetic data from all over Europe…

Alumni of BGI's Cognitive Genomics Lab, namely Steve Hsu and Laurent Tellier, are continuing the research they started in China with a new start-up venture in the United States. The pair founded Genomic Prediction, a company that is presenting American consumers with radical new choices. Genomic Prediction is now offering human embryo screening with the 'inexpensive evaluation of hundreds of thousands of genetic variants', dramatically eclipsing the scope of tests like NIFTY that currently promise to help parents have quality children.

The speed at which genomic technological advances were impacting the fertility sector was both breathtaking and concerning, thought Susie.

11.12 First International Summit on Human Genome Editing, 2015

When time allowed, Susie also undertook some further research into the history of the international summits concerning human genome-editing technology. She read that the first international summit was held in Washington DC in December 2015. Jennifer Doudna and George Church were reportedly present along with other world-renowned CRISPR scientists, corporate lobbyists, members of Congress and others from the political world in Washington, start-up companies, investment firms, Big Pharma corporations and people from the MITRE Corporation, a non-profit organisation with federal funding to work on top-secret cybersecurity, health care, defence and intelligence programmes.[314]

Susie read that: [315]

> *CRISPR seemed like it was a thing of abstract speculation in 2015, more science fiction than reality. American scientists were calling for a global moratorium on genetic engineering experiments that could lead to mutations in our collective gene pool. CRISPR presented an opportunity to "take control of our genetic destiny, which raises enormous peril for humanity", said summit leader George Daley in an interview with the New York Times. Later, Daley told me that this event in Washington had been organized in response to the fast pace of CRISPR research in China. He said that Chinese scientists 'do not have a deep tradition of bioethical inquiry'.*

11.13 NIH and NIAD

Susie also made time around her busy schedule to learn more about the role and work of the US National Institute of Health (NIH), to further expand her understanding of the bigger picture around genomics and biotechnology. She learnt that it is the primary US government agency responsible for biomedical and public health research. It funds scientists worldwide and partners with academia, industry, government and NGOs. She read that the NIH is one of the premier sites for genetic research in the US. In 2016, it had a budget of £32 billion. It had also been a national coordinating centre for the Human Genome Project. In addition, it had ongoing initiatives focusing on cancer, Alzheimer's disease and HIV. As she read on, she came across an article which made concerning reading about the atmosphere on the NIH campus and reported concerns about bioterrorism and espionage:[316]

> *...I found that the familiar buildings had become strange. Fears of bioterrorism and foreign espionage had produced new security protocols. The FBI were aggressively sweeping up Chinese scientists in a 'vast dragnet', with nearly 200 active investigations, according to the New York Times. Amidst international tensions and stiff competition in the field of biotechnology, many Chinese American researchers were being accused of stealing trade secrets.*
>
> *Every day when I arrived at the NIH front gate, an armed guard escorted me out of my vehicle. I dutifully hauled all my stuff out of the car and sent it through an X-ray machine. While I walked through a metal detector and presented my government-issued photo ID, guards searched my car outside. Everyday life for scientists and other commuters was now clouded with an atmosphere of paranoia.'*

Expanding her research, she learnt more about the role and work of the National Institute of Allergy and Infectious Diseases (NIAID) NIAD, an agency within the NIH. She read that in 2017, NIAD awarded grants of more than $6 million to Professor Ralph S Baric to accelerate the development of new drugs to fight deadly coronaviruses.[317] She also came across an account which stated NIAD's research priorities and mission areas included HIV, biodefense and emerging infectious diseases:[318]

1. *Expanding the breadth and depth of knowledge in all areas of infectious, immunologic, and allergic diseases.*
2. *Developing flexible domestic and international research capacities to respond appropriately to emerging and re-emerging disease threats wherever they may occur.*

Human Immunodeficiency Virus/Acquired Immunodeficiency Syndrome (HIV/AIDS)

The goals in this area are finding a cure for HIV-infected individuals; developing preventative strategies, including vaccines and treatment as prevention; developing therapeutic strategies for preventing and treating co-infections such as TB and hepatitis C in HIV-infected individuals; and addressing the long-term consequences of HIV treatment.

Biodefense and Emerging Infectious Diseases (BioD)

The goal of this mission area is to understand how these deliberately emerging (i.e., intentionally caused) and naturally emerging infectious agents cause disease and how the immune system responds to them.

Infectious and Immunologic Diseases (IID)

The goal of this mission area is to understand how aberrant responses of the immune system play a critical role in the development of immune-related disorders such as asthma, allergies, autoimmune diseases and transplant rejection. This research helps improve the understanding of how the immune system functions when it is healthy or unhealthy and provides the basis for the development of new diagnostic tools and interventions for immune-related diseases.

11.14 US Military Gene-Editing Programme

One wet Sunday morning, Susie came across a report about alleged US military forays into human gene editing, which stated:[319]

> *Later, after a long internet scavenger hunt, I discovered a $100 million US military gene-editing program 'to support bio-innovation and combat bio-threats'. A YouTube video, hiding in plain sight, reveals plans to edit the DNA of Soldiers. Steve Walker, the director of the Defense Advanced Research Projects Agency (DARPA), spilled the beans while talking on a public panel with William LaPlante, senior vice president at MITRE. Military researchers were planning experiments to see if they could "protect a soldier on the battlefield from chemical weapons and biological attacks by controlling their genome," Walker said, "having the genome produce proteins that would automatically protect the soldier from the inside out."*

This article made her pause for thought, as it gave further context around potential biotechnology innovations and countermeasures associated with dual-use technology.

11.15 China's People's Liberation Army (PLA) and Genomics

It also proved fruitful to expand her knowledge of Chinese military genomic policy. In doing so, she came across an account which reported:[320]

In 2015, then-president of the Academy of Military Medical Sciences He Fuchu argued that biotechnology will become the new "strategic commanding heights" of national defense, from biomaterials to «brain control» weapons…

Biology is among seven "new domains of warfare" discussed in a 2017 book by Zhang Shibo, a retired general and former president of the National Defense University, who concludes: "Modern biotechnology development is gradually showing strong signs characteristic of an offensive capability," including the possibility that "specific ethnic genetic attacks" could be employed.

The 2017 edition of Science of Military Strategy, a textbook published by the PLA's National Defense University that is considered to be relatively authoritative, debuted a section about biology as a domain of military struggle, similarly mentioning the potential for new kinds of biological warfare to include 'specific ethnic genetic attacks'.

Following these lines of thinking, the PLA is pursuing military applications for biology and looking into promising intersections with other disciplines, including brain science, supercomputing and artificial intelligence…

...Indeed, the PLA's medical institutions have emerged as major centers for research in gene editing and other new frontiers of military medicine and biotechnology. The PLA's Academy of Military Medical Sciences (AMMS) which China touts as its 'cradle of training for military medical talent' was recently placed directly under the purview of the Academy of Military Science...

Building on this, Susie read reports that a gag order had been placed on the Wuhan Institute of Virology (the WIV) on 1 January 2020 by the Chinese Communist Party (CPP).[321] Further accounts reported that a major general from the PLA, who was China's top military microbiologist, took over the WIV from mid-January 2020.[322] This indicated close interaction between the WIV and the Chinese PLA, Susie thought, and it suggested that activity at the WIV had been put on a sort of war footing. This left her wondering whether this was to wage war on the viral outbreak or whether there was perhaps more to it than that; she suspected that it might potentially be the latter, given the picture emerging from her research.

11.16 Anti-CRISPR Technology

When time allowed, Susie also turned to research on what was being done to develop technology to counter CRISPR genomic technology's use to create biological weapons. In 2016, James Clapper, US Director of National Intelligence, included CRISPR on the agency's annual 'Worldwide Threat Assessment' for the first time as a weapon of mass destruction.[323] As a result, in 2017, the Pentagon's Defense Advanced Research Projects Agency (DARPA) launched a Safe Genes programme to support ways to defend against genetically engineered weapons. It dispensed $65 million in grants, making the US military the largest single source of money for CRISPR research, including to George Church and Jennifer Doudna.[324] She read on in the same account:[325]

> *Doudna's grants, which would eventually total $3.3 million, covered a variety of projects, including looking for ways to block a CRISPR editing system. The goal was to create tools that, as the announcement put it, "might someday be capable of disabling weapons employing CRISPR"...*
>
> *They focused on a method that some viruses use*

> *to disable the CRISPR systems of the bacteria they are attacking. In other words, bacteria developed CRISPR systems to ward off viruses. It was an arms race the Pentagon could understand: missiles being countered by defense systems being countered by anti-defense systems. The newly discovered systems were dubbed "anti-CRISPRs".*

She read a further report which stated:[326]

> *The labs that received Safe Genes grants gathered once a year with Renee Wegryzn, the program manager of DARPA's Biological Technologies Office. Doudna went to one meeting in San Diego in 2018 and was impressed by how good Wegrzyn was at promoting military funding, just as DARPA had done in the 1960s when it was creating what became the internet.*

Susie also read reports that the annual budget for the roughly 200 programmes that were under way at any one time at DARPA was about $3 billion. The report went on to say that with its unconventional approach, speed and effectiveness, DARPA had created a 'special forces' model of innovation.[327] In addition, she read that by 2021, anti-CRISPR technology had been developed, partly funded by the 2017 DARPA grant, to create a reversible epigenetic gene editor using the same technology basis as for the Moderna and BioNTech Covid-19 vaccines. She carefully noted reports that this technology did not alter the DNA sequences themselves (meaning no gene editing) and instead changed the way they are read in the cell. This was possible because genes could be silenced or activated based on chemical changes to the DNA strand; essentially, via the addition of chemical tags to certain places in the DNA strand.

Susie sat back and reflected on the rapid speed with which developments were happening in the fields of genomics and biotechnology. It was positive to note reported developments in anti-CRISPR technology. However, it left her wondering about the potential issues and risks associated with further developments, given this technology's immense and transformational power.

11.17 Coronavirus, HIV and CRISPR-Cas9 Research and Development

Through further reading, Susie learnt that the development of Covid-19 vaccines had also led to HIV vaccine trials. These HIV trials were being run by teams at Oxford University's Jenner Institute (which developed the AstraZeneca Covid-19 vaccine) as well as by US company Moderna.[328] Susie was interested to note that Moderna was partly funded by the Bill & Melinda Gates Foundation and it combined B-cell strategy (which makes antibodies) with the mRNA delivery technology used for Covid-19.[329] The Oxford team used a genetically modified chimpanzee adenovirus that uses T-cells rather than antibodies. The T-cells target and destroy cells infected with HIV.[330] From her research, Susie also learnt that adenoviruses are a group of common viruses that infect the lining of the eyes, airways and lungs, intestines, urinary tract and nervous system. They cause common cold or flu-like symptoms including: fever, sore throat, acute bronchitis (inflammation of the airways of the lungs), pneumonia (infection of the lungs), pink eye (conjunctivitis) and acute gastroenteritis (inflammation of the stomach or intestines causing diarrhoea, vomiting, nausea and stomach pain).

In the coming weeks, Susie mulled over everything she had learnt in her research. It was a lot to take in and digest, and the landscape was evolving rapidly. It was complex and multifaceted, which made for additional challenges in trying to make sense of everything. Genomic technology, and specifically

CRISPR Cas-9 technology, was now playing a central role in the fight against Covid-19 around the world. It was also being used to develop new therapies against HIV, and there it was again, she thought; another correlation between Covid-19 and HIV. It seemed like the technology was coming full circle from a 'dual use' perspective in terms of creating a cause (virus) and vaccines as a cure. If Covid-19 was a manmade gain-of-function virus with an HIV insert, it would make sense that vaccine technology designed to combat Covid-19 could also be applied to combat HIV.

Susie also sat back to take stock of where things were at in the UK. She surmised that a swift and effective response was needed to deal with this rapidly evolving landscape. There continued to be a clear and present danger in the event of further viral outbreaks and that was very concerning. There also needed to be a paradigm shift in understanding and further action to address Chinese genomic capability and the associated risks. This would require close partnerships with international partners to address genomic technology. The UK also needed to review and increase its spending on genomic infrastructure and prioritise genomic funding for the security services and the military. Added to this, the UK needed to better understand the genomic technology landscape and the associated risks which represented a threat to its national security, health, wealth and way of life. Having undertaken all of this additional research, Susie also realised that the picture she had constructed outpaced that which appeared in the news and public debate. Given what had happened in recent months, she was not overly surprised by this and yet it was still unsettling to see it happening in real life. It also begged the question, what was she going to do with the further analysis and information she had put together?

Susie was conscious that she continued to experience additional activity on her social media. It seemed that every time she did a concerted research push at the weekend, it triggered new accounts popping up the following week. Whilst she was not as fazed about this as she had been initially, it still made her feel anxious and under pressure. She sat back in her office chair and stared out of the bay window as she considered her options. She sensed that this heavyweight online presence had increased recently and it was getting more persistent again. She wondered if they were aware that she had joined up more dots and put together further analysis of the big picture. If so, that did not bode well. She felt alone and increasingly concerned as she mulled things over in her mind. It was a heavy load to carry and it was an unwelcome burden, having unwittingly become embroiled in all of this. The more they pursued her and popped up in her world, the more questions and concerns were raised. It also triggered this innate determination from deep within her to want to get to the bottom of things. She had never felt like this before and it was as if a whole new side of her had been unleashed in recent months; one that continually surprised and unsettled her.

After several hours and more than one mug of tea, Susie reluctantly concluded that she should put her head above the parapet again with the security services. Her analysis went far beyond that which she had shared with them last autumn. It was far more in-depth and wide-ranging and it painted a far more serious picture. Overall, she did not feel that she was left with much choice, and she wanted to do all she could to do the right thing.

With a heavy sigh, she looked up the telephone number for her counter terrorism contact and dialled his number. After a few rings, her call was answered and to her surprise she found herself taking with Charles, who had visited her last year. He remembered her and quickly said that his colleague, Andrew, was away from his desk, which is why he had answered the call.

He then rapidly asked her to explain why she had called. She proceeded to explain that she had put together further research and analysis. She added that what she had put together seemed to outpace what was publicly understood and that the sums of money allegedly spent on gain-of-function viral research appeared far higher. Charles listened carefully and then calmly but firmly asked her to send over her latest analysis. Susie was a bit taken aback and explained that her PowerPoint presentation was not quite finished. He retorted that it did not matter and he reiterated his request that she send it straight over. Susie somewhat reluctantly agreed to do so, given the tone of his voice, and with that the call swiftly ended. Susie sat back in her chair with a jolt. She had not expected them to be so interested. Given the urgency of the request from Charles, she wasted no time in sending a short email to the email address at counter terrorism, attaching her unfinished PowerPoint presentation. She did not like sending incomplete work out like this. However, this was not a usual situation, she told herself firmly. They would not have made the request lightly either, she thought, and she wondered where it would all lead.

Chapter 12

Spring-Summer 2021

12.1 President Biden Launches Covid-19 Investigation, May 2021

Soon after sending over a second PowerPoint presentation to the security services, Susie noticed that calls were intensifying for US President Joe Biden to investigate the origins of the Covid-19 pandemic. This quickly led on to a statement by President Biden on 26 May 2021 confirming that he had asked the US Intelligence Community to further investigate Covid-19 and report back in ninety days:[331]

> *Back in early 2020, when COVID-19 emerged, I called for the CDC to get access to China to learn about the virus so we could fight it more effectively. The failure to get our inspectors on the ground in those early months will always hamper any investigation into the origin of COVID-19.*
>
> *Nevertheless, shortly after I became President, in March, I had my National Security Advisor task the Intelligence Community to prepare a report on their most*

up-to-date analysis of COVID-19, including whether it emerged from human contact with an infected animal or from a laboratory accident. I received that report earlier this month, and asked for additional follow-up. As of today, the U.S. Intelligence Community has 'coalesced around two likely scenarios' but has not reached a definitive conclusion on this question. Here is their current position: 'while two elements in the IC leans toward the former scenario and one leans more to the latter – each with low or moderate confidence – the majority of elements do not believe there is sufficient information to assess one to be more likely than the other'.

I have now asked the Intelligence Community to redouble their efforts to collect and analyse information that could bring us closer to a definitive conclusion, and to report back to me in 90 days. As part of that report, I have asked for areas of further inquiry that may be required, including specific questions for China. I have also asked that this effort include work by our National Labs and other agencies of our government to augment the Intelligence Community's efforts. And I have asked the Intelligence Community to keep Congress fully apprised of its work.

The United States will also keep working with like-minded partners around the world to press China to participate in a full, transparent, evidence-based international investigation and to provide access to all relevant data and evidence.

Susie sat back in her office chair and sipped her mug of Earl Grey tea thoughtfully. It was not an entirely unexpected announcement following Joe Biden's inauguration as the 46th President of the United States on 20 January 2021, but she wondered whether it would actually get to the bottom of things, given all of the complex dynamics at play. It was reported in the press as a 'dramatic turnaround from the administration's policy until now of leaving the investigation to the World Health Organization'.[332] She noted that it had also led to reports of a further deterioration in US-China relations:[333]

> *...The Chinese foreign ministry spokesman, Zhao Lijian, said it was 'extremely unlikely' the virus had come from a laboratory in Wuhan, pointing to the findings of a March report by a World Health Organization mission.*
>
> *Zhao said: "[The US'] one aim is to use the pandemic to pursue stigmatisation and political manipulation to shift the blame. They are being disrespectful to science, irresponsible to people's lives, and counterproductive to concerted global efforts to fight the virus."*

12.2 US State Department's Fact Sheet, January 2021

Susie stared out of her office window as she continued to drink her tea and stroke Rina, who had jumped up onto her lap for a late-afternoon cuddle. She reflected thoughtfully on matters and cast her mind back to a fact sheet that had been published by the outgoing US Department of State of President Trump's administration just a few months earlier on 15 January 2021. That fact sheet had stated that the US government did not know exactly where, when or how the Covid-19 virus was transmitted initially to humans or whether it was through contact with an infected animal or the result of a laboratory accident in Wuhan in China. However, it had laid out a number of serious concerns:[334]

1. *Illnesses inside the Wuhan Institute of Virology (WIV):*
   - *The U.S. government has reason to believe that several researchers inside the WIV became sick in autumn*

2019, before the first identified case of the outbreak, with symptoms consistent with both COVID-19 and common seasonal illnesses. This raises questions about the credibility of WIV senior researcher Shi Zhengli's public claim that there was 'zero infection' among the WIV's staff and students of SARS-CoV-2 or SARS-related viruses...

- *The CCP has prevented independent journalists, investigators, and global health authorities from interviewing researchers at the WIV, including those who were ill in the fall of 2019...*

2. *Research at the WIV:*
    - *The WIV has a published record of conducting 'gain-of-function' research to engineer chimeric viruses. But the WIV has not been transparent or consistent about its record of studying viruses most similar to the COVID-19 virus, including 'RaTG13', which it sampled from a cave in Yunnan Province in 2013 after several miners died of SARS-like illness.*
    - *...As part of a thorough inquiry, they must have a full accounting of why the WIV altered and then removed online records of its work with RaTG13 and other viruses.*

3. *Secret military activity at the WIV:*
    - *...For many years the United States has publicly raised concerns about China's past biological weapons work, which Beijing has neither documented nor demonstrably eliminated, despite its clear obligations under the Biological Weapons Convention.*
    - *Despite the WIV presenting itself as a civilian institution, the United States has determined that*

the WIV has collaborated on publications and secret projects with China's military...

- *The United States and other donors who funded or collaborated on civilian research at the WIV have a right and obligation to determine whether any of our research funding was diverted to secret Chinese military projects at the WIV.*

That hard-hitting fact sheet by the outgoing US Department of State had got Susie thinking, and tied in with her own independent research and analysis. She had been particularly interested to note the concerns that the virus outbreak might have happened earlier than December 2019 and that it had reportedly sickened three members of staff at the Wuhan Institute of Virology (the WIV) over the autumn of 2019. She had also been interested to read concerns about the WIV's reported gain-of-function virus research, including virus 'RaTG13', and the lack of access to the WIV's records. Furthermore, she had been struck by the reported concerns about alleged secret Chinese military activity at the WIV and alleged biological bioweapons work. She wondered whether these high-level concerns might have accounted for the strange military encounters and activity she had been experiencing.

US President Biden's May 2021 announcement of a further investigation into the origins of Covid-19 was food for thought, surmised Susie. However, the announcement was couched in more neutral terms than the outgoing US Department of State's fact sheet in January 2021. There was also little doubt it was going to be a difficult exercise to reach any form of consensus. With that, she sighed slowly to herself as Rina jumped down from her lap and padded across her office towards the door, signalling it was time for food. She realised she should think about cooking her own evening meal as well; a good meal, a relaxed evening and an early night would do her good.

12.3 Vanity Fair Article on the Origins of Covid-19, June 2021

A few days later, on 3 June 2021, Susie became aware of an article in *Vanity Fair* which sparked more debate about a potential lab-leak origin of the Covid-19 pandemic. She was interested to read it reported significant conflicts of interest around investigating the virus' origins:[335]

> *A months long Vanity Fair investigation, interviews with more than 40 people, and a review of hundreds of pages of U.S. government documents, including internal memos, meeting minutes, and email correspondence, found that conflicts of interest, stemming in part from large government grants supporting controversial virology research, hampered the U.S. investigation into COVID-19's origin at every step. In one State Department meeting, officials seeking to demand transparency from the Chinese government say they were explicitly told by colleagues not to explore the Wuhan Institute of Virology's gain-of-function research, because it would bring unwelcome attention to U.S. government funding of it.*
>
> *…But for most of the past year, the lab-leak scenario was treated not simply as unlikely or even inaccurate but as morally out of bounds. In late March, former Centers for Disease Control director Robert Redfield received death threats from fellow scientists after telling CNN that he believed COVID-19 had originated in a lab. "I was threatened and ostracized because I proposed another hypothesis," Redfield told Vanity Fair. "I expected it from politicians. I didn't expect it from science."*

It was sobering to read that some people looking into the origins of Covid-19 had reportedly received death threats; that must have been truly terrifying, thought Susie. It also brought into closer focus the complex dynamics and multifaceted aspects surrounding the origins of the virus. She was further interested to read that there were reportedly only three places in the world that were working on bat-related coronaviruses, one of which was the Wuhan Institute of Virology, which agreed with her own research and analysis:[336]

> *Dr. Richard Ebright, board of governors professor of chemistry and chemical biology at Rutgers University, said that from the very first reports of a novel bat-related coronavirus outbreak in Wuhan, it took him 'a nanosecond or a picosecond' to consider a link to the Wuhan Institute of Virology. Only two other labs in the world, in Galveston, Texas, and Chapel Hill, North Carolina, were doing similar research. "It's not a dozen cities," he said. "It's three places."*

Susie also read officials had reportedly taken note, just as she had, of a 2015 scientific paper by Shi Zhengli and the University of North Carolina epidemiologist Ralph Baric:[337]

> *...As they combed open sources as well as classified information, the team's members soon stumbled on a 2015 research paper by Shi Zhengli and the University of North Carolina epidemiologist Ralph Baric proving that the spike protein of a novel coronavirus could infect human cells. Using mice as subjects, they inserted the protein from a Chinese rufous horseshoe bat into the molecular structure of the SARS virus from 2002, creating a new, infectious pathogen.*
>
> *This gain-of-function experiment was so fraught that the authors flagged the danger themselves, writing,*

> *'scientific review panels may deem similar studies... too risky to pursue'. In fact, the study was intended to raise an alarm and warn the world of 'a potential risk of SARS-CoV re-emergence from viruses currently circulating in bat populations'. The paper's acknowledgments cited funding from the U.S. National Institutes of Health and from a nonprofit called EcoHealth Alliance, which had parceled out grant money from the U.S. Agency for International Development.*

It was again sobering to read about the perceived dangers attached to this risky type of so-called gain-of-function virus research from the scientists involved and their warning of a potential coronavirus re-emergence as far back as 2015. Susie also revisited with interest an account of the World Health Organization's (the WHO's) investigation of the origins of the Covid-19 pandemic and its visit to Wuhan in China:[338]

> *...On January 14, 2021, Daszak and 12 other international experts arrived in Wuhan to join 17 Chinese experts and an entourage of government minders. They spent two weeks of the monthlong mission quarantined in their hotel rooms. The remaining two-week inquiry was more propaganda than probe, complete with a visit to an exhibit extolling President Xi's leadership. The team saw almost no raw data, only the Chinese government analysis of it.*
>
> *They paid one visit to the Wuhan Institute of Virology, where they met with Shi Zhengli, as recounted in an annex to the mission report. One obvious demand would have been access to the WIV's database of some 22,000 virus samples and sequences, which had been taken offline. At an event convened by a London organization on March 10, Daszak was asked whether the group had*

> *made such a request. He said there was no need: Shi Zhengli had stated that the WIV took down the database due to hacking attempts during the pandemic. "Absolutely reasonable," Daszak said. "And we did not ask to see the data… As you know, a lot of this work has been conducted with EcoHealth Alliance… We do basically know what's in those databases. There is no evidence of viruses closer to SARS-CoV-2 than RaTG13 in those databases, simple as that.*
>
> *…After two weeks of fact finding, the Chinese and international experts concluded their mission by voting with a show of hands on which origin scenario seemed most probable. Direct transmission from bat to human: possible to likely. Transmission through an intermediate animal: likely to very likely. Transmission through frozen food: possible. Transmission through a laboratory incident: extremely unlikely."*

Susie further noted that the *Vanity Fair* article reported that the WHO's director, Dr Tedros Adhanom Ghebreyesus '*…appeared to acknowledge the report's shortcomings at a press event the day of its release. "As far as WHO is concerned, all hypotheses remain on the table… We have not yet found the source of the virus, and we must continue to follow the science and leave no stone unturned as we do."* The WHO's investigation had not got to the bottom of things and it had been a classic example of complex politics, conflicts of interest, lack of transparency and obfuscation, she thought.

12.4 Results of US Intelligence Community's Investigation of Covid-19, August 2021

Susie therefore continued to keep a close eye on reports about the US' ninety-day investigation into the origins of Covid-19.

On 27 August 2021, she was quick to spot a statement by US President Joe Biden.[339] She noted wearily that the results of the US intelligence community's investigation were inconclusive and that the origins of the pandemic were reported in the press as 'still murky'. President Biden's statement went on to say:[340]

> *...Critical information about the origins of this pandemic exists in the People's Republic of China, yet from the beginning, government officials in China have worked to prevent international investigators and members of the global public health community from accessing it. To this day, the PRC continues to reject calls for transparency and withhold information, even as the toll of this pandemic continue to rise. We needed this information rapidly, from the PRC, while the pandemic was still new. Since taking office, my administration has renewed U.S. leadership in the World Health Organization and rallied allies and partners to renew focus on this critical question. The world deserves answers, and I will not rest until we get them. Responsible nations do not shirk these kinds of responsibilities to the rest of the world. Pandemics do not respect international borders, and we all must better understand how COVID-19 came to be in order to prevent further pandemics.*
>
> *The United States will continue working with like-minded partners around the world to press the PRC to fully share information and to cooperate with the World Health Organization's Phase II evidence-based, expert-led determination into the origins of COVID-19 – including by providing access to all relevant data and evidence. We will also continue to press the PRC to adhere to scientific norms and standards, including sharing information and data from the earliest days of the pandemic, protocols related to*

biosafety, and information from animal populations. We must have a full and transparent accounting of this global tragedy. Nothing less is acceptable.

This was accompanied by reports that the US intelligence community would declassify parts of its report over the next few days, and she hoped that would shed some further light on matters.[341] In the meantime, she noted that President Biden's statement made it clear that the matter had not been laid to rest and that they still continued to seek full transparency about the origins of the Covid-19 pandemic. The subsequent publication of an unclassified report by the US Office of the Director of National Intelligence made interesting reading. Susie noted that it stated that the virus 'probably emerged and infected humans through an initial small-scale exposure that occurred no later than November 2019 with the first known cluster of Covid-19 cases arising in Wuhan, China in December 2019'.[342]

The unclassified report went on to state that the US intelligence community had reached broad agreement in concluding that Covid-19 was 'not developed as a biological weapon' and that 'China's officials did not have foreknowledge of the virus before the initial outbreak of Covid-19 emerged'. That was a significant finding, she thought, and it suggested an unintentional origin. However, she noted that the US intelligence community remained divided over the most likely origin of Covid-19, with two hypotheses remaining on the table: (1) natural exposure to an infected animal and (2) a laboratory-associated incident. Susie also noted the carefully couched statement that:[343]

...After examining all available intelligence reporting and other information, though, the IC remains divided on the most likely origin of COVID-19. All agencies assess

that two hypotheses are plausible: natural exposure to an infected animal and a laboratory-associated incident.

- *Four IC elements and the National Intelligence Council assess with low confidence that the initial SARS-CoV-2 infection was most likely caused by natural exposure to an animal infected with it or a close progenitor virus – a virus that probably would be more than 99 percent similar to SARS-CoV-2...*
- *One IC element assesses with moderate confidence that the first human infection with SARS-CoV-2 most likely was the result of a laboratory-associated incident, probably involving experimentation, animal handling, or sampling by the Wuhan Institute of Virology...*
- *Analysts at three IC elements remain unable to coalesce around either explanation without additional information, with some analysts favoring natural origin, others a laboratory origin, and some seeing the hypotheses as equally likely.*

All in all, thought Susie, the origins of the Covid-19 pandemic had yet to be fully clarified. There was so much at stake, and the investigations and debates were set to continue to rumble on. The battle for control of the Covid-19 narrative had yet to be won.

Chapter 13

Autumn 2021–Spring 2022

13.1 Project DEFUSE: Defusing the Threat of Bat-Born Coronaviruses, 2018

Towards the end of September 2021, Susie came across news reports about a leaked scientific research proposal detailing high-risk coronavirus research that had been rejected by US military research agency the Defense Advanced Research Projects Agency (DARPA).[344] The grant had been prepared and submitted by EcoHealth Alliance led by Dr Peter Daszak on 27 March 2018 entitled 'Project DEFUSE: Defusing the Threat of Bat-born Coronaviruses'.[345] She immediately noted the sum requested was just over $14 million for a four-year research period; a large sum of money. Furthermore, she noted that the proposed work would have been carried out by team members at the Wuhan Institute of Virology, led by Shi Zhengli (the WIV) and Professor Ralph Baric's team at the University of North Carolina. The proposal described the creation of full-length infectious clones of bat SARS-related coronaviruses and the insertion of a 'furin cleavage site'.[346] The article went on to explain that 'The furin cleavage site enables the virus to more efficiently bind to and release its genetic material into a human cell and is one of the reasons that the virus is so easily transmissible and harmful'.[347] So, here was a research proposal, albeit rejected by DARPA, shortly before the Covid-19 outbreak which sought to make a SARS-like virus more infectious and transmissible in humans by inserting a 'furin cleavage site' to make the virus bind more efficiently to human cells. The proposed work would have involved the WIV in Wuhan in China, which subsequently became the epicentre of the Covid-19 outbreak as from December 2019. This raised further issues and questions in Susie's mind.

That same article also reported that the reasons for how the furin cleavage site ended up in the SARS-CoV-2 virus had become a 'major focus of the heated debate over the origins of the pandemic'.[348] Susie read on with interest that it reported:[349]

> *"...Some kind of threshold has been crossed," said Alina Chan, a Boston-based scientist and co-author of the upcoming book* Viral: The Search for the Origin of Covid-19. *Chan has been vocal about the need to thoroughly investigate the possibility that SARS-CoV-2 emerged from a lab while remaining open to both possible theories of its development. For Chan, the revelation from the proposal was the description of the insertion of a novel furin cleavage site into bat coronaviruses — something people previously speculated, but had no evidence, may have happened.*
>
> *"Let's look at the big picture: A novel SARS coronavirus emerges in Wuhan with a novel cleavage site in it. We now have evidence that, in early 2018, they had pitched inserting novel cleavage sites into novel SARS-related viruses in their lab," said Chan. "This definitely tips the*

> *scales for me. And I think it should do that for many other scientists too."*

She was further interested to read:

> *Richard Ebright, a molecular biologist at Rutgers University who has espoused the possibility that SARS-CoV-2 may have originated in a lab, agreed. "The relevance of this is that SARS Cov-2, the pandemic virus, is the only virus in its entire genus of SARS-related coronaviruses that contains a fully functional cleavage site at the S1, S2 junction," said Ebright, referring to the place where two subunits of the spike protein meet. "And here is a proposal from the beginning of 2018, proposing explicitly to engineer that sequence at that position in chimeric lab-generated coronaviruses."*

That said, the article went on to report that 'others insisted that the research posed little or no threat and pointed out that the proposal called for most of the genetic engineering work to be done in North Carolina rather than China'.[350] However, the article also reported that according to several scientists interviewed, the proposed viruses presented a threat nevertheless:[351]

> *...The authors of the grant proposal make the case that because the scientists would be using SARS-related bat viruses, as opposed to the SARS virus that was known to infect humans, the research was exempt from "gain-of-function concerns." But according to several scientists interviewed by The Intercept, the viruses presented a threat nevertheless.*
>
> *"The work describes generating full-length bat SARS-related coronaviruses that are thought to pose a risk of*

human spillover. And that's the type of work that people could plausibly postulate could have led to a lab-associated origin of SARS-CoV-2," said Jesse Bloom, a professor at Fred Hutchinson Cancer Research Center and director of the Bloom Lab, which studies the evolution of viruses.

...While the grant proposal does not provide the smoking gun that SARS-CoV-2 escaped from a lab, for some scientists it adds to the evidence that it might have. "Whether that particular study did or didn't [lead to the pandemic], it certainly could have," said Nunberg, of Montana Biotechnology Center. "Once you make an unnatural virus, you're basically setting it up in an unstable evolutionary place. The virus is going to undergo a whole bunch of changes to try and cope with its imperfections. So who knows what will come of it." The risks of such research are profound and irreversible, he said. "You can't call back the virus once you release it into the environment."

Sitting back and reflecting on this, Susie concluded that this was further evidence of the complex, high-level and interrelated forces at play in the bigger picture. It shed further light on what was interpreted to be gain-of-function virus research. It also showed how an embargo on this dangerous research might be side-stepped using SARS-related bat viruses and not the SARS virus known to infect humans. *Was this just biological semantics?* she muttered to herself. Again, the article did not definitively confirm the origins of the Covid-19 pandemic. But it did shed further light on events leading up to it, she thought soberly, and the dangers associated with risky virus and vaccine research.

13.2 Train Journey Home

Around this time, Susie also noted wearily that the strange increase in activity was still happening on the fringes of her social media accounts. It had certainly lessened since her discussions with the security services the previous autumn, but it had not completely gone away either. Whilst she could not be entirely sure, she wondered if people were still keeping an eye on her movements. There had been one incident recently when she had travelled into London for a launch party for a new life sciences initiative. She had enjoyed herself at the event, met some interesting people and it had been nice to meet up in person after some many months stuck at home during the pandemic restrictions. She had stayed over in London as it had been a late night and then travelled home on the train the following day; that was when she had wondered whether she was being watched. She had sat down at an unoccupied table in the corner of one of the quiet carriages. The train was fairly empty and she had been glad of the quiet after the party the night before and an opportunity to catch up on some reading. Looking to her right, she had noticed a man sat at the table adjacent to her on the other side of the carriage. He was on his own and seemed occupied with his computer. He had not caught her eye, but there had been something about him that caught her attention, although she was not quite sure why. He had perhaps been in his forties and he had looked strong, fit and capable.

As her train journey continued, all of a sudden, a noisy and somewhat eccentric couple had come through the double doors behind Susie and sat down opposite her at the table. Her heart had sunk as she could have done without their presence, knowing that Covid-19 levels were on the rise again and because it made it more difficult to read. The woman had proceeded to noisily argue with her male companion about the lack of legroom and her preference for first-class seating. Their heated and somewhat over-the-top discussion had dragged on, which had disturbed her reading and headspace. Eventually, they had got up and moved further down the carriage to sit on their own.

It had all seemed a bit strange, but she had been relieved when they finally moved on and she returned to her reading. Shortly afterwards, the train inspector appeared through the double doors behind her and pointedly asked her whether the blue coat on the overhead shelf belonged to her. She had immediately stopped what she was doing and looked up to see what looked like a lightweight blue jacket on the shelf above. She had then felt a familiar cold shiver and her stress levels began to rise, which had been unwelcome. The coat was not hers, nor had she been aware of it when she had sat down. Almost instantly, the man at the table adjacent to her had leapt up and started to take charge of the situation. He had spoken quickly to the train inspector, saying that it was not hers, and he had pointed at the couple who had moved down the carriage. His actions had been rapid, efficient and effective, and it had come as a relief as she was still anxious about travelling on her own. The whole incident had happened quickly, but it had left her wondering whether it had just been a simple case of a misplaced jacket or whether there had potentially been more to it than that. The man had then proceeded to sit back down and busy himself with his work, travelling all the way until she left the train, without catching her eye or engaging with her. As she drove back home, she had wondered if the whole thing had just been a bit of a coincidence and if she had just been reading far too much into the incident. However, she was still left with a nagging thought that the man on the train might have been there to keep a bit of an eye on her. She did not want to get paranoid and start imagining things, but at the same time events over recent months had been far from normal and it was not the first time she had been left feeling as if she was being watched.

Despite her best efforts and a heavy legal workload, she was unable to dial down her mind's continued preoccupation with the Covid-19 pandemic, the forces behind it and world events. It was infuriating but thoughts would pop into her head at the most inopportune times. She found herself looking at the news and items on the internet in a different light, which saddened her and continued to change her outlook. Her recent experiences had widened her outlook and made her much less accepting of life. She saw things differently now and she was able to join up dots in a way she had not previously known. It was as exhilarating as it was concerning, and it was often difficult to discern between the two as they were so closely interrelated. It was also frustrating as things kept building up and developing in her mind. They filled her headspace and absorbed her free time until she got to a point where she felt compelled to capture everything in yet another spider's web on her office whiteboard and another PowerPoint. It was like she was stuck in a loop, having been here before. However, what she did know was that it would provide some relief to work her thoughts out like this. It was like a pressure valve and she knew she would feel a bit lighter and clearer once she had done it. Trying to stay positive, she told herself that it would take things forward and give her something to do to feel more on top of the situation.

13.3 The Wellcome Trust

Publication of new books on Covid-19 were a rich source of information. As such, there was an illuminating account published by Sir Jeremy Farrar, Director of the Wellcome Trust; an expert on infectious disease and member of the UK SAGE committee on Covid-19 who was reportedly one of the first people to alert the world about the unfolding pandemic. His book came out over the summer of 2021. It opened with an account of events on New Year's Eve 2019 whilst he was in an airport lounge. This immediately drew Susie's attention as it mentioned not just early knowledge of the virus outbreak but also his links with Chinese scientist Professor George Gao:[352]

> *I was scanning my phone when I saw a report of a mystery pneumonia spotted by doctors at a hospital in China. I sent a short message to George Gao, head of the Chinese Center for Disease Control and Prevention (China CDC) in Beijing, and an old friend. ...He phoned me back. Very soon, George told me, the world would be hearing about a cluster of cases of a new pneumonia from Wuhan in China. The cases had already been reported to the World Health Organization. ...I remember him telling me that we wouldn't need to worry because it wasn't severe acute respiratory syndrome (SARS), and that we must keep in touch.*

Upon his return to work, Sir Jeremy Farrar then contacted two of his '*most senior colleagues*'. What was particularly interesting was the previous senior leadership position held by of one of these individuals within the UK security services, Susie thought. Here was further reference of interaction between a key scientist and the scientific establishment and someone with connections to the intelligence community, a pattern that was continuing to emerge from her research:[353]

> *When I went back to work on Friday 3 January 2020, I emailed two of my most senior colleagues: Eliza Manningham-Buller, the Chair of the Wellcome Trust and former director general of the UK intelligence agency MI5, and Mike Ferguson, her deputy. I would not normally trouble them about a small, distant outbreak – but this one in China felt different. If it turned out to be different, the Wellcome Trust, where I have been director for eight years, would be called upon for its expertise and money. The charity had long worked in the field of infectious*

diseases, with researchers all over the world, it played a key role in the research response to the Ebola outbreaks of 2014 and 2018, including funding vaccine research and clinical trials.

His account went on to reference the interrelationship between public health experts, the security and intelligence community and the military in the US concerning the Covid-19 outbreak, shedding further light on these complex high-level associations:[354]

At Davos [2020], Richard Hatchett from CEPI [Coalition for Epidemic Preparedness Innovations] began looping me into emails with people in the US who were trying to parse the size of the threat and how to get ahead of it. The group included figures in Homeland Security, healthcare companies, the army and public health; they would each bring one or two other voices into the loop to crowdsource information.

It was also sobering to read Sir Jeremy Farrar's account of his early concerns that the virus might be a lab leak of a gain-of-function virus and the fraught international political landscape surrounding this:[355]

...And my starting bias was that it was odd for a spillover event, from animals to humans, to take off in people so immediately and spectacularly – in a city with a biolab. One standout molecular feature of the virus was a region in the genome sequence called a furin cleavage site, which enhances infectivity. This novel virus, spreading like wildfire, seemed almost designed to infect human cells.

To say that all this worried me would be an understatement. US-China politics were in a bad place in January 2020; a trade war that started in 2018 with import tariffs was escalating, with high-profile Chinese companies being put on export blacklists. It was obvious that people would soon begin hunting for a scapegoat for what was rapidly turning into a global health disaster. Trump was seeking to blame the virus on China and was calling it the 'China virus' and 'kung flu'. The security services in the US were on high alert for any hint that would prop up the accusations.

...In effect, one idea that was spreading was that the novel coronavirus might be a bioweapon. I remember sitting in the kitchen with my wife Christine and saying, "This could be an engineered virus. It could be a lab accident – or worse." Saying it out loud felt like a bombshell.

...With extremely tense US relations and an unpredictable American president determined to see a biological threat through the distorting lens of nationalism, it didn't feel too melodramatic to wonder if an engineered virus, either accidentally leaked or intentionally released, might be the sort of thing countries could go to war over.

He followed this up with an illuminating account of relationships between the scientific and security and intelligence worlds and the reasons for this, likening infectious disease epidemics to wars because they can spread chaos and be politically destabilising. This really resonated with Susie, given her growing understanding and concerns about biological research and virulent viruses:[356]

...This issue [the origins of the SARS-CoV-2] needed urgent attention from scientists – but it was also the territory of the security and intelligence services.

> *I had overlapped with the security services once before, when I was trying to drum up interest in the record Ebola outbreak in West Africa, which started in 2013. Epidemics are as politically destabilising as wars; they spread chaos along with disease. Back then I had trudged to Whitehall to try to convince the security services that the outbreak mattered, because it was threatening to creep into conflict zones.*
>
> *...Andrew Parker was the head of the UK intelligence MI5 at that time; he has since moved on, but we also spoke about the coronavirus outbreak in early 2020, when he was visiting Wellcome chair Eliza Manningham-Buller, his predecessor at MI5.*
>
> *When I told Eliza about the suspicions over the origins of the new coronavirus, she advised that everyone involved in the delicate conversations should raise our guard, security-wise. We should use different phones; avoid putting things in emails; and ditch our normal email addresses and phone contacts.*

Sir Jeremy Farrar then went on to give an account of an important meeting held over the first weekend of February 2020 between international scientific experts to discuss the origins of the coronavirus outbreak. It was interesting to note that these experts held influential scientific positions in the US, Britain, Australia, the Netherlands and Germany Susie pondered:[357]

> *The next challenge was to find an appointment for a secure conference call that could bring in extra voices. We settled on Saturday 1 February 2020 at 7 pm GMT, which was 2 pm for Tony* [Fauci – Head of the US National Institute of Allergy and Infectious Diseases] *and 6 am Sunday for Eddie* [Holmes – a British evolutionary biologist

> and virologist and a National Health and Medical Research Council Australia Fellow and Professor at the University of Sydney] *in Australia. Kristian* [Anderson – Professor in the Department of Immunology and Microbiology at the Scripps Research Institute in La Jolla, California] *and Eddie asked Andrew Rambaut* [Professor of Molecular Evolution at the University of Edinburgh] *and Bob Garry* [Tulane University, School of Medicine, Department of Microbiology and Immunology, New Orleans] *to dial in. The others on the call were: Francis Collins* [Head of the US National Institutes of Health]*; Ron Fouchier* [a Dutch virologist and Deputy Head of the Erasmus MC Department of Viroscience]; *Marion Koopman* [a Dutch virologist who is Head of the Erasmus MC Department of Viroscience]; *Christin Drosten* [a German virologist *whose research focus is on novel viruses*]; *Stefan Pohlmann, a virologist at the German Primate Centre in Gottingen; Mike Fergurson, Wellcome's deputy chair and a biochemist; Paul Schrier, also from Wellcome; and Patrick Vallance* [UK government's Chief Scientific Advisor].

Following this meeting, Sir Jeremy Farrar sent an email to the group setting out his views on the origins of the pandemic and the proposed way forward. It was telling that he continued to keep both a lab leak of a manmade virus and a zoonotic animal-to-human transmission spillover event equally in mind, Susie pondered:[358]

> *On a spectrum if 0 is nature and 100 is release – I am honestly at 50! My guess is that this will remain grey unless there is access to the Wuhan lab – and I suspect that is unlikely!*

> *We agreed it had to be looked at quickly and forensically, ideally under the WHO umbrella, but that did not materialise (the agency was taken up with the emergency response). So, after those initial conversations, five scientists came together to take an investigation forward: Kristian; Eddie; Andrew; Bob; and W. Ian Lipkin, a Columbia University virologist who, in addition to being a well-known virus hunter and SARS veteran, was scientific adviser to the film* Contagion. *They resolved to undertake a fingertip search of the literature, rake through accumulating research on the virus, study the epidemiological data and scrutinise samples of the virus; all to detect the trace of an unseen hand.*

From this group, five scientists subsequently went on to publish the scientific paper *The Proximal Origin of SARS-CoV-2* on 17 March 2020, and in doing so established the early narrative about the zoonotic (animal-to-human transmission) origins of the pandemic, stating:[359]

> *Our analyses clearly show that SARS CoV-2 is not a laboratory construct or a purposefully manipulated virus.*

It was also enlightening to read the account of Sir Jeremy Farrar's further dealings with the security and intelligence worlds at the Munich Security Conference. This provided further insight into the complex landscape of international political and security relationships amongst the governing elite and their connections with the scientific community. It highlighted the difficulties with tracking biological threats and searching for biological weapons in countries. It also tellingly referenced the power struggle between the security community and scientists for control of dual-use technology to make viruses more virulent and deadly; a biotechnology arms race:[360]

> *"Are you a spy?" asked the taxi driver, as I jumped into his cab at Munich Airport on Friday 14 February 2020. I was on my way to the Munich Security Conference, which takes place in one of the city's hotels every year and, with its focus on global security, seems to draw an even more exclusive crowd than Davos.*
>
> *...It is not the sort of conference to which you can blag an invitation. Mine came through Sam Nunn, the Democratic senator who set up the Nuclear Threat Initiative, which has since broadened its remit to look at other security threats, including biosecurity...*
>
> *A nuclear or terrorist threat is very much like the challenge we face in public health and epidemiology: seeing the signal for the noise...*
>
> *That difficulty is compounded by the inability to go into countries and look for biological threats in a way that agencies can demand access to countries to search for chemical or nuclear weapons. ...Another parallel between terrorism and biosecurity is the variety of actors who can stir up trouble: technological advances mean that big states and rich institutions no longer have a monopoly on building bombs or bioweapons. The counterpart of the lone gunman could be a hobbyist genetically modifying viruses in her garage.*
>
> *Maintaining a scientific presence in the security world also achieves another end: making sure that decisions on dual-use technology, such as gain-of-function research that scientists like Ron Fouchier practise, are not monopolised or controlled by the security community.*

Dual-use technology, like the techniques to make viruses more contagious or deadly, can seem very scary. But shutting them down would mean critical science, needed for threat surveillance and safety, not being done or being carried out under the radar.

It was further illuminating to note Sir Jeremy Farrar's account of the establishment of the UK's Joint Biosecurity Centre to combat the Covid-19 pandemic and the security service's model format upon which it was reportedly based:[361]

The Joint Biosecurity Centre, set up in May 2020 and modelled on the Joint Terrorism Analysis Centre based in MI5, has gone a long way to becoming a nerve centre. It pulls in information from SAGE and from other sources, such as mobile phone data, which can help to model behaviour changes and adherence to lockdowns. It has been excellent at turning huge amounts of data into usable information that can feed into policy and has genuinely transformed the UK pandemic response for the better.

13.4 Project Veritas Disclosure, January 2022: US Marine Corps Major Joseph Murphy's Report Concerning the Origins of Covid-19

In mid-January 2022 came news that Project Veritas (a US investigative group) had publicly published a report by Marine Corps Major Joseph Murphy concerning the origins of Covid-19. The report, dated August 2021, had been sent to the Department of Defence (DoD) Office of the Inspector General (OIG) for investigation five months earlier. Susie studied it carefully, noting it provided a working hypothesis that Covid-19 was a manmade gain-of-function virus that had initially been rejected by the US Department of Defence but then approved and funded by Dr Fauci via the NIH/NIAID, stating:[362]

1. *SARS-CoV-2 is an American-created recombinant bat vaccine or its precursor virus. It was created by an EcoHealth Alliance program at the Wuhan Institute of Virology (WIV), as suggested by the reporting surrounding the lab-leak hypothesis. The details of this program have been concealed since the pandemic began. These details can be found in the EcoHealth Alliance proposal response to the DARPA PREEMPT program Broad Agency Announcement (BAA) HR00118S0017, dated March 2018 – a document not yet publicly disclosed.*

   …Joining this analysis with US intelligence collections on Wuhan will aid this determination.

   When synthesized with the EcoHealth Alliance proposal, US collections confirm EcoHealth Alliance was performing the work proposed… For instance, WIV personnel identified in intelligence reports are named in the proposal, these people use the lexicon of the proposal in the collections, and the virus variants proposed for experimentation are identical to those gleaned by collections. Moreover, I am also privy to information obtained by congressional office investigators and by DRASTIC, which further corroborated that the program detailed in the BAA response was conducted until it was shut down in April 2020.

   The purpose of the EcoHealth program, called DEFUSE in the proposal, was to inoculate bats in the Yunnan, China caves where confirmed SARS-CoVs were found. Ostensibly, doing this would prevent another SARS-CoV pandemic… Being defense-related, it makes sense that EcoHealth submitted the proposal first to the Department

> *of Defense, before it settled with NIH/NIAID. The BAA response is dated March 2018 and was submitted by Peter Daszak, president of EcoHealth Alliance.*
>
> *DARPA rejected the proposal because the work was too close to violating the gain-of-function (GoF) moratorium, despite what Peter Daszak says in the proposal (that the work would not).*

She further noted the reference to US intelligence-gathering activity in the Marine Corps Major's report (referred to as collections). This seemingly tied in with her previous research findings that the US Embassy in Beijing had sent US science diplomats to visit the Wuhan Institute of Virology (the WIV) several times between January and March 2018. The US officials had reportedly been so concerned by what they found that they had sent two diplomatic cables categorised as sensitive but unclassified back to Washington DC warning about inadequate safety at the WIV lab, which was conducting risky studies on coronaviruses from bats. One of the cables reportedly warned that the WIV's work on bat coronaviruses and their potential human transmission represented a risk of a new SARS-like pandemic. They had reportedly raised concerns that the WIV had a serious shortage of appropriately trained technicians and investigators needed to safely operate a BS Level 4 laboratory. Moreover, the cables also reportedly warned that the Chinese researchers had found that various SARS-like coronaviruses could interact with the human receptor ACE2 and that the research strongly suggested that SARS-like coronaviruses from bats could be transmitted to humans to cause SARS-like diseases. This US intelligence-gathering aspect might account for part of the reason why there was a US-China scientific collaboration at the WIV backed by US funding, Susie pondered, over and above the more obvious public health pandemic prevention aspect. It might also provide a vehicle by which the US could seek to monitor Chinese scientific and genomic activity and the dual-use issues and international security risks associated with manipulating dangerous viruses to make them more virulent and transmissible.

It was also concerning to note that the report hypothesised that Covid-19 was a manmade chimeric virus with the aim of infecting and immunising bats, which leaked and spread rapidly because it was aerosolised. The ability to aerosolise novel manmade gain-of-function viruses with the capacity to infect, sicken and kill large numbers of people was a fundamental issue and risk for the world that needed to be addressed, she thought soberly:[363]

2. *SARS-CoV-2, hereafter referred to as SARSr-CoV-WIV, is a synthetic spike protein chimera engineered to attach to human ACE2 receptors and inserted into a recombinant bat SARS-CoV backbone. It is likely a live vaccine not yet engineered to a more attenuated [weakened form] state that the program sought to create with its final version. It leaked and spread rapidly because it was aerosolized so it could efficiently infect bats in caves, but it was not ready to infect bats yet, which is why it does not appear to infect bats. The reason the disease is so confusing is because it is less a virus than it is engineered spike proteins hitch-hiking a ride on a SARSr-CoV... since initial escape in August 2019.*

So, pondered Susie, here was US military analysis that suggested that Covid-19 first leaked in August 2019. If that was right, it might explain why China suddenly took its virus database at the WIV offline on 12 September 2019 and started to take other measures. Honing in even further, Susie noted US Marine

Corps Major Joseph Murphy's assessment of early treatments for Covid-19 and his reasoning for why gene-encoded mRNA vaccines work so poorly:[364]

> *...the SARSr-CoV-WIV's illness is readily resolved with early treatment that inhibits the viral replication that spreads the spike proteins around the body (which induce a harmful overactive immune response as the body tries to clear the spikes from the ACE2 receptors). Many of the early treatment protocols ignored by the authorities work because they inhibit viral replication or modulate the immune response to the spike proteins, which make sense within the context of what EcoHealth was creating. Some of these treatment protocols also inhibit the action of the engineered spike protein. For instance, Ivermectin (identified as curative in April 2020) works throughout all phases of illness because it both inhibits viral replication and modulates the immune response. Of note, chloroquine phosphate (Hydroxychloroquine, identified April 2020 as curative) is identified in the proposal as a SARSr-CoV inhibitor, as is interferon (identified May 2020 as curative).*
>
> *The gene-encoded, or 'mRNA', vaccines work poorly because they are synthetic replications of the already-synthetic SARSr-CoV-WIV spike proteins... The mRNA instructs the cells to produce synthetic copies of the SARSrCoV-WIV synthetic spike protein directly into the bloodstream, wherein they spread and produce the same ACE2 immune storm that the recombinant vaccine does.*

Although vaccines using new genomic technology to combat Covid-19 had been developed quickly and started to be used across the world from the end of 2020, they had not provided a complete solution for the global pandemic, Susie noted. Given the Covid-19 virus' ability to mutate and spread rapidly, it necessitated multiple vaccines to seek to offer some form of ongoing protection against contracting severe disease and death. The vaccines did not necessarily prevent individuals from contracting (or re-contracting) Covid-19 as it evolved, nor did they offer a complete defence against virus transmission. As such, the UK government had launched regular campaigns encouraging Britons to come forward for Covid-19 booster vaccinations. These campaigns focussed in particular on those that were elderly or medically vulnerable and susceptible to falling sick and dying from the disease, and she thought of friends and family who she knew had already had multiple Covid-19 boosters.

She further noted the US Marine Corp Major's working hypothesis that SARS-CoV-WIV virus was not designed to kill but to immunise bats, which may explain why many people did not appear to contract the disease or were asymptomatic (save for the old and those with underlying health issues or some sort of genetic predisposition):[365]

> *...SARSr-CoV is not meant to kill the bats, but to immunize them. This nature may explain its general harmlessness to most people, and its harmfulness to the old and comorbid, who are in general more susceptible to vaccine reactions. The asymptomatic nature is also explained by the bat vaccine-intention of its creators (a good vaccine does not generate symptoms). Such effects would be expected of an immature vaccine, or a vaccine being reversed engineered from a more virulent form into an attenuated form. The spike protein effect on ACE2 receptors exacerbates the harmfulness in accordance with age and comorbidity.*

Overall, US Marine Corps Major Joseph Murphy's assessment of the manmade origins of Covid-19 was thought-provoking. The penultimate paragraph of his report also resonated with Susie as it posited that the Covid-19 outbreak might have been the result of an imprudent attempt to stop bats infecting humans at source on public health grounds, stating:[366]

> *...I arrived at a hypothesis that what leaked from the WIV could be a bat vaccine or its precursor. It was feasible that the US would try to avoid a SARS-CoV outbreak by stopping it at its source, not by halting its infection amongst people, but by halting the infections amongst the bats. Americans are creative, even if imprudent, and technologically confident enough to try it. This concept seemed to fit within the PREEMPT program construct as well, and DRASTIC had discovered that some earlier specimens within the USAID PREDICT program were obtained in Africa and sent to the WIV.*

13.5 Publication of Redacted Emails on Covid-19 Origins in January 2022

In mid-January 2022 came news and publication of a letter by James Comer, a member of the US Committee on Oversight and Reform, and Jim Jordan, a member of the US Committee on the Judiciary, raising further concerns and questions about what was known about the origins of Covid-19 in the early stages of the pandemic. An article in *The Intercept* on 12 January 2022 stated:[367]

> *...[It] paints a damning picture of U.S. government officials wrestling with whether the novel coronavirus may have leaked out of a lab they were funding, acknowledging that it may have, and then keeping the discussion from spilling out into public view.*
>
> *...[It] was followed by pages of notes on emails that*

were first obtained through the Freedom of Information Act by BuzzFeed News and the Washington Post, but were heavily redacted when published in June 2021. The redacted emails included the agenda for a February 1, 2020, telephone conference between National Institute of Allergy and Infectious Diseases director Anthony Fauci; his then-boss, former National Institutes of Health director Francis Collins; and several of the world's leading virologists. The communications contained extensive notes summarizing what was said during the call, but their substance was hidden at the time.

...On February 2, Jeremy Farrar, an infectious disease expert and the director of the Wellcome, sent around notes, including to Fauci and Collins, summarizing what some of the scientists had said on the call. Farzan, a Scripps professor who studied the spoke protein on the 2003 SARS virus, 'is bothered by the furin site and has a hard time explaining that as an event outside the lab (though, there are possible ways in nature, but highly unlikely)'... Farzan didn't think the site was the product of 'directed engineering', but found that the changes would be 'highly compatible with the idea of continued passage of the virus in tissue culture'.

...[Robert] Garry, a professor at the Tulane University School of Medicine, said on the call that he had aligned the SARS-CoV-2 genome with that of RaTG13, a 96-percent similar virus isolated from bats at the Wuhan Institute of Virology... Garry found that the spike proteins of RaTG13 and SARS-CoV-2, which makes the latter so infectious, were nearly identical. The key distinction was in the ability of the new virus's spike protein to interact with furin, which Garry found too perfect to make natural sense. "I just can't figure out how this gets accomplished in nature," he said.

Sitting back and reflecting on this, Susie wondered why all of these email communications had been redacted in the first place and what they were seeking to stop becoming public knowledge. She proceeded to ponder the transcribed notes of an email from Dr Ron Fouchier to the group of experts on 2 February 2020 which allegedly stated:[368]

> *Any accusation that nCoV-2019 might have been engineered and released into the environment by humans (accidental or intentional) would need to be supported by strong data, beyond a reasonable doubt. It is good that this possibility was discussed in detail with a team of experts. However, further debate about such accusations would unnecessarily distract top researchers from their active duties and do unnecessary harm to science in general and science in China in particular.*

Delving deeper into the redacted emails of the group of experts in 2020, Susie noted that they also discussed a BioRxiv preprint Indian paper from January 2020 [subsequently withdrawn] about the new coronavirus which alleged it had four inserts similar to the HIV-1 virus. In particular, she noted an email between Courtney Billet at the NIH/NIAID and Anthony Fauci on 2 February 2020 which stated:[369]

> *Re: Seeking comment on Indian paper about new Coronavirus*
>
> *FYI re the paper from the Indian researchers. Talk about trying to put the genie back in the bottle! Yeesh [Courtney Billet].*
>
> *Geeeez [Dr Anthony Fauci].*

The reference to '*trying to put the genie back in the bottle*' was an interesting choice of language and it made Susie pause for thought. Looking the phrase up for context, she noted that the Collins Dictionary defined the phrase as 'if you say that the genie is out of the bottle or that someone has let the genie out of the bottle, you mean that something has happened which has made a great and permanent change in people's lives, especially a bad change'. Following further internet research, she came across another definition in the Free Dictionary which defined the phrase as meaning 'to attempt to revert a situation to how it formerly existed by containing, limiting, or repressing information, ideas, advancements, etc., that have become commonplace or public knowledge'. Almost always used in the negative to denote the impossibility of such an attempt'. If this phrase had been used with these meanings in mind, then it might suggest that there had been some validity to the Indian paper. If so, it might also potentially suggest that it had been repressed and account for its swift withdrawal, albeit there was no clear evidence to indicate this, she mused.

Susie then pondered the forces at play in a note from the author, Prashant Pradhan, on the BioRxiv comment section quoted in the redacted email correspondence on 2 February 2020 from John Mascola at NIH/VRC to the expert group:[370]

> *This is a preliminary study. Considering the grave situation, it was shared in BioRxiv as soon as possible to have creative discussion on the fast evolution of SARS-like corona viruses. It was not our intention to feed into the conspiracy theories and no such claims are made here. While we appreciate the criticisms and comments provided by scientific colleagues at BioRxiv forum and elsewhere, the story has been differently interpreted and shared by social media and news platforms. We have positively received all criticisms and comments. To avoid*

further misinterpretation and confusions world-over, we have decided to withdraw the current version of the preprint and will get back with a revised version after reanalysis, addressing the comments and concerns.

The redacted email correspondence also included further internal exchange at the NIH/NIAD on 2 February 2020 between Barney Graham and Nissa Hiatt and Jennifer Routh:[371]

Re: Seeking comment on Indian paper about new Coronavirus

Hi Barney –

We consulted with HHS and ASF. OCGR is going to send a note to the reporter to decline, noting that the paper is not peer-reviewed. Please let us know if you receive similar requests.

Thanks,

Jen

The response from Barney Graham read:

Hi Nissa and Jen,

This is one we don't want to answer without high-level input, but wanted you to know about the rising controversy.

BG

This raised further questions in Susie's mind about why there was a reluctance to address the Indian preprint paper 'without high-level input' and to whom precisely that might pertain. She also came across further email correspondence on 2 February 2020 between Francis Collins (head of NIH) and Dr Anthony Fauci (head of NIAD):[372]

In case you haven't seen, attached is the Indian paper claiming HIV sequences have been inserted into 2019-nCoV, which has been roundly debunked.

I found Jon Cohen's piece in Science to be a pretty useful summary (Francis Collins).

The Indian paper is really outlandish. Agree about Jon Cohen's nice summary (Anthony Fauci).

Looking at Jon Cohen's article in *Science* on 31 January 2020 also made Susie ponder. The article asserted that SARS CoV-2 originated from a zoonotic animal-to-human spillover event. It also went on to quote, amongst others, Peter Daszak of the EcoHealth Alliance:[373]

Every time there's an emerging disease, a new virus, the same story comes out: This is a spillover or the release of an agent or a bioengineered virus. It's just a shame. It seems humans can't resist controversy and these myths, yet it's staring us right in the face. There's this incredible diversity of viruses in wildlife and we've just scratched the surface. Within that diversity, there will be some that can infect people and within that group will be some that cause illness.

Reflecting on her own research findings, and with the benefit of the passage of time over the subsequent two years, it seemed to Susie that there was now more evidence to support arguments that SARS CoV-2 might be a lab leak of a manmade gain-of-function virus and that HIV inserts might potentially be possible too (albeit this was not a mainstream view).

13.6 Genetic Modification Technology in Humans

Reflecting further in the weeks that followed, Susie decided to distil down her third PowerPoint presentation so that it encapsulated the high-level big picture as clearly as possible. If she could condense her thinking, it would make it easier to understand and communicate and it might make it more impactful if she subsequently shared it. She had covered so much ground and there was so much to say that it seemed like a herculean task. She sat back and paused as she slowly thought through strategy. Her legal training had taught her that the art of a good outcome was all in the preparation. This was no different, she told herself. She decided to focus on key emerging themes and actionable insights; a subtle but significant difference in approach. Her main aim was to try and capture the serious issues and challenges ahead so she could sit back and say she had done her bit. She did not want to look back in the months and years to follow and know deep down that she could have done more, should have done more, to address all that she had come to understand.

First, she boldly set out that genetic modification technology in humans was already in use and it was here to stay. It had the potential to be used for great good or harm; the 'dual-use dilemma'. This technology could increasingly be used to cure diseases and offer hope to many. It would increasingly enable us to move to preventative and precision medicine; a different healthcare model which promised better outcomes and better quality of life in the years ahead. However, it could also be used for darker and more dangerous purposes to create dangerous viruses, causing mass disruption and death or over time even potentially seek to genetically edit people to create so-called 'super humans' or even 'super soldiers'. As such, this technology had massive public health, national security and economic implications moving forward which needed close scrutiny and oversight.

13.7 Public Health, National Security and Economic Implications

Then she set out the risks that, moving forward, gene-editing technology could be used to create and aerosolise dangerous gain-of-function viruses with the capacity to cause widespread disruption and death. She highlighted the risks that this technology could, in the wrong hands, potentially be used to target specific cohorts of people, for example, particular ethnic groups or state populations. It also had the potential to be used as a means of targeting and assassinating specific individuals, including politicians, rulers, key workers and military personnel. She proceeded to lay out a potential scenario whereby rogue actors might potentially spray dangerous manmade and tailored viruses into air vents, air-conditioning and climate control systems or public buildings, airports, airplanes, trains, buses, cars and ferries to cause mass disruption, injury or, worse still, death. This was scary stuff, she thought.

She went on to highlight the risks that dangerous manmade and tailored viruses could potentially be attached to weapons and missiles. These could then potentially be used to attack armed forces' ships, bases and other strategic facilities. Added to this, they might also potentially be used to cause mass disruption of states as well as to cause massive economic loss, fear, illness, death, restrictions and distraction.

13.8 Genetic Modification: Virus Aerosolisation and HIV

Susie then went on to illustrate the potential risk posed by dangerous manmade aerosolised viruses with the following statements by an Italian reporter Paolo Barnard in a publication called *The Origin of the Virus,* following an investigation into the origins of the Covid-19 pandemic with two well-known scientists Professor Angus Dalgleish and Dr Steven Quay:[374] [375]

> *"I was telling people, I know enough about HIV that if I wanted to I could probably get HIV to infect through the airborne route." Professor Simon Wain-Hobson put it to me in this way... He's one of the world's top retrovirologists... a senior researcher at the Pasteur Institute in Paris.*
>
> *"...I thereby realized in that moment that scientists today can manipulate a virus like HIV in order to transform it into a mass pathogen which is much easier to transmit than it naturally would be."*
>
> *"...It is horrifying to imagine AIDS being transmissible like the flu."*

It made for uncomfortable and difficult reading, Susie thought. No one wanted to have to face these sorts of potential risks, but it was not good enough to simply stick one's head in the sand either. If scientists were aware and actively discussing this sort of potential application, it was important that it was communicated and understood by those leading and safeguarding nation states too.

13.9 Potential Wider Significance of Chinese Gene-Edited Children

Next, Susie started to address the potential wider significance of the three Chinese gene-edited babies born in China in November 2018 (twins Lulu and Nana) and a further baby (Amy) in 2019. Their genomes had been permanently genetically edited at the embryo stage with the intention of making them immune to HIV. In doing so, this world-first experiment was held to have crossed a red line by the global scientific community, having recklessly and permanently changed the babies' genomes before the technology was deemed sufficiently safe and accurate for such use.[376]

Moving on, she outlined that this real-life clinical experiment by Chinese scientist He Jiankui in 2018 could potentially be seen in different wider terms as well. Put simply, it was also possible to view it as an early incomplete proof-of-principle attempt to create genetically structurally altered humans that are virus and disease resistant by removing receptors enabling viruses to enter and replicate in cells in the human body; applicable not just to HIV but to other viruses which engage similar gene functionality (for example, taking into account the apparent correlation between CCR5 genetic functionality in HIV and Covid-19).

If genetic editing of the Chinese babies' genomes was looked at in wider proof-of-principle terms, it could also potentially represent an alternative way to seek to prevent or counter viruses and the onset of diseases; a fundamentally different approach to developing drugs or vaccines. Since many viruses adapt and mutate to evolve, survive and thrive, they can require annually updated vaccines to offer some level of protection on a continuous basis; as seen by the annual influenza vaccine rollouts or the repeated Covid-19 booster vaccines. Vaccines and drugs can be costly to develop, range in efficacy and take time to develop and update, giving many viruses the opportunity to get ahead, causing sickness, disruption and, in worst case scenario, death.

If the Chinese gene-edited babies affair was viewed more widely as a proof-of-principle experiment (albeit an early incomplete attempt), it potentially engaged complex issues over and above it simply being a reckless clinical experiment by a rogue scientist. Instead, it would then engage the 'dual-use dilemma' which accompanies human genome-editing technology. Firstly, it might potentially over time be used to prevent people contracting nasty viruses causing virulent diseases and help shift to precision and preventative medicine. But secondly, this approach might potentially have serious national security implications as well; potentially making genetic changes in people which could make them more or less susceptible to viruses and disease by removing or changing mechanisms in the human body which enable viruses to enter human cells and replicate. In other words, the creation of genetically modified humans could potentially prevent virulent disease (e.g. HIV), including gain-of-function viruses (with structural genetic modification) causing mass disruption or death. This would be a new and different approach from current vaccines and treatments used in treating non-genetically structurally altered human populations.

However, the Chinese gene-edited babies were not born fully immune to HIV; a virus which had proven notoriously difficult to cure. The issue was that the clinical experiment had not been entirely successful in gene editing terms in creating immunity to HIV, not least because there are multiple strains or variants of HIV. Professor Henry T Greely, Professor of Law and Professor by Courtesy of Genetics and Director of the Stanford Center for Law and the Biosciences at Stanford University, succinctly explained this in an article:[377]

> *CD4 cells are a type of T cell, white blood cells that fight infection and play other important roles in the immune system. They get their name from the CD4 protein they carry on the outside and the inside of their cell membranes. CD4 proteins serve as receptors for external molecules, like the proteins on a virus. CD4 cells appear to be the most crucial type of T cell for HIV infection and its progression to AIDS.*
>
> *Most HIV infections begin when the virus latches onto the CD4 protein on the surface of CD4-positive T cells. But for infection to occur, the virus also needs to attach itself to*

a second cell surface protein. This second protein is often CCR5, but it can also be another protein called CXCR4. When HIV is connected to both CD4 and one of the other receptors, it fuses into the cell.

The most common strain of HIV in humans, dubbed R5 HIV-1 (for the CCR5 receptor), appears to require CCR5 in order to infect CD4 cells. But another strain, called X-4 HIV-1, uses CXCR4 instead of CCR5. Some strains of X-4 HIV-1 can use either CCR5 or CXCR4. And the less common and less deadly strain known as HIV-2 uses many receptors in addition to CD4...

The bottom line is that the proteins made by the CCR5Δ32 gene variant that He [Jiankui] tried to create in Lulu and Nana do not necessarily prevent infection with HIV... CCR5Δ32 doesn't interfere with the ability of X-4 and some HIV-2 strains to infect CD4 cells...

My message here is that CCR5Δ32 does not guarantee immunity to HIV infection. It works only for strains of HIV-1 that use both the CD4 and CCR5 cell surface receptors to infect T cells. Even if the version of CCR5 that he gave Nana does indeed protect her, it would only be from infection with the R-5 strains of HIV — not from X-4 strains and also not from other variants that the virus will inevitably evolve."

By widening the terms of reference of the clinical experiment leading to the birth of the Chinese gene-edited babies, a more complex and nuanced situation was arguably produced. Added to this, it was quite possible that the Chinese scientist He Jiankui had laudable intentions in seeking to confer HIV immunity upon the babies. However, that did not necessarily rule out a potentially more serious and significant wider concept at play that fed into 'dual-use' technology by means of other actors with a different agenda.

News about the progress and development of the Chinese gene-edited babies also continued to be shrouded in secrecy in China. Whilst there were a few brief reports that they were doing well, there was little information and evidence with which to assess matters beyond that which had been shared publicly by He Jiankui prior to his prosecution and imprisonment. Given the global interest that continued to surround them and the significance of the circumstances of their conception and birth, this also raised issues and questions. Why was there so much secrecy and what were the reasons for this? Arguments that the children's privacy, along with that of their families, needed to be protected seemed insufficient. After all, further analysis and updates about their progress and development could be released on a non-identifying basis (even if full copies of their genomes could not be released without identifying them). Were the three Chinese gene-edited children being monitored as part of a secret ongoing Chinese study? Susie found it hard to believe they were not in some form of follow-up programme, given the Chinese State's continued push for biotechnology supremacy. The opportunity to monitor the development of the world's first gene-edited children and in particular observe whether the CCR5 gene edit made them more or less resistant to infectious diseases, or even cognitive enhancement, was arguably too important an opportunity to overlook, she pondered.

It was further potentially significant that the Wuhan Institute of Virology (WIV) genome database had remained inaccessible to the international scientific community since 12 September 2019. This continued to weigh on Susie's mind and left her feeling uneasy; it was another incident that simply did not pass the smell test. It was at the very least a further example of secrecy and lack of transparency, she thought soberly. Was it possible that this was done to protect Chinese genomic and virology research and development and potentially dual-use technology initiatives? Was it also possible that it might have been done as part of a clean-up or even a cover-up operation by the Chinese authorities concerning the emergence of the Covid-19 pandemic?

13.10 Chinese Genomic Military-Civil Fusion

Highlighting another aspect, she set out that China has adopted a national strategy of military-civil fusion in biotechnology.[378] This created an even more complex and nuanced picture as China is at the forefront of breakthroughs in CRISPR-Cas gene editing.[379] This could be construed in terms of responses to threats of infectious diseases. It was also potentially possible that it extended to military applications seeking to obtain biological dominance in future warfare (new methods of confrontation). If this was the case, it could potentially include the creation of new synthetic pathogens which are more toxic, contagious and resistant, leveraging supercomputing for processing large-scale genetic information and human enhancement.[380]

Added to this, reports from US intelligence suggested that China has conducted 'human testing' on members of the People's Liberation Army in the hope of developing soldiers with 'biologically enhanced capabilities', according to John Ratcliffe, the Director of National Intelligence (December 2020).[381] [382] Susie went on to explain that the distinction between offensive and defensive bioweapons research is subtle.[383] Even a relatively benign pathogen could become a bioweapon if one party has conferred immunity to its population and an opponent has not.[384]

As such, Susie explained that genetic databases have national security implications. This is because knowledge of the DNA profile of a country's population could potentially lead to the development of disease pathogens specifically targeted at genetic vulnerabilities amongst its citizens.[385] It was also only a matter of time before DNA collection became a standard part of the biometric data collected by countries from foreign visitors, which was an added nebulous issue that needed to be considered carefully.[386]

13.11 Genetic Modification: SARS-CoV-2 and HIV Inserts

Moving on, Susie set out that there was now some evidence suggesting that SARS-CoV-2 had HIV-type genetic inserts as well as a furin cleavage genomic insert which made it more virulent, transmissible and able to mutate in humans (a gain-of-function virus) and which challenged vaccines whose efficacy wanes over time. She went on to explain that when working with dual-use biotechnology that could potentially be deployed on a defensive/offensive basis, the aims include understanding and/or developing (1) a virus/potential bioweapon and (2) a vaccine or mechanism to prevent/counter this. However, as conventional vaccines could not yet cure HIV, a different approach was required. If this line of thinking had merit, then it might potentially widen the significance of the Chinese gene-edited babies in 2018–19. They might then have potentially been the subject of early incomplete proof-of-concept attempts to genetically structurally alter them to be resistant to HIV and other diseases by changing CCR5 functionality present in approximately 10% of Caucasian populations.

Susie then proceeded to set out that BLAST is the NCBI/NIH (US government) repository for genomic sequences.[387] She referenced an article which ran through the BLAST database four alleged sequences in SARS-CoV-2 viral genome which had been laid out in an early pre-print scientific paper, *Uncanny similarity of unique inserts in the 2019-nCoV spike protein to HIV-1 gp120 and Gag* (published 31 Jan 2020), a few days after the genome sequence was released and then swiftly withdrawn.[388] The article reported that the results from the BLAST database showed matches to synthetic viruses from post-Covid and RaTG13 (added to the BLAST database post-Covid). It went on to report that the only remaining virus listed was HIV-1. The article then questioned the odds that HIV-1 would appear in all three searches.[389] The article further asserted that these three alleged genomic inserts – which it stated were all from HIV – were all at binding sites of the coronavirus and were in addition to a fourth genomic insert (a furin cleavage site) that does not appear to exist in nature.[390]

A follow-up article by the same author went on to say that the HIV-Gp-120 genome inserts were all located at the outermost strategic points in the whole SARS-CoV-2 viral spike.[391] The article stated that this was significant because it suggested (1) that this was a non-random event and (2) it was likely to help bypass T-cell immunity. The article asserted that it was specifically designed with fragments cut in, or passaged, to pick them up. It went on to state that the binding sites were part of the mechanism that HIV-1 uses to bypass the immune system and gain entry to the cells that keep the human immune system working (T-cells).[392] The article added that running these Gp-120 genome inserts through the BLAST database showed that they did not match any viruses fully and the closest match was to HIV-1.[393] Furthermore, the article said that the function of these inserts – that did not exist before 2019 in any coronavirus – was clearly stated as the intention of the DARPA DEFUSE proposal by EcoHealth Alliance in 2018.[394]

Susie then highlighted some reported unexpected findings about SARS-CoV-2 and its association with HIV by UK scientist Professor Angus Dalgleish:[395]

...Its Spike Proteins have inserted sequences which are structurally similar to other types of Spikes found on the surface of the HIV virus, that causes AIDS. How can this have happened in a bat coronavirus that is so distant from the HIV retrovirus? It is important to be aware that HIV proviruses were used in 2010 by Zheng-Li Shi and her colleagues at the Wuhan Laboratories in experiments aiming at selecting among bat coronaviruses those that learnt to best infect human cells through the ACE-2 receptors, a feature that closely suggests other isolates were part of the Gain of Function (GOF) experiments at the WIV...

...The SARS-CoV-2 Spike protein has clear evidence of inserts containing amino acids like Arginine which were 'built' with highly unusual 'instructions' for coronaviruses and which have been associated with enhanced pathogenicity in other pathogens, such as the 1997 H7N1 Hong Kong flu. In addition, these inserts carry positive charges that, together with inserts homologous to components of the HIV virus, enable SARS-COV-2 to latch onto negatively charged human cells' membranes via the so called extra-Arginine 'bridges', entirely bypassing the use of specific ACE receptors. In conclusion, these SARS-COV-2 Spike Proteins have a very high charge with an isoelectric point of 8.24 compared with only 5.67 for the 2003 SARS Spike Proteins. This extra electric charge could explain the extreme pathogenicity seen with Covid-19.[396]

Inserts are not uncommon either but the SARS-Cov-2 ones have been ignored as not unexpected when it is not at all a foregone conclusion. The fact that these contain HIVgp120 sequences which are used in experiments as a retroviral vector to insert ACE2 receptors in different

> *cells (and also to enable the extra-Arginine 'bridges' as previously explained) was brushed over by saying they could have occurred by chance, when in fact they are well-known GOF techniques and should have run alarm bells.*[397]

Susie then proceeded to point out that this genomic analysis raised a number of issues and questions that warranted further analysis to help determine its strength and validity. If this genomic assessment was correct, then it was potentially indicative that the Covid-19 virus was a manmade gain-of-function virus that escaped or was released and not a zoonotic spillover event from nature.

13.12 Origins of SARS-CoV-2 and Events in Wuhan During Last Quarter of 2019

There were also further indications that SARS-CoV-2 might potentially be a gain-of-function virus and the result of a potential lab release (not a zoonotic spillover event), whose first epicentre was in Wuhan, China in the last quarter of 2019. Susie set out that there were some additional accounts which indicated that it was potentially possible that the emergence of SARS-Cov-2 happened earlier than first thought, somewhere between September and November 2019 (and even possibly in August 2019 as suggested by Marine Corps Major Joseph Murphy in his report dated August 2021). If so, it might have coincided in Wuhan with certain events. Firstly, it might have coincided with the removal of the Wuhan Institute of Virology's (WIV) genomic database on 12 September 2019, raising questions about whether this was coincidental or an intentional act. Secondly, it might potentially have coincided with the Seventh World Military Games held in Wuhan from 18–27 October 2019, where military athletes reportedly fell ill. These military games included 10,000 competitors who competed from over one hundred countries, and this might then potentially have been the virus' first super-spreader event.

There were some reports that there was no mobile (cell phone) activity in a high-security portion of the Wuhan Institute of Virology from 7–24 October 2019, which might indicate a 'possible hazardous event' sometime between 6 and 11 October.[398] In addition, there were reports that Wuhan, a city of 11 million, appeared closed down during the Military Games: empty markets, few pedestrians, only a handful of cars on the road, closure of local business and manufacturing. Furthermore, on 11 October 2019, the Fuze Science and Technology Park in Wuhan's Qiaokou district reportedly received a notice from the district government demanding it suspend production in all its factories for half a month during the Military World Games. Moreover, on 15 October 2019, over one hundred factories in the park were reportedly closed.[399] During the Military Games, it was also reported that all residents living below the twelfth floor in the two buildings facing the stadium were evacuated, and their windows sealed. Hotels nearby were all closed, and the gas supply turned off for one month.[400] There were also reports that the Wuhan government banned all non-motor vehicles from the streets ahead of the Games, as well as shutting down the Xinhua General Market and a meat processing company nearby on the pretext of 'substandard fire control measures'.[401]

13.13 Future of Human Genetic Modification

Susie also concluded that assisted reproductive technology and its use in laboratories or fertility clinics was now at the frontier of human genetic modification. Pre-conception genetic structural modification of humans potentially represented a new and different way to seek to prevent disease and health problems from occurring, although fundamental questions remained about its safety and efficacy. She then went on to ask whether western democracies were doing enough as a result of this rapidly evolving technology to address what was happening in other authoritarian places around the world, including in China.

It was a positive step that the UK government had recently announced that £800 million of taxpayer funds would be deployed to fund a new Advanced Research and Invention Agency (Aria), modelled on the US Defense Advanced Research Projects Agency (DARPA). It would partly focus on genomic research and it would not be subject to freedom of information interest requests.[402] It was also noteworthy that in 2019, DARPA announced that it had invested over US$65 million (£45 million) to improve the safety and accuracy of genome-editing technologies.[403]

Susie proceeded to finesse her latest PowerPoint presentation over the following few days. It brought her research and analysis up to date and distilled down and built upon the content of her previous two presentations. She felt some relief, having committed what was in her head to her computer screen. The question now was whether she should pluck up the courage to send it to Andrew, her point of contact for the security services. Having come this far, she figured it was probably worth sending it on to them. What was the worst that could happen? she asked herself. With that, she picked up the telephone and called Andrew's telephone number. He answered and, following a short discussion, it was agreed that she would send it over. Having finally pressed send on her computer keypad and watched her email and attached PowerPoint presentation disappear from sight, she sat back in her chair and heaved a sigh of relief. It was sent. She had followed through and passed on her analysis and that was realistically all she was in a position to do. She pushed back her chair to stretch her legs, picked up her mug and wandered into the kitchen to find and feed Rina and decide what to have for dinner.

She also continued to keep an eye out for further information and articles about the origins of the Covid-19 pandemic in her limited spare time. After all her research and analysis, it was just difficult to switch off and focus her mind on other things. Following yet another late-night internet surfing session, she came across an article entitled *The Myth of the Blind Watchmaker* by Charles Rixey.[404] Charles Rixey was a member of DRASTIC, an independent group of researchers from around the world who worked together with the aim of discovering the origins of Covid-19 and addressing associated issues. As such, she took careful note because it represented further potential evidence that SARS-CoV-2 had HIV genetic inserts. It was a hard-hitting article which went on to allege that the HIV inserts were known amongst senior officials from very early on in the pandemic, as far back as January 2020:[405]

> *...They knew instantly that the discovery of HIV spike inserts within the SAR-CoV-2 viral genome [set out in a pre-print research paper on 31 January 2020 entitled 'Uncanny similarity of unique inserts in the 2019-nCoV spike to HIV-1 gp120 and Gag' and withdrawn shortly thereafter] made it impossible for the virus to be natural; mixing elements of HIV-1's spike protein with CoV sequences and/or backbones has been part of HIV-1/CoV vaccine research since at least 2006 [at least 2007 for the WIV, and at least as recently as 2018]. They knew about the Furin cleavage site [FCS] – the single biggest genomic contributor to SARS-CoV-2s ability to become a pandemic virus.*

Susie was conscious, however, that this was not the mainstream view and that it encompassed serious allegations that had yet to be fully aired and debated. It left her feeling more unsettled than ever.

Chapter 14

Autumn 2022–Winter 2023

The end of summer and the arrival of autumn 2022 seemed to pass in a bit of a blur for Susie. It had been an unseasonably long hot summer, bringing many social distractions and opportunities to catch up with family and friends. Her legal work proceeded briskly until the beginning of August, when it slowed down a little for the month, providing some welcome breathing space. It had been a fast-paced year and one that had brought its fair share of surprises. She knew more about world events and had joined up even more dots along the way. It was still strange to see things slowly play out in the news, given all that she had learnt over the last few years. It was unsettling, she thought ruefully as she watched the reports and the heated debates unfold. She wondered what would happen next and whether the world at large would ever really get to the bottom of the origins of the Covid-19 pandemic. Life pre-pandemic seemed just a distant memory now, and the pace of change was fast and furious, which continued to bring its own opportunities and challenges.

14.1 International Genomics Summit in Las Vegas

Over the next few days, she came across an article which promoted a new international genomics summit in Las Vegas. It caught her attention as much as anything because of the calibre of speakers, which included Barack Obama and Bill Gates as well as a string of other highly accomplished scientists, medics, technology experts and policymakers. *Wow,* thought Susie; that promised to be quite some event. As she sat back in her office chair and sipped at her mug of Earl Grey tea, it crossed her mind that perhaps she should try and attend this summit. It would be absolutely fascinating, she told herself, and quite unlike anything else she had been to in the past. It would give her the opportunity to listen first-hand to what these important and influential people had to say at the cutting edge of the rapidly evolving genomic field. It would also enable her to meet some new people and plug into the genomic space in a new way. She took another sip of tea as she mulled things over further. It was certainly a bold move and something very different from her usual sector events. On the other hand, it was a long way to travel to and she would not know anybody when she got there. She would also have to fit her legal work round it. She could not decide and, with a sigh, she turned her attention to her emails, and the rest of the day's work took over.

However, she could not get the possibility of attending the genomics summit out of her head, despite her best efforts, over the next few days. It looked so interesting, and the lure of listening to such prominent leaders and experts in the field was very enticing. It would also be a good learning opportunity, she told herself, and would build on her understanding of genomics, which was an added benefit. With that, she took another look at the conference website and concluded that it looked incredibly well organised. She sat back in her chair to ponder matters. She could not get rid of a nagging voice in the back of her mind telling her to just do it and go. After all, when was she likely to have the opportunity to do something like this again?

On the spur of the moment, and very uncharacteristically, she decided to take a chance and go for it. With that, she decisively took her credit card from her purse and made a booking through the conference website as an in-person attendee before she changed her mind. Then she called her friendly local travel agent, Martin, to book her flights. Next, she called the conference hotel direct to book a room at the block-booked discount rate. There, she was going, she thought, subject to getting her ESTA visa status renewed. She hoped that getting a new ESTA would not prove to be a problem, given all that had happened over the last couple of years. She speedily completed her ESTA application online and submitted it, hoping for the best. Then she got up and ambled into the kitchen and out onto the patio, to find Rina lolling about in a flowerbed soaking up the last of the summer sun.

A few hours later, Susie received email confirmation that her ESTA had been approved. There, she was definitely going, she thought with a smile. It was all booked and there was no going back now. This would be her first in-person conference since before the pandemic, and she would need to prepare herself for being with around 2,500 people for the first time in a long time. It would also be her first trip to the US for a few years, given all the pandemic disruption the world had encountered. She rechecked the conference website and started to read the Covid-19 safety guidelines. They were quite strict, which was both daunting and reassuring. She guessed that all of the headline speakers and heavy-hitting attendees would not want to get sick if they could possibly help it. First, she needed to upload her proof of Covid-19 vaccination. Then on arrival at the conference she needed to undergo onsite Covid-19 testing with their in-house medical team. She just had to hope she passed that test after travelling all that way, she thought soberly. It would be very disappointing to get there only to find she had contracted Covid-19 and was then ineligible to attend, she thought. She also wondered whether all of these safety arrangements would soon be a thing of the past, confined to the pandemic and its aftermath, or whether this was a sign of things to come as everyone seemed to be so much more safety-conscious these days. As she read on, she learnt that after passing the Covid-19 health screening she could register for the conference and she would then be furnished with a digital pass which would give her access to the conference venue. It all sounded quite strict, but then again she imagined security would be tight, given the important line-up of speakers and attendees. She also noticed a heavyweight IT specialist pop up on her LinkedIn account a couple of days later, and she told herself that this was probably because she had just registered for the summit; they were likely doing some online due diligence and vetting of the delegates.

A few weeks before she was due to fly out to Las Vegas, it suddenly dawned on her that she had better check her wardrobe and make sure she had suitable clothes for the trip. She needed to feel comfortable but look smart as well. Looking through her work clothes, most of them looked quite dull, in muted colours suitable for life at court. They were also getting on a bit, having hung around in her wardrobe since before the pandemic. She felt a sudden urge to brighten things up and she decided to try and buy a couple of new outfits with a bit of colour. She knew, however, that this was easier said than done. She was not great at online shopping and her size acted against her too; there was much less choice when you were looking for petite clothing. As a result, clothes shopping was usually a bit of a palaver. With that, she gritted her teeth and fired up her laptop to check women's clothing sites. After what seemed like ages, she managed to order a small batch of clothes from a petite clothing range and she completed an online purchase and hoped for the best. Even if just some of the stuff fitted, that would be great.

In the rest of the run-up to her trip, she worked hard to get through her workload. She booked Rina into her favourite cattery; the one with personal heaters and double-glazed windows overlooking country views. She checked her travel insurance and ordered some US dollars so she had cash for taxis and other things, just in case. Rina knew she was going away, having spotted her suitcase in the spare room. She had caught her scowling and jumping in it to give it a suspicious sniff, and she felt a pang of guilt knowing Rina was going to be locked up whilst she was away. She checked the fridge and ran down the rest of her fresh food supplies, making sure she left nothing perishable. She also let Tony and Emilia know her travel dates, so they could keep an eye on her house in her absence; that was very much the village way.

Her flight to Las Vegas came round quickly, not least because she had booked fairly last minute. It was strange to transit through Terminal 3 at Heathrow, and the whole experience was fairly brutal; noisy, busy, fast-paced and grubby. She much preferred travelling from Terminal 5. It was a relief when she hit the passenger waiting areas after a brief wander round the duty-free shops. Then, she boarded the plane for the long flight, vowing to sleep as much as she could on the way. Luckily, the flight was not full and so it was reasonably quiet.

On arrival in Las Vegas, Susie hopped into a taxi and made her way over to the conference hotel. It was enormous, with a grand atrium and wall-to-wall marble. As she walked over to the reception area to check in, she looked round to begin to get her bearings. Instantly, she noticed what looked like security men by the entrances and by the escalators leading up to the first floor. She supposed that was inevitable, given the speaker line-up, particularly when it included a former US president. It took a while to complete all of the check-in procedures and she was relieved when she finally received her room key and was directed to her room on the seventh floor. It would be good to freshen up, get changed and take a short nap before dinner.

Feeling somewhat refreshed later that evening, she decided to venture out for a meal. She wandered through the cavernous gaming lounges, noting the lack of windows and clocks, designed to help people lose track of time, she thought. She stepped outside and was hit by a front of hot air, hotter than she expected, given the time of day. She then took a short stroll down the main strip, taking in the sights along the way, stopping to enjoy the famous water and fountains display at the Bellagio Hotel. She quite enjoyed the anonymity of being here, amongst the noisy throngs of tourists, and she felt excited about the conference agenda for the following day. With that, she found what she hoped was a good Italian restaurant for a light meal. The food was good, surprisingly good. The waiter was attentive and friendly and the atmosphere in the restaurant was happy and relaxed. A relaxing end to the evening, she thought, as she slowly made her way back to her hotel and up to her room on the seventh floor, where she fell asleep quickly after her long-distance flight in a large comfortable bed.

The next morning, she woke up early and made her way down to the conference to get the Covid-19 onsite testing done. The results took about an hour or so to come through, so she found a coffee shop in the hotel lobby and treated herself to a hot drink and a pastry. As she came to the end of her large mug of Earl Grey tea, she was pleased to receive an email confirming that she had tested negative for Covid-19 and that she was now cleared to register for the conference. That was a big relief, as she had been waiting nervously. She got up quickly and made her way over to the large registration area on the first floor, passing more security guards and a sniffer dog on her way. Security was tight and you could see they were on alert, she thought. Having registered digitally, she received her conference pass with a lanyard bearing her name and a personalised QR code, which she thought was all quite high tech compared with the sort of events she was used to attending back in the UK. It was not long before she noticed that the security guards relaxed a little once they saw her conference pass, meaning she was a bona fide delegate.

The conference area was light, spacious and well planned. There were lots of seating areas, inspiring boards and banners to look at, and even a whole sweet station where you could stock up on snacks for the conference sessions. She was struck by how friendly everyone was and how easy it was to get chatting with people. People were clearly here to network. She had not expected to feel so welcome amongst such a different crowd and it lifted her spirits even further. There was a full conference schedule and it was not long before she was whisked through to the large conference arena for the main opening event. She was intrigued by the buzz and sense of energy in the room, fuelled by high-tech lighting and upbeat music. The main sponsor delivered an inspiring speech about the power of genetics and how genome sequencing was going to be a game changer from a healthcare perspective, not least in the fight against cancer. Looking down at the conference schedule on the conference app on her phone, she noted with some anticipation that Barack Obama was due to speak that afternoon.

During the breakout session, she did her best to mingle with the other attendees. She got talking to some ladies who specialised in genomic sequencing at a local university laboratory. Then she met a genomic technology company owner and then she got chatting with an investor from London who was looking to add to his billion-pound investment portfolio and ride the genomic technology wave. The rest of the morning session passed quickly and before she knew it she was busy having lunch, queuing at one of the multiple food stations round the outside pool overlooking the Las Vegas skyline. The food was hot and the choice was good, and she was careful not to eat too much as this tended to make her sleepy and she wanted to be wide awake to hear from Barack Obama.

Following lunch, everyone filed back into the main conference arena, where there was an informative session on using genomic sequencing to detect, prevent and cure cancer at an earlier stage to improve prognosis and outcomes. As the session came to a close, a group of security guards suddenly moved in. Then a short announcement followed that the doors to the mainstage area would remain closed and everyone needed to stay in their seats ahead of the arrival of Barack Obama. As she adjusted to the enhanced security measures, she looked round and could sense a palpable level of excitement and anticipation amongst the attendees. A few minutes later, the lights dipped and the audience started to clap as Barack Obama walked out waving and smiling before settling himself into an armchair in the middle of the stage.

Susie found Barack Obama's session fascinating. He spoke engagingly about what it was like to live and work in the White House and the demands of being President of the United States of America. He proceeded to discuss leadership and the importance of bringing people along to get work done and effect change. He was also optimistic in his outlook about the power and promise that genomic technology offered, peppering his conversation with family anecdotes and speaking openly about the impact of losing one of his own relatives to cancer. It was great to see him in action. He was polished, slick and professional in his delivery. You could see he was used to public speaking and engaging with large crowds. He also came across as very human, and it was uplifting and inspiring to see such a positive ambassador for genomic science and medicine.

Following Barack Obama's session, she was glad there was a coffee break as she needed to stretch her legs and grab a snack to top up her blood sugars. Jet lag was a funny thing, she thought, as she realised she was still adjusting to the time difference. Whilst she was standing by one of the hot drinks stations waiting to make a cup of tea, she turned to her side and got talking with the two men next to her. They were friendly and explained that they worked for the main company sponsoring the event; one said he was a chief operating officer and the other said he was responsible for strategy and global market affairs. They were smartly dressed, probably in their forties or early fifties, and conversation flowed easily. They were interested to learn more about what she did and what had motivated her to come from the UK to attend the event. She explained that she was a life sciences lawyer and that she had a special interest in genomics and its interplay with health and the fertility space. They nodded attentively, saying they were interested to hear her thoughts on the fertility sector in particular. Meeting their eyes and smiling, Susie explained that much of the focus so far had been on using genomics to start to move from healthcare to health design. This was a good thing, she added hastily, in that it offered new ways of diagnosing and treating rare diseases and identifying and preventing cancer. It promised a whole new way of managing health and it was exciting to see the advances that had already been made and what people were doing right now to make this happen. She added that the event was really inspiring and that it was great to see so many leaders and subject experts take the lead in bringing about change.

She went on to say that she also wanted to see greater use of genomic technology in the fertility space. Over time, and with the advent of more effective technological advances, there were opportunities to offer more options before starting a family too, including: genetic screening of prospective parents to identify disease risk, greater accuracy in genomic screening of embryos and genomic medicine applications for gametes and embryos. She added that she appreciated the sensitivities around this and that it came with social, ethical and legal issues too. However, this technology would increasingly over time provide more opportunities to enable the birth of healthy babies. It would increasingly reduce the risks of serious disease from the point of pre-conception and the biological roulette associated with natural conception as well. She continued that it was an important conversation and one that she appreciated was not easy. People held strong views both for and against, but raising awareness and enabling people to make informed choices and use this technology judiciously had its benefits.

She then explained to the two men that there were other reasons for needing to think carefully about the use of genomic technology in the fertility space. She mentioned the birth of the Chinese gene-edited babies in 2018 and the attempt that had been made to edit their embryos pre-conception to make them resistant to HIV. She explained that these births had already happened and that the significance and implications of this clinical experiment had yet to be fully appreciated. She added that it was important to think about the potential risks of this technology being used recklessly and for nefarious purposes in future. It was therefore important to ensure there was effective regulation and governance too at nation state and international levels. She added that thought needed to be given to appropriate sharing of research and development and technological advances too. At this point, she noticed the two men's countenance change and that their body language had become discernibly tense. She also caught a look of concern flash briefly across one of the men's faces. They pressed her further and she found herself flagging concerns about the collection and use of personal genomic information, rapid advances in gene editing and the 'dual-use' genomic technology dilemma that was playing out particularly in the study of viruses, so-called gain-of-function virology and vaccine design and use. She went on explain how so much of what was happening around us was connected to genomic technology and how the Covid-19 pandemic had increased the rate of change and uptake and application of this technology exponentially. There was still much work to be done to adapt to this rapidly evolving landscape and the opportunities and threats, power, wealth and influence promised by genomic technology. She added that the lack of clarity around the origins of the Covid-19 pandemic was also cause for continued concern, leaving the world's populations exposed to future viral outbreaks and pandemics.

Susie's turn came to make a cup of tea at the drinks station and as she busied herself for a few moments, she noted in her peripheral vision that the two men were talking quietly together. She turned back to them to explain that she was going to return to her seat in the mainstage arena so that she could get a good view for Bill Gates' upcoming talk. They nodded, giving her an intense stare as they did so. Their manner suddenly seemed a bit off, she thought, as she slowly wound her way back to her seat, not wanting to spill her hot drink over her new dress. She wondered briefly if something she had said had hit a bit of a nerve, but there was not much time to dwell on this as the rest of the day's agenda kicked back in with a swing. People were excited to hear from the highly successful billionaire Bill Gates too, she thought. The atmosphere was energised again as people bundled in to take their seats, albeit just a little bit less so than in the lead-up to Barack Obama, she thought.

The rest of the summit passed quickly, too quickly as far as Susie was concerned. It had been great to take some time out from her busy life in the UK and soak up all that was on offer at this event. She had met some really interesting people and listened to some fascinating talks about things like the Galleria test, which was a new multi-cancer early detection test that could detect a common cancer signal across more than fifty types of cancer through a simple blood draw. The Galleria test had really grabbed her attention and she hoped it would soon be available more widely in the UK beyond the current clinical trial.

She therefore had mixed feelings when it was finally time to make her way back to the airport for her flight home. She was glad she had attended this world-leading event and it had given her much to think about. She was, however, looking forward to getting home, collecting Rina from the cattery and sleeping in her own bed again. The British Airways flight was long, although as it was overnight she was able to get some sleep, which helped. As the plane landed smoothly at Heathrow, she looked round to see the familiar tired and weary looks on her fellow travellers' faces. Travelling was hard, she thought, unless you were pampered in Business or First Class. She gathered her belongings together and steadily followed the passengers ahead of her to passport control. It felt good to be back on home territory, knowing that in a couple of hours' time she would be home. Having cleared border control and eventually collecting her suitcase, she made her way over to valet parking to collect her car. Valet parking was a lifesaver after a long-haul overnight flight, she thought. She collected her keys and made her way to her car. Having put her suitcases in the boot, she sat down in the driver's seat, needing to adjust it to shorten the legroom; a giant of a person had clearly been driving her car, she thought with a smile. She then adjusted the rear-view mirror and carefully drove home, taking care not to exceed the multiple different speed limits along the way, courtesy of various roadworks.

14.2 US Energy Department Assessment in February 2023

By late February 2023, Susie had taken note of further developments in the news about the origins of the Covid-19 pandemic. News broke that the US Department of Energy had assessed, albeit with 'low confidence', that the origins of the Covid-19 pandemic were the result of a lab leak in China. Susie read with interest a CNN article which reported:[406]

> *...Intelligence agencies can make assessments with either low, medium or high confidence. A low confidence assessment generally means the information obtained is not reliable enough or is too fragmented to make a more definitive analytic judgment or that there is not enough information available to draw a more robust conclusion.*
>
> *The latest assessment furthers adds to the divide in the US government over whether the Covid-19 pandemic began in China in 2019 as the result of a lab leak or whether it emerged naturally. The various intelligence agencies have been split on the matter for years. In 2021, the intelligence community declassified a report that showed four agencies in the intelligence community had assessed with low confidence that the virus likely jumped from animals to humans, whilst one assessed with moderate confidence that the pandemic was the result of a laboratory accident.*
>
> *Three other intelligence community elements were unable to coalesce around either explanation without additional information.*

The article went on to report that a Chinese spokesman disputed the findings of the US Department of Energy stating that a lab leak was highly unlikely and that:[407]

The parties concerned should stop stirring up arguments about laboratory leaks, stop smearing China and stop politicizing the issue of the virus origin.

A news report in the *Wall Street Journal* the day before, 26 February 2023, provided further commentary that:[408]

The shift by the Energy Department, which previously was undecided on how the virus emerged, is noted in an update to a 2021 document by Director of National Intelligence Avril Haines's Office.

...The Energy Department now joins the Federal Bureau of Investigation in saying the virus likely spread via a mishap at a Chinese laboratory. Four other agencies, along with a national intelligence panel, still judge that it was likely the result of a natural transmission, and two are undecided.

...The FBI previously came to the conclusion that the pandemic was likely the result of a lab leak in 2021 with 'moderate confidence' and still holds this view. The FBI employs a cadre of microbiologists, immunologists and other scientists and is supported by the National Bioforensic Analysis Center, which was established at Fort Detrick, Md., in 2004 to analyze anthrax and other possible biological threats.

As such, there was still no official consensus about the origins of the Covid-19 pandemic over three years since it first emerged in Wuhan, China in December 2019. Susie wondered if this might in part be due to political reasons, for fear of what might have to be said or done should the origins of the pandemic and any associated liability become clear. Was it from a pragmatic perspective just too much of a 'hot potato' that no one wanted to touch?

14.3 BGI Units Added to US Sanctions List, March 2023

Then came further news reports that the Biden administration had levied further trade sanctions against China. A news report by Reuters reported:[409]

> *The Biden administration on Thursday added 37 companies to a trade blacklist, including units of Chinese genetics company BGI and Chinese cloud computing firm Inspur, in a move that promises to further ratchet up tensions with Beijing.*
>
> *The Commerce Department, which oversees export controls, added BGI Research and BGI Tech Solutions (Hongkong) over allegations that the units pose a 'significant risk' to contributing to Chinese government surveillance.*
>
> *The actions of these entities concerning the collection and analysis of genetic data present a significant risk of diversion to China's military programs.*
>
> *Reuters previously reported BGI was collecting genetic data from millions of women for sweeping research on the traits of populations, and collaborates with China's military.*
>
> *Also listed was BGI's forensics subsidiary, Forensics Genomics International.*

An article in the *Independent* added further context, stating:[410]

> *Three BGI units were among Chinese companies added to an 'entity list' last week that limits access to U.S. technology on security or human rights grounds. The Commerce Department cited a risk BGI technology might contribute to surveillance. Activists say Beijing is trying to create a database of genetic information from Muslims and other Chinese minorities.*

> *...The 'entity list' designation requires BGI Research, Forensic Genomics International and BGI Tech Solutions (Hongkong) Co., Ltd. to obtain government permission to acquire sensitive U.S. Technology.*

As such, the biopolitical landscape seemed as complex, if not more complex, than ever, Susie thought. US-China tensions were still running high, and the US' latest decision to sanction units of Chinese genomics company BGI indicated that it continued to be concerned about Chinese genomic activity and surveillance practices on both security and human rights grounds. Susie also wondered whether security grounds might have been the larger of the motivating factors at play.

14.4 The Third International Summit on Human Genome Editing, 6–8 March 2023

Events at the Third International Summit on Human Genome Editing from 6–8 March 2023, held at the Francis Crick Institute in London, also made Susie ponder matters further. It was convened by the UK Royal Society, UK Academy of Medical Sciences, US National Academies of Sciences and Medicine and the World Academy of Sciences. In its closing statement, it set out that its aim in holding the event was to:[411]

> *...Discuss progress, promise, and challenges in research, regulation, and equitable development of human genome editing technologies and therapies.*

The summit took place as a hybrid event, with around 400 in-person attendees from the global scientific, academic, medical and policymaker communities, with a further 1,600 individuals attending online.[412] Day one of the conference included a variety of sessions, starting with a session 'Regulation in

China following the 2018 clinical misuse of Heritable Human Genome Editing'. The two Chinese speakers determinedly delivered updates stressing the extent of the measures China had taken to introduce regulation of gene-editing technology since the Chinese gene-edited babies affair in 2018 and strongly condemned the scientific practices of Chinese scientist He Jiankui. However, concerns remained about China's attempts to regulate gene-editing practices. Dr Joy Zhang of Kent University, a speaker at the summit and an expert on the governance of gene editing in China, raised concerns about Chinese securitisation of biotechnology and how it had become a matter of national sovereignty and national security, limiting international collaborations and overseas involvement. She added that China was planning to govern this area by restricting the flow of knowledge and governing through a nationalistic lens, which was causing global concerns. She went on to say that China was also focusing on ethics, but ethical governance in practice was still confined to traditional methods, and it did not sufficiently cover entrepreneurs and the private sector. She proceeded to comment in a BBC News report that:[413]

> *My biggest concern is that the new measures fail to cover a chronic and increasing problem in trying to deal with private ventures that are taking place outside of conventional scientific institutes.*
>
> *The new rules may struggle to keep up with the burgeoning innovation that is happening in China.*
>
> *...I, like many people, had been wondering whether there had been an individual or institution in China that had been backing or protecting He Jiankui.*
>
> But she said that she now thought that *we are looking at a simple case of regulatory negligence.*
>
> That led her to believe that *without getting*

> *clarifications on Dr He's case, the recent talk of good governance is hypocritical.*
>
> *I worry less about* [what] *He Jiankui is up to and more about* [what] *the Chinese authorities are doing.*

The same BBC News report further reported that:[414]

> *The summit organiser, Professor Robin Lovell-Badge from the Crick Institute, where the meeting is being held, said he was concerned that there was still too much secrecy in Chinese research.*
>
> *"I understand why China wants to be leaders in technology, but there are some areas that require special attention and gene editing is one of them," he said. "It has to be done properly and with the appropriate governance and oversight, and I'm concerned that they are not there yet."*

Filippa Lentzos of King's College, London went on to deliver a session explaining that there was a security frame around human genome editing. She highlighted issues around the security of personal genetic data, explaining this could be used to customise a biological weapon programmed into a virus to attack an individual and that these sorts of scenarios are technically possible and could be used to incapacitate or kill. She added that covert assassination attempts had already proven to be a very real threat, referencing the biological attack on Sergei Skripal in 2018 in Salisbury, England. She went on to say that Wikileaks had produced evidence of secret US national human intelligence collections of individuals' fingerprints, DNA and iris scans, including those of UN officials and key civilians. Furthermore, the Pentagon had instructed US armed services personnel not to undertake direct-to-consumer DNA tests.

She also raised concerns about China's surveillance of minority populations, which had resulted in the US recently adding units of BGI to its trade blacklist. She went on to say that there was a significant programme of Chinese genomic surveillance as set out in an ASPI (Australian Strategic Policy Institute) report in June 2021 whereby tens of millions of people with no history of criminality had provided their genomic data, representing 5–10% of the male population. Moreover, she explained that the pre-natal Nifty Test developed by BGI Genomics had captured genetic information of more than 8 million women by July 2020. Given advances in genomic science, she explained that all of this genomic data could be put to nefarious use, including suppression and targeted weapons. As a result, the security dimension around genomic science and technology and security concerns needed to be on the table as well.

Reflecting on this and other sessions at the summit, it was evident that great progress had been made since the last summit in 2018, which had been overshadowed by He Jiankui's clinical gene-editing experiment and news of the birth of the Chinese gene-edited babies. The personal account delivered in-person by Victoria Gray, the first person to be cured of sickle cell disease in a US clinical trial using CRISPR gene-editing technology, had been uplifting and inspiring. However, it also raised big and thought-provoking questions about equity and access to these new gene-editing technologies and therapies and their affordability moving forward, since they were expected to be very expensive, potentially costing millions of dollars. As such, themes of equity, access, social justice and cost tracked across the three-day summit, and issues and challenges associated with this featured in many of the sessions and debates.

Day three of the summit focused in part on heritable gene-editing technology, producing lively sessions, both for and against its use. Proponents against argued that ongoing research into genetic editing of embryos with CRISPR Cas-9 technology continued to produce off-target edits and concerns, meaning it was not yet sufficiently safe or accurate for clinical use. Proponents for potential use of heritable gene-editing technology raised arguments that if scientific advances could ensure safety and accuracy, it offered potential ways to overcome infertility and enable individuals to become biological parents without passing on severe and fatal genetic diseases to their offspring. Having listened to the scientific updates, the attendees still had palpable concerns for the health and welfare of the Chinese gene-edited babies and the extent to which the CCR5 gene edit to their embryos had created unintended off-target DNA breakages and issues with their genomes. As such, the work of He Jiankui and the fate of the three Chinese gene-edited children continued to cast a palpable pall over the summit and the global scientific community.

Overall, the Third International Human Genome Editing Summit had been a carefully orchestrated event, Susie thought. It had navigated a range of issues and it was evident from the discussions that attendees were mindful of wider political dimensions and sensitivities too. The summit was, in essence, a form of 'soft power', she thought, which aimed to set the international tone and future direction for the development and use of human genome-editing technology. As such, its concluding recommendations were important benchmarks and further attempts to self-regulate and direct the global scientific community, including:[415]

> *Remarkable progress has been made in somatic human genome editing, demonstrating it can cure once incurable diseases. To realise its full therapeutic potential, research is needed to expand the range of diseases it can treat, and to better understand risks and unintended effects. The*

> *extremely high costs of current somatic gene therapies are unsustainable. A global commitment to affordable, equitable access to these treatments is urgently needed.*
>
> *Heritable human genome editing remains unacceptable at this time. Public discussions and policy debates continue and are important for resolving whether this technology should be used. Governance frameworks and ethical principles for the responsible use of heritable human genome editing are not in place. Necessary safety and efficacy standards have not been met.*
>
> *Governance mechanisms for human genome editing need to protect ongoing, legitimate research, while preventing clinics or individuals from offering unproven interventions in the guise of therapies or ways to avoid disease.*

The discussions and recommendations of the Third International Summit on Human Genome Editing were then disseminated in a subsequent article in *Nature* on 10 March 2023:[416]

> *More than four years after the first children with edited genomes were born, genome-editing techniques are still not safe enough to be used in human embryos that are destined for reproduction, organizers of the Third International Summit on Human Genome Editing announced at the conclusion of the meeting.*
>
> *…In addition to broader concerns about ethics and social justice, editing embryos would require a safe and effective genome-editing platform to minimize the chances of harming the embryos, the resulting child, and that child's descendants. Most research on genome editing in embryos, however, has been done using animal models such as mice, which might not accurately reflect what happens in human embryos. And although potential genome-editing*

therapies have been widely studied in adult human cells, embryos might respond differently than adult cells to the DNA damage caused by some genome editing tools.

Only a handful of laboratories have directly tried to edit the genomes of human embryos using the popular editing system CRISPR-Cas9, and several of these presented concerning results at the summit.

...An alternative to editing embryos would be to instead edit gametes, such as eggs and sperm, or the stem cells that give rise to them. This would also sidestep concerns that efforts to edit embryos might not succeed in all cells of the embryo, resulting in offspring that contain a mixture of edited and unedited cells. Several researchers at the summit reported progress towards generating gametes in the laboratory, but doing this with human cells destined for reproductive uses still poses challenges.

The summit organizers urged that researchers continue to explore each of these options, even as policy makers and the public grapple with what restrictions should be placed on heritable genome editing. "We are still keen that research goes ahead," said developmental biologist Robin Lovell-Badge of the Francis Crick Institute in London, who chaired the organizing committee for the summit. "In parallel, there has to be more debate about whether the technique is ever used."

This was an important reminder that there was ongoing scientific research into gene editing of human gametes (eggs and sperm) and their precursor cells, Susie thought. This was an area that merited close attention moving forward. The significance of human fertility, its biological legacy and falling world-wide fertility levels were not lost on her given her specialist legal expertise in life sciences.

14.5 Office of the Director of National Intelligence's Declassified Report, 23 June 2023

Susie continued to keep a keen eye on further US political developments regarding the origins of the Covid-19 pandemic. She followed repeated calls for the US Intelligence Community to declassify information potentially linking the Wuhan Institute of Virology (WIV) and the origins of Covid-19. This resulted in March 2023 with US President Joe Biden signing a bill declassifying information related to the origins of the pandemic.

On 23 June 2023, the Office of the Director of National Intelligence published a declassified report, *Potential Links Between the Wuhan Institute of Virology and the Origin of the Covid-19 Pandemic.* The report purported to set out the US Intelligence Community's '...understanding of the WIV, its capabilities, and the actions of its personnel leading up to and in the early days of the Covid-19 pandemic'.[417] However, Susie was not overly surprised to note that it did not '...address the merits of the two most likely origins hypotheses, nor does it explore other biological facilities in Wuhan other than the WIV'.[418]

The report opened by restating a summary of the US Intelligence Community's (IC) updated analysis of Covid-19 origins as of March 2023:[419]

> *All agencies continue to assess that both a natural and laboratory-associated origin remain plausible hypotheses to explain the first human infection.*
>
> - *The National Intelligence Council and four other IC agencies assess that the initial human infection with SARS-CoV-2 most likely was caused by natural exposure to an infected animal that carried SARS-CoV-2 or a close progenitor, a virus that probably*

would be more than 99 percent similar to SARSCoV-2.

- *The Department of Energy and the Federal Bureau of Investigation assess that a laboratory-associated incident was the most likely cause of the first human infection with SARS-CoV-2, although for different reasons.*
- *The Central Intelligence Agency and another agency remain unable to determine the precise origin of the COVID-19 pandemic, as both hypotheses rely on significant assumptions or face challenges with conflicting reporting.*
- *Almost all IC agencies assess that SARS-CoV-2 was not genetically engineered. Most agencies assess that SARS-CoV-2 was not laboratory-adapted; some are unable to make a determination. All IC agencies assess that SARS-CoV-2 was not developed as a biological weapon.*

The report itself was short, only nine pages in length, and two of those were taken up with an appendix and definitions of terms used, Susie noted. It was to her mind a veritable political '*tour de force*', carefully drafted in general terms. Despite its status as a 'declassified' intelligence report, it did not shed much in the way of new light on matters, nor clarify the origins of Covid-19. It only briefly referred to links between the WIV and the Chinese People's Liberation Army (PLA), stating that there was no clear evidence that viruses worked on were the originating virus for Covid-19:[420]

> *...Information available to the IC indicates that some of the research conducted by the PLA and WIV included work with several viruses, including coronaviruses, but no known viruses that could plausibly be a progenitor of*

SARS-CoV-2. For example, PLA researchers have used WIV laboratories for virology and vaccine-related work.

- *Between 2017 and 2019, the WIV funded and some of its personnel conducted research projects to enhance China's knowledge of pathogens and early disease warning capabilities for defensive and biosecurity needs of the military.*
- *Prior to collaborating on a vaccine for SARS-CoV-2, the WIV collaborated with the PLA on other vaccine and therapeutics relevant to coronaviruses. The IC assesses that this work was intended for public health needs and that the coronaviruses known to be used were too distantly related to have led to the creation of SARS-CoV-2.*

The report acknowledged that scientists at the WIV had carried out extensive research on coronaviruses but concluded that there was no direct evidence that a lab incident caused the Covid-19 pandemic:[421]

> *...We continue to have no indication that the WIV's pre-pandemic research holdings included SARSCoV-2 or a close progenitor, nor any direct evidence that a specific research-related incident occurred involving WIV personnel before the pandemic that could have caused the COVID pandemic.*

The report went on to set out a simplified timeline of events, not placing SARS-CoV-2 at the WIV until late December 2019 (following the viral outbreak), and stating that previous Chinese research work on bat coronavirus RaTG13 was not a direct originating virus:[422]

Information available to the IC indicates that the WIV first possessed SARS-CoV-2 in late December 2019, when WIV researchers isolated and identified the virus from samples from patients diagnosed with pneumonia of unknown causes.

- *In 2013, the WIV collected animal samples from which they identified the bat coronavirus RaTG13, which is 96.2 percent similar to the COVID-19 virus. By 2018, the WIV had sequenced almost all of RaTG13, which is the second closest known whole genome match to SARS-CoV-2, after BANAL-52, which is 96.8 percent similar. Neither of these viruses is close enough to SARS-CoV-2 to be a direct progenitor.*

The report then carefully and blandly navigated the issue of genetic engineering activity at the WIV, concluding that there was no direct evidence that this was the origin of the Covid-19 pandemic either:[423]

We assess that some scientists at the WIV have genetically engineered coronaviruses using common laboratory practices. The IC has no information, however, indicating that any WIV genetic engineering work has involved SARS-CoV-2, a close progenitor, or a backbone virus that is closely related enough to have been the source of the pandemic.

- *Scientists at the WIV have created chimeras, or combinations, of SARS-like coronaviruses through genetic engineering, attempted to clone other unrelated infectious viruses, and used reverse genetic cloning techniques on SARS-like coronaviruses.*

- *Some of the WIV's genetic engineering projects on coronaviruses involved techniques that could make it difficult to detect intentional changes.*

The report's assessment of much-publicised biosafety concerns at the WIV took the line that there was no known 'specific biosafety incident at the WIV that spurred the pandemic'. It only briefly referred to actual biosafety concerns. It also proceeded to highlight Chinese efforts to improve biosafety standards and training rather than presenting a damning picture of issues that fell short of what was required to safely work with dangerous and deadly viruses and pathogens:[424]

> *...Before the pandemic, the WIV had been working to improve at least some biosafety conditions and training. We do not know of a specific biosafety incident at the WIV that spurred the pandemic...*

- *Nearly a year after the accreditation of the WIV's BSL-4 laboratory in 2017, China's decisions of which pathogens required higher biocontainment protocols remained opaque, while the facility had a shortage of appropriately trained personnel.*
- *In mid-2019, WIV officials were evaluating and implementing biosafety improvements, training, and procurements in the context of a growing body of broader biosecurity PRC legislation. In November 2019, the WIV, in cooperation with other CAS entities, hosted a biosafety training course for WIV and non-WIV personnel that included speakers from the China Centers for Disease Control and Prevention. Given the timing of the event, this*

training appears routine, rather than a response to a specific incident.

- *As of January 2019, WIV researchers performed SARS-like coronavirus experiments in BSL-2 laboratories, despite acknowledgements going back to 2017 of these virus' ability to directly infect humans through their spike protein and early 2019 warnings of the danger of this practice...*
- *An inspection of the WIV's high-containment laboratories in 2020 – only months after the beginning of the COVID-19 outbreak's emergence – identified a need to update aging equipment, a need for additional disinfectant equipment, and improvements to ventilation systems.*

The report concluded that whilst several WIC researchers fell ill over the autumn of 2019, 'their symptoms were consistent with but not diagnostic of COVID-19'. It went on to stress that:[425]

> *The IC continues to assess that this information neither supports nor refutes either hypothesis of the pandemic's origins because the researchers' symptoms could have been caused by a number of diseases and some of the symptoms were not consistent with COVID-19.*

As a result, there was still no official consensus about the origins of the Covid-19 pandemic despite more than three years' worth of investigations since it first emerged in Wuhan, China in December 2019. Once again, this left Susie wondering whether this was politically motivated out of concerns for what might happen if the origins of the Covid-19 pandemic ever became clear. Was it still just too much of a sensitive issue?

14.6 US Select Subcommittee on the Coronavirus Pandemic: 'The Proximal Origin of a Cover-Up', 11 July 2023

Determined to keep pace with the latest developments as they unfolded, Susie took a keen interest in the hearing of the US Select Subcommittee on the Coronavirus Pandemic on 11 July 2023 and their written report released the same day. It reviewed in depth the forces behind, events and figures associated with the preparation and impact of the scientific paper *The Proximal Origin of SARS-CoV-2,* published by leading scientists on website Virological on 16 February 2020 and in *Nature Medicine* on 17 March 2020. This paper was instrumental in establishing and shaping the early narrative that the Covid-19 pandemic was the result of a zoonotic animal-to-human viral spillover event and not a lab release of a gain-of-function virus. In particular, she noted the reported scale of this scientific paper's impact:[426]

> *Since Proximal Origin was published, it has been accessed 5.84 million times. Further, it has garnered the third most attention of any paper of a similar age across all journals and the second most attention of any paper of a similar age in Nature Medicine. Finally, it has received the fifth most attention of any paper ever tracked.*

It was further illuminating to note the extent of the research and persistent 'drilling down' that had been undertaken by the US Select Subcommittee in preparing its report:[427]

> *As of July 11, 2023, the Select Subcommittee has received more than 8,000 pages of documents from the U.S.-based Proximal Origin contributors and conducted five transcribed interviews – resulting in almost 25 hours of testimony. This report is the culmination of that work.*

In essence, the US Select Committee's report stated that the aim of the Proximal Origin scientific paper was to downplay and quash theories that the Covid-19 pandemic derived from a lab release of a gain-of-function virus. In addition, it concluded that the scientific analysis and reasoning behind the paper was flawed and based on 'unsupported assumptions'. Susie was especially interested to read the report's findings that this scientific stance was adopted to prevent blame being aimed at China for the Covid-19 pandemic, stating:[428]

> *This theme – of scientists attempting to be international relations experts – prevails throughout the conception, drafting, and publication of Proximal Origin and explains the hesitancy to blame China or otherwise say COVID-19 may have been the result of Chinese negligence.*
>
> *Around this same time, Dr. Andersen shared his concerns regarding the possibility the COVID-19 pandemic was the result of a lab leak and that it had properties that may have been genetically modified or engineered – specifically the furin cleavage site – with Dr. Holmes. According to Dr. Holmes, Dr. Andersen texted, "Eddie, can we talk? I need to be pulled off a ledge here."*
>
> *Dr. Andersen went on to express concerns regarding two distinct aspects of the virus – the receptor binding domain (RBD) and the furin cleavage site. Dr. Andersen also found a paper written by Dr. Ralph Baric and Dr. Zhengli Shi (Baric/Shi Paper) that purported to have inserted furin cleavage sites into SARS. As recounted by Dr. Farrar, this paper was a 'how-to-manual for building the Wuhan coronavirus in a laboratory'. Dr. Holmes responded, "Fuck, this is bad" and "Oh my god, what worse words than that."*

Overall, the US Select Subcommittee's report painted a complex picture of interconnected relationships between politics, scientists and international security with conflicting global interests and agendas; a picture that had steadily emerged from Susie's own research and analysis. The report went on to state:[429]

> *The first possible motive to downplay the lab leak theory is an interest by those involved to defend China and play diplomat...*
>
> *1. Dr. Rambaut*
> *Dr. Rambaut, on February 2, 2020, communicating over a private Slack channel with Drs. Andersen, Holmes, and Garry, wrote, '**given the shit show that would happen if anyone serious accused the Chinese of even accidental release**, my feeling is we should say that given there is no evidence of a specifically engineered virus, we cannot possibly distinguish between natural evolution and escape so **we are content with ascribing it to natural process**'.*
>
> *...2. Dr. Andersen*
> *In response to Dr. Rambaut's message above, Dr. Andersen replied, '**Yup, I totally agree** that that's a very reasonable conclusion. **Although I hate when politics is injected into science – but it's impossible not to, especially given the circumstances**'.*
>
> *...3. Dr. Fouchier*
> *Dr. Fouchier, in emails following the February 1 conference call, stated, '...further debate about such accusations would unnecessarily distract top researchers from their active duties and **do unnecessary harm to science in general and science in China in particular**'.*

> *...4. Dr. Collins*
> *Dr. Collins, in emails following the February 1 conference call, stated, '...the voices of conspiracy will quickly dominate,* ***doing great potential harm to science and international harmony****'.*

Susie was also interested to read the US Select Subcommittee's reference to the intelligence and security services in the run-up to the preparation of *The Proximal Origin of SARS-CoV-2*. Here, once again, the intelligence and security services dimension cropped up, albeit in the background. The report highlighted an email from Dr Anthony Fauci to Sir Jeremy Farrar on 31 January 2020 concerning a conversation with Kristian Anderson in which Kristian raised concerns about genetic features in the Covid-19 virus. Specifically, that email stated that if on gathering together a group of scientists his concerns were validated then:[430]

> *...He should do this very quickly and if everyone agrees with this concern, they should report it to the appropriate authorities. I would imagine that in the USA this would be the FBI and in the UK it would be MI5. It would be important to quickly get confirmation of the cause of his concern by experts in the field of coronaviruses and evolutionary biology.*

It was further interesting to note the US Select Subcommittee's report that the forces behind events and figures associated with the preparation and impact of the scientific paper were not just confined to the published scientific authors in that:[431]

> *Through its investigation, the Select Subcommittee has learned that Dr. Fauci and the NIH exerted more*

> *influence over the conference call than previously disclosed. Further, by the end of the February 1 conference call, Dr. Fauci had suggested the drafting of a paper regarding the potential of a lab leak to Dr. Andersen twice. This suggestion was what 'prompted' Dr. Andersen to draft Proximal Origin.*
>
> *...In addition to Dr. Fauci and Dr. Collin's involvement, Dr. Farrar led the drafting process and made at least one uncredited direct edit to* Proximal Origin. *Dr. Farrar, however, is not credited as having any involvement in the drafting and publication of* Proximal Origin, *when in fact he led the drafting process and made direct substantive edits to the publication.*[432]
>
> *...On April 16, 2020, more than two months after the original February 1 conference call and a month after* Proximal Origin *was published, Dr. Collins emailed Dr. Fauci expressing dismay that* Proximal Origin *did not successfully squash the lab leak theory. He stated, "I hoped the* Nature Medicine *article on the genomic sequence of SARS-CoV-2 would settle this..." Then Dr. Collins asked Dr. Fauci, "Wondering if there is something NIH can do to help put down this very destructive conspiracy... Anything more we can do?".*[433]

Overall, the US Select Subcommittee's report had a narrow focus in addressing the origins of the Covid-19 pandemic and the forces behind, events and figures associated with the preparation and impact of the scientific paper *The Proximal Origin of SARS-CoV-2.* However, the report's analysis also supported repeating themes in Susie's wider-ranging research and analysis; producing an even more complex and nuanced picture about the use of gene editing and the global race for control of biotechnology.

14.7 Observations: Gene Editing and Genomics

There was still much that the Third International Human Genome Editing Summit in March 2023, the US Office of the Director of National Intelligence's declassified report in June 2023 and the US Select Subcommittee on the Coronavirus Pandemic Report dated 11 July 2023 did not fully address. This weighed on Susie's mind in the days and weeks that followed. The ongoing biotechnology arms race for control of powerful and transformative gene-editing technology was continuing unabated; involving complex interconnected relationships between the global political, security and scientific elite as well as conflicting interests and agendas between nations. This created a rapidly evolving landscape fraught with multifaceted challenges and risks. As such, she surmised that you could not look at the science in isolation from the interconnected wider aspects, which extended far beyond questions of access, equity, social justice and affordability of human genome editing technology to improve human health. The global biotechnology race to harness and control the power, wealth and influence that genomic technology promised and the associated 'dual-use' dimension needed to be clearly articulated, acknowledged and effectively managed too. The nefarious ways in which genomic material and data could be used together with the risks associated with the creation and release of dangerous and virulent gain-of-function viruses capable of causing mass disruption, death, economic loss and political destabilisation were very real. Furthermore, global governance and oversight was insufficient and difficult to enforce, she thought soberly.

Added to this, public discourse and narrative around the Chinese gene-edited children was seen through a lens of it being a one-off 'bad science' experiment by a reckless Chinese scientist before the science was deemed safe. It was not being considered in wider proof-of-principle terms (albeit an early incomplete attempt), whereby it potentially represented an alternative way to seek to prevent or counter viruses and the onset of diseases; a fundamentally different approach to developing drugs or vaccines by structurally genetically modifying humans at a preconception stage. If seen in these wider terms, it would then engage the 'dual-use dilemma' associated with human genome-editing technology. On the one hand, it might potentially over time be used to prevent people contracting nasty viruses causing virulent diseases and help shift to precision and preventative medicine. However, it might also potentially have serious national security implications; making genetic changes in people which could make them more or less susceptible to viruses and disease by removing or changing mechanisms in the human body which enable viruses to enter human cells and replicate. In other words, the creation of genetically modified humans could potentially prevent or enhance susceptibility to virulent disease, including gain-of-function viruses (with structural genetic modification) causing mass disruption or death. This would then potentially cause all sorts of complex issues, implications and outcomes when comparing non-genetically structurally altered human populations with those cohorts with genetic structural alterations. It could also alter the fragile international geopolitical and biopolitical balance.

There was also a question in Susie's mind about whether the three Chinese gene-edited children were being monitored as part of a secret ongoing Chinese study. To her way of thinking, it was hard to countenance that they were not in some form of follow-up programme, given the Chinese State's continued push for biotechnology supremacy. The opportunity to monitor the development of the world's first permanently gene-edited children and in particular observe whether the CCR5 gene edit made them more or less resistant to infectious diseases, or even cognitive enhancement, was surely too important an opportunity to overlook, she pondered; especially when it could be done away from scrutiny from the rest of the world.

Then there was China's adoption of a national strategy of military-civil fusion in biotechnology. This created an even more complex and nuanced picture as China is at the forefront of breakthroughs in CRISPR-Cas9 gene editing. This could be construed in terms of biotechnological responses to threats of infectious diseases. It was also potentially possible that it might extend to military applications seeking to obtain biological dominance in future warfare (new methods of confrontation), despite the difficulty in directly evidencing this.

There was also some evidence suggesting that SARS-CoV-2 had HIV-type genetic inserts (albeit this was not a mainstream view) as well as a furin cleavage genomic insert which made it more virulent, transmissible and able to mutate in humans (a gain-of-function virus). If so, this together with other evidence, gave weight to contentions that Covid-19 might be a lab release of a virulent manmade gain-of-function virus using genomic technology, albeit there was no direct evidential 'smoking gun'. This application of genomic science and technology raised all sorts of serious risks and issues.

Overall, the global debate around the merits of deploying gain-of-function virus experiments and the struggle for control of immensely powerful biotechnology continued to rumble on, Susie thought ruefully. She wondered what the future implications of this would be for humanity, wishing, not for the first time, that she was not so acutely aware of the bigger picture.

14.8 Two Men and a Black 4-Wheel Drive Vehicle

As summer 2023 drew to a close and autumn began, Susie made a journey into London for a series of life sciences sector meetings. Having picked up her Audi from the station after a busy day, she started to make her journey home, blasting the radio as she drove to help clear her mind. Looking in her rear-view mirror, she noticed that a large black 4-wheel drive vehicle was still behind her and that it had been there since she left the train station. She felt the hairs on the back of her neck stand up as she drove on, sensing she was being followed.

She wondered whether this was the result of all that she had come to know about the international biological and technological arms race to harness and control the power, wealth and influence that rapid advances in genomics and synthetic biology promised the twenty-first-century world; a race that was so important that it involved the military, Big Pharma, the Industrial Complex and information technology giants, as well as government officials, private entities, the intelligence services, key scientists and international scientific collaborations. With that, the large black 4-wheel drive vehicle flashed its lights to get her to pull over. As she slowly put the gear stick into park mode, she felt a knock on the driver's window by one of the men. He looked wiry and fit in nondescript dark clothing, and she anxiously wound down the window and swallowed hard, wondering what he and his companion wanted from her.

Endnotes

1 November 2017 UK Government Industrial Strategy to boost productivity and earning power of people across the UK, https://www.gov.uk/government/news/government-unveils-industrial-strategy-to-boost-productivity-and-earning-power-of-people-across-the-uk.

2 UK Genomics Summit held in Parliament on 31 October 2018 by the House of Commons Science & Technology Committee and the Department of Health and Social Care, https://committees.parliament.uk/committee/135/science-and-technology-committee/news/100885/genomics-summit-held-in-parliament-on-31-october-2018/.

3 "World's first gene-edited babies created in China, claims scientist", the *Guardian*, 26 November 2018, https://www.theguardian.com/science/2018/nov/26/worlds-first-gene-edited-babies-created-in-china-claims-scientist.

4 Antonio Regaldo, "Exclusive: Chinese Scientists are creating CRISPRbabies", *MIT Technology Review*, 25 November 2018, https://www.technologyreview.com/2018/11/25/138962/exclusive-chinese-scientists-are-creating-crispr-babies/.

5 The Cambridge Analytica Scandal, Wikipedia, https://en.wikipedia.org/wiki/Facebook%E2%80%93Cambridge_Analytica_data_scandal.

6 Nicola Davis, "Sperm counts among western men have halved

in last 40 years", the *Guardian*, 25 July 2017, https://www.theguardian.com/lifeandstyle/2017/jul/25/sperm-counts-among-western-men-have-halved-in-last-40-years-study.

7 "'Remarkable' decline in fertility rates", BBC News, 9 December 2018, https://www.bbc.co.uk/news/health-46118103.

8 Claire Duffin, "Average age of mothers hits 30", the *Telegraph*, 16 July 2014, https://www.telegraph.co.uk/women/mother-tongue/10971560/Average-age-of-mothers-hits-30.html.

9 Elena Burton, "Same-sex couples and singles use of fertility treatment hits UK record", Reuters, 8 May 2019, https://www.reuters.com/article/us-britain-fertility-lgbt-idUSKCN1SF1QH.

10 The Nuremberg Code, Wikipedia, https://en.wikipedia.org/wiki/Nuremberg_Code#:~:text=The%20Nuremberg%20Code%20(German%3A%20N%C3%BCrnberger,after%20the%20Second%20World%20War.

11 The Declaration of Helsinki, World Medical Association, https://www.wma.net/policies-post/wma-declaration-of-helsinki-ethical-principles-for-medical-research-involving-human-subjects/#:~:text=The%20World%20Medical%20Association%20(WMA,identifiable%20human%20material%20and%20data.

12 Universal Declaration on the Human Genome and Human Rights, Wikipedia, https://en.wikipedia.org/wiki/Universal_Declaration_on_the_Human_Genome_and_Human_Rights.

13 Sara Reardon, "NIH reiterates ban on editing human embryo DNA", *Nature*, 29 April 2015, https://www.nature.com/articles/nature.2015.17452.

14 Rob Stein, "House Committee Votes to Continue Ban on Genetically Modified Babies", NPR, 4 June 2019, https://www.npr.org/sections/health-shots/2019/06/04/729606539/house-committee-votes-to-continue-research-ban-on-genetically-modified-babies.

15 Kevin Curran PhD, "How on earth are we currently regulating human genetic modification?", updated 1-3-2019, Rising Tide Biology, https://www.risingtidebio.com/human-gene-therapy-regulations-laws/.

16 Matthew Campbell and Dong Lyu, "China's Genetics Giant Wants Everyone to Live to at Least 99", Bloomberg Law, 13 November 2019, https://news.bloomberglaw.com/pharma-and-life-sciences/chinas-genetics-giant-wants-everyone-to-live-to-at-least-99.

17 Matthew Campbell and Dong Lyu, "China's Genetics Giant Wants Everyone to Live to at Least 99", Bloomberg Law, 13 November 2019, https://news.bloomberglaw.com/pharma-and-life-sciences/chinas-genetics-giant-wants-everyone-to-live-to-at-least-99.

18 Matthew Campbell and Dong Lyu, "China's Genetics Giant Wants Everyone to Live to at Least 99", Bloomberg Law, 13 November 2019, https://news.bloomberglaw.com/pharma-and-life-sciences/chinas-genetics-giant-wants-everyone-to-live-to-at-least-99.

19 Matthew Campbell and Dong Lyu, "China's Genetics Giant Wants Everyone to Live to at Least 99", Bloomberg Law, 13 November 2019, https://news.bloomberglaw.com/pharma-and-life-sciences/chinas-genetics-giant-wants-everyone-to-live-to-at-least-99.

20 Sui-Lee Wee, "China Uses DNA to Track Its People, With the Help of American Expertise", The *New York Times*, 21 February 2019, https://www.nytimes.com/2019/02/21/business/china-xinjiang-uighur-dna-thermo-fisher.html#:~:text=New%20York%20Times-,China%20Uses%20DNA%20to%20Track%20Its%20People%2C%20With%20the%20Help,system%20of%20surveillance%20and%20control-.&text=As%20a%20subscriber%2C%20you%20have,articles%20to%20give%20each%20month.

21 Harry de Quetteville, "'I had nightmares about Hitler': meet Jennifer Doudna, the woman who unleashed the gene genie", The *Telegraph*, 14 December 2019, https://www.telegraph.co.uk/health-fitness/body/had-nightmares-hitler-meet-jennifer-doudna-woman-unleashed-gene/.

22 Lisa M. Krieger, "Lethal flu strains, dirty radiation bombs – can humans survive?", Bay Area News Group, the *Mercury News*, 21 December 2019, https://www.mercurynews.com/2019/12/21/lethal-flu-strains-dirty-radiation-bombs-can-humans-survive/.

23 Daniela Wei, K Oanh Ha and Kristen V Brown, "Chinese parents test DNA to check if kids will become prodigies", by Bloomberg,

19 November 2019, https://www.bloomberg.com/news/features/2019-11-19/china-baby-dna-tests-used-by-parents-to-check-for-prodigy-kids.

24 Matthew Campbell and Dong Lyu,"China's Genetics Giant Wants Everyone to Live to at least 99", 13 November 2019, Bloomberg Businessweek, https://news.bloomberglaw.com/pharma-and-life-sciences/chinas-genetics-giant-wants-everyone-to-live-to-at-least- 99.

25 Matthew Campbell and Dong Lyu,"China's Genetics Giant Wants Everyone to Live to at least 99", 13 November 2019, Bloomberg Businessweek, https://news.bloomberglaw.com/pharma-and-life-sciences/chinas-genetics-giant-wants-everyone-to-live-to-at-least-99.

26 Matthew Campbell and Dong Lyu,"China's Genetics Giant Wants Everyone to Live to at least 99", 13 November 2019, Bloomberg Businessweek, https://news.bloomberglaw.com/pharma-and-life-sciences/chinas-genetics-giant-wants-everyone-to-live-to-at-least-99.

27 Matthew Campbell and Dong Lyu,"China's Genetics Giant Wants Everyone to Live to at least 99", 13 November 2019, Bloomberg Businessweek, https://news.bloomberglaw.com/pharma-and-life-sciences/chinas-genetics-giant-wants-everyone-to-live-to-at-least-99.

28 Sui-Lee Wee, "China Uses DNA to Track its People, With the Help of American Expertise", 21 February 2019, The *New York Times*, https://www.nytimes.com/2019/02/21/business/china-xinjiang-uighur-dna-thermo-fisher.html.

29 Sui-Lee Wee, "China Uses DNA to Track its People, With the Help of American Expertise", 21 February 2019, The *New York Times*, https://www.nytimes.com/2019/02/21/business/china-xinjiang-uighur-dna-thermo-fisher.html.

30 "International commission on the clinical use of human germline genome editing", the Royal Society, https://royalsociety.org/topics-policy/projects/genetic-technologies/international-commission/.

31 "WHO launches global registry on human genome editing", 29 August 2019, news release.

32 "WHO expert advisory committee on developing global standards for governance and oversight of human genome editing: report of the first meeting", Geneva, Switzerland, 18–19 March 2019, https://www.who.int/publications/i/item/WHO-SCI-RFH-2019-02.
33 *Innovators* Magazine, January 2019, https://issuu.com/innovatorsmag/docs/innovators_magazine_jan_19_web/1.
34 "2002–2004 SARS Outbreak", Wikipedia, https://en.wikipedia.org/wiki/2002%E2%80%932004_SARS_outbreak.
35 "Three Gorges Damn", Britannica, https://www.britannica.com/topic/Three-Gorges-Dam/History-and-controversy-of-the-Three-Gorges-Dam.
36 Jon Cohen, "Chinese researchers reveal draft genome of virus implicated in Wuhan pneumonia outbreak", *Science Magazine*, 11 January 2020, https://www.science.org/content/article/chinese-researchers-reveal-draft-genome-virus-implicated-wuhan-pneumonia-outbreak.
37 Lily Kuo, "Coronavirus: panic and anger in Wuhan as China orders city into lockdown", the *Guardian*, 23 January 2020, https://www.theguardian.com/world/2020/jan/23/coronavirus-panic-and-anger-in-wuhan-as-china-orders-city-into-lockdown.
38 "Novel Coronavirus (2019-nCoV): Situation Report – 2" (22 January 2020), https://reliefweb.int/report/china/novel-coronavirus-2019-ncov-situation-report-2-22-january-2020.
39 The WHO statement that there is evidence of human-to-human transmission of Covid-19 in Wuhan, Twitter, 22 January 2020, https://twitter.com/who/status/1248352846971637760.
40 "Statement on the first meeting of the International Health Regulations (2005) Emergency Committee regarding the outbreak of novel coronavirus (2019-nCoV)", The WHO Statement, 23 January 2020, https://www.who.int/news/item/23-01-2020-statement-on-the-meeting-of-the-international-health-regulations-(2005)-emergency-committee-regarding-the-outbreak-of-novel-coronavirus-(2019-ncov).
41 "Statement on the second meeting of the International Health Regulations (2005) Emergency Committee regarding the

outbreak of novel coronavirus (2019-nCoV)", The WHO Statement, 30 January 2020, https://www.who.int/news/item/30-01-2020-statement-on-the-second-meeting-of-the-international-health-regulations-(2005)-emergency-committee-regarding-the-outbreak-of-novel-coronavirus-(2019-ncov).

42 "WHO declares Public Health Emergency on novel coronavirus", Pan American Health Organization (PAH), 30 January 2020, https://www.paho.org/en/news/30-1-2020-who-declares-public-health-emergency-novel-coronavirus.

43 Shiv Nalapat, "China appoints 'Terminator of Ebola' in Wuhan – Major General Chen Wei, China's foremost bio-warfare expert", TimesNowNews.com, updated 18 February 2020, https://www.timesnownews.com/international/article/china-appoints-terminator-of-ebola-in-wuhan-major-general-chen-wei-chinas-foremost-bio-warfare-expert/554930.

44 Bill Gertz, "Chinese Maj. Gen. Chen Wei takes leading role in coronavirus fight", *Washington Times*, 16 February 2020, https://www.washingtontimes.com/news/2020/feb/16/chinese-maj-gen-chen-wei-takes-leading-role-in-cor/.

45 Shiv Nalapat, *"China appoints 'Terminator of Ebola' in Wuhan – Major General Chen Wei, China's foremost bio-warfare expert"*, TimesNowNews.com, updated 18 February 2020, https://www.timesnownews.com/international/article/china-appoints-terminator-of-ebola-in-wuhan-major-general-chen-wei-chinas-foremost-bio-warfare-expert/554930.

46 Wuhan Institute of Virology, Wikipedia, https://en.wikipedia.org/wiki/Wuhan_Institute_of_Virology.

47 "Precautionary SAGE 1 minutes: Coronavirus (COVID-19) response", GOV.UK, 22 January 2020, https://assets.publishing.service.gov.uk/government/uploads/system/uploads/attachment_data/file/1058442/S0369_Precautionary_SAGE_meeting_on_Wuhan_Coronavirus__WN-CoV____1_.pdf.

48 "Covid-19 pandemic on Diamond Princess", Wikipedia, https://en.wikipedia.org/wiki/COVID-19_pandemic_on_Diamond_Princess.

49 Li Wenliang: Coronavirus kills Chinese whistleblower doctor", BBC News, 7 February 2020, https://www.bbc.co.uk/news/world-asia-china-51403795.

50 Brett Dahlberg and Elena Renken, "New Coronavirus Disease Officially Named COVID-19 by The World Health Organization", NPR, 11 February 2020, https://www.npr.org/sections/goatsandsoda/2020/02/11/802352351/new-coronavirus-gets-an-official-name-from-the-world-health-organization.

51 "WHO Director-General's opening remarks at the media briefing on COVID-19 – 11 March 2020", The World Health Organization, 11 March 2020, https://www.who.int/director-general/speeches/detail/who-director-general-s-opening-remarks-at-the-media-briefing-on-covid-19---11-march-2020.

52 "WHO Director-General's opening remarks at the media briefing on COVID-19 – 11 March 2020", The World Health Organization, 11 March 2020, https://www.who.int/director-general/speeches/detail/who-director-general-s-opening-remarks-at-the-media-briefing-on-covid-19---11-march-2020.

53 "Public Health Screening to Begin at 3 U.S. Airports for 2019 Novel Coronavirus ('2019-nCoV')", Centers for Disease Control and Prevention (CDC) press release, 17 January 2020, https://www.cdc.gov/media/releases/2020/p0117-coronavirus-screening.html#:~:text=Starting%20January%2017%2C%202020%2C%20travelers,Los%20Angeles%20(LAX)%20airports.

54 "First Travel-related Case of 2019 Novel Coronavirus Detected in United States", Centers for Disease Control and Prevention (CDC) press release, 21 January 2020, https://www.cdc.gov/media/releases/2020/p0121-novel-coronavirus-travel-case.html.

55 Dan Mangan and Christina Wilkie, "Trump declares national emergency over coronavirus", CNBC, 13 March 2020, https://www.cnbc.com/2020/03/13/trump-will-hold-a-press-conference-at-3-pm-et-to-discuss-coronavirus-response.html.

56 "Travel Advice against all non-essential travel: Foreign Secretary's statement", press release by Foreign & Commonwealth Office and The Rt Hon Dominic Raab MP, 17 March 2020, https://

www.gov.uk/government/news/travel-advice-foreign-secreatary-statement-17-march-2020.

57 Kristian G. Andersen, Andrew Rambaut, W. Ian Lipkin, et al., "The proximal origin of SARS-CoV-2", *Nature* Public Health Emergency Collection, 17 March 2020, https://www.ncbi.nlm.nih.gov/pmc/articles/PMC7095063/.

58 "Two first coronavirus cases confirmed in Italy: prime minister", Reuters, 30 January 2020, https://www.reuters.com/article/us-china-health-italy-idUSKBN1ZT31H.

59 "Italian government suspends all flights to and from mainland China and confirms two coronavirus cases January 30; confirm flight reservations", Crisis24, 31 January 2020, https://crisis24.garda.com/alerts/2020/01/italy-air-traffic-suspended-to-and-from-china-due-to-novel-coronavirus-as-of-january-30.

60 Lorenzo Tondo, "Coronavirus Italy: PM extends lockdown to entire country", the Guardian, 10 March 2020, https://www.theguardian.com/world/2020/mar/09/coronavirus-italy-prime-minister-country-lockdown.

61 "Health minister Nadine Dorries becomes first MP to test positive for coronavirus", itvNEWS, 11 March 2020, https://www.itv.com/news/2020-03-11/nadine-dorries-becomes-first-mp-to-test-positive-for-covid-19.

62 "Prime Minister's statement on coronavirus (COVID-19): 23 March 2020", GOV.UK, https://www.gov.uk/government/speeches/pm-address-to-the-nation-on-coronavirus-23-march-2020.

63 "Coronavirus: Prime Minister Boris Johnson tests positive", BBC News, 27 March 2020, https://www.bbc.co.uk/news/uk-52060791.

64 Emma Newburger, "British PM Boris Johnson admitted to hospital for tests over 'persistent' coronavirus symptoms", CNBC, 5 April 2020, https://www.cnbc.com/2020/04/05/british-pm-boris-johnson-admitted-to-hospital-for-tests-over-persistent-coronavirus-symptoms.html.

65 "Coronavirus: Boris Johnson moved to intensive care as symptoms worsen", BBC News, 7 April 2020, https://www.bbc.co.uk/news/uk-52192604.

66 "Boris Johnson discharged from hospital seven days after being admitted for coronavirus symptoms", the *Independent*, 12 April 2020, https://www.independent.co.uk/news/uk/politics/boris-johnson-news-coronavirus-update-hospital-discharge-today-a9461461.html.
67 Josh Rogin, "State Department cables warned of safety issues at Wuhan lab studying bat coronaviruses", the *Washington Post*, 14 April 2020, https://www.washingtonpost.com/opinions/2020/04/14/state-department-cables-warned-safety-issues-wuhan-lab-studying-bat-coronaviruses/.
68 Josh Rogin, "State Department cables warned of safety issues at Wuhan lab studying bat coronaviruses", the *Washington Post*, 14 April 2020, https://www.washingtonpost.com/opinions/2020/04/14/state-department-cables-warned-safety-issues-wuhan-lab-studying-bat-coronaviruses/.
69 Josh Rogin, "State Department cables warned of safety issues at Wuhan lab studying bat coronaviruses", the *Washington Post*, 14 April 2020, https://www.washingtonpost.com/opinions/2020/04/14/state-department-cables-warned-safety-issues-wuhan-lab-studying-bat-coronaviruses/.
70 Josh Rogin, "State Department cables warned of safety issues at Wuhan lab studying bat coronaviruses", the *Washington Post*, 14 April 2020, https://www.washingtonpost.com/opinions/2020/04/14/state-department-cables-warned-safety-issues-wuhan-lab-studying-bat-coronaviruses/.
71 Josh Rogin, "State Department cables warned of safety issues at Wuhan lab studying bat coronaviruses", the *Washington Post*, 14 April 2020, https://www.washingtonpost.com/opinions/2020/04/14/state-department-cables-warned-safety-issues-wuhan-lab-studying-bat-coronaviruses/.
72 "Coronavirus: Trump stands by China lab origin theory for virus", BBC News, 1 May 2020, https://www.bbc.co.uk/news/world-us-canada-52496098.
73 Richard Partington, "UK unemployment to double and economy to shrink by 14%, warns Bank of England", the *Guardian*, 7

May 2020, https://www.theguardian.com/business/2020/may/07/uk-economy-to-shrink-by-25-percent-and-unemployment-to-double- warns-bank-of-england-coronavirus.

74 "'We're facing a double pandemic': UN body warns of 'mega-famines'", Aljazeera, 7 May 2020, https://www.aljazeera.com/news/2020/5/7/were-facing-a-double-pandemic-un-body-warns-of-mega-famines.

75 "Secretary-General Denounces 'Tsunami' of Xenophobia amid COVID-19, Calling got All-Out Effort against Hate Speech", United Nations Press Release, 8 May 2020, https://press.un.org/en/2020/sgsm20076.doc.htm.

76 "Prime Minister's statement on coronavirus (COVID-19): 10 May 2020", GOV.UK, 10 May 2020, https://www.gov.uk/government/speeches/pm-address-to-the-nation-on-coronavirus-10-may-2020.

77 Matthew Brown, "Fact check: A Bill Gates-backed pandemic simulation in October did not predict COVID 19", USA TODAY, 26 March 2020, https://eu.usatoday.com/story/news/factcheck/2020/03/26/fact-check-bill-gates-backed-pandemic-exercise-didnt-predict-covid-19/5081854002/.

78 Event 201, John Hopkins Center for Health Security, https://www.centerforhealthsecurity.org/our-work/exercises/event201/.

79 Event 201 Players, John Hopkins Center for Health Security, https://www.centerforhealthsecurity.org/our-work/exercises/event201/players/.

80 Event 201 video recordings, John Hopkins Center for Health Security, https://www.centerforhealthsecurity.org/our-work/exercises/event201/videos.html.

81 Event 201 Players, John Hopkins Center for Health Security, https://www.centerforhealthsecurity.org/our-work/exercises/event201/players/.

82 Event 201 Players, John Hopkins Center for Health Security, https://www.centerforhealthsecurity.org/our-work/exercises/event201/players/.

83 Event 201 Players, John Hopkins Center for Health Security, https://www.centerforhealthsecurity.org/our-work/exercises/

event201/players/.

84 Event 201 video recordings, John Hopkins Center for Health Security, https://www.centerforhealthsecurity.org/our-work/exercises/event201/videos.html.

85 Event 201 Players, John Hopkins Center for Health Security, https://www.centerforhealthsecurity.org/our-work/exercises/event201/players/.

86 Event 201 Players, John Hopkins Center for Health Security, https://www.centerforhealthsecurity.org/our-work/exercises/event201/players/.

87 Event 201 Players, John Hopkins Center for Health Security, https://www.centerforhealthsecurity.org/our-work/exercises/event201/players/.

88 Event 201 Players, John Hopkins Center for Health Security, https://www.centerforhealthsecurity.org/our-work/exercises/event201/players/.

89 Event 201 Players, John Hopkins Center for Health Security, https://www.centerforhealthsecurity.org/our-work/exercises/event201/players/.

90 Event 201 Players, John Hopkins Center for Health Security, https://www.centerforhealthsecurity.org/our-work/exercises/event201/players/.

91 Event 201 Players, John Hopkins Center for Health Security, https://www.centerforhealthsecurity.org/our-work/exercises/event201/players/.

92 Event 201 Players, John Hopkins Center for Health Security, https://www.centerforhealthsecurity.org/our-work/exercises/event201/players/.

93 Event 201 video recordings, John Hopkins Center for Health Security, https://www.centerforhealthsecurity.org/our-work/exercises/event201/videos.html.

94 Event 201 Players, John Hopkins Center for Health Security, https://www.centerforhealthsecurity.org/our-work/exercises/event201/players/.

95 Event 201 video recordings, John Hopkins Center for Health Security,

https://www.centerforhealthsecurity.org/our-work/exercises/event201/videos.html.

96 Event 201 video recordings, John Hopkins Center for Health Security, https://www.centerforhealthsecurity.org/our-work/exercises/event201/videos.html.

97 Event 201 Recommendations, John Hopkins Center for Health Security, https://www.centerforhealthsecurity.org/our-work/exercises/event201/recommendations.html.

98 Aditya Panda, Archana Padhi, B. Anjan Kumar, "CCR5 Δ32 minorallele is associated with susceptibility to SARS-CoV-2 infection and death: An epidemiological investigation", Center for Biotechnology Information, U.S. National Library of Medicine, 10 July 2020, https://www.ncbi.nlm.nih.gov/pmc/articles/PMC7347491/.

99 Rajeev K. Mehlotra, "Chemokine receptor gene polymorphisms and COVID-19: Could knowledge gained from HIV/AIDS be important?", National Center for Biotechnology Information, U.S. National Library of Medicine, 26 August 2020, https://www.ncbi.nlm.nih.gov/pmc/articles/PMC7448762/.

100 YouTube video clip of He Jiankui discussing the birth of the Chinese gene-edited babies, 2018, https://www.youtube.com/watch?v=th0vnOmFltc

101 Xinzhu Wei, Rasmus Nielsen, "CCR5-Δ32 is deleterious in the homozygous state in humans", *Nature Medicine*, 3 June 2019, https://www.nature.com/articles/s41591-019-0459-6.

102 Ian Sample, "Gene mutation meant to protect from HIV 'raises risk of early death'", the *Guardian*, 3 June 2019, https://www.theguardian.com/science/2019/jun/03/gene-mutation-protect-hiv-raises-risk-early-death.

103 "Expert reaction to mutated CCR5 gene and mortality", Science Media Centre press release, 3 June 2019, https://www.sciencemediacentre.org/expert-reaction-to-mutated-ccr5-gene-and-mortality/.

104 Jon Cohen, "The untold story of the 'circle of trust' behind the world's first gene-edited babies", *Science Magazine*, 1 August 2019, https://www.sciencemag.org/news/2019/08/untold-story-circle-trust-behind-world-s-first-gene-edited-babies.

105 Jon Cohen, "The untold story of the 'circle of trust' behind the world's first gene-edited babies", *Science Magazine*, 1 August 2019, https://www.sciencemag.org/news/2019/08/untold-story-circle-trust-behind-world-s-first-gene-edited-babies.

106 Derek Lapiska interview with Professor Michael W. Deem, who delivered the Professional Progress Award Lecture at the AIChE Annual Meeting in Minneapolis in October 2011, https://www.aiche.org/chenected/2011/10/interview-professor-michael-w-deem-rice-university.

107 Jon Cohen, "The untold story of the 'circle of trust' behind the world's first gene-edited babies", *Science Magazine*, 1 August 2019, https://www.sciencemag.org/news/2019/08/untold-story-circle-trust-behind-world-s-first-gene-edited-babies.

108 Jiankui He and Michael W. Deem, "Low-dimensional clustering detects incipient dominant influenza strain clusters", Protein Engineering, Design & Selection vol.23 no. 12 pp. 935–946, published online, 29 October 2010, https://www.ncbi.nlm.nih.gov/pmc/articles/PMC2978544/.

109 Jiankui He and Michael W. Deem, "Structure Response in the World Trade Network", *Physical Review Letters* PRL 105, 198701 (2010), 5 November 2010, https://journals.aps.org/prl/abstract/10.1103/PhysRevLett.105.198701.

110 Michael W. Deem, Pooya Hejazi, "Theoretical Aspects of Immunity", *Annual Review of Chemical and Biomolecular Engineering 2010*, 1: 247–276, https://www.ncbi.nlm.nih.gov/pmc/articles/PMC4487771/#:~:text=Our%20immune%20system%20protects%20us,T%20cell%20mediated%20cellular%20response.

111 Jiankui He and Michael W. Deem, "Structure Response in the World Trade Network", *Physical Review Letters* PRL 105, 198701 (2010), 5 November 2010, https://journals.aps.org/prl/abstract/10.1103/PhysRevLett.105.198701.

112 Jon Cohen, "The untold story of the 'circle of trust' behind the world's first gene-edited babies", *Science Magazine*, 1 August 2019, https://www.sciencemag.org/news/2019/08/untold-story-circle-trust-behind-world-s-first-gene-edited-babies.

113 Jon Cohen, "The untold story of the 'circle of trust' behind the world's first gene-edited babies", *Science Magazine*, 1 August 2019, https://www.sciencemag.org/news/2019/08/untold-story-circle-trust-behind-world-s-first-gene-edited-babies.

114 Zhoufang Li, Guangjie Liu, Jiankui He, et al., "Comprehensive analysis of the T-cell receptor beta chain gene in rhesus monkey by high throughput sequencing", National Center for Biotechnology Information, US National Library of Medicine, 11 May 2015, https://www.ncbi.nlm.nih.gov/pmc/articles/PMC4426732/.

115 Jon Cohen, "The untold story of the 'circle of trust' behind the world's first gene-edited babies", *Science Magazine*, 1 August 2019, https://www.sciencemag.org/news/2019/08/untold-story-circle-trust-behind-world-s-first-gene-edited-babies.

116 Jon Cohen, "The untold story of the 'circle of trust' behind the world's first gene-edited babies", *Science Magazine*, 1 August 2019, https://www.sciencemag.org/news/2019/08/untold-story-circle-trust-behind-world-s-first-gene-edited-babies.

117 Jon Cohen, "The untold story of the 'circle of trust' behind the world's first gene-edited babies", *Science Magazine*, 1 August 2019, https://www.sciencemag.org/news/2019/08/untold-story-circle-trust-behind-world-s-first-gene-edited-babies.

118 Jon Cohen, "The untold story of the 'circle of trust' behind the world's first gene-edited babies", *Science Magazine*, 1 August 2019, https://www.sciencemag.org/news/2019/08/untold-story-circle-trust-behind-world-s-first-gene-edited-babies.

119 Jon Cohen, "The untold story of the 'circle of trust' behind the world's first gene-edited babies", *Science Magazine*, 1 August 2019, https://www.sciencemag.org/news/2019/08/untold-story-circle-trust-behind-world-s-first-gene-edited-babies.

120 Hank T. Greely, "CRISPR'd babies: human germline genome editing in the 'He Jiankui affair'", *Journal of Law and the Biosciences*, October 2019: 6(1) 111–183, https://www.ncbi.nlm.nih.gov/pmc/articles/PMC6813942/.

121 Hank T. Greely, "CRISPR'd babies: human germline genome editing in the 'He Jiankui affair'", *Journal of Law and the Biosciences*,

October 2019: 6(1) 111–183, https://www.ncbi.nlm.nih.gov/pmc/articles/PMC6813942/.

122 Jon Cohen, "The untold story of the 'circle of trust' behind the world's first gene-edited babies", *Science Magazine*, 1 August 2019, https://www.sciencemag.org/news/2019/08/untold-story-circle-trust-behind-world-s-first-gene-edited-babies.

123 Hank T. Greely, "CRISPR'd babies: human germline genome editing in the 'He Jiankui affair'", *Journal of Law and the Biosciences*, October 2019: 6(1) 111–183, https://www.ncbi.nlm.nih.gov/pmc/articles/PMC6813942/.

124 Jon Cohen, "The untold story of the 'circle of trust' behind the world's first gene-edited babies", *Science Magazine*, 1 August 2019, https://www.sciencemag.org/news/2019/08/untold-story-circle-trust-behind-world-s-first-gene-edited-babies.

125 Jon Cohen, "The untold story of the 'circle of trust' behind the world's first gene-edited babies", *Science Magazine*, 1 August 2019, https://www.sciencemag.org/news/2019/08/untold-story-circle-trust-behind-world-s-first-gene-edited-babies.

126 Jon Cohen, "The untold story of the 'circle of trust' behind the world's first gene-edited babies", *Science Magazine*, 1 August 2019, https://www.sciencemag.org/news/2019/08/untold-story-circle-trust-behind-world-s-first-gene-edited-babies.

127 Antonio Regalado, "He Jiankui faces three years in prison for CRISPR babies", *MIT Technology Review*, 30 December 2019, https://www.technologyreview.com/2019/12/30/131061/he-jiankui-sentenced-to-three-years-in-prison-for-crispr-babies/.

128 Ian Sample, "Chinese scientist who edited babies' genes jailed for three years", the *Guardian*, 31 December 2019, https://www.theguardian.com/world/2019/dec/30/gene-editing-chinese-scientist-he-jiankui-jailed-three-years.

129 Ian Sample, "Chinese scientist who edited babies' genes jailed for three years", the *Guardian*, 31 December 2019, https://www.theguardian.com/world/2019/dec/30/gene-editing-chinese-scientist-he-jiankui-jailed-three-years.

130 Tim Ripley, "'Medical spies' tracking PPE criminals", *The Sunday*

Times, 13 September 2020.

131 Aditya K. Panda, Archana Padhi, B. Anjan Kumar Prusty, "CCR5 Δ32 minorallele is associated with susceptibility to SARS-CoV-2 infection and death: An epidemiological investigation", Elsevier Public Health Emergency Collection, 10 July 2020, https://www.ncbi.nlm.nih.gov/pmc/articles/PMC7347491/.

132 "Programmable DNA scissors found for bacterial immune system", Science Daily. 28 June 2012, https://www.sciencedaily.com/releases/2012/06/120628193020.htm.

133 "A Programmable Dual-RNA–Guided DNA Endonuclease in Adaptive Bacterial Immunity", *Science Magazine*, 17 August 2012, https://science.sciencemag.org/content/337/6096/816.

134 "World's first gene-edited babies created in China, claims scientist", the *Guardian*, 26 November 2018, https://www.theguardian.com/science/2018/nov/26/worlds-first-gene-edited-babies-created-in-china-claims-scientist.

135 "He Jiankui defends 'world's first gene-edited babies'", BBC News, 28 November 2018, https://www.bbc.co.uk/news/world-asia-china-46368731.

136 "Second International Summit on Human Genome Editing: Continuing the Global Discussion", National Center for Biotechnology Information, U.S. National Library of Medicine , 10 January 2019, https://www.ncbi.nlm.nih.gov/books/NBK535994/.

137 "Chinese scientist who edited babies' genes jailed for three years", the *Guardian*, 31 December 2019, https://www.theguardian.com/world/2019/dec/30/gene-editing-chinese-scientist-he-jiankui-jailed-three-years.

138 "Chinese scientist who produced genetically altered babies sentenced to 3 years in jail", *Science Magazine*, 30 December 2018, https://www.sciencemag.org/news/2019/12/chinese-scientist-who-produced-genetically-altered-babies-sentenced-3-years-jail.

139 Covid-19 pandemic, Wikipedia, https://en.wikipedia.org/wiki/COVID-19_pandemic.

140 Jon Cohen, "China's CRISPR push in animals promises better meat, novel therapies, and pig organs for people", *Science Magazine*, 31

July 2019, https://www.science.org/content/article/china-s-crispr-push-animals-promises-better-meat-novel-therapies-and-pig-organs-people.

141 Zhoufang Li, Guangjie Liu, Jiankui He , et al., "Comprehensive analysis of the T-cell receptor beta chain gene in rhesus monkey by high throughput sequencing", National Center for Biotechnology Information, U.S. National Library of Medicine, 11 May 2015, https://www.ncbi.nlm.nih.gov/pmc/articles/PMC4426732/.

142 Jon Cohen, "The untold story of the 'circle of trust' behind the world's first gene-edited babies", *Science Magazine*, 1 August 2019, https://www.sciencemag.org/news/2019/08/untold-story-circle-trust-behind-world-s-first-gene-edited-babies.

143 Henry T. Greely, "CRISPR'd babies: human germline genome editing in the 'He Jiankui affair'", *Journal of Law and the Biosciences*, October 2019: 6(1) 111–183, https://www.ncbi.nlm.nih.gov/pmc/articles/PMC6813942/.

144 Jon Cohen, "The untold story of the 'circle of trust' behind the world's first gene-edited babies", *Science Magazine*, 1 August 2019, https://www.sciencemag.org/news/2019/08/untold-story-circle-trust-behind-world-s-first-gene-edited-babies.

145 Henry T. Greely, "CRISPR'd babies: human germline genome editing in the 'He Jiankui affair'", *Journal of Law and the Biosciences*, October 2019: 6(1) 111–183, https://www.ncbi.nlm.nih.gov/pmc/articles/PMC6813942/.

146 Aditya K. Panda, B. Anjan Kumar Prusty, "CCR5 Δ32 minorallele is associated with susceptibility to SARS-CoV-2 infection and death: An epidemiological investigation", National Center for Biotechnology Information, U.S. National Library of Medicine, 10 July 2020, https://www.ncbi.nlm.nih.gov/pmc/articles/PMC7347491/.

147 Rajeev K. Mehlotra, "Chemokine receptor gene polymorphisms and COVID-19: Could knowledge gained from HIV/AIDS be important?", National Center for Biotechnology Information, U.S. National Library of Medicine, 26 August 2020, https://www.ncbi.nlm.nih.gov/pmc/articles/PMC7448762/.

148 Chunxia Qi, Xiaopeng Jia, Lingling Lu, et al., "HEK293T Cells are

Heterozygous for CCR5 Delta 32 Mutation", National Center for Biotechnology Information, U.S. National Library of Medicine, 4 April 2016, https://www.ncbi.nlm.nih.gov/pmc/articles/PMC4820142/.

149 "Data Privacy and China's Covid-19 Genetic Research", Clearance Jobs, 13 June 2010, https://news.clearancejobs.com/2020/06/13/data-privacy-and-chinas-covid-19-genetic-research/.

150 Charlie Campbell/Yuxi, Yunnan and Alice Park, "Where Did Coronavirus Originate? Inside the Hunt to Find Out", *TIME*, 23 July 2020, https://time.com/5870481/coronavirus-origins/.

151 Charlie Campbell/Yuxi, Yunnan and Alice Park, "Where Did Coronavirus Originate? Inside the Hunt to Find Out", *TIME*, 23 July 2020, https://time.com/5870481/coronavirus-origins/.

152 Jon Cohen, "The untold story of the 'circle of trust' behind the world's first gene-edited babies", *Science Magazine*, 1 August 2019, https://www.sciencemag.org/news/2019/08/untold-story-circle-trust-behind-world-s-first-gene-edited-babies.

153 Henry T. Greely, "CRISPR'd babies: human germline genome editing in the 'He Jiankui affair'", *Journal of Law and the Biosciences*, October 2019: 6(1) 111–183, https://www.ncbi.nlm.nih.gov/pmc/articles/PMC6813942/.

154 Ning Jiang, Jiankui He, Joshua A. Weinstein, et al., "Lineage Structure of the Human Antibody Repertoire in Response to Influenza Vaccination", National Center for Biotechnology Information, U.S. National Library of Medicine, 6 August 2013, https://www.ncbi.nlm.nih.gov/pmc/articles/PMC3699344/.

155 Jon Cohen, "The untold story of the 'circle of trust' behind the world's first gene-edited babies", *Science Magazine*, 1 August 2019, https://www.sciencemag.org/news/2019/08/untold-story-circle-trust-behind-world-s-first-gene-edited-babies.

156 Henry T. Greely, "CRISPR'd babies: human germline genome editing in the 'He Jiankui affair'", *Journal of Law and the Biosciences*, October 2019: 6(1) 111–183, https://www.ncbi.nlm.nih.gov/pmc/articles/PMC6813942/.

157 Jon Cohen, "The untold story of the 'circle of trust' behind the

world's first gene-edited babies", *Science Magazine*, 1 August 2019, https://www.sciencemag.org/news/2019/08/untold-story-circle-trust-behind-world-s-first-gene-edited-babies.

158 Henry T. Greely, "CRISPR'd babies: human germline genome editing in the 'He Jiankui affair'", *Journal of Law and the Biosciences*, October 2019: 6(1) 111–183, https://www.ncbi.nlm.nih.gov/pmc/articles/PMC6813942/.

159 Jon Cohen, "The untold story of the 'circle of trust' behind the world's first gene-edited babies", *Science Magazine*, 1 August 2019, https://www.sciencemag.org/news/2019/08/untold-story-circle-trust-behind-world-s-first-gene-edited-babies.

160 Henry T. Greely, "CRISPR'd babies: human germline genome editing in the 'He Jiankui affair'", *Journal of Law and the Biosciences*, October 2019: 6(1) 111–183, https://www.ncbi.nlm.nih.gov/pmc/articles/PMC6813942/.

161 Jon Cohen, "The untold story of the 'circle of trust' behind the world's first gene-edited babies", *Science Magazine*, 1 August 2019, https://www.sciencemag.org/news/2019/08/untold-story-circle-trust-behind-world-s-first-gene-edited-babies.

162 Henry T. Greely, "CRISPR'd babies: human germline genome editing in the 'He Jiankui affair'", *Journal of Law and the Biosciences*, October 2019: 6(1) 111–183, https://www.ncbi.nlm.nih.gov/pmc/articles/PMC6813942/.

163 Jon Cohen, "The untold story of the 'circle of trust' behind the world's first gene-edited babies", *Science Magazine*, 1 August 2019, https://www.sciencemag.org/news/2019/08/untold-story-circle-trust-behind-world-s-first-gene-edited-babies.

164 Henry T. Greely, "CRISPR'd babies: human germline genome editing in the 'He Jiankui affair'", *Journal of Law and the Biosciences*, October 2019: 6(1) 111–183, https://www.ncbi.nlm.nih.gov/pmc/articles/PMC6813942/.

165 Jon Cohen, "The untold story of the 'circle of trust' behind the world's first gene-edited babies", *Science Magazine*, 1 August 2019, https://www.sciencemag.org/news/2019/08/untold-story-circle-trust-behind-world-s-first-gene-edited-babies.

166 Henry T. Greely, "CRISPR'd babies: human germline genome editing in the 'He Jiankui affair'", *Journal of Law and the Biosciences*, October 2019: 6(1) 111–183, https://www.ncbi.nlm.nih.gov/pmc/articles/PMC6813942/.

167 Jon Cohen, "The untold story of the 'circle of trust' behind the world's first gene-edited babies", *Science Magazine*, 1 August 2019, https://www.sciencemag.org/news/2019/08/untold-story-circle-trust-behind-world-s-first-gene-edited-babies.

168 Henry T. Greely, "CRISPR'd babies: human germline genome editing in the 'He Jiankui affair'", *Journal of Law and the Biosciences*, October 2019: 6(1) 111–183, https://www.ncbi.nlm.nih.gov/pmc/articles/PMC6813942/.

169 Jon Cohen, "The untold story of the 'circle of trust' behind the world's first gene-edited babies", *Science Magazine*, 1 August 2019, https://www.sciencemag.org/news/2019/08/untold-story-circle-trust-behind-world-s-first-gene-edited-babies.

170 Henry T. Greely, "CRISPR'd babies: human germline genome editing in the 'He Jiankui affair'", *Journal of Law and the Biosciences*, October 2019: 6(1) 111–183, https://www.ncbi.nlm.nih.gov/pmc/articles/PMC6813942/.

171 Jon Cohen, "The untold story of the 'circle of trust' behind the world's first gene-edited babies", *Science Magazine*, 1 August 2019, https://www.sciencemag.org/news/2019/08/untold-story-circle-trust-behind-world-s-first-gene-edited-babies.

172 Henry T. Greely, "CRISPR'd babies: human germline genome editing in the 'He Jiankui affair'", *Journal of Law and the Biosciences*, October 2019: 6(1) 111–183, *https://www.ncbi.nlm.nih.gov/pmc/articles/PMC6813942/.*

173 Jon Cohen, "The untold story of the 'circle of trust' behind the world's first gene-edited babies", *Science Magazine*, 1 August 2019, https://www.sciencemag.org/news/2019/08/untold-story-circle-trust-behind-world-s-first-gene-edited-babies.

174 Henry T. Greely, "CRISPR'd babies: human germline genome editing in the 'He Jiankui affair'", *Journal of Law and the Biosciences*, October 2019: 6(1) 111–183, https://www.ncbi.nlm.nih.gov/pmc/

articles/PMC6813942/.

175 Jon Cohen, "The untold story of the 'circle of trust' behind the world's first gene-edited babies", *Science Magazine*, 1 August 2019, https://www.sciencemag.org/news/2019/08/untold-story-circle-trust-behind-world-s-first-gene-edited-babies.

176 Henry T. Greely, "CRISPR'd babies: human germline genome editing in the 'He Jiankui affair'", *Journal of Law and the Biosciences*, October 2019: 6(1) 111–183, https://www.ncbi.nlm.nih.gov/pmc/articles/PMC6813942/.

177 Jon Cohen, "The untold story of the 'circle of trust' behind the world's first gene-edited babies", *Science Magazine*, 1 August 2019, https://www.sciencemag.org/news/2019/08/untold-story-circle-trust-behind-world-s-first-gene-edited-babies.

178 Henry T. Greely, "CRISPR'd babies: human germline genome editing in the 'He Jiankui affair'", *Journal of Law and the Biosciences*, October 2019: 6(1) 111–183, https://www.ncbi.nlm.nih.gov/pmc/articles/PMC6813942/.

179 Xinzhu Wei, Rasmus Nielsen, "CCR5-Δ32 is deleterious in the homozygous state in humans", *Nature Medicine*, 3 June 2019, https://www.nature.com/articles/s41591-019-0459-6.

180 "Expert reaction to mutated CCR5 gene and mortality", UK Science Media Centre, 3 June 2019, https://www.sciencemediacentre.org/expert-reaction-to-mutated-ccr5-gene-and-mortality/.

181 "Expert reaction to mutated CCR5 gene and mortality", UK Science Media Centre, 3 June 2019, https://www.sciencemediacentre.org/expert-reaction-to-mutated-ccr5-gene-and-mortality/.

182 "Expert reaction to mutated CCR5 gene and mortality", UK Science Media Centre, 3 June 2019, https://www.sciencemediacentre.org/expert-reaction-to-mutated-ccr5-gene-and-mortality/.

183 Jon Cohen, "To feed its 1.4 billion, China bets big on genome editing of crops", *Science Magazine*, 29 July 2019, https://www.sciencemag.org/news/2019/07/feed-its-14-billion-china-bets-big-genome-editing-crops.

184 Jon Cohen, "To feed its 1.4 billion, China bets big on genome editing of crops", *Science Magazine*, 29 July 2019, https://www.

sciencemag.org/news/2019/07/feed-its-14-billion-china-bets-big-genome-editing-crops.

185 Jack Ellis, "Syngenta restructures, rebrands, and relaunches after taking $5.6bn Chinese biz on board", AFN, 18 June 2020, https://agfundernews.com/syngenta-group-relaunches-after-taking-5-6bn-chinese-biz-on-board.html#:~:text=Click%20here.,foreign%20company%20%E2%80%94%20in%20Febraury%202016.

186 Jack Ellis, "Syngenta restructures, rebrands, and relaunches after taking $5.6bn Chinese biz on board", AFN, 18 June 2020, https://agfundernews.com/syngenta-group-relaunches-after-taking-5-6bn-chinese-biz-on-board.html#:~:text=Click%20here.,foreign%20company%20%E2%80%94%20in%20Febraury%202016.

187 Jack Ellis, "Syngenta restructures, rebrands, and relaunches after taking $5.6bn Chinese biz on board", AFN, 18 June 2020, https://agfundernews.com/syngenta-group-relaunches-after-taking-5-6bn-chinese-biz-on-board.html#:~:text=Click%20here.,foreign%20company%20%E2%80%94%20in%20Febraury%202016.

188 "FBI director: China is 'greatest threat' to US", BBC News, 8 July 2020, https://www.bbc.co.uk/news/world-us-canada-53329755.

189 "Special Report: COVID opens new doors for China's gene giant", Reuters, 5 August 2020, https://www.reuters.com/article/us-health-coronavirus-bgi-spec ialreport-idUSKCN2511CE.

190 Kevin Davies, "Guilty as charged. A Chinese court delivered a three-year prison sentence and hefty fine to He Jiankui, the rogue gene editor. Does human embryo editing stand a chance of rehabilitation?", *GEN, Genetic Engineering & Biotechnology News*, 1 February 2020, https://www.genengnews.com/insights/guilty-as-charged/.

191 Jeanne Whalen and Elizabeth Dwoskin, "California rejected Chinese company's push to help with coronavirus testing. Was that the right move?", the *Washington Post*, 2 July 2020, https://www.washingtonpost.com/business/2020/07/02/china-bgi-california-testing/.

192 "Special Report: COVID opens new doors for China's gene giant", Reuters, 5 August 2020, https://www.reuters.com/article/us-health-coronavirus-bgi-spec ialreport-idUSKCN2511CE.

193 Kevin Davies, "Guilty as charged. A Chinese court delivered a three-year prison sentence and hefty fine to He Jiankui, the rogue gene editor. Does human embryo editing stand a chance of rehabilitation?", *GEN, Genetic Engineering & Biotechnology News*, 1 February 2020, https://www.genengnews.com/insights/guilty-as-charged/.

194 Jeanne Whalen and Elizabeth Dwoskin, "California rejected Chinese company's push to help with coronavirus testing. Was that the right move?", the *Washington Post*, 2 July 2020, https://www.washingtonpost.com/business/2020/07/02/china-bgi-california-testing/.

195 "Special Report: COVID opens new doors for China's gene giant", Reuters, 5 August 2020, https://www.reuters.com/article/us-health-coronavirus-bgi-spec ialreport-idUSKCN2511CE.

196 Kevin Davies, "Guilty as charged. A Chinese court delivered a three-year prison sentence and hefty fine to He Jiankui, the rogue gene editor. Does human embryo editing stand a chance of rehabilitation?", *GEN, Genetic Engineering & Biotechnology News*, 1 February 2020, https://www.genengnews.com/insights/guilty-as-charged/.

197 Jeanne Whalen and Elizabeth Dwoskin, "California rejected Chinese company's push to help with coronavirus testing. Was that the right move?", the *Washington Post*, 2 July 2020, https://www.washingtonpost.com/business/2020/07/02/china-bgi-california-testing/.

198 "Special Report: COVID opens new doors for China's gene giant", Reuters, 5 August 2020, https://www.reuters.com/article/us-health-coronavirus-bgi-spec ialreport-idUSKCN2511CE.

199 Kevin Davies, "Guilty as charged. A Chinese court delivered a three-year prison sentence and hefty fine to He Jiankui, the rogue gene editor. Does human embryo editing stand a chance of rehabilitation?", *GEN, Genetic Engineering & Biotechnology News*, 1 February 2020, https://www.genengnews.com/insights/guilty-as-charged/.

200 Jeanne Whalen and Elizabeth Dwoskin, "California rejected Chinese company's push to help with coronavirus testing. Was that the right move?", the *Washington Post*, 2 July 2020, https://www.washingtonpost.com/business/2020/07/02/china-bgi-california-testing/.

201 "Special Report: COVID opens new doors for China's gene giant", Reuters, 5 August 2020, https://www.reuters.com/article/us-health-coronavirus-bgi-spec ialreport-idUSKCN2511CE.

202 Kevin Davies, "Guilty as charged. A Chinese court delivered a three-year prison sentence and hefty fine to He Jiankui, the rogue gene editor. Does human embryo editing stand a chance of rehabilitation?", *GEN, Genetic Engineering & Biotechnology News*, 1 February 2020, https://www.genengnews.com/insights/guilty-as-charged/.

203 Jeanne Whalen and Elizabeth Dwoskin, "California rejected Chinese company's push to help with coronavirus testing. Was that the right move?", the *Washington Post*, 2 July 2020, https://www.washingtonpost.com/business/2020/07/02/china-bgi-california-testing/.

204 "Special Report: COVID opens new doors for China's gene giant", Reuters, 5 August 2020, https://www.reuters.com/article/us-health-coronavirus-bgi-spec ialreport-idUSKCN2511CE.

205 Kevin Davies, "Guilty as charged. A Chinese court delivered a three-year prison sentence and hefty fine to He Jiankui, the rogue gene editor. Does human embryo editing stand a chance of rehabilitation?", *GEN, Genetic Engineering & Biotechnology News*, 1 February 2020, https://www.genengnews.com/insights/guilty-as-charged/.

206 Jeanne Whalen and Elizabeth Dwoskin, "California rejected Chinese company's push to help with coronavirus testing. Was that the right move?", the *Washington Post*, 2 July 2020, https://www.washingtonpost.com/business/2020/07/02/china-bgi-california-testing/.

207 "Special Report: COVID opens new doors for China's gene giant", Reuters, 5 August 2020, https://www.reuters.com/article/us-health-coronavirus-bgi-spec ialreport-idUSKCN2511CE.

208 Kevin Davies, "Guilty as charged. A Chinese court delivered a three-year prison sentence and hefty fine to He Jiankui, the rogue gene editor. Does human embryo editing stand a chance of rehabilitation?", *GEN, Genetic Engineering & Biotechnology News*, 1 February 2020, https://www.genengnews.com/insights/guilty-as-charged/.

209 Jeanne Whalen and Elizabeth Dwoskin, "California rejected Chinese company's push to help with coronavirus testing. Was that the right move?", the *Washington Post*, 2 July 2020, https://www.washingtonpost.com/business/2020/07/02/china-bgi-california-testing/.

210 "Special Report: COVID opens new doors for China's gene giant", Reuters, 5 August 2020, https://www.reuters.com/article/us-health-coronavirus-bgi-specialreport-idUSKCN2511CE.

211 Kevin Davies, "Guilty as charged. A Chinese court delivered a three-year prison sentence and hefty fine to He Jiankui, the rogue gene editor. Does human embryo editing stand a chance of rehabilitation?", *GEN, Genetic Engineering & Biotechnology News*, 1 February 2020, https://www.genengnews.com/insights/guilty-as-charged/.

212 Jeanne Whalen and Elizabeth Dwoskin, "California rejected Chinese company's push to help with coronavirus testing. Was that the right move?", the *Washington Post*, 2 July 2020, https://www.washingtonpost.com/business/2020/07/02/china-bgi-california-testing/.

213 "Special Report: COVID opens new doors for China's gene giant", Reuters, 5 August 2020, https://www.reuters.com/article/us-health-coronavirus-bgi-spec ialreport-idUSKCN2511CE.

214 Kevin Davies, "Guilty as charged. A Chinese court delivered a three-year prison sentence and hefty fine to He Jiankui, the rogue gene editor. Does human embryo editing stand a chance of rehabilitation?", *GEN, Genetic Engineering & Biotechnology News*, 1 February 2020, https://www.genengnews.com/insights/guilty-as-charged/.

215 Jeanne Whalen and Elizabeth Dwoskin, "California rejected Chinese company's push to help with coronavirus testing. Was that

the right move?", the *Washington Post*, 2 July 2020, https://www.washingtonpost.com/business/2020/07/02/china-bgi-california-testing/.

216 Georgia Everett, "China collects DNA from millions of men and boys", *BioNews*, 22 June 2020, https://www.bionews.org.uk/page_150357.

217 Genomic Surveillance Inside China's DNA dragnet", Policy Brief Report No.34/2020, Australian Strategic Policy Institute (ASPI), 2020, https://s3-ap-southeast-2.amazonaws.com/ad-aspi/2020-06/Genomic%20surveillance_1.pdf?QhPFyrNVaSjvblmFT24HRXSuHyRfhpml=.

218 Georgia Everett, "China collects DNA from millions of men and boys", *BioNews*, 22 June 2020, https://www.bionews.org.uk/page_150357.

219 Genomic Surveillance Inside China's DNA dragnet", Policy Brief Report No.34/2020, Australian Strategic Policy Institute (ASPI), 2020, https://s3-ap-southeast-2.amazonaws.com/ad-aspi/2020-06/Genomic%20surveillance_1.pdf?QhPFyrNVaSjvblm FT24HRXSuHyRfhpml=.

220 Georgia Everett, "China collects DNA from millions of men and boys", *BioNews*, 22 June 2020, https://www.bionews.org.uk/page_150357.

221 "Genomic Surveillance Inside China's DNA dragnet", Policy Brief Report No.34/2020, Australian Strategic Policy Institute (ASPI), 2020, https://s3-ap-southeast-2.amazonaws.com/ad-aspi/2020-06/Genomic%20surveillance_1.pdf?QhPFyrNVaSjvblmFT24HRXSuHyRfhpml=.

222 Aditya Panda, Archana Padhi, B. Anjan Kumar. "CCR5 Δ32 minorallele is associated with susceptibility to SARS-CoV-2 infection and death: An epidemiological investigation", National Center for Biotechnology Information, U.S. National Library of Medicine, 10 July 2020, https://www.ncbi.nlm.nih.gov/pmc/articles/PMC7347491/.

223 Rajeev K. Mehlotra, "Chemokine receptor gene polymorphisms and COVID-19: Could knowledge gained from HIV/AIDS be

important?", National Center for Biotechnology Information, U.S. National Library of Medicine, 26 August 2020 https://www.ncbi.nlm.nih.gov/pmc/articles/PMC7448762/.

224 Rajeev K. Mehlotra, "Chemokine receptor gene polymorphisms and COVID-19: Could knowledge gained from HIV/AIDS be important?", National Center for Biotechnology Information, U.S. National Library of Medicine, 26 August 2020 *https://www.ncbi.nlm.nih.gov/pmc/articles/PMC7448762/.*

225 Fred Guterl, "Dr. Fauci Backed Controversial Wuhan Lab with U.S. Dollars for Risky Coronavirus Research", *Newsweek*, 28 April 2020, https://www.newsweek.com/dr-fauci-backed-controversial-wuhan-lab-millions-us-dollars-risky-coronavirus-research-1500741.

226 Eamon Javers, "U.S. blocked Chinese purchase of San Diego fertility clinic over medical data security concerns", CNBC, 16 October 2020, https://www.cnbc.com/2020/10/16/trump-administration-blocked-chinese-purchase-of-us-fertility-clinic.html.

227 Eamon Javers, "U.S. blocked Chinese purchase of San Diego fertility clinic over medical data security concerns", CNBC, 16 October 2020, https://www.cnbc.com/2020/10/16/trump-administration-blocked-chinese-purchase-of-us-fertility-clinic.html.

228 Eamon Javers, "U.S. blocked Chinese purchase of San Diego fertility clinic over medical data security concerns", CNBC, 16 October 2020, *https://www.cnbc.com/2020/10/16/trump-administration-blocked-chinese-purchase-of-us-fertility-clinic.html.*

229 Eamon Javers, "U.S. blocked Chinese purchase of San Diego fertility clinic over medical data security concerns", CNBC, 16 October 2020, https://www.cnbc.com/2020/10/16/trump-administration-blocked-chinese-purchase-of-us-fertility-clinic.html.

230 Fiona Hamilton, "Empty streets during the pandemic make it harder to follow suspects, says MI5 chief", *The Times*, 14/15 October 2020, https://www.thetimes.co.uk/article/china-changing-the-climate-of-spying-mi5-boss-warns-09hlzprzw.

231 "China to build more bio labs amid questions over role in virus origin", Business Standard, 15 April 2021, https://www.business-

standard.com/article/international/china-to-build-more-bio-labs-amid-questions-over-role-in-virus-origin-121041601115_1.html.

232 George F. Gao, Wikipedia – https://en.wikipedia.org/wiki/George_F._Gao.

233 George Fu Gao, Centre for Health Security, https://www.centerforhealthsecurity.org/event201/players/gao.html.

234 Wuze Ren, Xiuxia Qu, Wendong Li, et al., "Difference in Receptor Usage between Severe Acute Respiratory Syndrome (SARS) Coronavirus and SARS-Like Coronavirus of Bat Origin", *Journal of Virology*, Feb. 2008, p.1899–1907, https://jvi.asm.org/content/82/4/1899.

235 Shuo Su, Gary Wong, George F. Gao et al., "Epidemiology, Genetic Recombination, and Pathogenesis of Coronaviruses", Trends in Microbiology, March 2016, https://www.cell.com/trends/microbiology/fulltext/S0966-842X(16)00071-8.

236 Vanping Huang, William J. Liu, George F. Gao, et al., "A Bat-derived Putative Cross-Family Recombinant Coronavirus with a Reovirus Gene", PLOS Pathogens, 27 September 2016, https://journals.plos.org/plospathogens/article?id=10.1371/journal.ppat.1005883.

237 Joseph O. Obameso, Hong Li, George F. Gao, et al., "The persistent prevalence and evolution of cross-family recombinant coronavirus GCCDC1 among a bat population: a two year follow-up", 1 December 2017, https://engine.scichina.com/publisher/scp/journal/SCLS/60/12/10.1007/s11427-017-9263-6?slug=fulltext.

238 Min Zhao, Hangjie Zhang, George F. Gao et al., "Human T-cell immunity against the emerging and re-emerging viruses", *Science China Life Sciences*, 29 November 2017, https://www.ncbi.nlm.nih.gov/pmc/articles/PMC7089170/.

239 William J. Liu, Yuhai Bi, George F. Gao, et al., "On the Centenary of the Spanish Flu: Being prepared for the Next Pandemic", *Virologica Sinica*, December 2018, https://www.researchgate.net/publication/329825434_On_the_Centenary_of_the_Spanish_Flu_Being_Prepared_for_the_Next_Pandemic.

240 Milton Leitenberg, "Did the SARS-CoV-2 virus arise from a bat

coronavirus research program in a Chinese laboratory? Very possibly", Bulletin of the Atomic Scientists, 4 June 2020, https://thebulletin.org/2020/06/did-the-sars-cov-2-virus-arise-from-a-bat-coronavirus-research-program-in-a-chinese-laboratory-very-possibly/.

241 Milton Leitenberg, "Did the SARS-CoV-2 virus arise from a bat coronavirus research program in a Chinese laboratory? Very possibly", Bulletin of the Atomic Scientists, 4 June 2020, https://thebulletin.org/2020/06/did-the-sars-cov-2-virus-arise-from-a-bat-coronavirus-research-program-in-a-chinese-laboratory-very-possibly/.

242 Milton Leitenberg, "Did the SARS-CoV-2 virus arise from a bat coronavirus research program in a Chinese laboratory? Very possibly", Bulletin of the Atomic Scientists, 4 June 2020, https://thebulletin.org/2020/06/did-the-sars-cov-2-virus-arise-from-a-bat-coronavirus-research-program-in-a-chinese-laboratory-very-possibly/.

243 Milton Leitenberg, "Did the SARS-CoV-2 virus arise from a bat coronavirus research program in a Chinese laboratory? Very possibly", Bulletin of the Atomic Scientists, 4 June 2020, https://thebulletin.org/2020/06/did-the-sars-cov-2-virus-arise-from-a-bat-coronavirus-research-program-in-a-chinese-laboratory-very-possibly/.

244 Lucia Lopalco, San Raffaele, "CCR5: From Natural Resistance to a New Ant-HIV Strategy", Viruses, 5 February 2010, https://www.mdpi.com/1999-4915/2/2/574/htm.

245 Chunxia Qi, Xiaopeng Jia, Lingling Lu, et al., "HEK293T Cells Are Heterozygous for CCR5 Delta 32 Mutation", PLoS One, 4 April 2016, https://journals.plos.org/plosone/article?id=10.1371/journal.pone.0152975.

246 Eben Kirskey, "Inside the Global Race to Genetically Modify Humans, The Mutant Project", 2020, p89–90.

247 Eben Kirskey, "Inside the Global Race to Genetically Modify Humans, The Mutant Project", 2020, p94.

248 Sophie M. Andres, Sarah Rowland-Jones, "Recent advances in

understanding HIV evolution", NCBI, 28 April 2017, https://www.ncbi.nlm.nih.gov/pmc/articles/PMC5414815/.

249 Eben Kirsksey, "Inside the Global Race to Genetically Modify Humans, The Mutant Project", 2020, p35.

250 Eben Kirsksey, "Inside the Global Race to Genetically Modify Humans, The Mutant Project", 2020, p36–37.

251 Zhoufang Li, GuangjieLiu, He Jiankui, et al., "Comprehensive analysis of the T-cell receptor beta chain gene in rhesus monkey by high throughput sequencing", National Center for Biotechnology Information, U.S. National Library of Medicine, 11 May 2015, https://www.ncbi.nlm.nih.gov/pmc/articles/PMC4426732/.

252 Zhoufang Li, GuangjieLiu, He Jiankui, et al., "Comprehensive analysis of the T-cell receptor beta chain gene in rhesus monkey by high throughput sequencing", National Center for Biotechnology Information, U.S. National Library of Medicine, 11 May 2015, https://www.ncbi.nlm.nih.gov/pmc/articles/PMC4426732/.

253 Wuhan Institute of Virology (WIV), GlobalSecurity.org, https://www.globalsecurity.org/wmd/world/china/wiv.htm.

254 Tim Wyatt, "Research into deadly viruses and biological weapons at US army lab shut down over fears they could escape", *the Independent*, 06 August 2019, https://www.independent.co.uk/news/world/americas/virus-biological-us-army-weapons-fort-detrick-leak-ebola-anthrax-smallpox-ricin-a9042641.html.

255 "After mysterious shutdown, Fort Detrick still shrouded in secrecy", CGTN, 22-Feb-2021, https://news.cgtn.com/news/2021-02-18/After-mysterious-shutdown-Ford-Detrick-still-shrouded-in-secrecy-XZkLOGbxcc/index.html.

256 Tim Wyatt, "Research into deadly viruses and biological weapons at US army lab shut down over fears they could escape", the *Independent*, 06 August 2019, https://www.independent.co.uk/news/world/americas/virus-biological-us-army-weapons-fort-detrick-leak-ebola-anthrax-smallpox-ricin-a9042641.html.

257 Tim Wyatt, "Research into deadly viruses and biological weapons at US army lab shut down over fears they could escape", the *Independent*, 06 August 2019, https://www.independent.co.uk/

news/world/americas/virus-biological-us-army-weapons-fort-detrick-leak-ebola-anthrax-smallpox-ricin-a9042641.html.

258 Sam Husseini, "Peter Daszak's EcoHealth Alliance has Hidden Almost $40 Million in Pentagon Funding and Militarized Pandemic Science", *Independent Science News*, 12 January 2021, https://www.independentsciencenews.org/news/peter-daszaks-ecohealth-alliance-has-hidden-almost-40-million-in-pentagon-funding/.

259 Xing-Yi Ge, Peter Daszak & Zheng-Li Shi, et al., "Isolation and characterization of a bat SARS-like coronavirus that uses the ACE2 receptor", letter in Nature, 28 November 2013, https://www.nature.com/articles/nature12711.

260 Xing-Yi Ge, Peter Daszak & Zheng-Li Shi, et al., "Isolation and characterization of a bat SARS-like coronavirus that uses the ACE2 receptor", letter in *Nature*, 28 November 2013, https://www.nature.com/articles/nature12711.

261 "Understanding the Risk of Bat Coronavirus Emergence", NIH Project Report, number 1R01AI110964-01, https://reporter.nih.gov/project-details/8674931.

262 "Understanding the Risk of Bat Coronavirus Emergence", NIH Project Report, number 1R01AI110964-01, https://reporter.nih.gov/project-details/8674931.

263 "Understanding the Risk of Bat Coronavirus Emergence", NIH Project Report, number 1R01AI110964-01, https://reporter.nih.gov/project-details/8674931.

264 Sam Husseini, "Peter Daszak's EcoHealth Alliance has Hidden Almost $40 Million in Pentagon Funding and Militarized Pandemic Science", *Independent Science News*, 12 January 2021, https://www.independentsciencenews.org/news/peter-daszaks-ecohealth-alliance-has-hidden-almost-40-million-in-pentagon-funding/.

265 Sam Husseini, "Peter Daszak's EcoHealth Alliance has Hidden Almost $40 Million in Pentagon Funding and Militarized Pandemic Science", *Independent Science News*, 12 January 2021, https://www.independentsciencenews.org/news/peter-daszaks-

ecohealth-alliance-has-hidden-almost-40-million-in-pentagon-funding/.

266 Sam Husseini, "Peter Daszak's EcoHealth Alliance has Hidden Almost $40 Million in Pentagon Funding and Militarized Pandemic Science", *Independent Science News*, 12 January 2021, https://www.independentsciencenews.org/news/peter-daszaks-ecohealth-alliance-has-hidden-almost-40-million-in-pentagon-funding/.

267 Sam Husseini, "Peter Daszak's EcoHealth Alliance has Hidden Almost $40 Million in Pentagon Funding and Militarized Pandemic Science", *Independent Science News*, 12 January 2021, https://www.independentsciencenews.org/news/peter-daszaks-ecohealth-alliance-has-hidden-almost-40-million-in-pentagon-funding/.

268 Jeanne Whalen and Elizabeth Dwoskin, "California rejected Chinese company's push to help with coronavirus testing. Was that the right move?", the *Washington Post*, 2 July 2020, https://www.washingtonpost.com/business/2020/07/02/china-bgi-california-testing/.

269 Jeanne Whalen and Elizabeth Dwoskin, "California rejected Chinese company's push to help with coronavirus testing. Was that the right move?", the *Washington Post*, 2 July 2020, https://www.washingtonpost.com/business/2020/07/02/china-bgi-california-testing/.

270 Eben Kirskey, "Inside the Global Race to Genetically Modify Humans, The Mutant Project", 2020, p39.

271 Eben Kirskey, "Inside the Global Race to Genetically Modify Humans, The Mutant Project", 2020, p39.

272 Eben Kirskey, "Inside the Global Race to Genetically Modify Humans, The Mutant Project", 2020, p39.

273 Eben Kirskey, "Inside the Global Race to Genetically Modify Humans, The Mutant Project", 2020, p39.

274 Eben Kirskey, "Inside the Global Race to Genetically Modify Humans, The Mutant Project", 2020, p39.

275 Eben Kirskey, "Inside the Global Race to Genetically Modify

Humans, The Mutant Project", 2020, p40.
276 Jeanne Whalen and Elizabeth Dwoskin, "California rejected Chinese company's push to help with coronavirus testing. Was that the right move?", the *Washington Post*, 2 July 2020, https://www.washingtonpost.com/business/2020/07/02/china-bgi-california-testing/.
277 Eben Kirskey, "Inside the Global Race to Genetically Modify Humans, The Mutant Project", 2020, p40.
278 Eben Kirskey, "Inside the Global Race to Genetically Modify Humans, The Mutant Project", 2020, p41.
279 Eben Kirskey, "Inside the Global Race to Genetically Modify Humans, The Mutant Project", 2020, p46.
280 Matthew Campbell and Dong Lyu, "Chinese Genetics Giant BGI Wants to Tailor Medicine to Your DNA", Bloomberg Businessweek, 13 November 2019, https://www.bloomberg.com/news/features/2019-11-13/chinese-genetics-giant-bgi-wants-to-tailor-medicine-to-your-dna.
281 Matthew Campbell and Dong Lyu, "Chinese Genetics Giant BGI Wants to Tailor Medicine to Your DNA", Bloomberg Businessweek, 13 November 2019, https://www.bloomberg.com/news/features/2019-11-13/chinese-genetics-giant-bgi-wants-to-tailor-medicine-to-your-dna.
282 Eben Kirskey, "Inside the Global Race to Genetically Modify Humans, The Mutant Project", 2020, p47.
283 Eben Kirskey, "Inside the Global Race to Genetically Modify Humans, The Mutant Project", 2020, p43.
284 Elsa B. Kania, Wilson VornDick, "Weaponizing Biotech: How China's Military is Preparing for a New Domain of Warfare", Defense One, 14 August 2019, https://www.defenseone.com/ideas/2019/08/chinas-military-pursuing-biotech/159167/.
285 Matthew Campbell and Dong Lyu, "Chinese Genetics Giant BGI Wants to Tailor Medicine to Your DNA", Bloomberg Businessweek, 13 November 2019, https://www.bloomberg.com/news/features/2019-11-13/chinese-genetics-giant-bgi-wants-to-tailor-medicine-to-your-dna.

286 China gene firm providing worldwide COVID tests worked with Chinese military", the *Economic Times*, 30 January 2021, https://economictimes.indiatimes.com/news/international/world-news/china-gene-firm-providing-worldwide-covid-tests-worked-with-chinese-military/articleshow/80602726.cms.

287 China gene firm providing worldwide COVID tests worked with Chinese military", the *Economic Times*, 30 January 2021, https://economictimes.indiatimes.com/news/international/world-news/china-gene-firm-providing-worldwide-covid-tests-worked-with-chinese-military/articleshow/80602726.cms.

288 China gene firm providing worldwide COVID tests worked with Chinese military", the *Economic Times*, 30 January 2021, https://economictimes.indiatimes.com/news/international/world-news/china-gene-firm-providing-worldwide-covid-tests-worked-with-chinese-military/articleshow/80602726.cms.

289 "China gene firm providing worldwide COVID tests worked with Chinese military", the *Economic Times*, 30 January 2021, https://economictimes.indiatimes.com/news/international/world-news/china-gene-firm-providing-worldwide-covid-tests-worked-with-chinese-military/articleshow/80602726.cms.

290 China gene firm providing worldwide COVID tests worked with Chinese military", the *Economic Times*, 30 January 2021, https://economictimes.indiatimes.com/news/international/world-news/china-gene-firm-providing-worldwide-covid-tests-worked-with-chinese-military/articleshow/80602726.cms.

291 "China gene firm providing worldwide COVID tests worked with Chinese military", the *Economic Times*, 30 January 2021, https://economictimes.indiatimes.com/news/international/world-news/china-gene-firm-providing-worldwide-covid-tests-worked-with-chinese-military/articleshow/80602726.cms.

292 Group 42 (Emirati Company), https://en.wikipedia.org/wiki/Group_42_(Emirati_company).

293 "China gene firm providing worldwide COVID tests worked with Chinese military", the *Economic Times*, 30 January 2021, https://economictimes.indiatimes.com/news/international/world-news/

china-gene-firm-providing-worldwide-covid-tests-worked-with-chinese-military/articleshow/80602726.cms.
294 "China gene firm providing worldwide COVID tests worked with Chinese military", the *Economic Times*, 30 January 2021, https://economictimes.indiatimes.com/news/international/world-news/china-gene-firm-providing-worldwide-covid-tests-worked-with-chinese-military/articleshow/80602726.cms.
295 "China gene firm providing worldwide COVID tests worked with Chinese military", the *Economic Times*, 30 January 2021, https://economictimes.indiatimes.com/news/international/world-news/china-gene-firm-providing-worldwide-covid-tests-worked-with-chinese-military/articleshow/80602726.cms.
296 "China gene firm providing worldwide COVID tests worked with Chinese military", the *Economic Times*, 30 January 2021, https://economictimes.indiatimes.com/news/international/world-news/china-gene-firm-providing-worldwide-covid-tests-worked-with-chinese-military/articleshow/80602726.cms.
297 "China gene firm providing worldwide COVID tests worked with Chinese military", the *Economic Times*, 30 January 2021, https://economictimes.indiatimes.com/news/international/world-news/china-gene-firm-providing-worldwide-covid-tests-worked-with-chinese-military/articleshow/80602726.cms.
298 "China gene firm providing worldwide COVID tests worked with Chinese military", the *Economic Times*, 30 January 2021, https://economictimes.indiatimes.com/news/international/world-news/china-gene-firm-providing-worldwide-covid-tests-worked-with-chinese-military/articleshow/80602726.cms.
299 "China gene firm providing worldwide COVID tests worked with Chinese military", the *Economic Times*, 30 January 2021, https://economictimes.indiatimes.com/news/international/world-news/china-gene-firm-providing-worldwide-covid-tests-worked-with-chinese-military/articleshow/80602726.cms.
300 "China gene firm providing worldwide COVID tests worked with Chinese military", the *Economic Times*, 30 January 2021, https://economictimes.indiatimes.com/news/international/world-news/

china-gene-firm-providing-worldwide-covid-tests-worked-with-chinese-military/articleshow/80602726.cms.

301 "China gene firm providing worldwide COVID tests worked with Chinese military", the *Economic Times*, 30 January 2021, https://economictimes.indiatimes.com/news/international/world-news/china-gene-firm-providing-worldwide-covid-tests-worked-with-chinese-military/articleshow/80602726.cms.

302 Jeanne Whalen and Elizabeth Dwoskin, "California rejected Chinese company's push to help with coronavirus testing. Was that the right move?", the *Washington Post*, 2 July 2020, https://www.washingtonpost.com/business/2020/07/02/china-bgi-california-testing/.

303 Eben Kirskey, "Inside the Global Race to Genetically Modify Humans, The Mutant Project", 2020, p46.

304 Eben Kirskey, "Inside the Global Race to Genetically Modify Humans, The Mutant Project", 2020, p49.

305 Eben Kirskey, "Inside the Global Race to Genetically Modify Humans, The Mutant Project", 2020, p49.

306 Eben Kirskey, "Inside the Global Race to Genetically Modify Humans, The Mutant Project", 2020, p49.

307 Eben Kirskey, "Inside the Global Race to Genetically Modify Humans, The Mutant Project", 2020, p140 –141.

308 Matthew Campbell and Dong Lyu, "Chinese Genetics Giant BGI Wants to Tailor Medicine to Your DNA", Bloomberg Businessweek, 13 November 2019, https://www.bloomberg.com/news/features/2019-11-13/chinese-genetics-giant-bgi-wants-to-tailor-medicine-to-your-dna.

309 Eben Kirskey, "Inside the Global Race to Genetically Modify Humans, The Mutant Project", 2020, p142.

310 Eben Kirskey, "Inside the Global Race to Genetically Modify Humans, The Mutant Project", 2020, p142.

311 Eben Kirskey, "Inside the Global Race to Genetically Modify Humans, The Mutant Project", 2020, p50–51.

312 Eben Kirskey, "Inside the Global Race to Genetically Modify Humans, The Mutant Project", 2020, p51.

313 Eben Kirskey, "Inside the Global Race to Genetically Modify Humans, The Mutant Project", 2020, p144.
314 Eben Kirskey, "Inside the Global Race to Genetically Modify Humans, The Mutant Project", 2020, p52.
315 Eben Kirskey, "Inside the Global Race to Genetically Modify Humans, The Mutant Project", 2020, p53.
316 Eben Kirskey, "Inside the Global Race to Genetically Modify Humans, The Mutant Project", 2020, p.67.
317 Ralph S. Baric, UNC Gillings School of Global Public Health, https://sph.unc.edu/adv_profile/ralph-s-baric-phd/.
318 National Institute of Allergy and Infectious Diseases, Wikipedia, https://en.wikipedia.org/wiki/National_Institute_of_Allergy_and_Infectious_Diseases.
319 Eben Kirskey, "Inside the Global Race to Genetically Modify Humans, The Mutant Project", 2020, p74.
320 Elsa B. Kania and Wilson VornDick, "Weaponizing Biotech: How China's Military is Preparing for a New Domain of Warfare", Defense One, 14 August 2019, https://www.defenseone.com/ideas/2019/08/chinas-military-pursuing-biotech/159167/.
321 Bill Gertz, "Wuhan lab 'most likely' coronavirus source, US government analysis finds", the *Washington Times,* 28 April 2020, https://www.washingtontimes.com/news/2020/apr/28/wuhan-laboratory-most-likely-coronavirus-source-us/.
322 Bill Gertz, "Wuhan lab 'most likely' coronavirus source, US government analysis finds", the *Washington Times*, 28 April 2020, https://www.washingtontimes.com/news/2020/apr/28/wuhan-laboratory-most-likely-coronavirus-source-us/.
323 Walter Isaacson, "The Code Breaker", 2021, p. 259–260.
324 Walter Isaacson, "The Code Breaker", 2021, p. 259–260.
325 Walter Isaacson, "The Code Breaker", 2021, p. 260.
326 Walter Isaacson, "The Code Breaker", 2021, p.262.
327 Regina E. Dugan and Kaigham J. Gabriel, "'Special Forces' Innovation: How DARPA Attacks Problems", *Harvard Business Review*, October 2013, https://hbr.org/2013/10/special-forces-innovation-how-darpa-attacks-problems.

328 "After developing AstraZeneca vaccine, Jenner Institute sets its sights on beating HIV", *The Times*, 18 April 2021, https://www.thetimes.co.uk/article/after-developing-astrazeneca-vaccine-jenner-institute-sets-its-sights-on-beating-hiv-g09l76vx8.

329 "After developing AstraZeneca vaccine, Jenner Institute sets its sights on beating HIV", *The Times*, 18 April 2021, https://www.thetimes.co.uk/article/after-developing-astrazeneca-vaccine-jenner-institute-sets-its-sights-on-beating-hiv-g09l76vx8.

330 "After developing AstraZeneca vaccine, Jenner Institute sets its sights on beating HIV", *The Times*, 18 April 2021, https://www.thetimes.co.uk/article/after-developing-astrazeneca-vaccine-jenner-institute-sets-its-sights-on-beating-hiv-g09l76vx8.

331 White House Statement, 26 May 2021, https://www.whitehouse.gov/briefing-room/statements-releases/2021/05/26/statement-by-president-joe-biden-on-the-investigation-into-the-origins-of-covid-19/.

332 Vincent Ni and Julian Borger, "Biden move to investigate Covid origins opens new rift in US-China relations", 27 May 2021, https://www.theguardian.com/us-news/2021/may/27/biden-china-coronavirus-origins-beijing.

333 Vincent Ni and Julian Borger, "Biden move to investigate Covid origins opens new rift in US-China relations", 27 May 2021, https://www.theguardian.com/us-news/2021/may/27/biden-china-coronavirus-origins-beijing.

334 US Department of State, "Fact Sheet: Activity at the Wuhan Institute of Virology", 15 January 2021, https://2017-2021.state.gov/fact-sheet-activity-at-the-wuhan-institute-of-virology/index.html.

335 Katherine Eban, "The Lab-Leak Theory: Inside the Fight to Uncover Covid-19's Origins", *Vanity Fair*, 3 June 2021, https://www.vanityfair.com/news/2021/06/the-lab-leak-theory-inside-the-fight-to-uncover-covid-19s-origins.

336 Katherine Eban, "The Lab-Leak Theory: Inside the Fight to Uncover Covid-19's Origins", *Vanity Fair*, 3 June 2021, https://www.vanityfair.com/news/2021/06/the-lab-leak-theory-inside-

the-fight-to-uncover-covid-19s-origins.
337 Katherine Eban, "The Lab-Leak Theory: Inside the Fight to Uncover Covid-19's Origins", *Vanity Fair*, 3 June 2021, https://www.vanityfair.com/news/2021/06/the-lab-leak-theory-inside-the-fight-to-uncover-covid-19s-origins.
338 Katherine Eban, "The Lab-Leak Theory: Inside the Fight to Uncover Covid-19's Origins", *Vanity Fair*, 3 June 2021, https://www.vanityfair.com/news/2021/06/the-lab-leak-theory-inside-the-fight-to-uncover-covid-19s-origins.
339 White House Statement, 27 August 2021, https://www.whitehouse.gov/briefing-room/statements-releases/2021/08/27/statement-by-president-joe-biden-on-the-investigation-into-the-origins-of-covid-%E2%81%A019/.
340 White House Statement, 27 August 2021, https://www.whitehouse.gov/briefing-room/statements-releases/2021/08/27/statement-by-president-joe-biden-on-the-investigation-into-the-origins-of-covid-%E2%81%A019/.
341 Siladitya Ray, "Biden Reportedly Receives Inconclusive Report About Covid Origins From Intelligence Agencies", *Forbes*, 25 August 2021, https://www.forbes.com/sites/siladityaray/2021/08/25/biden-reportedly-receives-inconclusive-report-about-covid-origins-from-intelligence-services/?sh=1b1ae2412aaa.
342 Unclassified report of the Office of the Director of National Intelligence, https://www.dni.gov/files/ODNI/documents/assessments/Unclassified-Summary-of-Assessment-on-COVID-19-Origins.pdf.
343 Unclassified report of the Office of the Director of National Intelligence, https://www.dni.gov/files/ODNI/documents/assessments/Unclassified-Summary-of-Assessment-on-COVID-19-Origins.pdf.
344 Sharon Lerner and Maia Hibbett, "Leaked Grant Proposal details High-Risk Coronavirus Research", the Intercept, 23 September 2021, https://theintercept.com/2021/09/23/coronavirus-research-grant-darpa/.
345 EcoHealth Alliance, "Project DEFUSE: Defusing the Threat

of Bat-born Coronaviruses", 27 March 2018, https://www.documentcloud.org/documents/21066966-defuse-proposal.

346 Sharon Lerner and Maia Hibbett, "Leaked Grant Proposal details High-Risk Coronavirus Research", the Intercept, 23 September 2021, https://theintercept.com/2021/09/23/coronavirus-research-grant-darpa/.

347 Sharon Lerner and Maia Hibbett, "Leaked Grant Proposal details High-Risk Coronavirus Research", the Intercept, 23 September 2021, https://theintercept.com/2021/09/23/coronavirus-research-grant-darpa/.

348 Sharon Lerner and Maia Hibbett, "Leaked Grant Proposal details High-Risk Coronavirus Research", the Intercept, 23 September 2021, https://theintercept.com/2021/09/23/coronavirus-research-grant-darpa/.

349 Sharon Lerner and Maia Hibbett, "Leaked Grant Proposal details High-Risk Coronavirus Research", the Intercept, 23 September 2021, https://theintercept.com/2021/09/23/coronavirus-research-grant-darpa/.

350 Sharon Lerner and Maia Hibbett, "Leaked Grant Proposal details High-Risk Coronavirus Research", the Intercept, 23 September 2021, https://theintercept.com/2021/09/23/coronavirus-research-grant-darpa/.

351 Sharon Lerner and Maia Hibbett, "Leaked Grant Proposal details High-Risk Coronavirus Research", the Intercept, 23 September 2021, https://theintercept.com/2021/09/23/coronavirus-research-grant-darpa/.

352 Jeremy Farrar with Anjana Ahuja, "Spike, The Virus vs the People, The Inside Story", pp.1–2, First published July 2021.

353 Jeremy Farrar with Anjana Ahuja, "Spike, The Virus vs the People, The Inside Story", pp.9–10, First published July 2021.

354 Jeremy Farrar with Anjana Ahuja, "Spike, The Virus vs the People, The Inside Story", p.49, First published July 2021.

355 Jeremy Farrar with Anjana Ahuja, "Spike, The Virus vs the People, The Inside Story", pp.53–54, First published July 2021.

356 Jeremy Farrar with Anjana Ahuja, "Spike, The Virus vs the People,

The Inside Story", pp.55–56, First published July 2021.
357 Jeremy Farrar with Anjana Ahuja, "Spike, The Virus vs the People, The Inside Story", p67, First published July 2021.
358 Jeremy Farrar with Anjana Ahuja, "Spike, The Virus vs the People, The Inside Story", p68, First published July 2021.
359 Jeremy Farrar with Anjana Ahuja, "Spike, The Virus vs the People, The Inside Story", p70, First published July 2021.
360 Jeremy Farrar with Anjana Ahuja, "Spike, The Virus vs the People, The Inside Story", pp.83–84, First published July 2021.
361 Jeremy Farrar with Anjana Ahuja, "Spike, The Virus vs the People, The Inside Story", p126, First published July 2021.
362 Marine Corps Major Joseph Murphy, report on the origins of Covid-19, 13 August 2021, made public by Project Veritas, January 2022, https://assets.ctfassets.net/syq3snmxclc9/2mVob3c1aDd8CNvVnyei6n/95af7dbfd2958d4c2b8494048b4889b5/JAG_Docs_pt1_Og_WATERMARK_OVER_Redacted.pdf.
363 Marine Corps Major Joseph Murphy, report on the origins of Covid-19, 13 August 2021, made public by Project Veritas, January 2022, https://assets.ctfassets.net/syq3snmxclc9/2mVob3c1aDd8CNvVnyei6n/95af7dbfd2958d4c2b8494048b4889b5/JAG_Docs_pt1_Og_WATERMARK_OVER_Redacted.pdf.
364 Marine Corps Major Joseph Murphy, report on the origins of Covid-19, 13 August 2021, made public by Project Veritas, January 2022, https://assets.ctfassets.net/syq3snmxclc9/2mVob3c1aDd8CNvVnyei6n/95af7dbfd2958d4c2b8494048b4889b5/JAG_Docs_pt1_Og_WATERMARK_OVER_Redacted.pdf.
365 Marine Corps Major Joseph Murphy, report on the origins of Covid-19, 13 August 2021, made public by Project Veritas, January 2022, https://assets.ctfassets.net/syq3snmxclc9/2mVob3c1aDd8CNvVnyei6n/95af7dbfd2958d4c2b8494048b4889b5/JAG_Docs_pt1_Og_WATERMARK_OVER_Redacted.pdf.

366 Marine Corps Major Joseph Murphy, report on the origins of Covid-19, 13 August 2021, made public by Project Veritas, January 2022, https://assets.ctfassets.net/syq3snmxclc9/2mVob3c1aDd8CNvVnyei6n/95af7dbfd2958d4c2b8494048b4889b5/JAG_Docs_pt1_Og_WATERMARK_OVER_Redacted.pdf.

367 Maia Hibbett and Ryan Grim, "House Republicans Release Text of Redacted Fauci Emails on Covid Origins", the Intercept, 12 January 2022, https://theintercept.com/2022/01/12/covid-origins-fauci-redacted-emails/.

368 Maia Hibbett and Ryan Grim, "House Republicans Release Text of Redacted Fauci Emails on Covid Origins", the Intercept, 12 January 2022, https://theintercept.com/2022/01/12/covid-origins-fauci-redacted-emails/.

369 Maia Hibbett and Ryan Grim, "House Republicans Release Text of Redacted Fauci Emails on Covid Origins", the Intercept, 12 January 2022, https://theintercept.com/2022/01/12/covid-origins-fauci-redacted-emails/.

370 Maia Hibbett and Ryan Grim, "House Republicans Release Text of Redacted Fauci Emails on Covid Origins", the Intercept, 12 January 2022, https://theintercept.com/2022/01/12/covid-origins-fauci-redacted-emails/.

371 Maia Hibbett and Ryan Grim, "House Republicans Release Text of Redacted Fauci Emails on Covid Origins", the Intercept, 12 January 2022, https://theintercept.com/2022/01/12/covid-origins-fauci-redacted-emails/.

372 Maia Hibbett and Ryan Grim, "House Republicans Release Text of Redacted Fauci Emails on Covid Origins", the Intercept, 12 January 2022, https://theintercept.com/2022/01/12/covid-origins-fauci-redacted-emails/.

373 Jon Cohen, "Mining coronavirus genomes for clues to the outbreak's origins", *Science*, 31 January 2020, https://www.science.org/content/article/mining-coronavirus-genomes-clues-outbreak-s-origins.

374 Paolo Barnard, "The Origin of the Virus: the hidden truths behind

the microbe that killed millions of people", p10, First published September 2021.

375 Paolo Barnard, "The Origin of the Virus: the hidden truths behind the microbe that killed millions of people", p11, First published September 2021.

376 Henry T. Greely, "He Jiankui, embryo editing, CCR5, the London patient, and jumping to conclusions", StatNews, 15 April 2019, https://www.statnews.com/2019/04/15/jiankui-embryo-editing-ccr5/ .

377 Henry T. Greely, "He Jiankui, embryo editing, CCR5, the London patient, and jumping to conclusions", StatNews, 15 April 2019, https://www.statnews.com/2019/04/15/jiankui-embryo-editing-ccr5/ .

378 Elsa B. Kania and Wilson VornDick, "China's Military Biotech Frontier: CRISPR, Military-Civil Fusion and the New Revolution in Military Affairs", China Brief. Volume 19, Issue 18. October 8, 2019, https://jamestown.org/program/chinas-military-biotech-frontier-crispr-military-civil-fusion-and-the-new-revolution-in-military-affairs/.

379 Elsa B. Kania and Wilson VornDick, "China's Military Biotech Frontier: CRISPR, Military-Civil Fusion and the New Revolution in Military Affairs", China Brief. Volume 19, Issue 18. October 8, 2019, https://jamestown.org/program/chinas-military-biotech-frontier-crispr-military-civil-fusion-and-the-new-revolution-in-military-affairs/.

380 Elsa B. Kania and Wilson VornDick, "China's Military Biotech Frontier: CRISPR, Military-Civil Fusion and the New Revolution in Military Affairs", China Brief. Volume 19, Issue 18. October 8, 2019, https://jamestown.org/program/chinas-military-biotech-frontier-crispr-military-civil-fusion-and-the-new-revolution-in-military-affairs/.

381 Ken Dilanian, "China has done human testing to create biologically enhanced super soldiers says top US official", NBC News, 3 December 2020, https://www.nbcnews.com/politics/national-security/china-has-done-human-testing-create-biologically-

enhanced-super-soldiers-n1249914.
382 Yusef Paolo Rabiah, "From bioweapons to super soldiers: how the UK is joining the genomic technology arms race", The Conversation, 29 April 2021, https://theconversation.com/from-bioweapons-to-super-soldiers-how-the-uk-is-joining-the-genomic-technology-arms-race-159889.
383 Joseph V. Micallef, "Will Genomics Become the Next Arena of China-US Military Competition?", Military News, 23 March 2021, https://www.military.com/daily-news/opinions/2021/03/23/will-genomics-become-next-arena-of-china-us-military-competition.html.
384 Joseph V. Micallef, "Will Genomics Become the Next Arena of China-US Military Competition?", Military News, 23 March 2021, https://www.military.com/daily-news/opinions/2021/03/23/will-genomics-become-next-arena-of-china-us-military-competition.html.
385 Joseph V. Micallef, "Will Genomics Become the Next Arena of China-US Military Competition?", Military News, 23 March 2021, https://www.military.com/daily-news/opinions/2021/03/23/will-genomics-become-next-arena-of-china-us-military-competition.html.
386 Joseph V. Micallef, "Will Genomics Become the Next Arena of China-US Military Competition?", Military News, 23 March 2021, https://www.military.com/daily-news/opinions/2021/03/23/will-genomics-become-next-arena-of-china-us-military-competition.html.
387 Dr Ah Kahn Syed, "How to BLAST your way to the truth about the origins of Covid-19", Arkmedic's blog, 28 December 2021, https://arkmedic.substack.com/p/how-to-blast-your-way-to-the-truth?s=r
388 Dr Ah Kahn Syed, "How to BLAST your way to the truth about the origins of Covid-19", Arkmedic's blog, 28 December 2021, https://arkmedic.substack.com/p/how-to-blast-your-way-to-the-truth?s=r
389 Dr Ah Kahn Syed, "How to BLAST your way to the truth about

the origins of Covid-19", Arkmedic's blog, 28 December 2021, https://arkmedic.substack.com/p/how-to-blast-your-way-to-the-truth?s=r

390 Dr Ah Kahn Syed, "How to BLAST your way to the truth about the origins of Covid-19", Arkmedic's blog, 28 December 2021, https://arkmedic.substack.com/p/how-to-blast-your-way-to-the-truth?s=r

391 Dr Ah Kahn Syed, "Absolute proof: The Gp-120 sequences prove beyond all doubt that 'COVID-19' was man-made", Arkmedic's blog, 10 April 2022, https://arkmedic.substack.com/p/absolute-proof-the-gp-120-sequences?s=r

392 Dr Ah Kahn Syed, "Absolute proof: The Gp-120 sequences prove beyond all doubt that 'COVID-19' was man-made", Arkmedic's blog, 10 April 2022, https://arkmedic.substack.com/p/absolute-proof-the-gp-120-sequences?s=r

393 Dr Ah Kahn Syed, "Absolute proof: The Gp-120 sequences prove beyond all doubt that 'COVID-19' was man-made", Arkmedic's blog, 10 April 2022, https://arkmedic.substack.com/p/absolute-proof-the-gp-120-sequences?s=r

394 Dr Ah Kahn Syed, "Absolute proof: The Gp-120 sequences prove beyond all doubt that 'COVID-19' was man-made", Arkmedic's blog, 10 April 2022, https://arkmedic.substack.com/p/absolute-proof-the-gp-120-sequences?s=r

395 Prof. Angus Dalgleish, "The Origin of the Virus: the hidden truths behind the microbe that killed millions of people", p77, First published September 2021.

396 Prof. Angus Dalgleish, "The Origin of the Virus: the hidden truths behind the microbe that killed millions of people", p89, First published September 2021.

397 Prof. Angus Dalgleish, "The Origin of the Virus: the hidden truths behind the microbe that killed millions of people", p96, First published September 2021.

398 "Report says cellphone data suggests October shutdown at Wuhan lab, but experts are skeptical", NBC News, 9 May 2020, https://www.nbcnews.com/politics/national-security/report-says-cellphone-

data-suggests-october-shutdown-wuhan-lab-experts-n1202716.
399 Xio Baming, "The Human Price of Wuhan's Military World Games, Bitter Winter", 2 April 2020, https://bitterwinter.org/the-human-price-of-wuhans-military-world-games/?gclid=EAIaIQobChMItKTgwums9wIVyu3tCh2SHQghEAAYASAAEgK4TfD_BwE.
400 Xio Baming, "The Human Price of Wuhan's Military World Games, Bitter Winter", 2 April 2020, https://bitterwinter.org/the-human-price-of-wuhans-military-world-games/?gclid=EAIaIQobChMItKTgwums9wIVyu3tCh2SHQghEAAYASAAEgK4TfD_BwE.
401 Xio Baming, "The Human Price of Wuhan's Military World Games, Bitter Winter", 2 April 2020, https://bitterwinter.org/the-human-price-of-wuhans-military-world-games/?gclid=EAIaIQobChMItKTgwums9wIVyu3tCh2SHQghEAAYASAAEgK4TfD_BwE.
402 Yusef Paolo Rabiah, "From bioweapons to super soldiers: how the UK is joining the genomic technology arms race", The Conversation, 29 April 2021, https://theconversation.com/from-bioweapons-to-super-soldiers-how-the-uk-is-joining-the-genomic-technology-arms-race-159889.
403 Yusef Paolo Rabiah, "From bioweapons to super soldiers: how the UK is joining the genomic technology arms race", The Conversation, 29 April 2021, https://theconversation.com/from-bioweapons-to-super-soldiers-how-the-uk-is-joining-the-genomic-technology-arms-race-159889.
404 Charles Rixey, "The Myth of the Blind Watchmaker", 28 May 2022, ResearchGate, https://www.researchgate.net/publication/359855384_The_Myth_of_the_Blind_Watchmaker.
405 Charles Rixey, "The Myth of the Blind Watchmaker", 28 May 2022, ResearchGate, https://www.researchgate.net/publication/359855384_The_Myth_of_the_Blind_Watchmaker.
406 Jeremy Herb and Natasha Bertrand, "US Energy Department assesses Covid-19 likely resulted from lab leak, further US intel divide over virus origin", CNN, 27 February 2023, https://edition.cnn.com/2023/02/26/politics/covid-lab-leak-wuhan-china-intelligence/index.html.
407 Jeremy Herb and Natasha Bertrand, "US Energy Department

assesses Covid-19 likely resulted from lab leak, further US intel divide over virus origin", CNN, 27 February 2023, https://edition.cnn.com/2023/02/26/politics/covid-lab-leak-wuhan-china-intelligence/index.html.

408 Michael R. Gordon and Warren P. Strobel, "Lab Leak Most Likely Origin of Covid-19 Pandemic, Energy Department Now Says", *Wall Street Journal*, 26 February 2023, https://www.wsj.com/articles/covid-origin-china-lab-leak-807b7b0a.

409 Alexandra Alper and David Shepardson, "US adds units of China's BGI, Inspur to trade blacklist", Reuters, 3 March 2023, https://www.reuters.com/markets/us/us-adds-chinese-genetics-company-units-trade-blacklist-2023-03-02/.

410 "Chinese company rejects rights accusation after US sanctions", the *Independent*, 5 March 2023, https://www.independent.co.uk/news/ap-beijing-chinese-uyghurs-commerce-department-b2294374.html.

411 Statement from the Organising Committee of the Third International Summit on Human Genome Editing, London, 6–8 March 2023, https://royalsociety.org/news/2023/03/statement-third-international-summit-human-genome-editing/#:~:text=08%20March%202023&text=Remarkable%20progress%20has%20been%20made,understand%20risks%20and%20unintended%20effects.

412 The Third International Summit on Human Genome Editing, London, 6–8 March 2023, conference website, https://royalsociety.org/science-events-and-lectures/2023/03/2023-human-genome-editing-summit/.

413 Pallab Ghosh, "China's new human gene-editing rules worry experts", BBC News, 6 March 2023, https://www.bbc.co.uk/news/science-environment-64857311.

414 Pallab Ghosh, "China's new human gene-editing rules worry experts", BBC News, 6 March 2023, https://www.bbc.co.uk/news/science-environment-64857311.

415 Statement from the Organising Committee of the Third International Summit on Human Genome Editing, London,

6–8 March 2023, https://royalsociety.org/news/2023/03/statement-third-international-summit-human-genome-editing/#:~:text=08%20March%202023&text=Remarkable%20progress%20has%20been%20made,understand%20risks%20and%20unintended%20effects.

416 Heidi Ledford, "Why CRISPR babies are still too risky – embryo studies highlight challenges", *Nature*, 10 March 2023, https://www.nature.com/articles/d41586-023-00756-0#:~:text=About%2040%25%20of%20the%20embryos,were%20allowed%20to%20develop%20further.

417 Office of the Director of National Intelligence, "Potential Links Between the Wuhan Institute of Virology and the Origin of the Covid-19 Pandemic", 23 June 2023, https://www.dni.gov/files/ODNI/documents/assessments/Report-on-Potential-Links-Between-the-Wuhan-Institute-of-Virology-and-the-Origins-of-COVID-19-20230623.pdf.

418 Office of the Director of National Intelligence, "Potential Links Between the Wuhan Institute of Virology and the Origin of the Covid-19 Pandemic", 23 June 2023, https://www.dni.gov/files/ODNI/documents/assessments/Report-on-Potential-Links-Between-the-Wuhan-Institute-of-Virology-and-the-Origins-of-COVID-19-20230623.pdf.

419 Office of the Director of National Intelligence, "Potential Links Between the Wuhan Institute of Virology and the Origin of the Covid-19 Pandemic", 23 June 2023, https://www.dni.gov/files/ODNI/documents/assessments/Report-on-Potential-Links-Between-the-Wuhan-Institute-of-Virology-and-the-Origins-of-COVID-19-20230623.pdf.

420 Office of the Director of National Intelligence, "Potential Links Between the Wuhan Institute of Virology and the Origin of the Covid-19 Pandemic", 23 June 2023, https://www.dni.gov/files/ODNI/documents/assessments/Report-on-Potential-Links-Between-the-Wuhan-Institute-of-Virology-and-the-Origins-of-COVID-19-20230623.pdf.

421 Office of the Director of National Intelligence, "Potential Links

Between the Wuhan Institute of Virology and the Origin of the Covid-19 Pandemic", 23 June 2023, https://www.dni.gov/files/ODNI/documents/assessments/Report-on-Potential-Links-Between-the-Wuhan-Institute-of-Virology-and-the-Origins-of-COVID-19-20230623.pdf.

422 Office of the Director of National Intelligence, "Potential Links Between the Wuhan Institute of Virology and the Origin of the Covid-19 Pandemic", 23 June 2023, https://www.dni.gov/files/ODNI/documents/assessments/Report-on-Potential-Links-Between-the-Wuhan-Institute-of-Virology-and-the-Origins-of-COVID-19-20230623.pdf.

423 Office of the Director of National Intelligence, "Potential Links Between the Wuhan Institute of Virology and the Origin of the Covid-19 Pandemic", 23 June 2023, https://www.dni.gov/files/ODNI/documents/assessments/Report-on-Potential-Links-Between-the-Wuhan-Institute-of-Virology-and-the-Origins-of-COVID-19-20230623.pdf.

424 Office of the Director of National Intelligence, "Potential Links Between the Wuhan Institute of Virology and the Origin of the Covid-19 Pandemic", 23 June 2023, https://www.dni.gov/files/ODNI/documents/assessments/Report-on-Potential-Links-Between-the-Wuhan-Institute-of-Virology-and-the-Origins-of-COVID-19-20230623.pdf.

425 Office of the Director of National Intelligence, "Potential Links Between the Wuhan Institute of Virology and the Origin of the Covid-19 Pandemic", 23 June 2023, https://www.dni.gov/files/ODNI/documents/assessments/Report-on-Potential-Links-Between-the-Wuhan-Institute-of-Virology-and-the-Origins-of-COVID-19-20230623.pdf.

426 Select Subcommittee on the Coronavirus Pandemic, "The Proximal Origin of a Cover-Up: Did the 'Bethesda Boys' Downplay a Lab Leak?", Interim Majority Report, 11 July 2023, p.1, https://oversight.house.gov/wp-content/uploads/2023/07/Final-Report-6.pdf.

427 Select Subcommittee on the Coronavirus Pandemic, "The Proximal Origin of a Cover-Up: Did the 'Bethesda Boys'

Downplay a Lab Leak?", Interim Majority Report, 11 July 2023, p.2, https://oversight.house.gov/wp-content/uploads/2023/07/Final-Report-6.pdf.

428 Select Subcommittee on the Coronavirus Pandemic, "The Proximal Origin of a Cover-Up: Did the 'Bethesda Boys' Downplay a Lab Leak?", Interim Majority Report, 11 July 2023, p.5, https://oversight.house.gov/wp-content/uploads/2023/07/Final-Report-6.pdf.

429 Select Subcommittee on the Coronavirus Pandemic, "The Proximal Origin of a Cover-Up: Did the 'Bethesda Boys' Downplay a Lab Leak?", Interim Majority Report, 11 July 2023, p.20–22, https://oversight.house.gov/wp-content/uploads/2023/07/Final-Report-6.pdf.

430 Select Subcommittee on the Coronavirus Pandemic, "The Proximal Origin of a Cover-Up: Did the 'Bethesda Boys' Downplay a Lab Leak?", Interim Majority Report, 11 July 2023, p.8, https://oversight.house.gov/wp-content/uploads/2023/07/Final-Report-6.pdf.

431 Select Subcommittee on the Coronavirus Pandemic, "The Proximal Origin of a Cover-Up: Did the 'Bethesda Boys' Downplay a Lab Leak?", Interim Majority Report, 11 July 2023, p.17, https://oversight.house.gov/wp-content/uploads/2023/07/Final-Report-6.pdf.

432 Select Subcommittee on the Coronavirus Pandemic, "The Proximal Origin of a Cover-Up: Did the 'Bethesda Boys' Downplay a Lab Leak?", Interim Majority Report, 11 July 11 2023, p.26, https://oversight.house.gov/wp-content/uploads/2023/07/Final-Report-6.pdf.

433 Select Subcommittee on the Coronavirus Pandemic, "The Proximal Origin of a Cover-Up: Did the 'Bethesda Boys' Downplay a Lab Leak?", Interim Majority Report, 11 July 2023, p.50, https://oversight.house.gov/wp-content/uploads/2023/07/Final-Report-6.pdf.